A6   1st Edition   35p

D0613826

Set in Oxford in 1952

A CUP OF TEA FOR MR. THORGILL

A CUP OF TEA
FOR MR. THORGILL

BY

STORM JAMESON

'. . . la vie éternelle n'est pas remise à plus tard, elle commence dès maintenant, à l'instant même . . . il est en nous à la façon d'une parcelle de levain, il commence à croître, à travailler, quelqu'un à commencé à se nourrir de nous et à opérer en nous à nos depens son mystérieux travail . . . Il faut pratiquer l'Espérance.'

LONDON
MACMILLAN & CO LTD
1957

MACMILLAN AND COMPANY LIMITED
London Bombay Calcutta Madras Melbourne

THE MACMILLAN COMPANY OF CANADA LIMITED
Toronto

ST MARTIN'S PRESS INC
New York

PRINTED IN GREAT BRITAIN

Chapter 1

ALONE in the back of his brother-in-law's car, Rigden gave himself up to the pleasure of being driven through a countryside seemingly empty, and so smooth that it gives the impression of being more civilised than a capital city. Scattered villages, built of the softly warm Gloucestershire stone, appeared, moved close, withdrew into the folds of low hills rounded as though by hand — and by centuries of care and affection. Above them the sky was calmness itself. Calm and reassuring. There were very few trees. Groomed and polished, in the innocence of sunlight, the fields did very well without them.

His wife's voice caught Rigden's ear, not pleasantly. She was sitting in front, beside her brother, who was driving. An argument between them, begun soon after they left Oxford, dropped, taken up again, had become sharp, and she was speaking with the coldness, half exaggerated and false, which meant that she was trying not to lose her temper. Their two heads, seen from the back, were absurdly alike, the same size, perfectly round, and covered with thick dark strong hair, Paget's too closely cropped to show the curl in it. He was less than an inch taller than his sister, and very like her in looks: he had all her features, except her straight nose — his was arched and not so aggressive. Apart from that, they were so nearly a reflection of one another that many people supposed they were twins, or even — because of his slight-ness and deceptive fragility — that he was the younger.

'You always said you liked her,' Evelyn said.

'I do like her,' Thomas Paget said calmly.

'Then why say that she is living in adultery? Of all imbecile phrases.'

'It happens to be exact.'

'Exact or not, it's fudge. You're talking like a silly vulgar old woman.'

Unmoved, Paget said, 'My dear girl, a married woman living with a man who is not her husband is living in adultery. You don't mind that. Why do you mind my using the correct words to describe it? What kind of sentimental nonsense would you prefer?'

How they enjoy their quarrels, Rigden thought. It was the angry play of two cubs, physically closer to each other than to anyone else. Evelyn's jealous devotion to Tom, and Tom's submission to it, went back to their childhood in Ireland. Their mother, an Edwardian beauty with the carrion-crow instincts of a political hostess, bored by Ireland and by her husband's passion — his only one — for the life of a feudal landowner, left him and her children, her son not yet three and Evelyn a baby. They grew up like young savages; their father's servants taught them to ride and shoot, they were taught nothing else: for days at a time they stayed out of the house, sleeping under hedges or in a tenant's primitive cottage, where very often they shared a bed, the only one in the place. This life went on placidly until Thomas was twelve, when their father suddenly noticed them and packed Thomas off to school in England; he died the same year, and his absentee wife, forced to recall that she had two children, abandoned very reluctantly two important dinner-parties — in her world the measure of importance was a physical one, as in an African tribe — and came over from England to sell the house and land, and take her daughter away 'to be civilised' . . . Evelyn had never forgiven her. Nor had she ceased to feel, in her heart, that the way in which she and her brother lived during those first ten years of her life

2

had a taste, of reality, that nothing had had since. It was in search of it — and to escape from her mother and her mother's plans for her — that she got herself sent to Oxford . . . And there married . . . There were moments when her husband wondered how much his success with her had been sensual passion and how much the satisfaction of angering and disappointing her mother. Certainly she hadn't felt for him — or not then — the possessive loyalty she gave Tom. Still gave. There was no jealousy in Rigden; he had no grudge, he was devoted to Thomas Paget. He owed him a great deal — everything — the feverish happiness of his years as a penniless undergraduate, his social freedom — even, yes, his marriage . . .

He saw Evelyn seize her brother's arm, in fury. The car swung across the road, and the front off wheel mounted the grassy bank below a wall, all but overturning the car. Paget righted it, drove a few yards and stopped.

'You little fool,' he said coldly.

His sister looked at him with unabashed anger. 'You shouldn't say things that irritate me.'

'If there had been anyone on the road, or another car, we might have killed someone.' He turned his head. 'You all right, Nevil?'

'It would serve you right if we had been killed,' Evelyn said viciously.

Rigden leaned forward to touch her shoulder. 'I prefer you alive . . . I wasn't listening. What did Tom say?'

'No business of yours.' She shook his hand off. 'Don't interfere. This idiot——' she paused, and added a phrase of schoolboy indecency.

Her habit, when she was in a temper, of using gross words, vexed her husband. With a light shock, he thought: I believe she does it because she imagines that what she calls real people, workers, talk like that among themselves. . . . This had never struck him before, but he felt

3

sure of it. She knows nothing, he thought coldly. He thought of the careful decency of the language used by his father, a casual labourer bringing up his family in a London slum, in two rooms. Either of his parents would have punished him for coming out with an obscene word.

Strange, he thought, that I used to admire her for just such freedom from the conventions of my lower-class childhood. With a feeling of astonishment he remembered that when, at Oxford, he first became intimate with the two Pagets, the mere fact that they allowed him to take part — an entirely silent part — in such scenes filled him with elation; he remembered how extraordinary and exciting they seemed, part of an extraordinary world; he remembered his timid awe of two such brilliant people — an awe he took good care to hide. He began his friendship with them by worshipping Paget, and from there moved naturally to falling in love with the girl who was so like her brother to look at, his gratitude turning to incredulous amazement when she said she felt as he did — and they became lovers. . . .

No, he thought uneasily, I don't admire it, I dislike it.

Evelyn had begun to be ashamed of herself. In a gentle voice she said,

'Forgive me, please, Tom.'

Paget glanced at her briefly. 'You admit you were an idiot?'

'Yes, yes,' she said, 'I behaved badly, and I'm sorry.'

'That's all right,' Paget said, smiling broadly.

Her meekness, and her brother's amiable acceptance of it, in some way excluded Rigden. It was a familiar feeling. A moment later, Evelyn turned to him and said,

'I'm really sorry, Nevil.'

He smiled at her. Now I'm part of the family again, he thought ironically. The irony was for himself and his relief at being included again in the Paget world.

4

'You didn't do me any damage,' he said.

Paget laughed gently. 'Nevil is a damned sight too good for you, my girl.'

'I know it,' she said. Rigden's hand was gripping the back of the seat, and she laid her cheek against it for a second.

Paget started the car. They drove on in a contented silence until he said,

'I had Henry Gurney on the telephone just before I came out.'

'What did he want?'

'Nothing. Primrose had invited him for a drink next week.'

'And he was refusing,' Evelyn said.

'No. He said civilly: Thank your wife and tell her I'll come.'

'Ah,' said Rigden, 'he wants something.'

Paget laughed. 'Why don't you like him?'

'Do you?'

'I neither like nor dislike him,' Paget said. 'He's intelligent — and malicious. Without ill-will. He doesn't, I mean, want to assassinate any of his colleagues, it's a purely disinterested malice . . . But I can't talk to him — or to anyone so abysmally ignorant,' he added, with an arrogance just as disinterested. In Thomas Paget's eyes an educated man who understood nothing about modern science was worse than ignorant: he was a half-wit.

Rigden did not speak, and his wife said,

'I can't stand him. He doesn't like me, either. But who does he like? He's as tough as a boot and far less sensitive.'

'I believe you're wrong,' her brother said warmly. 'Any man who takes such pains to get himself disliked as Gurney does is defending himself. And why defend yourself unless you can be hurt?'

'You're too kind to him,' Evelyn said with contempt.

'He dropped that he was dining with the Master tonight. You'll be able to treat him as unkindly as you think he deserves.'

Bored, Rigden leaned back and watched the road. 'Wasn't that our turning?' he asked suddenly.

Paget stopped. 'Yes.'

He drove the car in reverse, too quickly — he hated to be caught out in a mistake — and turned into the narrow road, little better than a cart-track, which would take them to the farm where they meant to have tea. A hundred yards before they reached the farm, he stopped again, in the open gateway of a field.

'We're going to bathe first, aren't we?' he said.

'Yes, of course.'

The field they crossed fell gently towards a stream: the infant Thames, lying quiet in its cradle of alders and hawthorn. The path turned up-stream a short way, passing continually from sun to shadow: it came to an end where the stream widened to a pool, with sloping over-hung banks. The light sliding through the branches of the trees had the effect of a hand stroking the water.

'Who has the towels and things?' asked Paget.

'Oh, damn, they've been left in the car,' Rigden said. 'I'll get them.'

He turned to go back. 'No use,' Evelyn said carelessly, 'they aren't there. I forgot to put them in. We were half-way here before I remembered I'd left them lying in the bathroom.'

Paget laughed. 'Idiot.'

'It doesn't matter, does it?' she said, yawning, stretching her arms, 'we don't need them.'

She had her dress off, and the thin drawers she wore under it, before her brother had got rid of his shirt and trousers, and jumped into the pool from the bank a second

6

before he did. The water, not more than four feet deep, splashed above her head.

'Lovely,' she said, spluttering. 'Get undressed, Nevil, it's deliciously cold.'

'No, it's too much trouble,' Rigden said.

'Lazy devil.'

She tried to scoop water over him. He moved back out of reach and sat down. With a feeling of shame he realised that he was slightly shocked by this bathing naked, ten minutes from the farm. My lower-class upbringing again, he thought drily: my mother's anxious decency and modesty. A part of his mind cringed at the thought of his wife guessing what he felt. He should have rid himself by now of such unavowable shames, as he had rid his voice of its uncertain accent, and disposed, long since, of his shyness and awkwardness in company.

Seen through the water, Evelyn's body had a greenish pallor: she waded into the shallows at the edge, and it recovered its summer warmth. She was standing sideways to him, idly shaking the water from her hair, one pointed breast profiled against the magpie trunk of a birch. Half unwillingly, he let himself be submerged by his passion for her. She came out, scrambling up the bank, and laid a cold hand against his face.

'Feel,' she said.

Something like an electric charge passed from his body to hers. She turned away, smiling, and began to dry herself with the handkerchief she had pulled out of the pocket of his shirt . . . All sense of discomfort had vanished; he felt happy.

Paget had come out, and was dragging his shirt over his wet body. He came, an active shadow, between Rigden and the column of sunlight against which he was sitting. Strolling nearer, he said,

'I have something I must discuss with you.'

7

Rigden had an instant of blind panic, the sensations of a man who realises that he has walked on to a quicksand. 'Now?' he asked.

'Why not now?'

With an effort to speak easily, Rigden said,

'It's too fine.'

His brother-in-law sat down. Smiling, he said in a calm voice,

'What the devil has that to do with it?'

In spite of the smile, his tone had the effect of a cutting edge laid, without pressure, against the skin. It gave Rigden a humiliating sense of disapproval and, yes, rebuke, as though he had been frivolously vulgar. It angered him. Hiding his anger, he said,

'All right. I'm talking nonsense. Go on.'

Chapter 2

THE greater part of Oxford is detestable and hideous. No town, no city containing, as Oxford does, buildings of incomparable loveliness has been more heartlessly disfigured. A small kernel, partly mediaeval, corroded by shops, cars, buses, like a stream choked by ordures, is embedded, suffocating, in a flux of mediocre streets, from the neo-Ruskin dregs of North Oxford to the scurvy disgrace of new suburbs massacring every year another wood, another farm.

And nothing can be done about it, Henry Gurney thought. Except to thank God that, for a few of us, it is still possible to step from the squalor into quiet and decency. At a cost. There were not in the university a dozen people with whom he could spend an evening without being exasperated by their profound frivolity — frivolity at a deep level, below whatever you like of scholarship, sophistication, wit — dryness, and want of nature, and he was certain not to find any of these in the Master's drawing-room.

But — before the boredom he expected — there were the few moments it took to cross the courtyard to the house with its well-mannered seventeenth-century front ,and the abiding green of lawns and mulberry tree seen through a door in the west wall. Moments of pure happiness. How many of these moments can you count on receiving in any one year? With luck, two or three.

On a fine evening in June the house offered almost too much: a world as polished as the *Essay on Man* and as inimitable, the silence of a buried cloister in the incessant

9

clatter and stench of traffic — la recherche du temps perdu. The elms dividing lawns from kitchen garden were full of nightingales; later, when it grew dark, they would shrill in the leaves like a march-past of fifes. One nightingale is enchanting or bearable; four or five singing against each other make a devil of a row.

The door was opened to him by Towey, the Master's oldest servant and one of the few women Gurney was fond of: you could at least be certain that she was neither writing a witty and fashionably dotty novel, nor seeing herself playing a part in a modern comedy of manners.

'Good-evening, Towey.'

'Good-evening, Mr. Gurney.'

'Who is dining, d'y'know?'

'Miss Retta, of course.'

Of course. Few of the Master's dinner-parties were spared his sister. When he took the trouble to think seriously about Retta Spencer-Savage, Gurney did not deny that she was formidably clever — a circus cleverness, the trained rider galloping round the ring, now up on one foot, now seated backwards astride the crupper, now crashing through the hoop. A female don, three years younger than the Master, lively, insolent, ambitious, she was courted as much as feared. Or courted because feared: she was uncommonly sensitive, and snapped and bit recklessly, it seemed for the pleasure of biting, since she had so few frank enemies. As a very young woman she had been the mistress during a year or two of a famous man. The liaison was well-advertised, and lifted her at one move into a powerful and cultivated world — this at a time before power had spilled into too many hands. Even then she had a forked tongue, and the courage, a little impudent, to force society to accept her on her own terms. When the liaison broke off — on her growing exigence; she began to want marriage and to make scenes

— she kept her friends, the women as well as the men. Very adroitly, she turned her intellect loose in a field none of them wanted; she became a brilliant and reasonably erudite literary critic; then, making use of her brother, slipped into the newly-created School of Modern Literature at Oxford: now, at fifty-five, she was respectable and an institution. Thanks to our indulgent contempt for intellect, the passage from enfant terrible to being accepted as an institution is smoother in England than anywhere else . . . Not, in Retta Spencer-Savage's person, an engaging or lovable institution, Gurney reflected, and yet — since it was flesh and blood, it must house childish memories, moments of self-doubt, terror (of death and all that), even tenderness. Nonsense, he thought coldly, you are becoming romantic.

At some moment in her career she began to be called, or to call herself, Athene.

Looking at him slyly, Towey said,

'And the Master's cousin. Mr. Miles. He's staying here.'

Gurney was as surprised as she had meant him to be. Since the day, ten years ago, when Miles Hudson — with that backhanded exhibitionism he was able to pass off as the reserve and hauteur of a great writer — did not announce but let it be discovered that he had joined the Communist Party, the Master had refused to see him. For the past four years he had been living somewhere in North Africa. Less than a week ago, the *Daily Worker* in a flurry of jargon had signalled his 'return to the front line' — no doubt with a new masterpiece in his knapsack.

'What's he like now?' Gurney asked.

'Burned as black as your hat. And no pleasanter to do for than he was.'

'Well — who else?'

'Mr. and Mrs. Rigden.' She looked at him with her old woman's cynical smile: if she saw human nature from below, through its primitive habits, she saw it as decent enough to last. 'What is it you don't like about him, Mr. Gurney? He isn't nearly so bad as you think. And he works hard.'

'He's too pleased with himself, my dear Towey.'

A sardonic fold appeared at the ends of Towey's lips, as though she were accusing him of snobbery — every soul in the college knew (Rigden saw to that) that he had fought his way up on scholarships. The accusation was quite unjust: even in a man he detested Gurney admired energy — the energy, that is, of a pure passion, not the itch of tyrants and agitators. No. What irritated him was Rigden's brash self-confidence, exuding from him whenever he opened his mouth. He disliked, too, what he saw of Rigden's influence on his pupils . . . At first sight, you would say he was likeable: he had a narrow face, with fine bones, and a curiously vulnerable quickness in his glance and smile — but he was pushing and intolerably opinionated and cocksure.

'Maybe,' Towey said, with indulgent contempt for his obstinacy. 'They're in the drawing-room. You don't want me to announce you?'

'No.'

The drawing-room was in the eighteenth-century part of the house, at the end of a corridor: a long room, it overlooked a garden enclosed between the south and east wings: at this hour, with its many windows and faded green panels, you stepped into a light of extreme delicacy and smoothness, like slipping into the waters of a pool.

It was strange, but . . . even now, in spite of his rooted indifference to what people might think of him, he could not evade the moment of panic when he felt himself stripped by inquisitive glances. He covered himself at once. But it is impossible to remain on guard throughout the whole of an evening: and both his false and his real self were apt when he began talking to get out of control, and make a hare of him. Then why did he go out? Why accept invitations to make a fool of himself? A little because he had the wit to know that if he saw no one he would grow very queer, until fewer and fewer voices were able to reach him in his cell. But more, much more, because — at fifty — one passion had survived in him the death or yawning fatigue of all the others: his tyrannical curiosity about the human heart. It hid completely the one thing he most wanted to hide, a profound quivering diffidence and mistrust.

'Ah, my dear Gurney, there you are. A glass of sherry? Very dry?'

Familiarity had given him a sense of ease with the Master, whom he continued to respect as a remarkable character, more remarkable than his critics knew. John Spencer-Savage was handsome, with the rather feminine fullness and smoothness of a fashionable elderly actor. Thick hair like a white biretta, a shapely mouth, soft brown eyes sharpened by a point of irony. Not an uncommon type in the academic world, as in the Church; what was unusual in him was his double nature: an immensely learned classical scholar had given birth to a shrewd administrator — a shrewdness exercised in his own financial affairs as well as in the deftness with which he had tamed the Fellows, so clumsily handled by the previous Master that they were a knot of vipers.

'Thank you.'

A low rasping voice said, 'How do you do, Gurney?'

He turned to look down at Retta Spencer-Savage's yellow sagging cheeks and mouth of a hammer-headed shark. Odd, he reflected, that vain as she is she has never taken any trouble to keep her looks. She might be lazily indifferent to her physical ruin. Or — the supreme point of vanity — she might see herself decaying like the Parthenon — Athene as time had made her . . . Nothing of her handsome youth remained except a pair of fine sombre eyes; she was dewlapped and her body as shapeless and heavy as an old peasant's. When she was a handsome fly-by-night he had disliked her spiteful tongue and her reputation for stinginess and unkindness. As an institution, she did no worse than bore him.

Nevil Rigden and his wife were at the far end of the room, talking to Hudson. She glanced towards them, and swallowed her saliva as though she were helping herself to a dish she couldn't resist.

'Did you,' she asked, 'expect to see Miles here?'

'No.'

'Neither did I.' With a greedy excitement she added, 'He's a brilliant fellow but an assez mauvais sujet, my dear Gurney. He doesn't know wrong from right: right is what gives him pleasure, and wrong is anything he finds boring or vulgar. I daresay he's done more harm than any other living writer.'

'His politics?'

'Oh, no, no, not only his communism. That's a mental illness, and bad enough. But, long before that, he did what he could to teach a whole generation to mock its parents and behave sexually like rabbits.'

'I doubt,' Gurney said, 'whether even a famous writer has so much influence in this country.'

He thought: And I doubt whether you can so completely have forgotten your own life and habits as a female rake . . . In fact he agreed with her about Hudson, whose prodigiously clever mockery of conventions and moral codes — all the cleverer and more infectious for being conveyed in prose of classic simplicity and ease — must have corroded a great many hearts and young minds.

14

The rat beneath the piles, and all that. It may be natural for the young to turn against their parents and to sleep with each other in unabashed freedom, but nature is monstrous. A little hypocrisy is a good thing for a society.

He stared at Hudson. An admirable forehead, pale uncandid eyes under heavy lids, drooping at the outer corners, a fine nose, long sensually arrogant mouth, remarkably small ears. In manner he had nothing of his cousin's charm: he was urbane without grace, inclined, being blessedly certain of himself, to be mockingly insolent with duller people.

'You've met my cousin Miles, haven't you?' the Master said. 'Come and talk to him.'

As he crossed the room Gurney thought: The fellow must be five or six years older than I am. At least. Say fifty-six . . . He looked, with his smooth sun-darkened skin, a good twenty years less.

'I think you know Gurney,' said the Master.

Hudson nodded and smiled thinly, without speaking.

Evelyn Rigden said with energy, 'We were talking about Stephen Quin. Mr. Hudson knows him. He agrees with me that sending him down for good is wicked.'

'Miles,' the Master said easily, 'will agree with anything a pretty woman says, whether he thinks it nonsense or not. Make what you like of that, my dear.'

Is she pretty? Gurney asked himself. Yes, I suppose so . . . A healthy skin, clear greenish eyes under dark eyebrows, close-cut dark curls: a sort of good looks at once boyish and provocative: noticeably wide shoulders, and firm breasts, almost certainly naked under her thin dress.

She had no fear of the Master. Looking him in the face, she said,

'You think Quin ought to be thrown out?'

'Certainly I do. A little immorality and wildness if you like. And if you can afford it. But Master Quin made a

15

profession of drunkenness and lechery. It became very tiresome. He was unwashed, too.'

'He's only twenty and he's a genius,' Evelyn exclaimed.

Hudson smiled. 'That's possibly true. At least four or five of his poems are remarkable, and — most surprising — neither clever nor prudently disillusioned nor like anyone else's.' He looked inquisitively at Rigden. 'I see you don't agree with me.'

'I'm an historian, not a poet,' Rigden said drily, 'and I found young Quin quite intolerable. I can see no reason why, because a young man can afford to buy himself unlimited drink and women, he should come to Oxford to do it.'

His wife glanced at him without a trace of the kittenish charm she had been turning on Hudson. 'Don't be such a — a puritan, Nevil.'

Gurney watched her with delighted amusement. He liked her better for not keeping her charm as firmly fixed to her as a wig. It struck him — not for the first time — that she had a whipping side to her. She had virtues; she could be generous and gay; but something, perhaps in her nature, perhaps only that fantastic childhood in Ireland she enjoyed talking about, had left a hard sediment in her: she expected to be obeyed.

'A university is no place for a genius,' he said lightly: 'our young men now come here to qualify for jobs. And even if it were, it's no place for Quin. If a young man can't live and write his poetry without drinking and whoring, he becomes a bore. Let him find a society where he isn't a nuisance. That's all.'

The Master said genially,

'Don't get it into your head, my dear Evelyn, that the fellow was persecuted. I've been patient. And he had one very good friend, outside this college. Herbert West.

16

West picked him up one night — I dare say in his usual
unpleasant state — and since then he has looked after our
dear Quin with a kindness and patience only a saint — or
a complete fool . . .' His eyes sparkled, and he went on,
'I'm not sure that I know the difference between a saint
and a fool. And to tell you the truth — I'm not even sure
whether West himself has more silliness or more idealism.'

'And since you believe that idealists are scoundrels . . .'
Gurney said.

The Master smiled finely. 'Some of them may be deceiving themselves — or they may be so terrified of the
truth about human nature that they keep their idealism
clapped over their eyes . . .' His smile became malicious.
'I invited West to dine this evening. Perhaps he'll give
himself away.'

His sister had been out of the room. She came in at this
moment, and exclaimed,

'West! Did you say you'd asked him here? Oh, why?
I can't stand his highminded silliness. It's almost impossible to believe that anyone with a mind so open that it
gapes can be as silly as he looks, and often is. He *must*
be a hypocrite.'

The door opened. 'Dr. West,' Towey said.

He came forward with his sly timid smile, which Gurney
suspected him of rehearsing outside the door. But not,
he thought instantly, for any evil reason. He might be an
idealist, West; he was certainly not a scoundrel. Nor a
hypocrite. Nor could he really be simple: a simpleton
would never be able to hit the bull's-eye with his quixotic
gestures as regularly as West did. He had an astonishing
knack of rushing boldly into an advanced position the day
before it was due to become modish and profitable. He did
it in all purity and sincerity of heart, too. You had only
to look into his rapt bubble-witted eyes to be sure of
that.

The Master smiled at him warmly. 'We were just talking about you, my dear fellow — and your terrible protégé, Quin.'

'Ah, Quin,' West said with an effect of reproach, 'poor boy. I had a letter this morning from his mother.'

'Has he a mother?' Gurney asked. 'Who is she?'

'I haven't even the faintest idea,' said West. 'He never spoke to me about her. From her letter I gather that she divorced Quin's father, and married again. She wrote from Venice.'

'I hope,' said Evelyn impulsively, 'that she knows how terribly kind you were to her son. And I hope he was grateful.'

West said in a simple voice,

'Anything I did was done for a boy who is unquestionably a genius.'

The Master chuckled. 'He was ungrateful as well as quite unmanageable, and he had the most shocking table manners. Poor West put up with a lot. No doubt, my dear West, you'll get your reward, but I'm damned if I can see how.'

In a suave voice Hudson said,

'Couldn't you reward him — and the rest of us — with a little food? I'm famished.'

The Master raised his eyebrows. He said gravely,

'We're waiting, in fact, for Thomas Paget.'

'Well, who is he, my dear fellow? Ought I to know him?'

With the same gravity, as if talking to an ill-bred woman, the Master said,

'No. Why should you? You don't read papers on modern science, do you? Paget is the most brilliant of our young scientists — he's thirty-seven — a child — and for the last five years or so he has been the deputy head of the Institute of Advanced Theoretical Physics here. I'm told he knows far more about nuclear physics than the distinguished older man who is the head . . . What else do you want to know?'

Hudson yawned. 'Nothing. Except why he isn't here.'

'Shall we go in to dinner without your brother?' the Master asked Evelyn smoothly.

'Yes, why not?' she said, glancing at Hudson.

'Very well . . . No, here he is at last . . . My dear Paget.'

Watching the late-comer cross the room, Gurney felt a familiar stinging envy. There are a few men and women who have only to come casually into a room to charge it with their own energy and presence. Thomas Paget was one of them. It is a talent, or a trick, which has nothing to do with intelligence, although one can't easily imagine it belonging to a stupid man. Paget's intelligence was intimidating. All the more, Gurney thought, for being exercised in a world about which I am as fatally ignorant as nine hundred and ninety-nine thousand human beings out of a million: our lives are in the hands of a few men who know a great deal about certain properties of matter, but are no wiser or saner than the rest of us. Even before getting rid of all the dictators in the world, we have given ourselves new ones, infinitely more dangerous. They invent the H-bomb and we react like a hen which has found a knife lying on the ground and can only walk round and round it . . . What he envied in Paget was not his monstrous intellect, but a kind of spiritual elegance he had, a moral ease — and his superb energy. Yet he liked him. He liked the other man's kindness and gaiety, and even the streak of vanity, innocent enough, which is natural in small men able to make up in brains or force of will what they lack in physical height. Paget had, too, a charming simplicity. Gurney had been told that, with equals in his own field, he was woundingly arrogant. If it's true, he thought drily, he treats the rest of us kindly out of contempt . . . But he didn't believe it.

'Forgive me for being late,' Paget said. 'I was just leaving the house when a call came through from London. It wasn't one I could let anyone else deal with. I'm abjectly sorry.'

The Master smiled warmly. 'Do you know my cousin, Miles Hudson?'

'In print, of course, very well,' Paget said.

Hudson made no response to this friendliness. Looking down his prominent nose from an angle that accentuated the boldness of its nostrils, he said,

'Then you know as much as anyone need know about a writer.'

Was he stressing the distance between the great writer and the scientist he had never heard of? The effect was slightly and absurdly pompous. Paget smiled. 'You may be right. But I'm not sure. We must talk about it.'

'We'll go in to dinner now,' the Master said.

In the corridor, Gurney had Rigden and his brother-in-law immediately in front of him. Paget said something in a low voice to the younger man, who answered him by a glance of affection and — surprising Gurney a little — deference. One person that bumptious lout respects, he thought.

Spencer-Savage's enemies — he had several: he was too prosperous — were in the habit of saying that he paid his cook more than the salary of a senior tutor. The fellow is worth it, Gurney thought. He had produced an exquisite meal. The windows of the room were open on to the narrow terrace and its row of scented peonies; the servants moved noiselessly between table and olive-grey walls. Eating young duck, Gurney caught himself wondering whether the world will really be happier when these few remaining cells of privilege and rarefied tastes, offensive to an itching social conscience, have been wiped out and replaced by other, cruder forms of privilege? Perhaps. And perhaps the only difference will be that the privileges of bureaucrats, stoats in office, weigh far more crushingly on more people — as well as being sterile . . . I can live happily without anything the Master possesses, he thought, but only — an immense only — if I'm not deprived of pleasures I enjoy far more acutely: the first glass of cheap Anjou after landing in France; the first stroll through a foreign city, with its foreign smells and colours; the first moment when I slip my knife into an uncut book taken from the shelves of a provincial French bookshop.

He had Retta Spencer-Savage opposite him at the table. Knowing, as everyone in the room did, that she loathed and feared communists to the verge of insanity, he was amused by the way she behaved herself with Hudson, deferring to him, praising his earlier novels — not even her snobbery, inflated as it was, could force her to praise anything he had written since his *mental illness*. It was Athene at her most acute. And the great writer showed himself bleakly unappreciative and bored: the relief with which he turned to talk to Evelyn Rigden was shockingly clear. Possibly Athene did not notice it — Thomas Paget drew her attention away at once, deftly and gaily . . . She ought, Gurney thought callously, to know better than to try to impress Miles Hudson. Like all womanisers, he detests intellectual women.

The talk turned, very briefly, on politics. Herbert West said,

'Ten years ago most of my pupils had wandered very far to the Left; now they're swinging the other way — fast. Those of them who bother to have any politics at all, that is.'

'I don't believe it,' Evelyn cried.

'I assure you.'

'Then you must have a singularly dull lot of pupils. Or singularly mean and cautious.'

21

'No, no, far from it,' he said mildly.

Gurney leaned forward to speak directly to Hudson. 'Had you realised that the only effect of your persuasive voice over the last ten years has been to empty your church?'

Hudson smiled, with a little indulgence, and did not speak.

West turned his large pear-shaped head and solemn stare on Gurney as though he were bestowing them — John the Baptist handing round his own head.

'Oh, no,' he said, 'it's the fault of Russia. The young have had their rattle taken away from them. I mean — they know too much now. They're dubious or indifferent — or groping round for something less fly-blown.' He smiled sheepishly. 'I do my best,' he said in a modest voice. 'I tell them that humanity——'

'My God,' Gurney interrupted, 'I hope they don't listen to you. Humanity, my God! Couldn't you find anything more fly-blown? What itch makes you want to sacrifice human beings to these stupefying words? An altar in Trafalgar Square, and a victim or two or a thousand killed over it at every new moon would be far less murderous.'

'I don't know what either of you gentlemen think you mean,' Evelyn said fiercely. 'I believe in Russia with all my might and mind. If what Dr. West says about the young is true, we might as well cut our throats at once before the Americans do it for us. But I don't believe him.'

Her brother looked at her with a teasing smile. 'Now, my child, this is not the place to wave your rattle. You're shocking Athene — and if you're not very careful you'll break one of the Master's irreplaceable wine-glasses.'

She made a face at him, and was silent.

Hudson had a trick of tilting his head back, at the same

22

time settling it into his neck: it reminded Gurney of the
way an eagle or vulture in the zoo will sit sneering coldly
at visitors. He used this trick now.

'Nonsense! When I was young enough to believe her,
my charming scrupulous mother — the only perfectly
bred woman I have ever known — warned me that a feeling
of pleasure meant I was committing a sin. A year or two
later I realised that she was wrong. It was an extraordinary moment — something like a rage of joy. Any
sane man who blames his unhappiness on his intellect is
either a fool or impotent.'

'Or not, let's say, an unmitigated egoist,' said Gurney.

Hudson smiled briefly. 'Oh, if you like. But has any
writer written anything of value about an experience he
hadn't exhausted before he ran to his desk? Accept that,
and you accept my right to make use of any human being
who attracts me strongly — strongly enough for me to
satisfy my psychological curiosity and my sensuality in
one kill, with no obligations. I admit none — except to
my frankness as a writer. D'you ask a surgeon, with his
patient laid open on the operating table, to hesitate out of
pity, or moral prudence, or fear of inflicting pain? Of
course not. Then why ask a writer to stop an experiment
before he has discovered all there is to discover, and
become bored? Absurd!'

'How perfectly heartless!' Evelyn said impulsively.
She recovered herself at once, and smiled at Hudson. 'I
suppose that's silly.'

'Not at all,' Hudson said. 'You're quite right. What
use would a surgeon's knowledge and dexterity be to
him if he weren't something of a butcher?'

In another mood Gurney would have argued genially
that a great poem is worth any number of human victims.
Irritated by Hudson's bland vanity, he felt that the most
obscure human being is more to be cherished than a

23

masterpiece. In the same moment he felt a very pleasant access of hatred. He said calmly,

'And the things you experiment on — young women — probably inexperienced, certainly not your equals in, what was it you said? dexterity? Are they as quickly bored — and as happy to drop the experiment?'

The Master had been listening with half-closed eyes. 'My own pleasures are very simple,' he said in a smooth voice. 'A good wine. This hock, by the way — d'y'like it?'

Paget held his glass up to a light darkened by floating gold filaments. 'It's extremely pleasant.'

'Ah, but I don't think you drank any of my 1921 Moselle. That was a wine. 1921, y'know, was a dry hot summer and the wine needed special care, there was so much sugar in the must. It had to be left longer in the wood than usual, but the best of that year was beyond praise.'

He kept the talk on wines, and his travels in pre-war Germany, until the end of dinner. Afterwards, in the drawing-room, his sister made another bid for Hudson's attention. She told two amusing stories: she was what people of her age call an excellent raconteur — that is, she shaped her anecdotes between finger and thumb, giving the facts a sharp turn, and offered the morsel with a determined vivacity. One of her tricks was to build up a character as wholly admirable and lovable and then, with a nail she kept long for the purpose — rip him up neatly, leaving the poor fellow exposed to the world in all his disembowelled absurdity. Her stories bored Gurney. He detested them as heartless. Hudson made no pretence of listening. He shut his eyes, and it was left to Paget to lean forward alertly, with an air of enjoyment. His roar of laughter made her feel a success — and had the effect of starting her on a story about a Jewish professor in the college. It was spiteful and witty, and — from all he

knew about the man — a lie, Gurney thought sardonic-
ally, from beginning to end. For some personal reason,
something to do with an attack on one of her books by a
Jewish critic, she was nearly as fierce against Jews as
against communists. She could give other, purer reasons
for her ferocity.

Gurney remembered abruptly that this particular Jew
was a friend of Rigden's — perhaps hardly a friend, but a
close colleague. You won't find Athene so easy to flatter,
he thought cynically: I'll bet you hold your tongue.

He lost the bet. Rigden let her finish, then said drily,
'When did you say that Goodman did this ridiculous
and very improbable thing?'

Athene looked at him with astonished anger. 'Why d'you
call it improbable? It happened.'

'But when?'

'Only last Monday,' she told him in the voice of a
headmistress subduing a refractory pupil.

'You're quite sure it was Monday?'

'Of course. I'm absolutely sure. My good man, I never
confuse days, and that afternoon I——'

He interrupted her civilly. 'Then it's certainly untrue.
Goodman spent the whole of that day with me, in my
room, preparing his course for next year. He was there
until seven in the evening, then came home with me to
supper.'

'How can you be such a fool about the man?' Athene
said. 'Or are you telling me I'm a liar . . . No, no, don't
interrupt,' she warned her brother curtly, 'I want an
answer.'

'Of course not,' Rigden said quietly. 'You've been taken
in by someone's malicious invention, and I'd dearly like
to know who it was.'

Nothing he could have said was more certain to exasperate her. She laughed shortly. 'First you accuse me of

repeating scandal about an innocent. Then you imply that I can be taken in by it.'

'Forgive me,' he said, 'I didn't want to vex you.'

She won't forgive you, my boy, Gurney thought, sharply amused . . . The young man had committed an even deeper offence than he knew. After all, Athene was one of the people who had pushed him hardest for his present job, and she expected — naturally — that for the rest of his life he would feel obliged to her and respectful. He — as naturally — believed that he had been given it only because he deserved it — and this in spite of knowing, as he must, that merit is one of the weakest ingredients in a success . . . But why on earth, wondered Gurney, did he run such risks? Not, almost certainly not out of pity for the harmless, and unprofitable, Goodman. Probably only because, as the brightest boy in the class, he has no patience with silly chatter. She'll punish him for it, of course . . . The poor woman, he thought drily, is consumed by resentments, and by imaginary grievances — always the most stubborn and incurable. And as always, the person she resents most vindictively is herself and her youthful failure to make a brilliant marriage. She finds it — don't we all? — pleasanter, less painful, to punish herself and her humiliations outside, in other people . . . It was a very natural arrangement, very convenient, and he did not blame her for it. But certainly she had made a great many defenceless people pay bitterly for her undying sense of injury and her need to give herself absolution, and to feel important.

Not that Nevil Rigden was one of these inoffensive people.

'Heaven knows how these stories get round,' Thomas Paget said lightly.

With an engaging sincerity he began to talk to her about her new book — a velvet-pawed essay on three

26

women novelists. Athene was no fool: she guarded her future by going out of her way to praise young men, and her present by dancing before the most fashionable altars.

All this time Hudson had been sitting on a sofa, alone, in a very curious pose, knees wide apart, hands behind him on the sofa propping him up, head thrown back. One half of his face was in shadow, so that you saw one hooded eye, part of his long shapely mouth, and the thrust of a fleshy nose.

'Have you a new book coming?' Thomas Paget asked him.

'Yes.'

'Ah, good. When?'

'The end of next week.'

'I look forward to it,' said Paget.

The fold of irony enclosing Hudson's mouth deepened. 'I hope you'll like it.' He stood up, yawned, and looked at the Master. 'John, do you mind if I go off to bed? I have a month's sleep to make up.'

The Master lifted his hand. 'Do, my dear fellow,' he said carelessly.

Without glancing at anyone else, Hudson made off.

He took away with him the point of uneasiness that had ruined the dinner-party and prompted Athene to show the worst face of her vanity, but it was too late. Paget tried gaily to rescue the fragments of the evening. He got little help. The Master himself sat with a bland air of not caring what happened to his dinner-party, as though it were a joke that had fallen flat.

After five minutes West left, sidling out with a look of relief and simple fatuity.

Giving him just long enough to get clear of the house, the Rigdens stood up to leave. As he followed her through the double panels of the great doorway, Nevil Rigden touched his wife's arm; it was both apology and caress.

She turned to him at once. Gurney caught the look that passed between them. He felt a sharp bitter envy of them both, and another, less disgraceful emotion. For a moment grief got the better of him — then the lucidity he kept in reserve to be used on himself and his paroxysms of regret or ecstasy woke, and he thought: Is it only because they take so obvious a pleasure in each other that I dislike him? If it is, what an atrocious nature I have.

Chapter 3

HE had no intention of taking Athene home, although the shortest way to his rooms lay past her house. Let Paget do it, he thought, since he makes a profession of tact. Paget was already offering himself. He waited until the two of them had left, then rose to go.

The Master looked at him with a lively smile. 'No, no, don't go away yet. It's too early to think of going to bed, and I need a little distraction after an evening spent watching six people with nothing, absolutely nothing in common except their egoism . . . Notice that I've left you out of the count. Only because when you come here you leave yourself at home. Discreet of you, no doubt, but baffling.'

'Your cousin——' began Gurney.

'That pompous ass,' said the Master lightly. 'Y'know, I can't understand why people take writers seriously. You can never trust them to behave themselves. Miles is intelligent, cultivated — and I suppose one can talk of his thread of genius. He knows, too, that he is a fine writer, he doesn't have to convince himself of it every time he takes a pen in his hand. In short, he's — among other things — a block of vanity.'

'I can't believe he turned communist out of vanity,' Gurney said.

The Master smiled. 'Oh, he would climb up on anything to show off — even a pillory. Perhaps especially a pillory. He really loved his mother, y'know — she was a very beautiful woman, beautiful and pious — the daughter of a Swiss banker — that's where he gets his money from.

His books, and the dissolute life he leads, hurt her mortally. He knew it, and I daresay he has a conscience about it somewhere. That's why he enjoys being scolded and whipped — even invites it.'

'I didn't expect to see him here,' Gurney said with malice.

'Didn't you indeed? . . . Let's go outside for a few minutes. It's a warm night.'

It was very warm, and except for the nightingales, as silent as a village at night. The high walls enclosing the garden underlined a sky the colour of bluish plums: a cool breath moved between the lightly parted branches of the trees, and there was a scent of geraniums and stocks. The darkness was not dark.

Gurney had drunk enough to reach the level where, and only where, he moved freely. It was not drunkenness, it was release, indifference, a profound indifference, the certainty that he could cope with anything and anybody, mock at them or answer them in their own terms: it was not power, it was an exultant sense of power free from any need or impulse to use it. If he had been walking along a street, the faces of the passers-by would have come at him with obsessive sharpness: here, on the equivocally obscure terrace of the east wing, everything he noticed seemed barely able to contain its excess of life: shadows, a leaf, the manifold globe of a peony, a stone. They were concealing a phrase which if he could have caught it would have given away the quick of their existence, a sign, very reassuring to a man who has lost his own meaning, of the persistence of a material world. Drinking, the proper amount of wine, no more, was not his only way of coming at these moments of freedom — they were freedom, escape, not happiness: that is something else — but it was the only way under his control. Any other occasion when it happened was chance, a sign made to him from the material world itself — the suddenly heightened reality of a house wall or a tree or a wrinkled hand stretched out carelessly to feel the sun.

They sauntered across the grass, away from the house. In an abrupt tone the Master said,

'I called this morning on Loddon.'

This is what he wanted to talk about, thought Gurney. 'How is he?'

'Dying.' He paused, and went on in another, frankly moved voice, 'He is a good man, you know, Gurney — the only honest and perfectly incorruptible man I have ever known. He has no vanity, no personal ambition. I couldn't say that of a single other person I know. Even you are only incorruptible out of pride. Or — possibly — laziness.'

'Thank you,' Gurney said.

'I like very few people, y'know. There are fewer still I respect. Loddon is one.' He added carelessly, 'No doubt I meet the sort of people I deserve.'

Gurney smiled. After a moment he asked, 'Who will get his Readership? Do you know?'

'No. But I hope — Rigden.' He glanced at Gurney's face in the darkness and said, 'Yes, yes, I know. He's very young — thirty-four, is it? That humbugging monster Dalton will run Herbert West against him. I have nothing against West — he's conscientious and a hard worker — except that outside his field I have never known a sillier fellow, nor such an unforgivable parade of sincerity. Always in a dither of enthusiasm and misplaced devotion — and what a bore that is!'

'West — outside his work,' Gurney said, 'may be an ass. Is. But does it matter? Rigden is infinitely more obnoxious. Self-satisfied, aggressive — and knows everything. Even a little history.'

The Master laughed gently. 'I said you were incorruptible, my dear fellow. I knew you weren't honest.

31

Rigden has done some brilliant work on the nineteenth century, and will do a great deal more.'

'I'm not a judge,' Gurney said. 'Except of character. I should have said he has every fault of the ranker — desperate anxiety to get on, no scruples about the way he does it, no real generosity. And aggressive because' — this had only just struck him, and he was instantly sure of it — 'he's also uncertain. He struggled up from his class, out of his class: in some corner of him he's terribly afraid of tumbling back into it.'

'I had no idea you felt like that about him,' the Master said.

He knew perfectly well, Gurney thought.

With a familiar shock of clarity, he realised two things. The indiscretion with which the Master had talked about the Readership and Herbert West was intended to provoke indiscretions in return. And, by scandalously abusing Rigden, he had actually helped him — anyone, not only the Master, would realise that he was prejudiced . . . As always, he thought mockingly, your tongue has damaged no one but yourself.

'It puzzles me why you like the fellow,' he said.

'He's a good teacher,' the Master said coldly, 'and West is a very bad one.'

There was no point in holding his tongue now. 'Yes. But have you noticed that although he makes a song about disliking politicians and having no politics — not like West, who is idiotic enough to call himself an anarchist — the young men Rigden turns out are all political types? They all, I mean, believe in a kind of real-politik of power and success. I've talked — or listened — to them about their future, and I know. Most of them go into the civil service — because it's safe and because, as one of them explained to my pitiable innocence, it is the shortest road to the sort of power they covet. Power, entirely unadvertised, over the lives of ordinary people. In this country, now, there are two classes, only two, the administrators and the administrated — and they intend to belong to the first. In short, the commissar type. A bad thing — no country can keep its soul without a great many young men with the energy to make mistakes.'

'He did very well in the war,' the Master said with an effect of irrelevance.

Gurney did not speak. Part of the Master's liking for Nevil Rigden must spring from his aristocratic dislike of the middle-classes, and from the romantic notion he had — rooted in his total ignorance of the new society — that the lower orders are made up of simple people, without pretensions or affectation. Rigden, thought Gurney, is quite shrewd enough to play up to this grotesque error.

'Just as each of us has one saintly Jew,' he said lightly, 'you have your lower-class phoenix.'

The Master smiled, lazily. 'Neither you nor I, Gurney, have ever been driven to get on; we have never been hungry.'

Stung, Gurney thought for less than a minute of the double line of portraits in his elder brother's possession, Gurneys who had been servants of the State, soldiers, proconsuls. It struck him suddenly that the coldness of the solitude round him came from his refusal to let these dead, near or remote, speak through him. He had taken pains to stifle in himself all those voices that alone could give him what he lacked, the sense of a life less brutally short and meaningless than, when he allowed himself to look at it, his was. In the eyes of these others to whom he refused life he was a failure, a man who had made a hash of his life: and even his living friends thought of him with more indulgence than respect, certain as they were that he would never come to anything, it was too late, he had thrown away every chance. Oh, be damned to friends, he thought carelessly . . .

33

'Yes, that's true,' he said.

The Master was silent. Then, in a gentle voice, he said,
'I know you dislike Rigden. I know, too, that you don't
dislike him for any self-regarding reason. You are the only
man I talk freely to, without watching myself. D'you
think I don't know what that's worth?'

Surprised, touched, Gurney said,

'I owe you a great deal.'

It was true. Would anyone else have endured — not
merely endured, but treated with exquisite kindness — a
Senior Tutor who for months, a year, drank much too much,
quarrelled uselessly with his colleagues, and did his work
carelessly and badly?

As if he knew where the other man's thoughts had taken
him, the Master said,

'I never cross this part of the garden without remembering your wife standing just here. She was wearing a
green dress.'

There was a silence. Then Gurney said,

'Really? You have a good memory, better than mine. A
green dress? It can't have suited her.'

He saw, from the set of the Master's mouth, that he had
shocked him by his flippancy — as he had shocked other
people who spoke to him about Anne after she died. His
behaviour at that time had done him a great deal of harm.

The Master did not answer, and he said curtly,

'I must go, I have a lot of work to get through.'

When he had left the house, and was walking back to his
rooms, he thought with sudden anger that it was very
unlikely the Master had been shocked. Spencer-Savage's
half-closed eyes were as sharp as nails. He might only have
been sorry. Oh, God damn the fellow, he said to himself.
He could swallow being ignored, hated, disapproved: the
one intolerable thing would be for people he was forced to
see every day to know that he had suffered and could still

34

suffer, ludicrously . . . Anne, he thought, Anne. My poor child, my poor love . . . The pain, when it began, was always the same, a live nerve drawn out slowly. She was younger than he was, and at thirty, when she was caught in an air-raid in London and killed, she still looked like a girl, with a girl's untouched skin and thin arms. Nothing would reconcile him to her death, nothing.

Chapter 4

IN the morning old R. P. Thorgill came in to see him — just after breakfast, when his servant was clearing away. He stopped the man and said,

'You'll have a cup of coffee, Mr. Thorgill.'

'No, thanks. I've had m'breakfast.'

Gurney smiled. In all the twenty years he had known the old boy, Thorgill had never accepted anything offered him. He was a teetotaller, and he smoked his own evil tobacco. A northerner, he had come to Oxford thirty years ago, for one month, to fill the place of an organiser for the Workers' Education Association who was ill: during that month he fell in love with a girl from a village near Oxford, married her, and because she hated the very idea of the north did not go back. She was dead now, but he was too old, too set, to make a move, and he stayed on, as much out of his right place, as much the shrewd caustic deep-living northerner, as when he came. He was sixty-five and looked a great deal older: a starved childhood had twisted and stunted his body, so that his head, wrinkled like an old root, was too big for it.

He had come to ask Gurney to find him someone to give a course of lectures on modern history. More because he wanted the old Yorkshireman's opinion than for any good reason, Gurney said,

'What about Nevil Rigden? Would he . . . if I can get him to do it, would you like him?'

'No,' Thorgill said at once, 'I wouldn't.'

'Why not?'

The eyes sunk in Thorgill's ruined face had kept as much

innocence as scepticism. 'He's a johnny-come-up and I
don't trust him.'

'You came up yourself, didn't you?'

'Not so fast — and not that far I can't look back to
where I started.'

'Well, it's not likely he'd have taken it on,' Gurncy said.
'What sort of classes have you been getting?'

Thorgill pulled a contemptuous face. 'Poor. It's not
like it was, Mr. Gurney. They don't want to learn. Too
much done for them, too many easy distractions.'

'You're a socialist, aren't you?' said Gurney. 'You
wanted it this way.'

The old boy wouldn't rise. 'Oh, ay, I wanted it — for
the children. Not for th'rest. Let th'rest help themselves,
as I did. It's the onny way to keep your soul. Mind you,
Mr. Gurney' — a glint of derision in the pale eyes — 'it
won't be so bad up north. These southern chaps are as
soft as their country.'

Gurney asked, 'Is it only because he's jumped-up that
you won't have Rigden?'

'No.' He hesitated. 'I don't like that wife of his. She
came to see me one day, blaring in with that loud voice
she has. *How are you, Mr. Thorgill? Is this where you cook
for yourself? How clever of you.* I could a'thrashed her.'

'Has she a loud voice?' What he means, thought Gurney, is that she speaks to him clearly and distinctly, in the
voice of the ruling classes when they find themselves talking
mouth-to-mouth with the other ranks.

'Louder than it has any need to be.'

'She's a fine figure of a young woman — but you
wouldn't notice that.'

'Oh, ay, I noticed it,' Thorgill said drily. 'For a married
woman of her age to look like that — it's not what should
be. I'm telling you.' He got up to go. 'Find me a sound
man,' he said, 'none of your Rigdens.'

Chapter 5

GURNEY'S closest friend in Oxford was a foreigner, a Czech. A child of eight when his country was baptized at Versailles, Jan Eduard Vančura grew up with this young country, and even shared with it one of its godparents: his father was Beneš's friend, and it was Beneš who made to both children the promises a godfather is required to make — and kept them until nothing more was required of him except silence, except forgetfulness, except death. He was a kind distant godfather, allowing the child to call him 'uncle Eduard' and talking to him as if Jan were his own age. 'My uncle Eduard,' Vančura told Gurney, 'could find an answer for everything, even a child's grazed knee — always — until the day when, to be any use, he would have had to find one for baseness, treachery, cowardice, squalid murder.' When, seeking the answer to his first experience of treachery, Beneš came to England, Vančura came with him. He was already beginning to be known as a mathematician, and he found a minor post in Oxford, in Gurney's own college. After the war, he went home: three years later, warned by Jan Masaryk that he might be arrested any day, he went into exile again, without a now silenced Beneš, but with Masaryk's firm promise to join him. The first newspapers he saw after he reached England carried headlines about Masaryk's suicide, which he translated at once as murder . . . By now his reputation was high enough to draw the offer of a post at Harvard, highly-paid. He chose to stay in Oxford, in an obscure and very badly-paid position — for no reason, he told Gurney, except that he knew the worst about Europe and preferred

38

exile in a country which has about it a faint European flavour, even when it is betraying Europe, and even though what it calls dumplings are only pallid sour mounds of grease, with no flavour at all.

Gurney's affection for him was deepened by the feeling of security it gave to him to have a thin strip of neutral territory between himself and even a close friend. For all his intelligence and warmth, Jan Vančura was enough of a foreigner for this nearly imperceptible distance to remain; Gurney could talk to him without the danger of being too nakedly or pityingly or mockingly understood. What had drawn him to Vančura were the very qualities which made him unacceptable to his countrymen in their old-new skin — his total lack of patience, cunning, submissiveness to authority, and his paradoxical gaiety. Narrowly pinched as his life was in Oxford, he enjoyed it. He was one of those fortunate beings — not always the most unselfish or the noblest — who catch happiness as quickly as others catch colds.

He did not live alone. He and his Bella — the girl he had picked up when he came back to Oxford — perched like two birds on the top floor of one of the horrible North-Oxford rooming houses, owned, this one, by a German woman who closed her eyes to their unmarried state. This evening when Gurney went to see them, Bella was just going out: five evenings a week she taught in an art school. She was so bad an artist that she must, Gurney thought, keep her job by sheer industry, or because the director of the school liked her pale face and simple ways as much as he did himself. As a cook she was first-rate.

'Ah, Henry,' she said when he came in, 'I've left everything for your supper on a tray in the kitchen. Don't let Jan forget it and just go on drinking. I see you've brought two bottles.'

'I'll put one in the cupboard,' Gurney said.

'It won't stay there,' she said, smiling at him. 'Jan, remember to eat. Please.'

Vančura reached up from his chair to pat her shoulder. 'Run away, my darling, and draw another robin on a twig,' he said sweetly. He might have been speaking to a child. She did not move at once. 'Why a robin?'

'They are easy to get right. Your horses are awful.'

'I know.' She laughed a little. 'I'd give it up if I could.'

'If I didn't drive you to it,' he said, 'if I let you laze about at home instead of sending you out to work.'

'Heavens, I shall be late.' She touched his cheek lightly, and was gone.

'She was working before you knew her, wasn't she?' asked Gurney.

'Yes. But she would have married — there was someone.'

'You could marry her.'

'She's happy enough as she is.'

Gurney did not feel sure of this, but it was not his business. He opened a bottle, got the glasses out of the cupboard, and settled down to talk. It was a week since he had seen Vančura, and during this week — in a lucky absence of other excitements, and with all the hoo-ha an eminent modesty could spring — Miles Hudson had renounced his communism. His new book, *The Anatomy of Death* — just the title he would choose, Gurney thought — was out, and showed him stripping himself of his illusions with the same joyous energy he had used to analyse his earlier belief and his earlier love-affairs. One more experience exhausted, turned inside-out, its eviscerated body nailed to the door. Brilliantly clever, a little petulant, the book dealt surgically with the infection which, in our day, caused apparently sane men to brush aside as necessary and of no importance the killing, in death-camps, in the cellars under prisons, by torture, by forced famine, of millions of human beings — in the name of a god with several names:

40

historical necessity, the victory of the workers, the future, and so on, and so on, a libation of blood such as no earlier idol ever received.

All he said was true — and set down without a tremor of heart or nerves — neither of which, he would have explained if he had been as anxious to tell the whole truth about himself as he was to display its most spectacular sides, had ever, for one instant, been engaged.

His fame as a writer made his defection news: *The Times* devoted its second leader to the book on the day it came out, less genteel newspapers ran headlines, and an American lecture agent cabled offering him a tithe of the wages of a film star.

Vančura was very sarcastic about him. 'All these years he has done harm — from a position of complete safety and comfort, like a pilot dropping napalm bombs. Now, because he has stopped, he is thanked, adulated, rewarded. I feel a little sick.'

'Have you read his book?'
'Yes.'
'Well, what's wrong with it?'
'Nothing. It's a good book.'
'Then why are you complaining?' said Gurney. 'Drink.'
'He reasons impeccably — and he knows nothing,' Vančura said. 'Entirely bloody nothing.' He sat in his uncomfortable chair looking like a neatly-dressed savage: black hair brushed forward over a low forehead, thin fine mouth, aquiline nose, small dark lively eyes, tarnished and unfriendly. His rage, which puzzled Gurney, was making his hands shake. 'I'll tell you something I have never told anyone. Do you want to hear it?'

Almost certainly not, thought Gurney. The sorrowful tales of exiles bored him. Not so much bored as filled him with a desperate impatience: a pain, a misery, he could only helplessly watch, exasperated him with himself: one of the reasons he was so fond of Vančura was his friend's firm refusal to grieve.

'Go on,' he said.

Vančura's voice had the effect of a bent steel let go. 'I never bothered with politics, because I believed that I did less harm in the world as a mathematician. I had a friend from my childhood, an excellent musician, perhaps he had genius, who believed the opposite — that he must forget his music and be a faithful communist. He was my God completely honest. One day in 1933 his Party sent him to Germany, to work in the illegal Party there; he was caught, tortured, held his tongue, and after two years they released him and he came home to Prague — broken. A few months he was living quietly, then he was sent for by Moscow: he went, of course, and after a time I heard, I was told, that he had been shown up as a police spy and shot.' He leaned forward, his eyes, full of hatred, staring into Gurney's. 'Do you understand?'

Gurney hesitated. 'I don't think I do.'

'I didn't believe it, I believed there had been some hideous mistake. But it was just the time when a shake-up was going on in his Party, there were new leaders, the chaps who had known my friend disappeared, the others seemed only eager to vilify him. I didn't get at the truth until the week I was trying to run away. Then a communist, a man I knew well and had never liked, told me. He was in trouble himself.'

He stopped. His face was distorted and he passed his hand over it.

'Do you want to go on with this?' Gurney asked.

'Shut up . . . In Moscow they had told my friend that a certain German communist who was in Prague must have his mouth stopped: he was going about saying openly that, but for orders from Russia to treat the social democrats as worse scoundrels than the Nazis, Hitler would never have won. My friend was instructed to get rid of him, either shoot him or have him shot: he refused, and was murdered himself, in prison. I asked: How do you know this? and the bastard said: Because I saw to the German myself: your friend was wrong to refuse, he was a traitor, he put a man the Party had no further use for above the Party itself; he deserved what he got. I said: If you feel like that about him, why are you telling me the truth now? . . . God curse him, he didn't seem to have an answer to that one. Finally he thought it might be because he was in disgrace himself, and when he saw me he had had the impulse to clear my friend to just one living soul. After all — he was going to die — tonight, tomorrow — and he couldn't be rapped for it. Why don't you get away? I said, I'll help you. I thought: You damned fool, why burden yourself with the swine? But it was all right, he wouldn't come. He wanted to die, the Party had finished with him and he was losing everything he had given not only his whole life to, but his decency as a man. He said as much to me, and then he said, with a frightful contempt: And let me tell you, Vančura, that *our* indecency is less vile than the greed and spiritual senility of the other side, the side I know you're bolting to; but run, run, and if you're caught on the frontier don't imagine I denounced you, I'm not interested in rats.'

He was silent. Gurney asked, 'Was he killed?'

'I suppose so. Does it matter?' Vančura said. He wiped his face, trying to wipe off the useless grief and rage. His eyes, used down to their roots, defied Gurney to say the wrong thing.

Any touch of warmth would be the wrong thing. 'Would your friend have made the same choice — or would he have tried to escape?'

'He would have tried to escape,' Vančura said. 'He had, somewhere, another life, apart from his communism,

43

though he never lived it.' He hesitated, and said, 'That was what killed him. His other side. His pity for a man who was already lost.'

'It's an ugly story,' Gurney said.

The inadequacy of his words shamed him. One has to listen to these stories, he thought. Ought to listen. But what's the use? . . . It was a story, a thing told, not part of his life, not a twitch of agony in his nerves when he thought of it: he had not even the right to feel anger.

Vančura grinned. 'It wouldn't happen here, eh? That's what you're thinking.'

'No. I wasn't. But it wouldn't. Some infections don't take on us.'

'Perhaps. Perhaps not,' Vančura said. Suddenly he laughed. 'You'll find out one day whether they do or don't. This is a slow country. Everywhere else, time is so running.'

His English was fluent and idiomatic, but he had kept a few oddities. He hated to be corrected.

'Time runs so,' Gurney said.

'That's what I said — time is so running.'

'Have it your own way.'

'And always,' Vančura said carelessly, 'the chance of an atomic explosion cutting short the whole human adventure. Or flinging the survivors back to their aboriginal struggle against cold, hunger, disease . . . A struggle going on, mark you, over vast areas of the world, at this very moment. Human kind is still in its short petticoats.' He made a face. 'What an infant! What you call a leg of Satan, eh? Terrifying!'

'We shan't use the bomb,' Gurney said.

Talk about it bored and irritated him. It shut all doors, effaced all horizons. There was no space left for the mind to breathe, and he resented attempts to suffocate him.

Vančura burst out laughing again. 'What do you mean:

we? We — you — are the people who did use it. If the
Russians drop a hydrogen bomb on New York or London
next week, it will be the third atomic bomb, it will be
nemesis. No, no, my dear Henry, every argument, from
the greatest — Is freedom possible? — to the smallest —
Will you sleep with me today, tomorrow, some time? —
goes on now under the shadow of that event. I find it
intensely interesting . . . Would you like to eat now?'

He stood up and went into the tiny kitchen — it was
also the bathroom; a wooden top covered the bath and
made the table. Through the open door Gurney saw
Bella's canary in its cage; she had brought it with her from
her home, and she gave it the love she might have given
a child. She had left a careful supper: cold soup and a
mould of egg and chicken in aspic, with a salad. Gurney
opened the second bottle of claret; thanking God as he did
it that the things which had delighted him when he was
a young man — among them, good wine drunk in good
company — still gave him the same exquisite pleasure
they did then. And in Vančura's company he had the
final absolute reassurance of knowing that he could neither
shock nor offend: where his friends were concerned
Vančura had no jealousy, no vanity — he was as remarkable in that as in other ways.

His mouth full, Vančura said lightly,

'I tell you, there are too many people in the world. If
there were only a few of us, if human beings were rare like
rare birds, shouldn't we be a lot bloody kinder, and for-
giving each other? Suppose you and I were spending the
rest of our lives alone on one of those prison islands, eh?'

'The only thing I wouldn't forgive you then,' Gurney
said, 'would be dying.'

Chapter 6

GURNEY had accepted Mrs. Paget's invitation to come in for a drink before dinner only because he wanted to ask Paget, casually, whether he could find a job for a young cousin nearing the end of his military service. He was annoyed when he got there and she told him that her husband had been called to Paris, it was something quite unexpected and important and he had gone off right away, that morning.

'I put off some of the people we'd asked,' she said, 'and then I thought: Why bother?' She smiled at him. 'Do you mind?'

'Not in the least,' Gurney lied.

She gave him one of her bright vacant-seeming glances. As a younger woman Primrose Paget had been a beauty, in a fine lavish way. She was still under forty, but she had become blowsy; her enormous brown eyes, under surprised eyebrows, had a trick of rounding themselves, so that the pupils were like glittering jet buttons on a white surface. Her wide mouth could take on any shape, and she had another trick, a smile with closed lips which was at once sorrowful and comic, very like a clown's. She was partly Jewish, through her mother, and that touch of Jewish blood may have accounted for the astonishing mobility of her face with its rapid shifts between beauty and clownish vacancy. She worshipped her husband shamelessly, like a child or a slave. Gurney had the impression that her relations with Thomas Paget were very like Rigden's appeared to be with his wife: although loved, she was an appendage — valued, necessary — but not invited into the closed circle where

46

brother and sister admired each other with a bland ferocity. Extraordinary pair, thought Gurney — the brother so superbly intellectual and so gentle, and the sister, her mind crammed with avidly-held prejudices, a hawk, a young bright-feathered hawk. No doubt she could caress with her claws, and no doubt caresses of that sharp sort went a long way towards compensating her husband for anything he had to put up with in a marriage where, like Primrose, he was not given a great deal of respect. But how many husbands are respected, and how many merely indulged, cherished, needed? . . . One certain thing — dear simple Primrose would never, for a single breath, resent her husband's domination of her: she was silently and absolutely devoted.

'When is Thomas coming back?' he asked.

'I don't know. It depends,' she said vaguely. She raised her voice to carry into the next room. 'Hetty, my love. Hetty, are you bringing us something to drink? Mr. Gurney is here.'

The girl who came in, carrying a tray with glasses and decanters, smiled at Gurney shyly, and said,

'I didn't know how many to bring. Who is coming?'

'Almost no one, but never mind.'

Hetty — Henrietta — Smith was the Pagets' ward, if you liked to call it that. She was the daughter of one of Thomas Paget's friends who had been killed fighting in the Spanish war. Her mother, too, was dead, and the Pagets, without adopting her formally, had taken her to live with them. Primrose, who had no children, loved her with a nervous passion. Not only loved, but in a strange way relied on her, as though the girl were older than herself, an elder sister, with the stability and wisdom she lacked . . . Hetty was not eighteen yet. She had no coquetry, and seemed not to know that her face, a short oval, broad across the eyes, was within a year or two of great and unusual beauty. She had not learned yet to use her long limbs gracefully, and she was too impatient or too awkward to tie a bow . . . This year was her first in one of the women's colleges. She was not seriously intelligent, and she would have been happier if the Pagets had allowed her to become a nurse, but since Thomas Paget mocked at the idea she abandoned it. Very often she gave Gurney the impression of waiting, as a child patiently waits for its life to begin, its real life, not the one forced on it by well-meaning adult hands. She could still laugh with all a child's trusting and candid gaiety.

'Put that tray down and come here,' Mrs. Paget said.

She pulled still further out of place the scarf Hetty had knotted round her neck, and rearranged her hair, only letting her go as the door opened and the Rigdens and Dr. George Craddock came in together.

At the sight of Craddock, Gurney's annoyance at having wasted his time to come here became ill-temper. Craddock of all useless people. He couldn't stand the fellow. Rich, and a licensed enfant terrible, he taught modern philosophy — including for good measure his own 'concrete' version of existentialism. To a few chosen pupils, as to anyone else who would listen or could not shake him off, he demonstrated the *absurdity* of life with all the pleasure he would have got out of scratching a sore on his plump body. He was intolerably wordy. Words, moist with saliva, poured from him like water through a mill-race. He was also, quite openly, a fellow-traveller, going faithfully through all the rites: adoration of Russia, reverence for that fabled Beast, *the proletariat* — in his eyes the only vessel of moral health and virtue. True, he had never spoken to a worker, except to his manservant and his two highly respectable women, housemaid and cook, each of whom would have given notice if they had had a notion how he regarded them . . . All this implies that he was a fool: he was nothing of the sort, he was industrious, immensely learned, and still, at the age of fifty, in impotent revolt against a Catholic upbringing. Oxford is full of people suffering from delayed or ingrown adolescence, but only a few of them do any harm.

'Ah, Gurney,' he said in his effusive voice, 'I haven't seen you for an age. It must be quite three weeks. Not since your friend Hudson blew, as they say, his top.' He had a habit, when he smiled, of blinking, as though to stress his friendliness — See, I'm not even looking.

'He's not one of my friends.'

'Well, well, I'm glad to know that. I must say, he's a shoddy fellow, a monster of sexual conceit and — not to be too squeamish — a liar. A feeble liar.'

'Surely,' Gurney said, 'you used to admire his work. I remember an article you wrote——'

Craddock interrupted him, lifting his podgy hands. 'My dear fellow, that can only have been during his interlude of political decency, when he was making himself useful in agit-prop.' He took a naive pleasure in using what in his elderly-boyish way he thought of as passwords, dragging them in by their heels whenever he could.

'He's much worse than a silly fellow,' Evelyn Rigden said, 'he behaved abominably to a young woman I know in London — you know her, too, Primrose — she's almost half-witted, her parents are rich, and they had to buy him off, which I suppose is what he hoped when he took her up.'

'That's not a very clever story, is it?' said Gurney. 'And had you heard it when you were talking to him at the Master's? You made up to him quite shamelessly that night.'

She gave him a glance of annoyed dislike, and said,

'He has a trick of rubbing his middle finger against his thumb which reminds me of my mother.' Her dislike of her mother, savage though it was, had become a mental quirk: she shunned all the great commonplaces — reverence in the

49

face of death, pity for the weak, honour thy father and thy
mother and the rest of it — as though they were not only
vicious but unfashionable. 'I ought to have known when I
saw him doing it that there was something very wrong. I
I could tell you a lot of stories about him.'

Rigden said abruptly,

'Well, don't tell them. I'm sick of the sound of his
name.'

A note in his voice struck Gurney: not distaste so much
as uneasiness — as if he felt that, in her anxiety to damage
Hudson, she was inventing too recklessly.

She stared fixedly at her husband. 'You don't want to
defend him, do you?'

'No, of course not, but——'

'He and my mother are wicked in exactly the same way,'
she cried. 'There is nothing I should like better than to see
both of them on their knees scrubbing a poor woman's floor
for her, or cleaning latrines with their beautiful smooth
hands. That would really please me.'

'A lot you know,' Rigden said savagely, 'about poor
women and their floors. You know as much as Hudson
himself. As for hands — ' he grinned — 'what does yours
know about the dirt in old cracks, or a child's sore gum, or
the emptiness of a shabby purse? Your — ' he swallowed a
word — 'your socialism is all in your head.'

'That may be why I'm not forced to throw emotional
fits about it,' she said arrogantly. 'I can be rational.'

'Rational?' he said. 'You? You're so rational about your
mother that I——' he checked himself and said in a low voice,
'Never mind. I'm sorry.'

'The one evening Hudson came here to dinner,' Primrose Paget said, 'he wouldn't talk of anything except other
writers. He was horribly sarcastic and funny.'

Hetty said suddenly, 'I liked him. I thought he was
kind.'

Mrs. Paget smiled slyly. 'He took a great deal of notice of Hetty. He paid more attention to her than to anyone else in the room.'

'Aha,' said Craddock, 'the famous technique. I'm horrified by you, my child, yes, horrified. I had no idea you could be so easily seduced.'

'I can't, and I don't know why you say so,' the girl said.

She had blushed hotly. She was, Gurney saw, suffering the senseless ridiculous agony of the very young when they are made fools of in public. Before he could interfere, Rigden said,

'What rot. I know nobody less likely to be taken in by Miles Hudson, any Miles Hudson, than Hetty.'

The girl looked at him without speaking — it was a look that gave her away so nakedly, with so shocking an innocence that instinctively Gurney moved to hide her from the others. She's in love with him without knowing it, he thought. Or does she know? . . . For a moment he saw her as not only very young, but as alone in her unguarded innocence, and vulnerable . . . To draw attention from her, and to be rude to Craddock, he said,

'I'm damned if I understand you and your friends — the bien-pensant Left. You swoon when some wretched negro is lynched in the States — you even push bad faith to the point of pretending that it is an American custom — but you keep as silent as their graves about the thousands dying of disease and misery in labour camps in Russia. And about the murder of a small decent Baltic people. Why? I could understand it if you were afraid or stupid. You're neither — and you're not even a communist; you don't go out into the streets, you sit at home urging others on, like a pimp.'

Craddock smiled. No insult, however gross, reached him through his shell of complacency and vanity.

'Yes, yes,' he said, 'I know, my dear fellow, I know. But,

51

but, but a religion in its first flush of revelation is always a persecuting force. Think of the early Church, with its human bonfires.'

He laughed triumphantly, and dried the corners of his mouth. As your raisonneur always does, he believed that a clever analogy nailed any argument.

'It comforts me immensely,' Gurney said, 'to know that if your friends ever take us over, you will be shot out of hand, as a bourgeois intellectual — romantic and unreliable.'

Craddock said solemnly,

'I trust I should have the strength of mind not to resent an inevitable error.'

'No, no,' Gurney said, grinning at him, 'what you trust is that you can go on applauding executions in Eastern Europe while living safely in Oxford for the rest of your life.'

With a touch of mischief — she knew all about the girl's fear of being noticed — Evelyn said,

'Hetty, your father was a communist, wasn't he?'

'No,' Hetty said.

'Are you sure? I thought he was.'

The girl looked at her directly. 'No. But he was a hero. And he was with communists when he was killed.' Suddenly she looked very young, resolute, defenceless. 'That's why I don't believe any of those lies about them,' she said under her breath.

'You are right to think of him like that,' Gurney said gently.

Craddock put his head on one side and the blunt tips of his fingers together, in his pose when he lectured. 'My dear little Hetty, my dear Gurney, try to realise that the triumph of communism is what *must* happen. I say: must. To place yourself in opposition to the line of history proves of two things one. Either you can't think clearly, or you are acting in bad faith. Suppose, let us say, that you, or I, citizens of a communist state, discover that our dearest friend, or wife or husband, is talking against the government, and we denounce him — or her — is it a crime? No. Objectively no — since we are defending the, ah, workers' state. If, on the other hand, I denounce a communist in *this* country because he is, let us say, acting as a spy — that is, as a loyal agent of the class struggle — then, my dear girl, I commit a crime, a real crime. Do you understand? A crime, my child, cannot be separated, dialectically, from its context. It's as cosy as that.'

Hetty turned scarlet. 'I couldn't denounce a — a friend.'

'I could,' Evelyn Rigden said quietly.

Her husband looked at her with a smile. 'Oh, no, you couldn't, my darling.'

'I could and I would.'

They stared at each other for a moment before Rigden turned away.

Gurney had been watching them with curiosity. It amused him that — even when she was arguing like an idiot — Evelyn Rigden could subdue her husband's self-assurance so easily. Astonished him too.

'And you would be right, my dear Evelyn,' Craddock said, smiling and blinking. 'You would be thinking dialectically — that is, concretely — in the, ah, correct context.'

Mrs. Paget had been sitting silent, her eyes, as bright as a magpie's, staring at nothing. When suddenly she roused herself, stretching her mouth to its widest in a grimace of innocent astonishment, she seemed a prematurely old and knowing child.

'Oh, no, no, what nonsense!'

'Do you call it nonsense?' said Gurney. 'I'd call it the bitter dregs of sophistry. Any action, however cruel or sordid, becomes noble when you baptise it in the name of the class struggle . . . As Craddock would say, it's as cosy as that.'

He was sick to death of Craddock's clever frivolity, and bored by the rest of them. He was angry with himself, too, dejected by what at this moment he felt as the agonising futility of his life. Why the devil, he thought coldly, do I stay in Oxford? Why haven't I the courage to cut loose, to take the little money I could raise, and spend the rest of my life in mortal poverty and peace in a Greek or Turkish village, at that end of the Mediterranean? Why? At least I should discover there what I am — and how to live—lightly, easily — with insecurity and death. With reality, in fact.

'My dear chap——' Craddock began, quivering eagerly, like a dog.

'Primrose, my dear, I must go,' Gurney said. 'Tell Thomas I want to see him.'

He walked home. As he passed a house near the Parks, someone began to pick out on a piano the air of a once popular waltz. He knew it, and stopped dead, as if someone had hit him. With an effort he even remembered the name — *Temptation.* For a moment he saw Anne as she looked when he had seen her for the first time, waiting to be asked to dance to this same worthless tune: when he spoke to her she gave him a young calm smile in which he caught a flicker of relief that she was not going to be left without a partner at her first London dance... The joke is, he thought, that only bad music is able to start up so unbearable and humiliating a despair and grief. Great music, a great poem, has no such horrible degrading power . . . An elderly woman walking towards him stared at his face. The fear that she had noticed his ridiculous state, and was going to speak, gave him the energy to walk on.

Chapter 7

A FORTNIGHT later something happened that was like an echo of Craddock's grotesque nonsense. In the afternoon, the Master telephoned Gurney, asking him to come round at once. He went, and found Retta Spencer-Savage there. She was nobly dishevelled, Hecuba after the fall of Troy, and holding her hands crossed like a martyr's over her breasts. She gave him an unfriendly smile and went on talking at once, as though he knew what it was all about — a conversational trick of hers.

' . . . and if you don't agree with me, Gurney, at least you're not so insanely prejudiced in his favour that you can't even listen. All I'm asking either of you to do is to watch — and form your own judgment. You'll very quickly see that I'm right. Then you can call in someone trained to keep an eye on these gentlemen. If you won't . . . well, at least I've done my duty by warning you.'

'Warning us about what?' Gurney asked. 'Who is it?'

'Master Rigden, of course. You were here that evening.' She rolled her large dark eyes like a nervous horse, a sign with her of impatience and excitement.

Speaking flippantly, as though he still had some hope of teasing her out of it, the Master said,

'My sister believes that Rigden is a very sly communist. She wants us to take steps — I'm not sure what steps.'

'I simply wanted to warn you,' she repeated. 'If you refuse to do anything, you are responsible, not me. Both of you.' She rounded on Gurney. 'Haven't *you* anything to say?'

'I'm much too surprised,' he said.

This was quite untrue. He had been expecting some-

55

thing of this sort — ever since the evening when Rigden demolished her lying story about poor Goodman. Denouncing people as communists was a mania with her, a curious and unpleasant one but not, as manias go, and in a sceptical society, very dangerous. Why did she do it? Gurney thought that it was only an elderly version of the resentment, perhaps the fears, springing in her, when she was still a young woman on the make, against everybody she suspected of criticising her unconventional life. Even in those days she had complained bitterly of being persecuted. Then, as now, she had the same desperate need to be agreed with, approved, endlessly admired, and to play the distinguished woman. For all her intelligence, and although she was safe now, she suffered terribly from disapproval, real and fancied; her vanity was an open wound. To protect it, if you opposed her, she assumed first that you were a fool, then that you were malevolent and treacherous. Her spy mania had grown out of this, in the most natural way imaginable. Where she used to see everywhere treachery to herself she now saw, as well, treason to the state. The two together sent her into a frenzy, not always without its comic, even its cruel side.

Had she, Gurney wondered, even a remote suspicion that her motive, her deepest motive, in trying to make trouble for Nevil Rigden was a personal one? Probably not. There is nothing like a noble cause for putting a good face on personal needs and resentments — and even pleasures.

'Have you any proof?' the Master asked lightly.

'Proof? You have only to listen to his wife's talk. And the insane way he flew to the defence of that creature Goodman — who calls himself a socialist, which gives him a Jew means something at least as sinister and destructive as communism.' Her voice shook with passion. 'Besides, I can trust my instinct. Treachery gives out a certain peculiar vibration — nowadays I can pick it up as soon as I come anywhere near it. The other evening it was unmistakeable.'

Gurney laughed, and she looked at him with exasperated distaste.

'My dear girl,' the Master said very gently, 'I hope you don't tell people about these vibrations. They'll think you're mad.'

'I'm completely indifferent what people think about me!'

He gave her one of his unexpectedly sharp glances. 'Are you indeed? If Rigden hadn't offended you, would you have noticed his, what d'you call it, vibrations?'

She stood up. 'I'll leave you to your little ironies,' she said, with a finely sarcastic smile. 'They save you the trouble of thinking, don't they?'

He walked with her to the door, and stood there talking to her for a minute in an affectionate voice. Gurney could not hear what he said, but he was smiling when he shut the door on her and came back.

'She won't carry this nonsense anywhere else,' he said easily. 'I've told her she must hold her tongue. She will, too, now that she's shot her poison.'

He was fond of his sister. This slightly inhuman comment only meant that he had as few illusions about her as about himself or anyone else. He had — Gurney knew better than anyone — been through a great many painful scenes with her, without ever losing patience or kindness: he looked on her as a spoiled child, brilliant, unstable, pathologically vain, but a child. And since he believed that human beings are always, whatever pretences they put up, governed by vanity and self-interest, he forgave her readily enough. Even her malicious tongue amused him.

'She used to think very highly of Rigden,' Gurney said.

'Oh, when she forgets this affair she will again,' the Master said, yawning. 'Forgive me for dragging you into it. I wanted you here because I thought she would be impressed — knowing how you dislike him — by your scepticism. She distrusts me — she's quite certain that I have no strength of character.' He laughed under his breath. 'Odd how difficult it is for a woman to imagine strength apart from brutality and wickedness.'

Gurney frowned. 'Is it so obvious that I don't like Rigden?'

'My dear fellow,' the Master said, smiling, 'you have as much tact, with people you don't like, as a bear.'

'I hate charlatans,' Gurney said violently.

'Oh, come — we're all charlatans in our way. D'you think I should be where I am without the necessary grain — trick — call it what you like — of intimacy? False intimacy. Think of all the really successful men and women you know. Do you know a single one who didn't learn very young the trick of calling attention to himself in the right quarters? And another thing — ' his voice became light and charming — 'the fact that you, my dear boy, didn't take the trouble to be successful doesn't mean that you are simple and straightforward — or even modest. Does it?'

Gurney laughed. 'Perhaps not.'

The Master took hold of his arm. 'I want you to do something for me.'

'What is it?'

'I want you to drop in on Rigden at home, and tell him what you have just heard my sister saying about him. He must ignore it, of course, when he sees her, but tell him to be a little careful with her. Evelyn, too, would be wise to guard her tongue — but I doubt if she can or will. She's rather a goose.'

'Do you insist on my telling him?' Gurney said, staring.

'If you will,' the Master said gently.

He was amusing himself, of course, delighted to be able to indulge, at the Senior Tutor's expense, his equivocal sense of humour. Gurney knew it, and was vexed. Short of refusing outright, there was nothing he could do.

Chapter 8

THE Rigdens had a flat at the top of a large horrible house in the Banbury Road. The woman who opened the door to Gurney was a blond rawboned foreigner —he thought a German — drawn from the last dwindling reserves of willing or at least passive labour. When it is exhausted, or moves into greener fields, we shall have reached our future as a lower-middle-class Utopia with a bureaucratic *gratin*. He asked whether Mr. Rigden were in, the woman smiled and nodded, and he followed her into a sitting-room agreeably full of books, a writing-table, armchairs meant for sprawling legs — in short, the cocoon of a married don without children. He waited. After a minute or two Evelyn came in. She seemed surprised to see him, and said,

'Did you want Nevil? He's away.'

'I'm sorry,' Gurney said. 'I asked your woman for him. I thought she——'

'She doesn't understand a word yet. She's a Finn, and all she has grasped is that no one is to be sent away. What time is it? Please have a glass of sherry, I want one myself, and I don't drink alone.'

'Will he be back this evening?' asked Gurney.

'I hope so. I hope, before six. We're going down to the cottage for two nights.' Her voice hardened. 'His mother is ill. They sent for him and he went off this morning.'

Gurney took the glass she held out. 'Is it serious?'

She made a mocking face. 'She's been ill for months, I don't know what it is — I suppose, old age. She lives in London with Nevil's sister — in Deptford . . . that's the East End, you know.'

'Yes, I know,' Gurney said drily. Her tone irritated him.

'Once a month or so the sister sends for him — always for the last time. He rushes up, but of course it isn't the last time, she doesn't die, probably won't for years.' She drew her brows together in ill-temper. 'It wastes his time, and I can't make him stop doing it.'

'You don't care much for families, do you?' said Gurney. She gave him a clear look. 'I never see why we should let them make unreasonable demands. Nevil works so hard — he hasn't time to throw away on these death-bed rehearsals. His sister, of course, enjoys them. Persons of that sort do.'

If you weren't playing at being a socialist, Gurney thought, you would say: persons of that class. Do her justice, she never would say it, but the impulse had been there, almost audible in the inflexibility of her voice. He understood why old Thorgill disliked her. It was an unfair dislike, she tried hard, and she could not possibly have guessed that her clear authoritative tone stirred in the old Yorkshireman a bitterness older than his starved childhood, older even than himself.

He wondered how sharply her husband resented her attitude to his family. But perhaps, on his way up, he had come to share it?

'Why did you want Nevil?' Evelyn asked.

'It was nothing important. I'll see him later.'

'As you please.'

He tried to think of something friendly to say to her, and said, 'Hasn't he an article in the *Historical Review* this month? I heard something.'

Her face changed. 'You haven't read it?'

'Not yet.'

'It's terribly good,' she said gaily. 'He's writing better and better. Don't you think so?'

This eager admiration for her husband's intelligence was

attractive. For a moment Gurney liked her. Her careless rather rough good looks and abrupt manners had never impressed him as worth a second glance, and he disliked her half-conscious arrogance. With a little surprise he caught himself thinking that gaiety, candour, a lively mind and a firm supple body, were not without charm. In fact she has everything, he thought idly, except tenderness.

'You didn't stay very long at Primrose's party the other evening,' she said.

'I hadn't time.'

She laughed. 'You mean you hated everybody there.'

'Not quite,' he said coolly. 'That's an extraordinarily nice girl.'

She looked at him with smiling derision. 'You mean Hetty? She's all right, though I think she's a bit simple. But I can't stand the way Primrose thrusts her at us. If she were the girl's mother, one would make excuses for it—though I don't really see why we should: it wouldn't be any less silly.'

'Do you dislike all mothers,' Gurney asked, 'or only your own?'

She said drily, 'I dislike what I'm sure you would call family loyalty — if what you mean is that I ought to feel sorry for a nasty creature or an idiot merely because she was dumped on me by birth, or marriage. I'm never sorry for fools — even harmless ones.'

'And you consider your sister-in-law a fool?'

'She is about Hetty. And in some other ways.' She smiled without kindness. 'One thing about her, she adores Thomas. That covers a multitude of idiocies.'

Gurney stood up to go. 'How lucky—for Primrose,' he said, 'that you think so.'

Chapter 9

EVERY time he went back again to Deptford, Rigden found himself trying to see it as it had been when he was a child, before German bombs destroyed so many hundreds of squalid little houses, including the house he used to live in, and before the rawly efficient rebuilding. His sister's little house was new, its bricks scarcely grimed yet; the small rooms were light, no boards grey with ancient dust, no suffocating unpleasant smell. Most of the furniture was new and only too believably copied from a bad copy. When he and his sister were children they would have thought such rooms the last word in luxury. They pleased Catherine now, and although she might suspect that he admired them a little less, she could have no notion how much less. When he was with her he was not ashamed of having learned other tastes; he was uneasy, as though his skin had ceased to fit him. There were ten years between them (she was twenty-four), but on one level — the level which held a narrow cold room and a child asleep in a bed formed from two chairs pushed together against a wall — they were still close. On every other level they were separated by the whole of Rigden's present life. The only time he had brought Evelyn here was a hideous failure. What his mother's real feelings were about her he never knew; she said little, and that pitifully constrained. Catherine and Evelyn grated on each other like sand on glass. God knows, he thought wryly, what Evelyn had expected — certainly not the lower-middle class gentility of Cat's manner with a strange sister-in-law. It was a horrible afternoon, and they didn't try it again.

He rang, opened the door, and called. His sister came downstairs, running.

'Oh, you've come,' she said.

'Didn't you expect me to come? How is she?'

Coming here, he had thought of everything rather than of their mother. He did not want to hear when he came in that she had died — yet, somewhere in him, he wanted the strain to be over. A strain, he kept reminding himself irritably, that bore infinitely less heavily on him than on Catherine, who had to nurse the sick woman as well as look after a husband, a child, the house. She was young and strong, but that didn't make it less a burden, and one he didn't share. His share was the little money he sent every month — and these visits which interfered with his work. Again and again he had tried to feel remorse for the egoism which kept dragging his half-written book across the image of his mother so near her death. As if anything he would ever write was so magnificent that he could justly turn his back on what was going on in the human being who, when all was said and done, was part of his body and soul in a sense no other creature was. Inexplicable: at the moment when he could really do something for her, he hung back. It was horrible, inexcusable — and stronger than he was. Each wasted day drove him irritably mad, like an aching tooth.

'She's asleep. Don't go up yet,' Catherine said. She drew him into the kitchen and sat down, pushing her hair. 'Oh, Nev, I'm so tired, and she breaks my heart, she's forgotten you don't live here, and she expects you every time the door opens. I can see it in her.'

'Is that why you sent for me?' he asked.

'No. Yesterday the doctor said she was going, today she's better. But it won't last.'

'Why not?' he said with a spurt of bitterness. 'She must want to live.'

63

'I don't know,' Catherine murmured. 'What do you mean? . . . Sometimes now she thinks she's a child living in that farm she told us about, with the yellow field of buttercups. I never told you, did I, but last summer, before she got so ill, Jim and I took her down there for the day. And oh, our Nev, it had all gone — the fields, the stream, the farmhouse. And the big house was gone, that she gave you your name from — Nevil Place. Streets everywhere — she couldn't find a thing: she was terribly put out. Nice little houses they were, too; I could have done with any one of them.'

'I can't stay long,' he said.

'You never can. I suppose your wife complains.'

'No.'

His sister laughed shortly. 'I'll bet she does — and grudges every time you come here. Don't tell me. And looks down on us, too.'

The jeering note in her voice when she spoke of Evelyn irritated him. He said nothing. It was useless — like talking to her about books or politics. She read when she had time, but only the pap of stale dishonest emotions prepared for her. As for politics — she and Jim voted Labour out of habit, and it meant nothing: she had no vitriolic memories of the meanest sort of poverty, she and her husband were decent unthinking people, at their ease in the world handed to them.

'How is my niece?' he asked.

Catherine jumped up. 'Come and see.'

He followed her into the sitting-room and they bent together over the cot, looking at a flushed face and long dark eyelashes. 'She looks very well,' Rigdon said.

His sister glanced at him. 'Why don't you and Evelyn have children, our Nev? You're missing something.'

'I daresay,' he said lightly. 'We can't afford it.'

'That's nonsense!' She hesitated, changed her mind,

and said, 'You haven't noticed the new radio. We can't manage a telly yet, but we might next year, if . . . Listen, that's her calling, Nev — she's awake.'

She hurried away. He had not heard the faintest sound. Some part of her, he thought, as young and kind as the rest, never stops listening . . . In a few minutes she came running downstairs again, and sent him up.

You open the door into a room where someone is dying, and it is like any room: death keeps well out of sight: no need to think about it yet. Sunk deeply in the bed, his mother did not answer him when he spoke to her. She was flushed, and her blue eyes, empty and unfocussed, wavered across his face, then closed. He sat down and took her hand: for a minute it lay inert in his, then, as blindly as an infant's, the fingers moved and held on. He thought: It is the last jet of that persistence which kept her alive through the near-hunger, filth, disappointment, that killed my father . . . Another thought, more familiar, wiped this out. How long must I stay here? . . . A nerve from her body passed through her fingers into his, but he was infinitely far from her. Still holding her hand, he let himself think of anything else, of his work, of a problem in the chapter he had reached, of the airlessness of the room: at last he began to worry about reaching home in time to get away to the cottage. If he failed her Evelyn would be disappointed: angry, too — since his mother was not after all dying. He looked down at his watch: he had been in the house nearly two hours. He was ashamed of his boredom, ashamed of feeling that every minute he spent here was wasted — and he was impatient, a nervous, growing impatience. He tried gently to free his hand. At once his mother's fingers tightened their grip. In the end he had to use all his strength to push away these poor fingers — yes, push them . . . She opened her eyes for a moment, and said in a strange remote voice — how far had it to climb?

65

'Don't go.'

'I must,' he told her. 'I'll come back.'

She closed her eyes again, the lids as if bruised. He bent down and kissed her; her head had slipped sideways on the pillow; she did not move. He refused to let himself notice the anguish that woke furtively in him, like an animal. He could still feel on his skin the moment when her fingers gave way suddenly and let him free himself. He went downstairs and told Catherine,

'She's asleep again, I think. I must go.'

'You couldn't for once stop the night? I can make a bed for you on the couch — if you can bear to stay with us.'

'Don't be silly,' he said. He felt only impatience. 'You know I'd stay if I could, gladly. But I have to get back.' She looked at him with a mocking smile, and he said angrily, 'I work, you know.'

She said nothing, and he thought: Must we quarrel every time we meet now? She came to the door with him, and suddenly, as he was going, she threw her arms round him.

'Oh, our Nev, don't leave us.'

He said, 'I have to go, Cat. I'll come again soon, you know I come when I can.'

There were tears in her eyes. 'I don't mean . . . I know — when she's gone — you'll drop us.'

'Don't be silly.'

She clung to him for a moment with her hard young arms, then gave him a sharp push and slammed the door. He hurried off — seeing in the one same confused wretched moment a future of lame excuses, and the child lying on her two chairs where he could reach out from his own bed to touch her if she whimpered in the night . . . God Almighty, he thought furiously, is any of it my fault? Why should I feel guilty? She has the life she wants — and mine, after all, isn't easy.

66

He felt relief, too, the enormous relief of turning his back. By the time he reached Paddington he was in a sensible frame of mind and could keep both her and his mother at a distance, where in fact they belonged. He had missed the train he meant to take, and had to go by a slow one. He would be at least an hour and a half late . . .

'I knew you wouldn't be here in time,' Evelyn said drily. 'How was she?'

'Not really any different.'

'Then why did they send for you? I suppose your sister was making the usual fuss . . . Is it worth going to the cottage now? By the time we get there it will be dark.'

'Of course we'll go,' he said quickly.

He did not want to argue about it. Coming down in the train he had thought, with a crazy impatience to be there, of the two days and nights he would have with her in the cottage their friends called Rigden's Folly. It was five miles from any village, any other house, in the hilly country between Burford and Stowe, a room and a kitchen downstairs, another room above: that was all — it had been built for a shepherd, and when the estate came to pieces after a death no one wanted this isolated place with oil lamps and an outside pump; they bought it cheap, with the legacy from Evelyn's aunt. Its isolation was the thing they liked about it, Rigden because here he had her to himself, he shared her with no one, not even her brother; Evelyn because it reminded her of Ireland, and gave her back a faint flavour of all she had lost the day her mother's car drove up to the great shabby house where she and Thomas, pressed together like stray dogs, waited in a hostile silence for 'the woman' to speak to them . . . For as long as they were in the cottage, Nevil became part of that life — at least, he thought a little wryly, in so far as he dealt with oil lamps, worked the pump, and shared a fairly primitive bed.

'All right,' she said. 'Let's start at once.'

'I'll take the bags down to the car.'

'They're there already. I took them.'

She had meant to go, he thought . . . For several miles, until they were well out on the road, she did not speak. It was a warm evening. They were driving west, towards a sky scaled like a trout seen through dissolving ripples. As always when he had in front of him a space of time when he need make no effort to impress or amuse, Rigden was happy.

Evelyn spoke sharply. 'Why, if your mother is not worse, did your sister make you come up?'

'She had been very ill the night before, and Catherine was afraid.'

'It's such an absurd waste of time. I can't see why you should give way to your family's love of scenes. Do you *want* to be there when she dies?'

He knew — it had come up many times before — that she resented the idea of death: not her own death, about which she never thought, but that other people died vexed her as though they were trying to call attention to themselves with unforgivably bad taste and stupidity. As she did about religion, conventional morals, rites of any sort, she felt that death was an affront to a free mind . . . For no reason he could have traced, he heard his mother saying, 'Don't go,' in that sunk barely audible voice: his remorse and buried guilt rushed back; he wanted to punish some one for the way she had been left this afternoon by a son who had pushed her out of his life years ago, like shutting the door on a stray cat, and he said angrily,

'No. But why should I leave my sister to go through it alone, if I can help her?'

'There are people who enjoy a death-bed,' she said calmly.

He knew she meant him to understand that his sister had no self-control, no manners. An uncontrollable bitterness filled him.

68

'I don't ask you to like Catherine,' he said, 'you scarcely could — it's not your fault. But she's up against something you are never likely to be — since you would never let yourself be made responsible for an old dying woman . . . Don't let's talk about it.'

His wife was silent. A familiar feeling of tension invaded him, and he thought: Why are we going away, what's the use? . . . Without glancing at her he could see her stubbornly offended smile. Her body near him in the car was a tightly-coiled spring of contempt and rejection. He had an unpleasant sense of being cut off — from everything, from himself, the past, his life now, with its straining demands, and Evelyn. Obscurely he knew that anger would help him; he could escape into it from his intolerable dissatisfaction with himself — or he could stop the car and make love to her there and then, at the side of the road. Forcing himself to keep quiet, he drove on.

It was dark now, as dark as it can get in early July under a sky restless with stars: on either side of the road the country, drawn back into itself in sleep, allowed a remote pre-human past to rise gently to the surface. At the highest point of the ridge, he turned the car off the road into the narrow lane, no wider than a cart-track and as rough, which dropped steeply to the valley. In the darkness the air round them gave off a feeling of emptiness and depth. The head-lights were not much use here; he switched them off, and the circle of hills came at him out of the clear night, smooth and rounded. At the bottom, a humped bridge as old as the track crossed the stream running through the valley: the car began climbing again, slowly, grinding up the track, almost to the top of the hill. Their cottage was hidden away here to the left, in a fold of the ground.

Evelyn jumped out as he stopped, and ran to open the door. He collected their things, wondering whether she had forgiven him yet, and carried them in. Dropping them on the table, he felt round it for the lamp. Before he had touched it, Evelyn put an arm round him and said gently,

'I'm sorry, darling. I know you're anxious. I'm only angry because they worry you unnecessarily, and you have so much to do. Forgive me.'

'There's nothing to forgive,' he said, 'except my bad temper.'

'You're not bad-tempered, it's me, I have a foul temper, but I do love you. What can I do to show that I'm sorry I behave badly?'

An unguarded triumph filled him. 'You can take your things off.'

She took them off at once, without a word, and lay on them on the stone floor. Afterwards, Rigden started a fire with the wood they kept stacked in the kitchen; they fried sausages over it and ate them, with the half-bottle of wine, and laughed and talked nonsense, sitting together in the cell of warmth, peace, safety, formed by the flames and smoke of the dry wood and the friendly nearness of their bodies. When they ceased talking, the silence outside pressed itself against the walls of the cottage. Unless an owl hooted, or a wind shuffled through the grass, there were no near sounds here.

Evelyn said, 'I forgot to tell you. Gurney came to see you this evening.'

'What did he want?'

'He didn't tell me. I like him less than ever, he's malicious and unfriendly — and no friend of yours.'

'I don't dislike him,' Rigden said slowly. 'In a way I admire him. Partly, I suppose, because he's completely reckless, he says what he feels like saying, he doesn't care whether he offends people or amuses them, so long as they keep their distance. I shall never be capable of that sort of disinterest and indifference.'

70

A Cup of Tea for Mr. Thorgill

'Indifference you call it, do you? I call it playing the fool. Besides, he's a wicked Tory.'

'We don't have to think about him now,' her husband said. 'Or about anything — except sleep.'

'Do you want to go to bed?'

'Soon.'

In the room upstairs there was nothing except the bed pushed against the strip of window, with the roof coming down over it. Lying there, his hand across her smooth body, he thought: She never wanted to have children. Why?

Turning her head, Evelyn touched his shoulder with her mouth and asked, 'Are you asleep?'

'No.'

'Why not? What are you thinking about? Don't think.'

'Why don't you want us to have a child?' he said.

She did not speak at once. 'Do you really want that?'

Do I? he wondered very briefly. 'Yes.'

He had to stifle the sense that he was making himself ridiculous. After all, he thought, what does it matter? . . . They had talked about this before, and she had always said the same thing. She said it again now, gently.

'Then I'm not enough for you? Answer. Answer me, Nevil.'

There was only one answer he could make, and his body made it for him. Afterwards he sat up to look at her lying, relaxed, distant from him, in the serene indifference of sleep. With a kind of grief, remembering where he had been that day and the room where his sister would have left a night-light burning so that their mother should not be absolutely alone, he thought: Could I — without turning my back on them — have done all I have? Could I have succeeded? . . . For less than a second, he felt that his success was dry and trivial.

Chapter 10

EARLY next day the Master telephoned to Gurney and asked him if he had spoken to Rigden. When Gurney told him, 'No, he was in London,' he said, 'I'm not sorry. Thinking it over, I feel he should be told about it casually. I don't want to seem to be giving Retta's mania any importance. Come in on Monday, will you, at five? I shall be talking to Rigden then about this boy — Howard.'

'Howard? I thought we'd decided to send him down for a term?'

'Rigden wants to keep him,' the Master said carelessly. 'I'd like you to hear what he has to say.'

'Very well.'

When he walked into the Master's room on Monday, Rigden was there, and began talking at once: his tone implied that he regarded Gurney as the prosecuting counsel against young Howard, a disgracefully brutal one at that. Gurney listened to him for a time with growing boredom, then said,

'So far as I know, Howard has done no work the whole year. He came up with a scholarship and a reputation for intelligence; he has belied the last and he certainly doesn't deserve the other. I see no reason why public money should be wasted on a good-for-nothing. Let the army have him.'

He expected Rigden to fly out at this. To his surprise Rigden answered in a quite steady voice. 'A month ago I would have agreed with you. It was only at the end of term, after I'd read his papers, and when I called him in to tell him they were inexcusable, that I got the truth. He's

72

been living with an anxiety I'd call insane — if I weren't
so sure that the boy is as sane as I am. His background is
the same as mine — father a labourer — and all that. Until
he came here he lived at home, the only one of the family
who wasn't earning; he studied in a room full of people and
the wireless. He's brilliantly clever, but what got him here
was selfishness — the effort he made, and went on making,
to shut his ears to his parents' grumbles and the mockery
of brothers and sisters. He got here. The schoolmaster
who had been pushing him makes his scholarship money
up to what he can just live on; he ought to have gone
straight ahead — and he collapsed. He collapsed inwards
on his anxiety and his repressed fears and the sense he has
of having no one and nothing behind him . . . It might have
been me — except that I could be sure of my mother . . .
I got all this out of him. He cried. I swear on my head that
he's through the crisis now . . . and if we give him a chance
. . . I've written to the fellow in Leeds who's been backing
him, and told him I'll make myself jointly responsible with
him. If I'm wrong about the boy you can curse me at the
end of the year. But I'm right. I know it.'

The Master had listened as if he were half asleep. He
raised his eyelids a little, enough to glance at the Senior
Tutor with an inquisitive irony. 'Well, Gurney?'

Gurney had been moved — and disconcerted. It disconcerted him to find that Rigden was capable of a pene-
tration and a compassion he wouldn't have believed the
fellow had in him. Even now he wondered sharply whether
it were not part of a flourish he was making for the Master's
benefit. He said coldly,

'You're very sure of yourself — and of Howard.'

Rigden fell back into the aggressive tone he used with
people he considered obtuse. With almost everyone, that
is. 'I know what I'm talking about.'

'If the Master agrees with you,' Gurney said, his manner

at its driest and most insolent, 'I have nothing to say except: All right — go ahead and try.'

'I think that's agreed,' the Master said easily. In the same abrupt easy voice he went on, 'My sister came to see me the other day, Nevil — to denounce you. You must have offended her.'

'To—' Rigden's frown made him look bad-tempered — 'what did you say? What have I done?'

'Only you can tell us that, my dear Nevil,' the Master said, smiling. 'She believes you're a communist. You affect her nerves like one.'

Gurney took no trouble to hide his curiosity. A confident man dealing with an accusation — true or, as this one undoubtedly was, false — usually cannot help giving away his peculiar form of vanity. It depends where the accusation gets through — to his personal or his social dignity, himself or the self he enjoys keeping on view. He fixed his sharp pale eyes on Rigden, waiting for him to show himself.

Rigden laughed shortly and said,

'Everyone knows I was a communist for exactly two and a half weeks, in my first year at Oxford. I've never made any secret of it. I was twenty. I joined the Oxford Communist Party — and unjoined it as soon as I realised what an ass I'd made of myself. Is that what Miss Spencer-Savage means?'

'God knows what she means,' the Master said, 'she's a clever woman, they're always the worst.'

Rigden made a gesture of distaste, like a man brushing dirt off his hands. 'What can I do?'

'Do? Why, nothing. Ignore it —' a flickering glance under his eyelids — 'but be a little gentler with her. And tell Evelyn to be more discreet. No, don't tell her anything of the sort. Why shouldn't an attractive young woman talk nonsense? . . . That's enough about that. I had something else to say to you. I hope we can get you

74

Loddon's Readership. Don't let yourself feel certain. But you can hope. That wretch Dalton is running Herbert West. But I think — I say: I think — we've got round him. People don't like Dalton. Damned if I see why they should. A scholar who has taken to politics and broadcasting doesn't deserve to be respected.' A gleam of irony came into his eyes. 'If he had done it badly . . . but the fellow is a blatant success. Unforgivable.'

Rigden had flushed. He said half-audibly,

'Thank you. Thank you for telling me.'

The Master waved a hand. 'We'll see, we'll see. Nothing's certain . . . You must go away now, both of you. I have to talk to a German, who will no doubt be in that state of angry superiority chaps get into when they've lost a war. Pray for me.'

They crossed the courtyard together in silence. Except for a restless twitch of his mouth, Rigden showed no sign of being excited or happy. Turning it round on his tongue, Gurney thought. He felt a shocking bitterness. Of all men to take the place of the selfless austere Loddon . . . He checked himself sharply. How do you know, he mocked, that your anger is all on Loddon's behalf? How much of it is jealousy of the man who has never put a foot wrong on his way up?

Half under his breath, Rigden said,

'I should get some work done at last.'

Loddon has done no work for six years — is that what you mean? Gurney thought. He said nothing.

'Can I, do you think, tell my wife?'

'You can tell her you're in the running,' Gurney drawled.

'Yes, of course,' Rigden said swiftly, 'that's all it is.'

Unexpectedly, Gurney had a twinge of remorse. 'You can tell her your chances are good. The Master wouldn't have said anything to you at this stage if he weren't feeling reasonably sure.'

'You think that?' Rigden said.

He had spoken in a low voice, but with a trace of what Gurney took to be exultance. He detected some other emotion, less credible. Relief, he thought: the lifting of a desperate strain. But what the devil has he to feel desperate about? His future? . . . He smiled maliciously. Well, it's safe now . . .

'It has come to you very young,' he said. 'If it comes.'

Rigden stood still, as if the other man had put a hand on him. 'You think I'm full of myself, don't you? Cocksure. Vain. The scholarship type.'

'You have one or two reasons to be vain,' Gurney said smoothly.

'More than you know,' Rigden said.

He looked at Gurney with a quick half-friendly half-excited smile. Something about him — perhaps this young smile, or a sudden sense of him as defenceless, his guard down — surprised Gurney: for the first time since he had known the young man he felt a spring of sympathy — even liking.

'What do you know,' Rigden said, 'about Nev Rigden, Sally Rigden's little boy?'

'Your mother?' Gurney asked.

'Yes.'

'Your wife told me she was ill.'

'Yes.' Rigden's face changed. He walked on as rapidly as his long legs could move. 'You know how it is. When I was nine or ten, everything I hoped to do was going to be for her. Now —' he turned a savage face on Gurney — 'I saw her ten days ago, she's going to die, and all I could think about was how quickly could I get away . . . What happens? How did I get to the point where finishing a book is more important to me than any human being — except my wife, of course? It's — it's indecent.'

It struck Gurney as curious that excitement — the shock

76

of triumph — should break the young man open to the point of spilling confidences of this sort over a man who was not even his friend. He felt a prick of contempt — not so much for Rigden as for the human heart — then pulled himself together to behave as well as possible.

'Starting where you did,' he said slowly, 'among people who can't change — you grew out of them.'

Rigden smiled unhappily — another of those smiles younger than himself. 'Does everyone do that?'

'No,' Gurney said. He was thinking of old Thorgill.

'Well, there you are,' Rigden began. He stopped, and with an effect of jauntiness said, 'Won't you come in and have a drink?'

Gurney refused. He had had enough of the young man and his trouble, such as it was. He could not feel that it was terribly serious. Rigden was not the only young man (or woman) who had pulled himself up too quickly — to a height where he no longer felt safe or perfectly sure of himself. Before long he would get used to himself and his cleverness, and to speaking a language he had learned, not from any human mouth, but from his ambition, his energy, his youthful fever. He had more on the credit side of his page than his success — he had Evelyn and their self-satisfied, self-absorbed passion for each other. He doesn't need pity, Gurney thought ironically; least of all, mine.

Chapter 11

MORE than anything in the world at the moment, Gurney wanted to get out of England.

In the days before travel abroad was made so difficult that the only people able to move about freely are politicians and scoundrels like Sir X——Y—— and his wife or mistress, he spent every free moment in France. Since his first trip abroad, as a schoolboy, he had realised that the only way to endure, without becoming imbecile, the physical and mental climate of this island is by getting out of it as often as the need seizes you to escape. Undoubtedly the English are the salt of the earth, but a diet of salt gives one an intolerable thirst for sun, wine, unaffected delight in food and talk, spontaneous gestures — in short, happiness. Since the last war, this most innocent of pleasures has been largely destroyed. An honest man goes abroad on a short leash held by the bureaucrats who are our masters. Under no circumstances can he choose to prolong his happiness, or decide that eight or nine months spent in France would unstiffen his mind and dry an acid damp out of his bones: to stay so long, he would have to become an expatriate, a sort of animal Gurney had no wish to be. If he is caught taking away with him a few pounds more than the categorical sum, he will not merely be fined but insulted by some smooth jack-in-office in terms too insolent and hypocritical to be used to a thief or a murderer. The truth is that under the permanent terror of governments, all, whatever their label, equally ignorant of the art of happiness, and equally incompetent, he is allowed to exist and pay taxes, but not to live. This is one of the benefits

a century and a half of progress and enlightenment has
brought us . . . An Englishman kept at home against his
will is a dull warped Englishman, unable to see anything
in his own country beyond the vileness of its climate and
the parochial dullness of its men of letters. After a few
weeks or months abroad he comes back to it in a mood to
appreciate the commonsense and common kindness of nine
out of ten of the men and women he meets in a day spent
walking on some trivial errand about London, or any
English town or city.

Naturally, when an instinct so vital and deeply rooted as
their need to escape is in question, people otherwise honest
and scrupulous will invent ways of getting out of the
country illegally — for as long as it takes to lay up a stock
of energy large enough to last through another period of
mists, cold houses, distrust of happiness, and a sour dislike
of anything resembling elegance in thinking or living.
Gurney himself, scrupulous about money as he was,
unable to run up a debt at a shop, had an arrangement
with a French scholar which allowed him to spend time
in France or Italy without taking out of the country a
farthing more than the derisory sum allowed. He had never
been to Venice. This summer he intended to move very
slowly through France to northern Italy, and reach Venice
in September. He was working twelve hours a day to
clear up arrears of paper work and get away at the end of
July, so that when — one afternoon a few days after Nevil
Rigden's talk with the Master about young Howard —
Primrose Paget rang him up and asked him to come round,
he refused.

Her voice came back strangely loud: she had a gentle
voice. 'It's not a party. Please come. I want to see you.'

He said ungraciously, 'Is it important?'

'Yes, yes, important.'

He went, determined not to stay more than a few

minutes. He did not for a moment believe that anything she had to say to him was in the least urgent. Probably, if her husband were still away, she had been asked some question about him which she did not know how to answer. Without being stupid, she had an extraordinary fear of making a fool of herself, and would sit mute, smiling, at her own dinner parties. This might have been due to a humble sense of her husband's immense intellect. Yet, when Einstein visited Oxford, she had made friends with him at sight; they talked and laughed together like two children.

Gurney liked her, as he liked all simple unpretentious people. Primrose Paget was not only simple and modest, she was, especially in her gay moods, as appealing as a child or a clown: you felt that she had none of the ordinary defences which even the simplest human beings learn after a few experiences with their kind. The beauty still visible in her large flaccid body and heavy face only sharpened this sense of her as more defenceless than other women. So, oddly enough, did her devotion to her husband: there was some anxiety in it; she watched him like a conjurer's assistant waiting to jump forward at the critical instant.

She opened the door to Gurney herself.

Something, he saw at once, had happened to her — something more than an unanswerable question. She did not speak, and pulled him into the nearest room and closed the door. Leaning against it, she stared at him, eyes widely open, her queer vulnerable face without any expression.

'What is the matter?' he asked.

She did not answer, and his mind raced over the possible disasters: her husband was dead, he had left her. As gently as he could he asked,

'Has anything happened to Thomas?'

'No.' She repeated it. 'No, no, no.'

'Then what is it, my dear? Tell me. I'll help you. Is he away? Where is he?'

'He came back yesterday,' she said in a low voice.

'Then what——?'

Without taking her eyes off him she said,

'It's Hetty. A terrible thing has happened. Thomas said: No one can do anything. And I said: Of course, but Henry will know what to do; we'll ask him.' She moved, and came close to him. 'You don't mind?'

'You know I'll do anything I can for you,' he said. 'But what is it?'

She drew down the ends of her mouth so that it formed an ugly half-circle. 'Well, what can you do?' Her hands rose in a vague gesture. 'Where is Hetty? *I* don't know where she is. She was in London. She went up a week ago, at the end of term, to stay with a friend. And then on Saturday — that's two days ago, you know——' She began to cry: tears poured over her face; she made no effort to brush them away, and went on talking, words tumbling from a mouth stretched to cry. 'She had dinner with that man Miles Hudson; they went to — to wherever he lives, and he raped her. Poor child, poor child . . .'

Gurney was horribly startled. Almost at once it occurred to him that she might have gone off her head and be talking nonsense.

'How do you know this?'

She fumbled in the pocket of her dress for a moment. 'There was a letter from her this morning — for Thomas. He wouldn't give it to me to read, he read it to me . . . Have you a handkerchief?'

He gave her his. 'Why hasn't she come home?'

She made a tragically funny face. 'She doesn't want to come back to Oxford.' Her tears started again. 'Oh, if she doesn't come, what shall I do? I can't bear it. I want her. What shall I do?'

'Where is Thomas?' Gurney asked.

'Coming, he's coming,' she said absently. 'I wanted to see you first, I knew I should cry, and I can't cry in front of him, it worries him.' She gave him a look of reproach and disappointment, like a child discovering for the first time the poverty of adult kindness. 'Henry, I thought you would know what to do.'

'When I've talked to Thomas I may be able to think of something,' Gurney said. Without thinking at all, he added, 'You trust him, don't you?'

Almost as he was speaking, it struck him that he had made an ambiguous and very foolish remark, but she cried, 'Oh, yes, yes,' with an eager swiftness.

Paget came in at this moment. Her face changed as instantly and frankly as a child's: she left Gurney and ran to him. He put his arm round her for a moment.

'Good of you to come,' he said heavily. 'Primrose has been telling you, hasn't she?'

Until this moment Gurney had been concerned only with Primrose: now, when for the first time he thought directly of Hetty, he saw her young unformed face, offered to him dumbly, with all the meaning torn from it — like Anne's face when he was shown her after the raid. But Hetty isn't dead, he thought, she is simply . . . His mind stopped. What really had happened? *Where* was she?

'I'm not sure,' he said, 'that I understand it. Where is Hetty?'

'I wish to God we knew,' Paget said. His face twisted with anger. 'That scoundrel . . . We heard yesterday that she had run away from — from the house she was staying in. They knew, her friends knew she was going out to dinner with Hudson: no one sat up for her, she had a key: then, on Sunday morning, when she hadn't come back, they rang him up, and he made an ambiguous answer which left them under the impression that Hetty was still there, with him. When she still didn't come back, they rang me up . . . And this morning her letter to me . . . I'm going up to London, of course — I'm off now. We must find her.'

Primrose said suddenly and loudly, 'And he ought to be at the dentist's. He has terrible toothache.'

'Don't,' Paget said to her.

'What can I do?' Gurney asked.

Paget looked at him with a flicker of his practised charm. 'I wanted to see you before I went. I have no time to see Hetty's tutor, and I think she should be told. Would you see to it? I know it's something to ask of you, but——'

'Who is her tutor?'

'Retta Spencer-Savage.'

'Oh, my God, why tell her?' Gurney said. 'It seems quite unnecessary. Why tell anyone?' He felt the greatest reluctance to delivering the poor child into, of all hands, Athene's. He could see no good reason for trusting either her discretion or her kindness. 'Why not wait until you get her home before deciding what she needs — what ought to be done?'

Paget seemed to hesitate. '*If* we get her home,' he said. Primrose made a sound like a very young child trying not to whimper, and he stroked her arm, absently. 'I feel horribly uncertain. I think we need the advice of some woman, and who else is there? . . . I really should be obliged if you would see her for me.'

It was only afterwards that Gurney reflected consciously on their cruelty in passing over Primrose's advice as of no value. She did not say anything. She stood, arms hanging as if she had forgotten them, eyebrows raised as far as they would go, dark eyes round and fixed.

'Do you want me to talk to Miss Spencer-Savage?' Gurney asked her.

She glanced swiftly at her husband. 'Y-yes. Yes.'

'Very well.'

After he had left, it struck Gurney hard that he had been given only the barest outline of the story: there were gaps. He did not feel that he could go back. Paget was hurrying off to catch his train, and it would be indecent to ask Primrose any more questions. The poor woman was unhappy enough.

Chapter 12

Retta spencer-savage had the upper half of a house in the Parks. She was looked after by an elderly woman so well aware of her survival value as what used to be known as a good servant that she stood no nonsense from her employer. Their relation was a little that of a married pair, terribly used to each other, well past the age of sexual complicity and able to give their whole attention to clipping each other's vanities. There were quarrels, in which Athene behaved with less dignity than her servant, but they never separated. Neither forgave the other but, somehow, over a headache or a gloriously successful soufflé, they were reconciled.

There had been a quarrel that afternoon: Gurney recognised the signs on Gilmore's rigidly-closed lips. She showed him in in silence, and as she closed the door Athene burst into abuse of her. 'She's a devil, I should like to whip her, naked. That would teach her which foot to dance on.' When she was really angry, she fell back on a language she had picked up heaven knows where.

'Why don't you get rid of her?' Gurney said with a malicious smile.

'And then what? I should starve, I can't boil an egg. It would be either a foreigner, or some daily nuisance. No, no, I have to put up with her, she's my cross . . . What do you want?'

He told her. Not for the first time, she surprised him. She had so lively a notion of women as the insulted and injured, and Hudson had made his want of respect for her intellect so brutally plain, that he expected her to seize this chance to take the skin off him. Not a bit of it. To his dismay she turned on Hetty, striking through her at her own youthful failure, with a stupefying bitterness.

'Any girl of eighteen who allows a man of his age and reputation to take her to his flat knows what will happen. If you don't know that, I do. I was eighteen when Marly seduced me, and I knew perfectly well what I was doing. The one thing I didn't know was that he was pathologically vain and greedy — but I wasn't naive, and you can be sure Henrietta isn't. As for Hudson, he'll gaily and mercilessly make use of her in his next novel. It's all she deserves. At least she will have been useful to a great writer . . . Mind you, Gurney, I'm not suggesting that there is any likeness between my affair with Marly and Hetty's ridiculous accident — quite apart from the fact that she is far less intelligent and highly strung than I was and will suffer less. For a young woman to suffer as I did is unusual. And yet *I* recovered.'

Gurney said without anger,

'This girl may not have your indestructible egoism. Can I — I suppose I can — tell the Pagets that you'll be glad to have her come back? That must be what they want from you.'

'Primrose, I suppose, is off her head, and as inarticulate as usual.'

'She's very unhappy,' said Gurney.

Athene rolled her eyes at him. 'Why do men like Thomas Paget invariably marry half-wits? Is it because they don't want to make the effort of living with another intellect?'

'They may prefer living with loyalty and kindness,' Gurney said. 'But Primrose is not a half-wit. What am I to tell her?'

He had meant to hurt her. He realised he had done it when she said with a cold smile,

'I'd better talk to this paragon of devotion myself.'

86

'Perhaps you had.'

Knowing that if he stayed any longer he would behave worse, Gurney stood up. I could scarcely have managed more clumsily, he thought. But — intolerably vain and self-centred as Athene was — in the last resort she had a sense of responsibility to certain things and certain people, her pupils among them. She said quickly,

'No, no, tell the Pagets that the best thing they can do is to set the girl to work. I'm not going away this summer; if they like, I'll see her once a week. I may tell you that she can do with some coaching.' She smiled sharply. 'But there mustn't be a scandal. If there is, she can't come back to the college — even if she could face it. They — and she — must hold their tongues about this little episode — absolutely.'

'You can be certain they will,' Gurney said. 'Thank you.'

The next morning he had her on the telephone in a savage temper. A reporter from one of our tabloid newspapers had rung her up from London and asked her whether it was true that the writer Miles Hudson had seduced one of her pupils, a very young girl, in what he described as unusual circumstances. (Are the circumstances in which a seduction is usual laid down in the code supplied by their editors to journalists of his order? Gurney wondered.) She gabbled angrily in her deep strangled voice, and for a minute Gurney was too taken aback by the news even to try to interrupt her. Then he asked,

'But how did he get the story? Has anything more happened?' Paget? he thought. Hetty?

'I don't know how it got out,' Athene rushed on. 'But I know why *I* am being persecuted: newspapers of that sort live on the envy of the dull ignorant mass for an exceptional man or woman — especially woman. I have a great many enemies among clergymen and communists — not a week passes without at least one anonymous abusive letter.'

'Why clergymen?' Gurney asked.

'Especially Low clergymen, for some reason——'

He cut her short. 'What did you tell him?'

'Simply that there isn't a word of truth in it, and that he had better be careful. I spoke very calmly, since these creatures are adolescent in an unpleasant way . . .'

Gurney let her go on talking, and tried to make up his mind how much damage had been done. The story had been picked up — how? — by a paper skilled in treating filth so that it can be spread, more or less deodorised, on a million breakfast-tables, not all of them squalid. He was too angry to laugh at Athene's delusion that she was in danger from the mob (like Marie Antoinette) and the Low Church. The gutter-press is nothing to laugh at, he thought savagely: like a cracked sewer, it infects. That it had stumbled on Hetty's pitiful little story horrified him.

Athene's voice had stopped. He said,

'Neither of us can do anything useful. We must wait until Paget comes home.'

Athene said freezingly, 'I asked you whether I ought to get police protection.'

'Did you? I'm sorry . . . Good God, no, don't do that — they'll hardly consider one reporter a threat.'

'There may be others.'

'Let Gilmore deal with them,' he suggested.

She hung up, with ill-humoured sharpness.

Gurney tried to ring up Primrose, to ask her if she had been molested. No one answered the telephone, and he supposed she was letting it ring — and the door-bell, too, no doubt. He gave it up and went out, meaning to buy a copy of the offending paper, to see whether anything had been printed yet. In the High he ran into George Craddock, who knew all about it. He was in a mild state of salacity, his nearest approach to a sexual emotion, and —

of course — delighted to be able to add rape to Hudson's crime of *lèse*-Russia.

Gurney felt a spasm of distaste. 'Before you spread this charming story, why not wait until you are sure it's true?'

'Not only is it true,' Craddock said, smiling, 'but you'll find that a great many of the imbeciles who hurried to applaud his last vicious silly book will shy off it and off him.' He ran a grey tongue over his lip. 'As an apostle he's done for himself.'

Gurney said, 'I see . . .' He appeared to be seeing something obscenely unpleasant. 'If you can discredit Hudson you don't care that, at the same time, with the same filthy brush, you're injuring Hetty? Do you want to ruin the child? The least harm you'll do her is to make it very difficult for her to come back here. The worst — damn it, how would you feel if Hetty were your daughter?'

Craddock's eyes shifted a little as he made the effort to swallow this. He must have felt momently uneasy; then he tucked it all comfortably away inside the dialectic, and down it went.

'A weak point,' he said judicially, marking the pauses with his white pulpy hand. 'My dear Gurney, I shouldn't be justified — no one is — in sparing an individual, even a sweet child like Hetty — or, for that matter, a thousand, ten thousand Hettys — when what is at stake, if I may say so, is our future, our whole future — the end of a great fear — peace — hm, hm — peace.'

Gurney gave way to the impulse of a schoolboy. 'I never argue with deaf people,' he said.

He left the fellow stretching his mouth into a wavering indulgent smile, and went on to buy his paper. There was nothing in it about Hudson, not a hint.

It was only when he was walking home that he thought: Then how the devil *did* Craddock hear it?

Chapter 13

HE SPENT that evening with Vančura. Bella's art school had closed for the summer, and she was at home. During supper she was very gay. She would not allow either of the men to help her to clear away, and they heard her singing to herself in the kitchen in a low off-tone voice and talking softly to her canary. When she came back into the living-room she seated herself on the side of Vančura's chair: he put his arm round her, his hand resting in her lap, and went on talking: now and then she caressed this hand, lifting one after another the square short fingers with their spine of black hairs, playing with them. Jan is perfectly right, thought Gurney: she is childishly simple and she is happy.

Vančura had been reading, to review it in the obscure exiles' paper he wrote for, a book about the Cathars, singularly obstinate heretics who gave the mediæval Church the fright of its life until the last of them was burned, or buried to go on working quietly underground.

'They were absolutely correct,' he said, 'when they noticed that history is run by the devil: their mistake was to believe that there is something more than history. In that, our friends in Russia — and their disciples in the West — are right. History is all.' He lifted a sardonic eyebrow. 'I don't for all that understand how any man, not forced into it by terror — and not a sadist — is able to believe in a blissful end of history, life freed of the need to kill . . . History is a broken string of magnificent efforts — Goya, Mozart, Einstein — and a double thread of kindness and wilful cruelty. So it was and so it will be. Either

90

you obey it, or — like me — you run away. To a country where history is still in its age of blundering half-baked adolescence.'

'You're too kind to us,' said Gurney.

'I might have stayed to fight,' Vančura said, 'and been shot. As most of my friends were . . . The difference between them and me,' he said with a light bitterness, 'is that I care about my skin.'

'Why shouldn't you?' Bella said.

'You don't mind sleeping with a coward? No, of course not. Why should you?'

She lowered her head. 'You mean — because I'm stupid?'

'No.' With his free hand he touched hers. 'Because you are a very young woman — and you had the bad luck to fall into my hands before you knew what was good for you. And because you don't see me as I really am, a middle-aged refugee with a vile tongue. When you do, you'll leave me — and have the life you ought to have.'

'Then you don't trust me,' she said under her breath.

'Of course I do. As much as myself.'

She said slowly, 'But you don't trust — you don't believe in yourself. So . . .'

He smiled at her. 'So we are both talking nonsense. And boring Henry. Look at him!'

She did not move. Gurney said drily,

'You take yourself damned seriously, don't you? Are you asking us to agree that to get clear before you can be shot in the back of the head is a form of cowardice? You're insane if that's what you mean. But you don't mean it, you're showing off.'

My poor Bella, he thought, you don't believe me for a moment, do you? . . . And in fact he was lying, to console her. Vančura had given himself away with both hands. Against all reason — since what have you proved by waiting to be murdered? who, except the chief of police, gains anything by your whim? — he had no faith in himself left. And none in her — since self-contempt is a dye that colours off on everything you touch. Even his love for her — seen through what he knew about treachery — was nothing he could trust. Nor hers for him, nor her young kindness. Yes, poor Bella.

She freed herself gently from Vančura's arm, and stood up. 'I forgot to cover the cage,' she murmured.

When she had shut herself in the kitchen, Gurney said,

'Torment yourself if you like — if it amuses you — but why torment Bella?'

Vančura frowned at him. 'What d'you mean?'

'She's a shrewd young woman, for all she's ungrasping and simple. Do you imagine she can't see — and suffer from it — that you're pleased to have her here to take the chill off your exile . . . but that's all?'

'I — what nonsense,' Vančura said sharply.

'Be a little more careful with her . . . I begin to understand why you turned down the Harvard job. It wasn't only to stay in Europe. That's less than half the reason. Your exile has to be as poverty-stricken and uncomfortable as possible, to punish you for running away.' Gurney laughed. 'And I believed you were sane — saner than the general run.'

'When I want a lesson in sanity,' Vančura said thinly, 'I'll come to you for it.'

Bella came in. Her always pale cheeks were flushed, but she was smiling.

'Come here, Bella,' Vančura said.

She came at once, with her quick docility, and let him pull one of her ears and kiss her lightly. He smiled sharply and triumphantly, and slumped back in his chair to listen to the record Gurney had brought Bella for her small gramophone. Mozart. Even the wretched machine could not destroy it. It was an exercise in happiness, carried out with all the skill in the world.

The hard fold of Vančura's mouth became less bitter. 'Ah,' he said when it ended, 'what confidence he had, what knowledge. It was still daylight then; you lied and murdered for your personal profit, not coldly for an idea: happiness was a drive in the country, a state of grace, friends coming in to talk and drink.'

'Which is why Henry came,' said Bella. 'There's still a half-bottle in the cupboard.'

She brought it, and the glasses. The rest of the evening was like all the other evenings Gurney had spent in this shabby room, 'soirées pleines de grâce et douceur', because unlike anything else he knew in his daily life: no affectation, no clash of rival vanities, no self-interested anxiety to score off a colleague, nor even, which is forgiveable, to bare your wits. He had never heard Vančura tell a malicious story — not that he lacked malice, but he kept it in reserve, to use on himself. As for Bella . . . Glancing at her, Gurney saw that she had put out of her mind everything except her contentment with a life which gave her, surely, very few of the things a sturdy pretty young woman ought to have. But she is contented, he thought.

He did not envy Vančura his good luck. What he felt was an exasperated and inopportune pity. The fool doesn't know, he thought, how it should be treated — as something to be taken very gently between the hands. Since it won't last.

Chapter 14

WHEN two more days passed without anything more scabrous than mouth-to-mouth gossip, Gurney began to feel easy. And then, the third day, trouble blew up in the last place he expected it. Salacity — rape in unusual circumstances and the rest of it — can slip past the English law of libel only by a very few doors, and who the devil would have expected Thomas Paget, of all men, to open one? But he did it. Approached in London by a reporter from the same newspaper which had been annoying his wife and Retta Spencer-Savage, he set on him with his fists, split his lip open, broke his spectacles and camera and threw them after him into the street. He was charged with assault. In court he lost his temper again, badly, and in an acid outburst against all journalists he gave away the whole miserable story. The more mannerly papers had nothing to do except print it; the others put all four feet in the trough, with all the stomach in the world. The two names involved, Paget and Miles Hudson, made it a highly respectable scandal, scarcely needing touching up to go anywhere.

The affair puzzled Gurney even more than it angered him. No one would blame Thomas Paget for losing his temper, but he had been stupefyingly imprudent. Imprudence did not fit Gurney's idea of him as not only more intelligent but saner than most men . . . Perhaps it was the toothache, he thought. He did not feel like laughing.

During the morning the thought of Primrose nagged him until he did the last thing he wanted to do. He telephoned her, this time with better luck: the housekeeper answered,

94

and — obviously repeating a phrase she had used several
times already — said,

'Mrs. Paget is not available.'

He strangled his impulse to take this way out. 'Tell her
that Mr. Gurney is leaving Oxford this evening, and would
like to see her before he goes.'

She went away, and came back in a minute with a single
word.

'No.'

Very reluctantly, kicked into it by the image of Primrose
staring at the newspapers with the bewilderment of a child
who is being bullied, he went round to see the Rigdens.
Evelyn could tell him if there were anything he could do
before he left.

To his surprise, she had not been near her sister-in-law.
He let her see that he was taken aback, and she said roughly,

'My dear man, if I were Primrose, the only thing I
should want would be to be left alone. I shouldn't want
to talk about it, or answer any questions.'

'Strangers, yes,' Gurney said. 'But you're one of her
family — the only one here.'

She said with the same curtness, 'Primrose is the last
person I should like to see coming into the room if I were
in a difficulty, or ill.'

'And you think she must feel the same distrust of you?'
he said. 'Possibly you're right, but . . . she's alone, she's in
agony of mind about Hetty. I don't believe — however
low you rate yourself as a friend — that there's nothing
you can do for her.'

Rigden was in the room. So far he had kept quiet, as
though he resented Gurney's interference. With a repressed
violence, he said,

'There's only one person we need worry about — that's
Hetty herself. If instead of knocking down a reporter,
Tom had gone for that swine Hudson, I could understand it.'

95

His wife sent him one of her direct hard glances. 'Miles
Hudson is certainly a swine,' she said coolly. 'But he was
one before any of this happened, and I'm delighted he's
been shown up — and shown up like this, so that anyone,
even the stupidest and most gullible people, can see what
he is. It's a damned good thing.'

'What is a good thing?' asked Gurney. 'That your
brother lost his temper, or that Hetty has been raped?'

'You're being absurd,' Evelyn said. 'I'm quite certain
that Hetty asked for what she got, and there's no point in
being sorry for her. But that doesn't make Miles Hudson
any less contemptible. And I'm glad we can all say so
now — without being suspected of prejudice. Political
prejudice, I mean, of course.' She looked at Gurney with
candid amusement. 'I'm sorry you're shocked, but you
know, you would be. You have all the proper feelings.'

Her husband said violently,

'I agree with Gurney. Until Hetty turns up — and I
wish to God I knew where to look for her — I can't take
any interest in Hudson's politics or his morals or anything
else.' He went on in a calmer voice, 'You don't mean what
you're saying, Evelyn. Gurney knows that as well as I do.'

Evelyn had a trick of standing with her wide shoulders
held as far back as they would go: it gave her supple body
every advantage. She moved and placed herself squarely
in front of Rigden, as if challenging him to quarrel with her.

'I do mean it — every word. Why do you think you know
more about Hetty, or any other young woman, than I do?'

Rigden stared at her coldly. 'If you really believe she
was responsible for any of it — even partly responsible —
then you certainly don't know anything about her.'

Her eyes widened to show their clear whites. 'Nevil,
you're a fool about the silly girl.'

The contempt in her voice, and her husband's anger,
sprang a brief suspicion in Gurney's mind . . . Is he a

little — more than a little — in love with Hetty? . . . He let it drop at once. No one could see Rigden with his wife without noticing that he was still possessed by her. (The right word, Gurney thought.) But there was some tension between them. He had the impression that Rigden was quarrelling about the girl because she was the thing nearest to hand. Neither he nor Evelyn had any kindness to spare for Thomas Paget's wife — his fool of a wife, as Evelyn said.

Bored, he rose to go. 'If you can't tell me anything about Primrose——'

At this moment the Finnish woman came into the room with a telegram she held out to Rigden with the ends of her fingers, as if it might blow up. He read it — and looked at Evelyn, a hard blank look.

'What is it?' she asked.

'It's from Catherine. She wants to know why I haven't come . . . *Why haven't you come, she's going* . . .' He made a confused gesture. 'But how could I? I didn't know.'

A slightly uneasy and at the same time obstinate look came over Evelyn's face. 'I'm terribly sorry, Nevil. She rang up yesterday when you were out, and said your mother was worse. With Craddock coming in to talk about Hudson and all that, I forgot to tell you. Oh dear, I'm really very sorry. And I'm sorry about your mother, too. But perhaps Catherine is exaggerating again.'

He kept his eyes on her face. 'You forgot——?'

'She's said something like this before — more than once.'

'You could have given me the message,' Rigden said quietly. 'She might, as you say, be exaggerating — but in your place I wouldn't have counted on it.' He turned away. 'I must go. Excuse me, Gurney . . . I shall take the car,' he told his wife over his shoulder.

They heard him running down the stairs. The front door slammed. Looking from the window, Gurney saw him striding along the street towards the garage where they kept their shabby little car.

'Run after him,' he said to Evelyn.

'It's too late.' She looked at him with a half-embarrassed, half-mischievous smile. 'Besides, I'm almost sure it's another false start. His sister really does enjoy a good wallow. She sounded no more excited yesterday than any other time. How long is it since he was up there last? Not very long. Oh I'm sure it's all right.'

'I hope so,' Gurney said politely. 'I must go.'

As he reached the door Evelyn made one of her swift changes from mulish and irritating wilfulness to an ingenuous charm. Narrowing her eyes in a smile, she said,

'You were quite right about Primrose and I'm wrong. I'll go and see her this afternoon, at once. What can I take her to comfort her? . . . I know, I'll take the jar of Greek honey one of Nevil's pupils gave me last week. Don't laugh — you'd be surprised how easy it is to console Primrose, anyway for a few minutes. And she's greedy about honey; she doesn't spread it on bread, like anyone else, she eats it by the paw-ful, like a bear.'

There was not a trace of malice in her voice, nothing but satisfaction in having thought of something to give her sister-in-law.

Gurney did not laugh. He knew, much too sharply, that what catches at the mind in moments of intense grief is not likely to be either noble or extraordinary. Hadn't he, the day after Anne's death, caught himself watching, with acute pleasure, a shaft of light striking across the old wall opposite his window? It could as easily have been the taste of a glass of wine. The utter causelessness of these flashes of joy is no more curious than the indecency of their timing. And — why not admit it? — they make life infinitely more bearable. And cost nothing in self-respect. (Or very little.)

Chapter 15

CATHERINE said, 'She won't know you.'
She did not reproach him for coming when it was
no longer any use: perhaps she was too tired: there
was a line under her eyes which had not been there the
last time he was here; her youth had had its first irrecover-
able blow. She let him go alone into the little room full
of its double bed, and their mother lying in it, sunk.

He bent down and said, 'I'm here. It's Nev.'

Her eyes, those pale blue eyes, their colour almost gone,
moved towards him, nearly imperceptibly. And closed
again.

During the evening, he and Catherine went in and out
of the room with as little effort to move quietly as if it were
already empty. The woman lying there was terribly
present and infinitely far away, out of reach of their hands,
a drowned body drifting out to sea. Standing over her,
they talked about her as if she could no longer hear voices.
Her son felt uneasy when he did it, but he was ashamed to
show his discomfort: he waited until Catherine left him
alone with her, then he knelt down and spoke in her ear.
'You're not alone, I'm here.' There was no answer.
Nothing.

Later he shared a meal in the kitchen with Catherine's
husband, Jim, inarticulate and awkwardly friendly, as
always. They talked about the wireless and Jim's work.
When he moved, to go back upstairs, Jim cleared his throat
and said,

'Cat's pretty done up with this.'

'She must be.'

'I was wondering if she and th'child could have a few days with you when it's — well — over.'

'She wouldn't come,' Rigden said. Meaning (and he knew that Jim knew it): I hope she wouldn't. 'She won't leave you alone.'

He thought for a second that his brother-in-law was going to jeer at his bad faith. Jim's glance wavered and turned aside. He might even — a more scalding thought — be feeling a sort of pity. All he said was,

'I c'd manage.'

'We'll ask her,' Rigden said. He pushed out of his mind what he knew would be Evelyn's revulsion against squeezing Cat and a baby into the flat. She would do it, but she would be resentful, and he disliked annoying her as much as he disliked the thought that Cat would be unwelcome. It was an impossible situation.

He went back to the bedroom. For several nights he had been working late and he was heavy with sleep. He had only to close his eyes to feel his mind rocking over the edge into unconsciousness. He would have given anything to lie down. With a fretful impatience he thought: She won't go yet . . . It was half fatigue and half disbelief (of his body) in death itself. You can't see death, to push it away: you can't hear it in the room. How can you believe it is there? His mind felt nothing but its longing to sleep.

When, about one o'clock, the quick noisy breathing in the bed fluttered out, and Cat stood there and wept loudly, half in childish misery and half, he knew, from relief, he felt only the relief.

He left Catherine with the neighbour who had come in to help, and went downstairs, to lie uncomfortably on the couch in the sitting-room. He fell asleep at once. Footsteps on the pavement outside — a man going to work — roused him. It was still very early, and he dropped off again. This time he dreamed . . . He was in the room

which used to be kitchen, living-room and his parents'
bedroom. Vaguely, he was himself, a man of thirty-four,
and a young boy. He half saw and half was the boy: alert,
skinny, a thin white face with restless dark eyes. His
youngish mother was in the room; there were other
figures, indistinct: these disappeared, and his mother,
standing against the table, asked him to fetch something.
He wanted to do it, but he knew that he was going to leave
her; he had to, there was nothing he could do about it;
already the room was almost dark, and the figure of his
mother in it growing less clear. He felt a terrible guilt,
and tried to cry out, to tell her he would come back the
next night without fail: desperate, he repeated: 'I promise
I'll come, it's you I love, not the other one.' But it was no
use; the room, and the distant unseizable woman, wavered
and blew away like dark smoke.

He opened his eyes. It was a moment before he knew
where he was. In the same moment he was caught back
into that other room with its stained wallpaper and low
cracked ceiling, and into a moment which must have been
waiting years, at least twenty-two years, to rise again to the
surface with all its weight of a child's despair and rage.

He had come in from school to find his mother and two
other women drinking tea with her. The brown enamel
teapot was on the table, with the cups and a plate of the
rock cakes his mother made when she could: she had kept
her countrywoman's dislike for what she called contemptuously 'bought cakes'. The other two had been to the
cinema: they were telling her about it, in half-sentences,
very much, he thought now, as they would have emptied
a rag-bag on the table and fumbled in it for bright scraps,
forgetting or not knowing how they came to be there.

'... you could see she wanted him, but she thought he ...'

'... singing, she sang, la, la, and it was who ... who
was it, did you say? ...'

'Makes you think . . .'

Their voices had the sound of all half-noticed familiar noises, the talk in the streets, a tap dripping into the sink, the river noises heard only at night, tugs hooting, a steamer's whistle, a shout from the wharf. He scarcely listened. It was only after a time that he realised they had begun to talk about something else, furtively eyeing him to see how much he understood. What they were saying meant nothing. The meaning sprang at him suddenly, from some crack between the words they used and what was in their minds — and his mother's. She had told them, or they had guessed and were asking her about it, that she was going to have another child. Coming now, one of them said, it was downright bad luck. The other nodded, and as if counting slowly in some recess of her mind, said, 'One — and with the two you lost . . .'

He kept a blank stupid face. Not for a fortune would he have let them see that he felt sick with fury at the thought of the discomfort, the trouble it was going to be — to him, not to his mother. He didn't give her share in it a thought, except to feel confusedly angry with her.

When the two women took themselves off — 'Ta-ta, Sally . . . 'bye, Mrs. Rigden . . .' he watched his mother from the corner of his eye. She was doing nothing, but she walked about the room; she went out to the sink in the passage, and came back, and looked at him. If she were going to tell him now, he didn't want to hear: he kept his head down, reading.

She said quietly,

'Nev. I don't know what I'm going to do. Nev, are you listening to me?'

'What about?'

I know what she's going to say, he thought . . . He was wrong. She had a much nearer trouble . . . She always, he thought now, talked to me as if I were her own age . . .

Flushed, her chin trembling in a very unpleasant way, she told him, in a rush of words, that when, at the beginning of winter, she had bought his father an overcoat, she had been spending that month's rent money: three pounds. Ever since, by one shift or another, she had 'managed'. But had never managed to close the gap, and the thing now was desperate. 'I s'll have to tell your father,' she said in a voice he could hardly catch.

She looked at him unhappily, and somehow — something passed from her troubled mind to the mind of the twelve-year-old boy — he realised that she was bitterly ashamed of having lied when she pretended, preening herself a little about it, to have saved the money for that desperately-needed coat.

'If he wasn't so patient,' she cried. 'If he ever kept back any money for himself.' She hesitated. Her mouth worked in a way that horrified the boy. 'Oh, our Nev, to have a bit of money over!' Tears came into her eyes; she sat down and covered them with her hands.

He watched her. He was shaking. He knew what he was going to have to do, and he felt a bottomless sick grief. Without speaking, he got up and went to the loose bit of board in a corner of the room, pulled it up, and felt round under it for the thing he had hidden there. Soft fine dark leather — a note-case. He ran his fingers over it before dropping it in her lap.

'What's this?' she said.

'I picked it up over a month since,' he told her.

'Where?'

'I don't know exactly,' he said sullenly. 'A good way from us. There were two men coming out of a hotel at a corner, one of them let it drop; he never looked, and I took it.'

'You've had it all this time,' his mother said in a queer voice.

He said nothing. What he had meant to do was to go off somewhere with the money, he had no clear idea where, but it was to be the start, somehow, in some unimagined way, of a new life.

He watched her unfold the case. She took out a letter — and the four notes. There was a ten-shilling one and three pounds: she fingered each of them for a minute, as if it were something strange, then laid them a little away from her, on the table.

'Can I have the case?' he asked.

'Oh, no,' she said quickly, 'it isn't safe. You ought to have given it back, our Nev. It's too late now — the police . . .'

Before he could stop her she had thrown case and letter on the fire. He ran frantically to try to snatch it back before it blazed up. She dragged him away. He struggled, hitting at her with his free arm. Suddenly he knew it was no good. He gave in, and stood watching the leather curl and turn black. He tried to smile. He thought: I'm ashamed. He had no notion why he felt ashamed — but it had nothing to do with having stolen. It was deeper, more twisted, more humiliating . . .

He got up — and took this trivial memory upstairs with him to the now tidy darkened room. He had thought vaguely that he could give it back to her, with all his other memories, more harmless, indistinct, and faded, than very old photographs, of a Sally Rigden not a soul remembered except him. Her face, shut against him in a perpetual cold absence, rejected him and them. There was no way of reaching her. The nerve between them still held, and the pain, when he tried to tear himself free from her, was real and physical.

'Help me,' he said.

Even alive, she could not have helped him. Somewhere along the road — it began even before that evening, he thought — he had gone wrong, but where? Where?

Chapter 16

To wait until you are fifty before going to Venice is, Gurney supposed, a grave error. Its canals, its silences, its white light rippling upwards from the pitch-green surface of the water and thrown gently back from walls smelling of musk and seaweed, should underlie all other images of European cities, not be flung down on top of the heap. None the less, it gave him the same shock of pleasure he got from any foreign place he was seeing for the first time. (It is the first moment, entering the body through all its senses, which counts: the second and all the others are contentment, happiness, what you like; they are not this piercing shock of joy.) Venice is, too, only partly a European capital: the Adriatic leads directly to Istanbul and the honey of the East, by-passing Greece; the slowness of movement along the canals or on foot in the labyrinth of stone-flagged passages and narrow streets; the vast empty squares you stumble into by accident, enclosed by shuttered houses, a wine-shop, and a deserted half-ruined church, not a living soul, not so much as a cat, in sight; the walls of palaces on the smaller canals, with their windows eaten away by an inner shadow and their decaying steps, all share something, some knowledge, which owes nothing to Europe.

There had been an error, they told him at the hotel, in booking his room, and he would have to spend the first four nights in a hotel on the Lido. He did not believe it was an error — the clerk was altogether too suave — and he was vexed. But in the morning, when the light from the Adriatic flowed into his bedroom, and afterwards, crossing the lagoon in a light no less pure, but softened to the bright-ness of silk — in front of him the long crescent of houses drawn so subtly at the edge of the water that only a fool would try to pin them down to rectangles of pink, grey, yellow — he found that he was trembling with happiness, as at his sudden first sight of the Alps from the window of a pension in Lausanne, and as when he stepped ashore in France for the first time, aged sixteen, and the flat shabby houses facing the quay, the rusted iron of a balcony, the narrow black lettering above a striped sun-washed awning — *Café du Centre* — answered some deep need of his adolescent body: he walked towards them across the cobbled street as though he were coming home, as though he had known them in another time or another body: it was recognition, friendship — *parce que c'est toi, parce que c'est moi.*

Nothing, no disillusion, no grief, blunted him to these major chords of happiness.

Since it was the middle of September, there were not a great many English visitors. One evening when he had been there a week, he was surprised, and not best pleased, to hear his name spoken. He was sauntering, going no-where, in a dark little lane behind the Ca' d'Oro. He turned. Herbert West, his body neatly bisected by a ray of sunlight knifing its way between two houses, was smiling at him.

'I saw you getting on the vaporetto at the Accademia yesterday,' he said. 'I was in a gondola and I couldn't shout at you, we were in a hurry to get home.'

'What are you doing here?' asked Gurney. 'Where is home?'

'Come back to Florian's and have a drink with me,' West said in a kind voice, 'and I'll tell you. It's quite interesting.'

At Florian's, he walked along the terrace until he reached

a table placed in front of a column. 'I prefer this one. You get the finest angle on the cathedral.' He took up a noble pose of devotion, leaning against the pillar, on which he made the effect of a faint pencil mark.

It turned out that he was living in the Palazzo Savena, which belonged to the mother of the dissolute young poet they had thrown out of Oxford, Quin: she lived in Venice — when she was not living in New York with her second husband, an American, immensely rich. 'When she invited me I didn't know what I was coming to,' he said, smiling. 'It's a magnificent place, crammed full of valuable paintings and tapestries. You must come and see them, Gurney. Why not come next week? I shall be alone in it then, she and her husband are going away, but she has asked me to think of the palazzo as my second home, I'm to come there whenever I can leave Oxford. She means it, too; she's a simple generous woman, and I've become much attached to both of them, her husband is a dear, so unassuming. Surprising story, isn't it?'

'Very.'

It was nothing of the sort: it was exactly what would happen to West — that he would befriend a tiresome young drunkard, for no reason at all except goodness of heart and a sincere belief in the young man's genius, and be rewarded with a rich patroness and a second home in Venice. And he could not have foreseen it. He never foresaw the result of any of his quixotic acts, yet invariably they turned to his profit, as if he had been the shrewdest speculator in futures ever born. Gurney laughed and asked,

'Is Quin here?'

'Yes.'

'Still drinking?'

'I'm afraid so.'

'Never mind — he has served his purpose in life.'

'I don't know what you mean by that,' said West
gravely. 'I think it's a great pity. He'll kill himself. But
I'm enjoying myself here and I like to think that I can come
as often as I like — no worry about lire.'

'You've always been a lucky man,' Gurney said without
irony.

West considered this solemnly. 'Oh, I don't know about
that,' he said, turning his long face of a clever fool from side
to side of the great sunlit square laid out in front of them
like a stage from which some mediaeval procession in golds
and purples has just been cleared off to make room for the
crowd of ordinary Venetians with their air of languor
and gaiety, and supple disregard of appearances. 'Call no
man happy, you know. Time yet — I'm only forty. There
are a lot of things I should still like to get, and shan't . . . For
instance, I should like to be given poor Loddon's Readership
— but I'm told it's unlikely. What do you think of my
chances, Gurney?' He looked up with a shy neutral smile.
'I couldn't ask you that if we weren't sitting here, in Venice,
could I? That's one thing to be said for foreign countries
— they make one less ashamed of telling the truth.'

'I have no idea what your chances are,' Gurney said.

West nodded, and stood up. 'Well, come and see me.
Any day. I'm always in in the evening, after dinner.'

Gurney watched him make his jerky light-footed way
across the square: he had some affinity with the pigeons;
he moved with the same purposeful quickness and detach-
ment, always underfoot and always escaping at the last
second from any rough contact. Half-way across he
stopped briefly to speak to a man strolling towards Florian's,
and moved nimbly away again.

The man he had spoken to came on. It was Miles
Hudson.

Gurney had recognised him too late to move from the
terrace, and Hudson came directly towards him.

'Do you mind?' He put his hand on the chair West had just left, and sat down, legs well apart. He was wearing a linen jacket and trousers exactly the colour of the pillar behind him, but he did not, as West had done, disappear into it: his broad shoulders and lifted head came at you with an animal suavity. 'What's that fellow's name?' he demanded.

'West,' Gurney said. 'Dr. Herbert West.'

A curiosity he could not bring himself to disappoint kept him in his chair, at the same table with a man for whom he felt little more than contempt and detestation: he knew himself too well even to try to disappoint it by leaving at once: he would only regret it.

'Ah, I met him somewhere once,' Hudson said, yawning. 'And yesterday when I went to the Palazzo Savena, with a letter of introduction — I wanted to see two of the paintings — who should come into the gallery but this chap? He showed me round. His face reminded me vaguely of something other than a sheep and a pettish old maid, but he was so affable that I took it he was the butler, and if he hadn't vanished just as I was leaving I should have tipped him.'

'You met him in Oxford,' Gurney drawled, 'in your cousin's house.'

'The devil I did.' A nearly invisible smile of malice deepened the fold under his eyes. 'No, I don't remember.' He lifted a finger. The waiter moved towards him. 'What will you drink?' he asked, with a quick look at Gurney's empty glass.

'At the moment, nothing.'

Hudson ordered his own drink. 'How long have you been in Venice?'

It was the moment, it was perhaps the moment, to find out what — what besides vanity, the arrogance of a powerful intellect, unsatisfied sensuality — moved him. 'Before

I get up and leave you,' Gurney said, 'what can you tell me about Hetty Smith? Where is she?'

If he had expected to embarrass Hudson, or startle him, he did not know his man. Tilting his head back easily against the column, Hudson glanced at him under his heavy eyelids, with the same faint malice — or was it only reserve?

'What do you *think* happened?' he said.

'Oh, I know what happened. But where is she now?'

Hudson raised his eyebrows. 'Hasn't she gone home? Back to Oxford?'

The dislike Gurney felt for him, and his curiosity itself, began to be undermined by a sudden acid suspicion that the story was less a commonplace story of seduction than it seemed. To cover his uneasiness he spoke with deliberate insolence. 'If you really don't know where she is . . .'

'Why the devil should I bother to lie?' Hudson said, very quietly.

'She hadn't come back to Oxford when I left,' Gurney said. 'She wrote — once — to the Pagets — and told them she didn't intend to come back.' He smiled sharply. 'Perhaps you find it amusing?'

'No.' Hudson leaned forward. 'No, let me tell you . . . I'm not offering excuses. As it turned out — there are none. But — in fact — the story you must have heard — I heard it myself only yesterday, when a month's letters caught up with me — is not, let's say not entirely, true. It has been . . . manipulated.' His eyelids covered all but a pale segment of eye, very bright. 'Do you want to hear any more?'

'Go on.'

'Perhaps *you* will be amused . . . I came in that evening from my club and found the girl sitting at my desk, turning over letters and papers she'd emptied out of the drawers. To this day I don't know how she got in. My servant was out . . . I supposed — you'll credit it to my vanity — but it's not an unknown event — I supposed she had come to offer herself to the notorious writer. Not unknown, hardly even uncommon, and I saw no reason why I should disappoint her.' He went on coolly, 'It never entered my head that she was a virgin. Until it was too late I didn't know she was . . . And afterwards she bolted out of the room and out of the building as if I were the devil. I didn't feel inclined to run up Arlington Street after her. I did, next morning, try to find her — she left a handbag with a couple of telephone numbers in it, but I drew blank at both of them. The day after, I left for Spain. That's all. I assure you that's all.'

Gurney had no doubt whatever that he was speaking the truth. The incident was not important enough for him to be tempted to invent. So far as he was concerned it was not important at all. At the risk of appearing simple, he asked,

'Then — hadn't you offered to give her dinner that evening?'

Hudson stared. 'Good heavens, no. Why should I?'

Gurney's heart sank. Why had Hetty invented that part of the story? Far, far more disconcerting — why did she go to the flat? You can never be sure how anyone will behave, not even a very young girl, he thought — perhaps least of all a young girl . . . His mind turned back to the last time he had seen her, listening with smiling attention to the nonsense pouring from Craddock, her eyes fixed on his face with a child's bland interest in what it can just barely understand. With an effort, he pushed the whole confusing riddle to the back of his mind, to be looked at when he was alone.

'No, it wasn't excusable,' he said.

'I agree.' Hudson frowned — and yawned suddenly. 'But tell me why else she forced herself on me? An explanation — other than the obvious one — did occur to me later. But it was too grotesque . . . No. No, she can only have come out of — what shall we call it? — curiosity? If you insist that I oughtn't to have punished her for it, I won't argue with you . . . Of course,' he added lightly, 'you think I'm a scoundrel.'

'I think you behaved very like yourself,' Gurney said.

Hudson moved his chair into the sun, settling himself in it in the pose Gurney had seen before — tired rapacious eagle or gargoyle — but the mouth with its long full curve was human. So was the portentous vanity of what he had to say.

'My dear Gurney, there are moments when my . . . my eroticism, my capacity for pleasure, my greed, disgust me. But only a very few moments. The rest of the time I find it natural and right, like any perfectly healthy function. More important, it releases my energy to work. I'm certain, too, that after a lifetime of sensual happiness one dies without any regrets. It is people who have been starved of it, or have starved themselves, who regret the end of their youth, and fear death. They know they are dying unfulfilled . . . Perhaps, though, great saints use, and wear out, their energies on another level.' A fold at the ends of his mouth did duty for a smile. 'But how many of them took up saintliness only *after* Carthage!'

His familiar cold vice got the better of Gurney's distaste for the man. If he could have read anything in Hudson's heart by cutting it out, he would have tried to do just that. How the devil did Hudson reconcile his belief that he had the right to use his fame as a writer, and his money, to draw very young women into his bed, with his other belief that, to be worth anything, human beings must be free? Free to sleep with him and release his other energies? Gurney thought: Perhaps — minking himself in his monstrous egoism — he believes that what gives him pleasure is enough reward for them? Perhaps he avoids thinking about it — as we avoid seeing the animal we are eating? . . .

We are all egoists, all beasts of prey: most of us timidly; Hudson frankly and without any feelings of guilt.

'Why in heaven's name did you turn communist?' he asked suddenly.

The irony Hudson knew how to convey with every line in his face — with those doubling his lower lid as clearly as with the jagged cipher drawn from the fleshy wings of his nose to his jaw — became complacent.

'Oh, I could give you any number of clever reasons. The truth isn't at all clever. You can't be free in a vacuum. Unless in some way or another you *engage* yourself, you risk becoming the servant of your own egoism. I'm an atheist, but my mind will never escape wholly from the twist given it in childhood, by my saintly mother. You can see why communism, the revolution and so on and so on, appealed to me — as the one form of belief in eternal life which an atheist could accept. The up-to-date form of my mother's Christianity . . . I was far from suspecting that it could turn out to be eternal death . . . And I believed that it had been incarnated in Soviet Russia. Quite simple.'

'But was that all?'

'Not quite. I dislike the smell of poverty, it offends my nose and disturbs my peace of mind. On the face of it — communism was going to stop all that.'

'Why did you drop it?'

Hudson looked at him with a half-amused arrogance. 'Because I dislike the stench of cruelty even more. That stench, coming out of communist Europe, became altogether too strong for me.' He leaned across the table. 'Shall I tell you something? I knew — as long ago as 1948 — four years ago — I knew I'd made an honest fatuous mistake. I was wasting my time and ruining my chances of enjoying my life. But I held my tongue about it — for four years. For two reasons. Because I needed as long as that to prepare my counter-attack. It had to be remarkable — my pride was suffering a little, I'd been duped.' He laughed. 'Yes, yes, I duped myself . . . My other reason for waiting is simpler. I'm not merely a writer. I live. Several months out of the four years were spent — lived — with a young woman, an Arab.'

The cold impudence with which he had taken his time struck Gurney. He had amused himself — sharpening his knife and letting the faithful go on using his name for their purposes all the time he did it, relishing the scandal his communism raised against him, just as he was taking acute pleasure now in the stale abuse emptied on him by his ex-friends. Gurney remembered being told that he never took the trouble to read an article praising his work — no critic was fit to praise him. But he read abuse: it amused and stimulated him.

'The truth is,' he said slowly, 'your heart was never involved. And isn't now.'

'Oh, if you like,' Hudson said with indifference. 'The fact remains that I did — for a time — blame my Calvinist childhood for it — see Soviet Russia as the kingdom of heaven on earth. But you're perfectly right. When it turned out to be the kingdom of a new Popery — supported by armed policemen, tanks, and administrators with a natural talent for heartless obedience — I wasn't much distressed. As you say — my heart wasn't engaged . . . As a writer, I cared fatally. Every age, my dear Gurney, has its demonic passion. Ours is the passion for confession — my job as a writer is to pursue it to its very last hiding-place in the blackest most shocking impulse of minds and bodies. The only way I can do that is by embracing the whole living world: what, in the interests of style, I have to leave out is still present invisibly. I can't let myself create a false whole by killing and mutilating what I don't like. Russian communism does precisely this — not simply in daily life, by silencing or murdering its critics. It demands the same disgusting habits of mutilation from its writers. Impossible! You can't create by killing. And even the atheism professed by their top brass is perverse. Under cover of planning an earthly New Jerusalem — saints *à rebours* — they slip into the seat of God Almighty. An honest atheist like myself has no use for any God — neither the traditional one nor the infinitely more vacuous, more boring one labelled Humanity. Or History or Necessity or . . . May I order both of us another martini?'

'Yes, if you will,' Gurney said.

He had been unwilling to drink with Hetty's seducer, but that incident had become intolerably blurred.

Hudson beckoned the waiter. Holding his glass against the light, he leaned back with an air of alert contentment, like a man who has eaten a really excellent meal.

'Have you noticed,' he said, 'how startling a woman's black dress is in this light? Look at that one. It has the brightness of the most violent colours.'

'Do you,' Gurney asked, 'intend to go on assaulting your late friends?'

'Good God, no! I never gave the Party more than its fair share of my time. Why the devil should I waste energy on it now? I don't know any Party secrets — and if I did I wouldn't touch the sordid job of denunciations and the rest of it. I've chucked my bomb. Now I can write what I please.'

'Another confession?' Gurney asked maliciously.

Hudson glanced at him down his powerful nose. 'What do you think? . . . I know what you think. That I enjoy exposing myself. I do — but not in the way that makes you feel morally superior. I use myself *as an object* — without fear or favour. Not a man named Miles Hudson, but a human being — every human being. And I tell plainly what other men are too cowardly or too vulgarly discreet or too prudish to tell about themselves. That's all, that's all.'

His famous 'sincerity', thought Gurney. Which is as much an invention as any lie. As much part of his rapacious pride . . . He has done a great deal of harm. All his adult life he has been, morally and spiritually, a vortex of disintegration and doubt. A demon. A corrupting demon. Now he's going to make himself a new reputation as an archangel of sanity: he will be praised, honoured, given the O.M. And the young will cease to care tuppence about him. He won't notice it. His life of the higher hedonism will go smoothly on until his magnificent funeral — if he succeeds in dying before magnificent funerals become impossible. He will . . . A supremely fortunate, supremely cold man.

He could not feel in himself the smallest germ of desire to enjoy Hudson's good fortune. He shot over his own butts. He had minutes of intense happiness, always thanks to a small chance: like that of waking in a bedroom on the Adriatic to a light of unequalled suavity; or the moment in Nevers when he remembered that Stendhal had been there, and he bought, in a bookshop where Stendhal himself might have stood turning over pages, an edition of the *Memoires d'un touriste*, to be able to follow him through the streets and stare at the same view: other moments — sights, sounds, sensations — equally unreasonable and inexplicable, but starting up a pleasure barely endurable by mind or senses.

Immediately in front of him in the square, a small child, breaking loose from his mother, rushed at the pigeons strutting about the pavement: a dozen of them rose languidly, their wings catching the light from the lagoon on its rebound from the wall of the Doge's Palace: his face lifted to this same reverberating light, the child watched them in a silence more moving than a cry.

'Shall I tell you my finest memory of Venice?' Hudson said suddenly. 'It happened when I was very young. One night I was in a sort of bistrot, a shabby little place on the edge of a very narrow canal, completely silent and dark except for the light falling across it thinly from the café. There were only Italians in the place — all, if their clothes are anything to go by, very poor. At one table an elderly woman was sitting with three men. Quite suddenly — as if in answer to something one of them had said — she sang a few bars of *Don Giovanni*, in a low voice that was very weak, but perfectly and amazingly true. The waiter told me that she had been a concert singer, well-known in Venice, and now forgotten and poor. I know nothing more about her, I don't remember her name — and I shall hear her voice, as it was that evening, when I've forgotten every other I ever knew.'

Gurney felt a momentary liking for him. It made him incautious.

'Can you,' he asked, 'recall the actual sound of a voice?'

'Yes. Easily.'

'Are you sure? Even when the owner of the voice has been dead years?'

'Of course. Can't you?'

'No.' He used to think, of Anne's voice, that it would charm the ears of a stone image. After she died, he could no more hear it than he could feel the softness of her skin under his hand.

Hudson was looking at him with curiosity and a touch of pity. He noticed it at once, and his mind froze. Nothing was more possible than that the Master had talked to Hudson about him and about Anne. And in that case, he thought, I have just given myself away to the least merciful of egoists.

'You probably deceive yourself,' he said coldly.

Hudson did not take the trouble to pretend. 'I don't think so. You may be tone deaf.'

'I daresay,' Gurney said. He stood up. 'I must go.'

'Shall you be in Venice long?'

'I don't know.'

Hudson smiled very slightly. 'I'm leaving tomorrow morning.' He hesitated. 'If you hear anything——'

'About the girl? . . . You are the last person I shall tell.'

Hudson's smile became almost kind. 'Very well.'

Gurney nodded and left him. All the way across the square the thought of the other man's inquisitive pity burned him as though he had swallowed an acid. My own fault, he thought, raging: I laid myself open to it — clumsy ape that I am. If, even now, I haven't learned to guard myself — *ne pas être deviné* — I deserve nothing better . . . He felt sick with self-disgust.

Venice itself calmed him, but not by showing itself off: by a subtler trick. Between half-past eight and nine he was in the Piazzetta, listening to a concert given by the Banda C. Monteverdi. A dozen men in white uniforms played Strauss to a crowd of people standing rapt, as though anxious not to miss a note of the mediocre and horribly badly played music, or sauntering, never far from the band, between the Palace and the round arches at the near end of the Piazza San Marco with their lighted windows of shops or cafés, and round globes of white light. He listened absently, wondering at the amiability which kept all these Venetians entranced by the most atrocious playing in the world. Suddenly and gently — with an incomparable gentleness — the worn-down stone paving under his feet, and the faded pink, grey, and white marble, resembling brick, above the gallery of the Palace, were replaced by the flagstones of the small lost North Sea port of his childhood and first youth; a wind from a colder sea flowed through the chill air from the lagoon, and the growing darkness of a September night in Venice became a thinner colder half-light pricked here and there by street-lamps, plain, feeble, leaving in shadow a line of comfortless wooden seats under the sea-wall — exactly as the infinitely more elaborate lights near him failed to reach as far as a few benches in the shadowy cloister of the Palace . . . Created from absence, by a throw of the dice, the past rose from the darkness: the clock striking in a corner of the Piazza sounded three miles out in the North Sea, a floating bell-buoy to warn ships.

No, he told himself with contempt, you don't hear it . . . But he was no longer foolishly bitter — and not because he knew that he could, if he chose, go back to the unforgotten sea-wall and catch the tolling of the bell-buoy itself. I shall never go, he thought; it's a mistake to try to creep back into a cast skin . . . His sudden sense of freedom came from nearer at hand, from the happiness of a moment of escape. Ghosts cannot exist in Venice, in the devouring purity of an air washed by long stretches of water.

Except moments like this, nothing in my life is worth a toss, he thought lightly. I have thrown away, more or less deliberately, out of laziness, diffidence, fear of failure, far more success than I have had or now can have. These brief pleasures are all. Nothing, he thought, except death or (I suppose) extreme bodily pain, can spoil them for me . . .

'And except for one event,' he said aloud, 'not on the whole a bad life.'

Chapter 17

WHEN he had been back in Oxford a week, he came home one evening to find Nevil Rigden waiting to see him. He had come to talk about his work during the year. Just as he was leaving, Gurney remembered to ask,

'Oh, how is your mother?'

'My mother? Yes — she died,' Rigden said curtly.

'Did she? I'm very sorry,' Gurney said.

His attention caught, he was struck by a change in Rigden. He looked much older, and his manner had lost a little of its cockily aggressive self-confidence. That, thought Gurney drily, was all to the good, but there were other marks, of strain or fatigue, which were not improvements — notably a twitching muscle at the corner of an eye.

'I expected it,' Rigden said.

'Expected or not, a death hurts.'

'Yes.'

Gurney tried to find something friendly to say. 'Did you go away this summer?'

Rigden shook his head. 'No. Evelyn went off to Spain with friends of hers. I stayed here to try and finish a book.'

'Oh. Did you finish it?'

'No.' He eyed Gurney furtively, as though he expected to be laughed at. 'I wasted too much time.'

'Doing what?'

'Going up to London . . . I tried to find Hetty.' He laughed briefly. 'A total waste of time.'

Gurney knew already that she had not been found. The police had failed to trace her. Paget, going about it his own way, had failed. The two or three people who had spoken to Gurney about it since he came back were certain — sorrowfully, or with the profound satisfaction a disaster can be to onlookers whose human need for a victim it meets — that she was 'no longer alive'. ('Dead' would have been brutal.) The police, it seemed, were less certain. They had astonished Paget by telling him that every year a number of people, even a number of young people, manage to disappear without trace and without any suspicion that they have been killed or have done away with themselves: often, too, without anyone discovering why they had wanted to vanish.

'Where did you look?' asked Gurney.

'Oh, only in London.' He hesitated, and began to talk about his search, savagely, with a curious effect of suspense. The girl had one day told him, he said, that the only thing she really would like to do was to nurse in a children's hospital. With only this to go on, he had persuaded the police to give him a letter to the matrons of hospitals where there are children, and he had visited the lot, day after useless day: he carried a snapshot of Hetty stolen from Primrose Paget's desk, and asked every one of these matrons — many of whom in their astonishment treated him icily — whether she were sweeping floors in any of their wards. 'I can't tell you,' he said, 'what a horrible feeling of desolation you get in a room full of sick children. I felt thankful that Cat and I were nursed through our illnesses at home, in unhygienic safety.' . . . He had also walked the streets, miles of streets. His search became a nightmare of frustration, blindly prolonged. Why did he prolong it? He had no idea why — except, Gurney saw, that for some reason he was wholly unable to swallow the void into which the girl had disappeared from the moment she left the house to go to meet Hudson.

As he listened, Gurney tried to make up his mind whether

or not to tell him what Hudson had said: that there had been no invitation to dinner, no planned seduction. In the end, feeling that he had no right to keep back any scrap of evidence, he told him. He expected a burst of rage. But all Rigden did was to pass his hand over his face in a gesture of weariness, and say,

'It could be true . . . None of it really makes sense. One can only try.'

'My dear Rigden,' Gurney said gently, 'what more can you do?'

This reasonable remark seemed to exasperate Rigden. With a familiar jeering aggressiveness he said,

'What everyone is doing. I could give up thinking about her. Write her off. A total loss.'

The fellow's beginning to show off, Gurney thought. 'Is that what the Pagets have done?' he said drily. 'Thomas Paget doesn't strike me as a man without any heart.'

He was delighted to see that he had pricked Rigden. The young man stared at him, his face perfectly blank. After a minute he said,

'Tom——' and stopped on a sharply-drawn breath. He went on in a quieter voice, 'Did you know that Primrose is ill?'

'No. What's wrong with her?'

'Not exactly ill. But she has shut herself in the house, and won't see anyone — none of their friends. Tom is desperately worried.'

'Has your wife seen her?'

'No. She keeps Evelyn out, too,' Rigden said. He spoke as if this were the most astonishing of Primrose's sick whims.

Gurney frowned. 'There must be something one can do.'

'I don't think so,' Rigden said coldly.

A Cup of Tea for Mr. Thorgill

He left. After he had gone, Gurney noticed that he had forgotten the books he had been holding under his arm. One of them opened on a sheet of writing paper: a few lines written to him by Thomas Paget, about his mother — lines of such delicacy and compassion that Gurney caught himself wishing he were capable of writing them. They sharpened his liking for Paget, and his respect.

Chapter 18

H E hesitated a long time, days, before trying to see Primrose. He was not indifferent. Very far from it. Simply he could not make up his mind whether a visit from him would be looked on as anything but an intolerable nuisance. He could rarely convince himself that he would be welcome at such a time: the reputation he had with a great many people, as a callous unreliable egoist, had been built out of just such moments of diffidence. In the end, driven to it by his affection for Primrose, he decided to go to the house.

The afternoon he went was cold, with a bitter wind, and he was surprised to find the front door left open on to a path thick with fallen October leaves. He rang. No one answered. He went in and walked half-way along the passage; the door of the sitting-room was wide open, and Primrose was sitting there on a sofa, a tray beside her, eating pieces of bread with quick greedy movements of her hand between plate and mouth. She saw him and smiled widely.

'The front door was open,' he said. 'Forgive me for walking in. I rang.'

'I heard you,' she said calmly. 'Mrs. Johnson is out.'

'May I sit down?'

She moved the tray a little. 'Sit here.'

'You've been ill, haven't you?' he began.

'No.' She shook her head vigorously. 'But I didn't want to go out. Do you know what I thought? If Hetty rings up and I'm not here, she'll forget us again, and I shall lose her.'

Gurney's pity for her stung him. He thought that, with the complete egoism of the young, Hetty had in effect for-

124

gotten her. Or at least did not care enough for her to feel any conscience about neglecting her.

'She hasn't forgotten you,' he said, 'she's afraid of people here. Why don't you go away — the country, London, anywhere you like — and let it be known you've gone, and she'll probably come there, or write to you? Try it.'

A gleam of cunning came into her eyes. 'Oh, no, I don't want to go away.'

'Why not, my dear?'

'He would be alone,' she said, smiling. 'And he hasn't anyone else now. Who would make coffee for him?'

'He won't die of Mrs. Johnson's coffee,' Gurney said.

She laughed gaily. 'That's true, but——'

The front door shut noisily and steps came quickly along the passage. She turned her head, with a look of fear in her widely-open eyes. 'Who's that?' she cried out. 'Who's coming? Don't let them come in here, Henry.'

'It may be Mrs. Johnson,' Gurney said.

He got up to go and look. Before he reached the door of the room, it opened, and Paget came in. His face cleared when he saw Gurney, and the tray on the sofa, as though they had been having tea together.

'You're feeling stronger,' he said. 'Splendid. I'm so glad. Seeing Henry has done you good, I think.' He bent down to kiss her. She started up, pushing at the tray, which slid from the sofa to the floor.

'No,' she said, in a jerky terrified voice, 'no, no, no, no.'

Paget did not move. 'Don't, Primrose. What is it?' he said calmly.

Still staring at him with the eyes of a scared animal, she repeated,

'No! I'm afraid. No, Thomas.'

He made a helpless gesture. Turning, she hurried to the far side of the room, and cowered in an armchair, pressing her cheek against the back. Gurney stooped to gather the things scattered from the tray: a plate had been broken, and the pieces were all over the place. Paget did not move to help him. He watched, with his arms hanging and a dull look of bewilderment on his face.

'She's been like this for nearly a month,' he said. 'What am I to do?'

'Has a doctor seen her?' asked Gurney.

'He says there's nothing whatever wrong with her.'

Gurney disliked talking about her in her hearing, as if she were deaf, or couldn't understand that she was being discussed.

'Is there no one you could ask to stay here and look after her?'

'She won't have a nurse.'

'Not a nurse,' Gurney said, frowning. 'A relative or a friend.'

'I've been trying to get her to stay for a few weeks with friends of ours in the country, but she doesn't listen . . . I wish you would speak to her about it, my dear fellow.'

Gurney said reluctantly, 'Primrose.'

Primrose did not answer. He walked across the room and looked at her. Her eyes were closed and she did not move. For a moment, he thought she was pretending to be asleep, but when he looked at her closely there was no doubt about it, she had dropped off to sleep, like a child or a very old woman, in the moment of leaning back in her chair. The deep lids under her strong black half-hoops of eyebrows were motionless: she was smiling, a strangely equivocal smile, half knowing, half placidly amused.

He beckoned her husband. Paget came over and looked at her for a moment. One of the Paisley shawls admired by our grandmothers lay along the back of the sofa; he reached for it and covered her with it, gently and deftly.

'I'll go,' Gurney said.

Paget nodded. 'She may sleep like this for several hours.'

She woke up soon after Gurney had left, and began crying. Unable to soothe her, Paget telephoned to the doctor: when he came he persuaded her, with great difficulty, to go to bed, and gave her a sedative. He left a few tablets of barbiturate with Paget, to be given to her when she needed them. Some time during the night, she woke, got up — so quietly that the housekeeper, sleeping in the dressing-room to be near her, was not disturbed; nor was Paget in the room beyond it — and swallowed all the tablets. She had seemed to be taking no interest in anything, but she must have watched her husband carry them away to a cupboard in the bathroom. Then — or before she swallowed them — she wrote a short letter, laid it in the drawer of Paget's desk in his study, and went back to bed. When the housekeeper came in with her coffee, she had been dead for two or three hours.

Paget did not come on the letter until the afternoon, and then he handed it to the police. There were only a few lines, in her fine erratic hand. She begged him to forgive her for wanting to die; she could not live any longer without Hetty — 'without my poor child'. After her name she had scrawled, 'No, I can't forgive him — Miles Hudson. I can't.'

The buzz of flies which attends a suicide moved aside a little, to settle again on Hudson. This time not for long. The moral character of a writer, even a famous writer, is only tepidly interesting — except, possibly, to religious or fastidious people, and these, in the nature of society now, are not numerous or very powerful. But Gurney felt an impotent rage when he thought of Primrose's sad little letter being pored over by greasy eyes and rolled on dirty tongues. One or two newspapers, and a Left weekly, made a louder song about it than the others — waving it as a proof that Hudson's change of mind about communism was immoral because he was. Let them jeer at him and welcome, Gurney

thought savagely, but . . . Each time he remembered the
letter he saw Primrose writing it, with that effort it was to
her to write anything, frowning, mouth drawn into its
crazily bold half-circle — then creeping back like a mischievous child to bed, to lie down with, perhaps, that same
sly ambiguous smile . . . Why had her husband given it to
the police? In his place, Gurney thought, I would have kept
her weak cry of grief for myself.

Paget, when Gurney went to see him, spoke of the dead
woman in a rather curious tone. It was only afterwards that
it struck Gurney as peculiar — and then he reflected that ti
was very much what Paget might have said if he had been
talking about the death of an animal he had been fond of.

'The worst, the most unbearable thing was that there was
so little I could do for her. She didn't understand what I
said to her, of course, and I couldn't tell her that I was trying to help her. For days all I had been able to do was to sit
in the same room with her, and talk to her a little. She
wouldn't — you saw — let me touch her.'

'Until the trouble about Hetty, she was very happy,'
Gurney said.

'Yes. Yes, I think so.' He turned his face aside. 'That
was a bad business. I wish to God I had been able to
prevent it. Poor Primrose.'

Chapter 19

THAT same day Gurney went to talk to the Master in his rooms in the college. Crossing the quadrangle, he felt singularly light-hearted: during the night it had rained, and a light south wind had blown up clouds the greyish-white colour of olive-trees: these, and the yellow ochre leaves of a plane-tree, and the scent of wet earth, gave him a feeling of youth and confidence — as a fine autumn always did, far more than the spring, and with an incomparable suavity.

He found Rigden with the Master.

'Am I in the way? I can come back later.'

'I'm just leaving,' Rigden said.

The Master watched him gather his papers together. With the casualness he affected when he was going to make an indiscreet remark, he said,

'Nevil, I think you'll get the Readership. The wind's blowing your way.' He laughed gently. 'If anyone except Dalton had been supporting West . . . But he has insulted too many people for his support to be anything but a dead weight.'

For less than a second, Rigden's eyes brightened: the flame came and went as though nipped out. He let go the handle of the door and said,

'There's something I should tell you.'

'Yes?' the Master said, smiling. 'What is it?'

Rigden did not answer at once. Something, some hint of tension in his silence made Gurney glance at him sharply. The same physical tic he had noticed once before — a twitching muscle — caught his eye, and he had time to wonder whether the young man were in a fit state to discuss anything at all. Afterwards, he reflected that Rigden had hesitated very much in the way a suicide might, at the last second, feel a rending uncertainty. But he spoke calmly.

'You remember, sir, that Miss Spencer-Savage told you, at the end of last term, that she knew I was a communist. You spoke to me about it — and I told you it was all nonsense . . . In fact, it wasn't nonsense. She was right.' He paused very briefly, and went on, 'That is, until a short time ago she was right. I . . . But it's not easy to explain.'

Gurney felt a cold excitement. In a sudden explosion of light behind his eyes he realised something — not about Rigden: about himself. This wasn't the sort of treachery, wrong-doing, call it what you like, which sickened him: there *are* unforgiveable treacheries, but they are quite different — smaller, more murderous . . . He came back abruptly to the Master's over-warm room, and Rigden's face, strangely smooth and appeased. He thought: My God, he's done for himself. Why the devil did he tell us? . . . He looked at Spencer-Savage.

The Master's face showed neither astonishment nor anger. He might have been listening, with his usual sleepy interest, to an argument at his dinner-table, only troubling himself to take part in it when he wanted to provoke an indiscretion, or if it turned political, at which point he cut it short. This is politics all right, Gurney thought maliciously. What will he do?

Settling himself back in his chair, the Master said in a brusque voice,

'All the same, you'd better try.'

Rigden said, 'I reminded you at the time that I'd been a communist, a member of the Party, for two and a half weeks, my first year in Oxford, and that I'd left it . . . That was quite true. It wasn't the whole truth. The truth is — I left because I was advised to leave. I was told I could do more useful work if I were not a member. Not openly a member ... That was in 1939. Then the war came. Then until — until I stopped — I was doing various things. I —' he hesitated and said, 'Miss Spencer-Savage——'

The Master interrupted him. 'Never mind her. *What* were you doing — what was the point?'

'I wrote for them,' Rigden said quickly. 'Pamphlets. That kind of thing.'

'What else?'

'Nothing else,' Rigden said.

There was a brief silence. The Master picked up the ivory paper-knife he used, and balanced it on one of his long shapely fingers.

'It seems a curious, ah, hobby, for a sane man,' he said carelessly.

Rigden did not answer. It struck Gurney that he didn't realise at all clearly the effect his confession was making on the Master. He had been concentrated in himself, like a man waiting to be operated on, with no attention to spare for the impression his words and gestures may be making on others. Gurney felt a momentary pity for his blindness. Impulsively — with a vague idea of giving Rigden the chance to put himself in a better light — he said,

'My dear fellow — 1939 — that's thirteen years . . . It doesn't surprise me that you joined the Party: a great many young men of your decade joined it and have since become painfully respectable. What does surprise me is that — after being faithful so long — you broke out. Why?'

'I can't tell you in a few words,' Rigden said. He moved his hands awkwardly. 'There are some things you can't order yourself to accept — or be ordered, even——'

The paper-knife overbalanced and clattered to the floor. Rigden moved to pick it up, and was stopped by the Master's voice as if he had run into a wall.

'I'm not in the least interested in your reasons for being, or not being, a communist,' Spencer-Savage said. 'They're quite irrelevant — and I doubt if I should understand them. Not that I intend to try . . . The fact is, Rigden, you're a dishonest fellow — a liar — and that I find very distasteful.'

How like him to be more contemptuous than shocked, Gurney thought . . . Yet the Master's brutality startled him: the instant wiping out, as if it had never existed, of his affection for the young man. He might have been dealing with a clerk he had caught out in a disgraceful theft. Even for a man who has brought egoism to a quite remarkable degree of delicacy and highmindedness, he was being singularly callous. He may Gurney thought drily, be protecting himself against the shock of disappointment. But why — since he has the poorest opinion of human nature — is he even disappointed? A crack in his scepticism and indifference? Or only hurt vanity?

Rigden stared at him without any expression. At last he said under his breath,

'What can I say?'

'Better say nothing.' The Master turned to glance sharply at Gurney. 'You knew nothing about this, I take it?'

Gurney had an insane impulse to answer: Yes, I knew, and why bother? What does it matter?

'No.'

The Master seemed to hesitate. 'I'll send for you,' he drawled. With sudden roughness he added, 'You don't, do you, imagine that your — your untrustworthiness won't affect you and your position?'

In the same nearly inaudible voice, but quite steadily, Rigden said,

'You can at least trust me to know what to say to a young man who looks like being caught, as I was, by the —' he stammered a little — 'the logic of communism.'

'And what in God's name is that?' the Master said with an off-hand contempt. 'Logic? Infernal nonsense . . . You'd better go.'

Gurney said quickly, 'I'll see you later, Rigden.'

Rigden did not look at him, and gave no sign of having heard. He was already crossing the room, with an odd clumsiness, as though he had to feel his way between bookcases and leather armchairs. The door had barely closed on him before the Master exclaimed,

'What did I always tell you, Gurney? You can't make a decent fellow out of a nobody by educating him. All this business of educating people right and left — regardless of where they come from — lunacy, my dear boy, lunacy. About as sensible as trying to grow wine in Scotland. I thought I knew that fellow, and it turns out that I don't understand a damned thing about him, I don't know why he chose to behave like a pickpocket, I don't know anything. He might be a performing animal. I'm completely baffled.'

'I feel a certain sympathy for him,' Gurney said.

Exasperated, the Master said coldly,

'By God, if a remark or an action is completely and utterly indefensible, one can count on you to defend it. Why the devil do you go out of your way to irritate people? You're not a fool. Could you bring yourself to talk sensibly for a moment?'

'I didn't feel that we were getting much of the story,' Gurney said coolly.

'Oh, you didn't? How much filth can you swallow?'

Gurney smiled. 'Oh, come — is it as serious as that?'

The Master looked up at him without a trace of his habitual carelessness and sweetness of temper. 'What is serious is that I've been actively pushing forward a young man capable of deceiving and making an ass of me — without my having the faintest suspicion. And as for why he wanted to do it . . . No, I'll be damned if I can understand him. Do you?'

'No,' Gurney said unwillingly. 'I don't.'

For the first time he noticed in the Master one of his sister's more atrocious habits. Or instincts. Both of them judged men and women by the degree of their usefulness to the Spencer-Savage myth of social infallibility. Put Athene in the wrong, and she not only detested you, she knew at once that you were a low treacherous fellow, capable of any wickedness. Her brother seemed kinder, more nearly reasonable and impartial. But was it anything more than his natural lazy urbanity, his dislike of scenes, and inbred lack of respect for human nature? He's more like her than I knew, Gurney thought. Scratch his charming indifference, and you come on the same touchiness, hardness, vanity.

'What are you going to do?' he asked.

The Master frowned. 'Damned if I know. I can't tell you yet. I must think about it.'

Something that was neither his demon of curiosity, nor his impulse to provoke Spencer-Savage, jerked Gurney into saying,

'I doubt if you know what you're thinking about. Let me look into it a little more before you decide anything.'

The Master's mood changed suddenly. He went off into one of his abrupt surprisingly heartless laughs.

'D'you know what? I shall have to apologise to Retta. It's intolerable. She'll be more sure of herself and her what-d'you-call-it, her vibrations, than ever. She'll go round smelling out sinners under every damned dinner-table in Oxford.'

'Why tell her? Why tell anyone until you've had time to consider it?'

'Oh, these things always get out,' the Master said lightly. 'No good trying to hide them.'

Chapter 20

DURING the evening Gurney called on Vančura. He wanted his advice, or at least his opinion, before seeing Rigden.

Vančura listened, and made a contemptuous grimace. 'My dear chap, what's the trouble? You've had them in Oxford before, these excited adolescents begging a hairy communist to rape them. It comes of being coddled. They feel vaguely that in other countries young men have a harder time of it, and they want to be involved, that's all. It's generous and silly — and absolutely meaningless.'

'In the first place,' Gurney said, 'Rigden is not an adolescent, and was never coddled; he came out of a London slum before the war. And in the second, he didn't put his long ears back after a few weeks and bolt from the Party as soon as he smelled that it wasn't an atheists' Sunday-school. He resigned. But only because he was told he could be more useful behind the scenes. That's to say, he's been faithful for more than ten years——'

Vančura glared at him. 'You didn't tell me that.'

'I'm telling you now,' Gurney said.

'You say he joined the Party, then left — ostensibly — and went on working for it? He told you this himself?'

'Yes, of course.'

'Listen, Henry,' Vančura said, with an air of tired patience. 'If what you're telling me is true, your chap is — possibly — interesting. I say possibly, because how do I know in this scandalous country whether black is black or only a fog coming up? But every dear old auntie should know, and you obviously don't, that the only interesting

135

communists — I say: the only ones — are not members of the Party, they're members of anything you like, the civil service, I.C.I., a research establishment, a profession; they work under the direction of an official in this country of the Soviet army or police — and for all I know you're an agent yourself. But I don't think so — you stink of innocence and indiscretion.'

'Thank you,' Gurney said.

Vančura grinned sharply. 'It could be the double bluff, of course . . . No, no, I absolve you. But your young man . . . My poor friend, don't you know that any local communist party is what Germans call the *sitz-Direktor* — the chap in a black-market firm who goes to prison? In Moscow the English party is looked on — it and its leaders — as derisory. That's why they're left in peace. You could arrest the lot without shaking the bed. My friend in Prague, when he was still in favour, told me that Stalin said to him: I sh— an English comrade every morning . . . If the Party ever became politically important here, its leaders would be removed and others, with real claws, supplied from stock. It follows that your young friend knows — possibly — all kinds of things you ought to hear. Ask him.'

Unwilling to offend him by smiling, Gurney said, 'Forgive me, you may be right, but——'

'But you don't believe me,' Vančura interrupted.

'I'm not much impressed. My dear Jan, it's all much too neatly conspiratorial. Conspiracy isn't one of our habits.'

Vančura smiled sourly. 'You English are the most simple-minded sceptics in Europe. I don't know about America.'

'Nonsense,' Gurney said. He laughed. '"Why, sometimes, I've believed as many as six impossible things before breakfast."'

'What's that?'

'It comes in *Through the Looking-Glass* . . . the White Queen——'

Vančura exploded in black rage. 'Of all the affectations that make me want to spit in the face of this country, that is easily the most irritating and unbearable. You tell an Englishman he's got the plague and he comes back with a quotation from a book he read in his nursery — always the same book.'

'No,' Gurney said, 'it could be *Alice in Wonderland*.'

'My God!'

The door of the bedroom opened a couple of inches, and Bella brought her round face close to the crack to see why he was shouting: she vanished, shutting the door again quietly, when she knew that Gurney had seen her.

'No, no, leave us our dodos,' he said, 'they do no harm.'

'I'm not so sure.'

Gurney laughed at him again. 'Live in England another fifty or a hundred years, and——'

'This country isn't going to last so long as that,' Vančura snapped. But he had calmed down. 'A pity.'

'You know nothing about us,' Gurney said equably. 'As for Rigden — there's only one thing I really would like to know. Why did he break? He stalled on that.'

'Ah,' Vančura said. 'The answer to that one is in his character, and I don't know him. I can tell you one thing. Simply finding out that the thing you're serving is inhuman, an inhumanly efficient police state, isn't enough. The chap I told you about — the one who was going to be killed, *and knew it* — went on believing. Died a believer. *Though thou slay me, yet will I,* and the rest of it . . .' A gleam of savage amusement came into his small eyes. 'Let me talk to your young man.'

Gurney cocked an eye at him. 'Is that a good idea?'

'I know what to ask him. You don't.'

By no means sure that he wanted to hand Rigden over — *my* bird, he thought — he said,

'I'll think about it. I won't promise anything, but I——'

The bedroom door opened again, widely this time. Bella was wearing hat and coat, and carrying a large suitcase, which must have been heavy: it dragged her strong young body over to one side. Without speaking to either man, she went straight through the room to the kitchen, unhooked the cage with her canary, and came back with it into the sitting-room.

'I'm going now, Jan,' she said quietly. She looked at Gurney with a serious smile. 'I'm glad you're here, Henry.'

Vančura did not get up. He frowned at her and said,

'Where are you going?'

'You don't need to know that,' she answered, 'and I'd rather not tell you.'

'What do you mean?' he demanded. 'What are you doing with that bird?'

'He's mine,' Bella said, 'I can't go without him. I'm leaving you.'

She was standing, suitcase in one hand, cage in the other, and talking with her habitual simplicity and politeness. Vančura got to his feet. 'I don't understand.' Dropping his head so that his low forehead with its fringe of black hair almost disappeared, he stared at her from angry lustreless eyes as though she were an enemy. She stood still, and repeated gravely,

'I'm leaving you.'

'What is all this about?' he asked.

'Bella, my dear, I'll go,' Gurney said, 'you don't want me here, if you're going to quarrel with Jan.'

She said in the same polite still voice, like a child repeating something learned by heart, 'But I'm not quarrelling, and if you don't mind, Henry, I'd like you to stay. Then you can look after him a little.'

Gurney supposed that she wanted him because, with a third person in the room, she was less likely to lose her self-control.

'You can't go, Bella,' he said.

'I must.'

Vančura took a step towards her. 'Why?'

'I can't stand any longer being lived with as though I were a child or a half-wit, useless to you except in bed. And of course as a cook.'

She was speaking without a trace of bitterness or anger, and although what she said might have come from a vain woman, it clearly did not. She has less vanity, Gurney thought, than any human being I ever knew . . . If she had any at all, it was buried in her so deeply, under so many habits of serviability and gentleness, that her lover might have been forgiven if he had treated her carelessly (it is only vanity one has to be careful not to offend). He had gone one worse, and behaved as though kindness — he was never unkind — would make up to her for lack of trust and complete ruinous disbelief in her honesty. Ruinous of all security, all warmth.

'You——' Vančura began. He stopped, as though he were short of breath: the blood had left his face, its place taken by a dull grey shadow. After a minute he went on, 'You shock me, Bella. What have I done, what did I ever say to make you feel that?'

She said firmly,

'You enjoy my cooking, you make love to me, and when you're in a bad mood you go out of the house and stay out until you can come home full of little jokes for the child; she mustn't, whatever happens, if you have had bad news from Prague, if you are wretched, be shown any of it. Why, she might run away!' For the first time her voice shook a little. 'I didn't ask you to think the world of me. Only to take things as they come.'

She had put suitcase and cage down and retreated behind them. Vančura watched her with an incredulous look of pain.

Gurney thought sorrowfully: I couldn't, if I were a woman in love with him, let it go on. Do women, even the straightforward simple Bella, enjoy dragging a punishment out — because they intend to comfort afterwards? Flatten the poor sinner to the earth, so that picking him up is a fiercer joy? . . . But did Bella mean to comfort him?

'How could I lay a weight of that sort on you?' said Vančura heavily. 'I have no right.'

She looked at him with the unforgiving contempt of the young for adult lies. 'You were afraid for yourself, not for me. You thought that if you tied yourself to me too closely you might suffer. No, no, something much worse — you might begin to live, and live happily, the way people can even in the cellar of a bombed house, if they set themselves to it.' She tried to smile. 'It's quite simple. You can do wonders with a pot of geraniums.'

Or a canary, thought Gurney.

Vančura groaned under his breath. 'And now you *are* running away.'

'But you expected me to leave you,' she cried.

He did not answer for a full minute. Watching his face, Gurney had a faint sense of what was going on in him, the bitter reluctance to take the risk of belief in another human being, the effort, a torturing effort, to humble himself. He'll have to humble himself now, Gurney thought, if he wants to keep her. After all, he thought ironically, she's too young to go on hoping. She wants a proof. And even then, will she . . .?

Vančura said, 'No. I didn't expect it.'

Bella did not answer. She turned, pulling her hat off with one hand and seizing the cage in the other, and went into the kitchen, where she hung it carefully back on its hook. Vančura stumbled blindly towards her.

Chapter 21

GURNEY decided easily that he ought to see Rigden alone — and make up his mind afterwards whether to let Vančura talk to him. He gave very little importance — in effect, none — to Vančura's fantasy about amateur secret agents: in other countries, no doubt, where ill-feeling and dislike of the government have to find dubious ways of coming out, like a case of suppressed measles, but not in this country, where a malcontent has only to go out into the street on a cold day to gather up people anxious to join him in grinding his teeth — only, in all innocence and simplicity, to desert him in better weather. Not only that. He felt some responsibility towards the young man, not a great deal, but enough to think it unfair to loose a man like Vančura on him without warning.

The next day, when he was climbing the stairs to the Rigdens' flat, it occurred to him that he did not know how far Evelyn was involved — if at all. This brought him up short. He might — if Rigden had had to confess to his wife as well as to the Master — find himself walking into the middle of another emotional crisis. At this point he almost turned back. His two passions — the exquisite happiness of walking for the first time along the streets of a foreign town, and the pleasure, equally sharp, of learning something fresh about the human heart — sprang, no doubt about it, from the same root, but the first had no limits of enjoyment: if his last glance offered him the sun rising over strange roofs he would die happy. The second reached its limit as soon as it was a question of real anguish.

The complications of vanity, ambition, jealousy of a more successful colleague, are fair game, however much suffering they cause (only a fool supposes that the pains of vanity are not really pain), and however ridiculous the sufferer's antics. What he feared touching were those pains into which vanity does not enter: the pain of a death, the pain of disillusion, itself a sort of death, and as hard and bitter sometimes as the real thing.

He need not have hesitated. With almost her first words Evelyn made it perfectly clear that she had known nothing about her husband's secret. Hearing about it had been a shock, but what she seemed chiefly to feel was anger that he had kept it from her all these years — anger and hurt pride, without a trace of compassion or anxiety or pity. And with a feminine logic that Gurney felt she rather overdid, she was very angry with him, too, for giving it away.

She was standing in the middle of the room, hands in the pocket of black trousers, eyes coldly bright as glass.

'Why need he have told anyone?'

Rigden looked at her with a slight smile. 'You know as well as I do, Evelyn, that I couldn't do anything else.'

'It's no crime to be a communist,' she said quickly. She turned on Gurney. 'Is it?' she insisted.

'It's one thing to be an avowed open communist,' Gurney said, 'and quite another to deceive us all, deliberately, by keeping it dark.'

'Why?'

He shrugged his shoulders. 'Oh, if you don't see that that makes it suspect . . .'

'Suspect of what?' she demanded. 'Nevil hasn't done anything wrong.'

'Don't talk so much,' her husband said gently.

She sent him an irritated glance. 'There was no sense in starting all this fuss. It was unnecessary and idiotic. You're being just as bloodily sentimental about this as you

are about everything else — your sister, Hetty Smith . . . I
do believe, if it hadn't been for her . . .' She stopped, and
went on calmly, 'I'm sorry, Nevil, I'm talking nonsense.
But you must admit I have some excuse for being furious.
You've probably ruined yourself, and it's all absurd. It
need never have happened.'

Gurney noticed sharply that she had not been able to
resist speaking of Hetty. In the same moment he wondered
which of her husband's crimes was pinching her worse.
That he had damaged himself by confessing? Or that he
had acted without consulting her, in a way she didn't
approve? He felt momentarily sorry for the young man:
he had enough to handle, without her furious female will
cracking down on him. He looked tired behind his pallor,
with that tiredness of the young which seems deathly, and
is wiped out by a night's sleep: the strange thing was that
he no longer looked anxious.

'I'm sorry, my darling,' he said now. 'We shall never
agree about this. Don't let's discuss it. It's not pleasant for
Gurney, he didn't come here to listen to a family quarrel.'

'Why did you come?' Evelyn asked Gurney, sullenly.

'To talk to your husband.'

'About this?'

'Yes.' He added coolly, 'I think, if you don't mind, I'd
rather talk to him alone.'

She did not move. Staring fixedly at her husband, she
asked,

'Suppose you lose your job here — what will you do?'

'I don't know yet,' he answered. 'I haven't thought
about it.'

'You'd be ruined. You'd have to take some wretched job
or other — a clerk or a schoolmaster — with no time and
no energy to write your books.'

'Probably,' he said.

She went on mercilessly hammering the same nail. 'In

fact, what you've done is utterly irresponsible — an act of individual folly.'

'If you like to call it that,' Rigden said. The sudden tightening of his thin jaw stretched the skin over his cheeks; the bones stood out like clenched knuckles. 'Yes, I agree. But I couldn't do anything else.'

'Why not?'

Rigden lost his patience with her. 'Would you rather I'd gone on with — with what I was doing?' he shouted.

Gurney was regretting sharply that he had come. He disliked the sight of uncontrolled feeling, and the tension between husband and wife had become disagreeable. Evelyn said drily,

'Of course not.'

'Very well, then,' Rigden said. He glanced furtively at Gurney. 'After all,' he said, with an effort to speak calmly, 'we don't know yet that I'm going to lose my job.' He hesitated. 'I can't really see why I should.'

Evelyn swung round. 'Mr. Gurney, what will the Master do? Do you know?'

The temptation to give them what hope he could got the better of Gurney's caution. The worst doesn't always happen, he thought.

'No, I don't,' he said. 'He's certainly angry. And disturbed by what he regards — very rightly — as a shocking and unjustifiable deception. Your best hope is that his respect for people goes no deeper than their social virtues . . .' He thought suddenly: Am I doing him an injustice? Why did he love and admire poor Loddon except for his *goodness*? . . . 'He may persuade himself that this is no more mischievous or tiresome than the intrigues and private manias he has to deal with all the time inside the college. He has always said that idealists are either blackguards or dupes — the chances are that he'll decide he never expected anything better of your husband.'

In the tail of his eye he saw Rigden wince slightly. 'Besides, he's too shrewd to want a scandal. Shrewd and rather lazy . . . All this — the laziness especially — may end in his doing nothing at all. But don't expect him to decide at once — he'll wait for a wind.'

'Have you said the very worst you think?' Evelyn demanded.

'It's only my opinion,' he warned her.

A flash of joy crossed her face. Walking over to her husband, she touched his cheek lightly. 'Forgive me if I've been harrying you, my darling. It's because I'm crazy with anxiety about you, I don't mind anything else, only about you and your work. I mind terribly about you.'

Rigden said, 'I know.'

'Now I'll leave you and Nevil alone,' she said to Gurney with a friendly smile. 'Don't be too hard on him, will you? He may be an idealist, but he's not, I assure you, a blackguard. And no one knows as much about him as I do.'

Gurney noticed that, as she passed him, she gave Rigden the long hard glance any wife might give any husband, warning him not to offer drinks, or to remember that his guest must be got out of the house before six. If he understood the signal he had been sent, Rigden's expression — alert and serious — did not change.

Chapter 22

As soon as his wife had gone, Rigden asked, 'Were you telling her the truth?'

'I told her what, on the whole, I believe,' Gurney said.

Rigden looked quickly away from him. 'If I'm let off,' he said, slowly, stumbling over words, 'if I can go on teaching . . . It may be more than I deserve, but I can be useful. I know that.'

Gurney thought: If yesterday he was a man on the edge of a risky operation, now he's in that state of slack quiescence when it's all over. It won't last — a day or a few hours, before the pains of convalescence set in — but for the moment he's escaped, and sees himself living a new simpler life . . . He felt a brief dismay. If against everything one knew about him, the Master decided to be stiff, the young man's hopes would come to a sudden unpleasant end.

The idea that he had reached the point of feeling anxious about Nevil Rigden's future made him grin.

Rigden had been watching him. 'You think I'm a rat, don't you?' he said, with something of his usual aggressiveness.

'I don't pretend to understand you,' Gurney said coldly.

Rigden did not answer for a moment. In a quieter voice, he said,

'I don't suppose I should ever be able to tell you enough about it — or about myself — to make you see why it seemed a decent way to behave. I'd tell you anything I could, but it's fairly hopeless.'

'Oh, for pity's sake, I don't want to hear why you turned

communist,' Gurney said, 'I can imagine a dozen reasons, all to the last degree commonplace. All I want to know is why you changed your mind. You're not like Craddock, a clever ass. You're not a sentimental.' He smiled maliciously. 'Though I'm damned if I know why I say that. I know nothing about you.'

'Nothing except that I'm a practised liar,' Rigden said.

'I doubt if you enjoyed that side of it,' Gurney said, smiling.

He was feeling his way in the other man's mind now. In his present mood Rigden would probably answer almost any question. Everything depended on finding the right question — the trip-wire that would split things wide open . . . Suddenly he had it.

'Tell me what Hetty Smith has to do with all this,' he said.

Rigden's face changed, hardening. 'Hetty? Nothing. How could she?'

'You're lying,' Gurney said.

Until he said it he had not been sure; the question had sprung out of the confused notion lying about his mind that Hetty and Hetty's pitiful disaster had started trouble between Rigden and his wife that was not sexual jealousy — or not only sexual jealousy. Now he was certain. The change in Rigden, from something like serenity to a defensive coldness, was too noticeable.

'You know as much about her as I know myself,' Rigden said quickly, too quickly. 'I told you I'd been trying to find her.'

'Yes, yes,' Gurney said. 'And now tell me why Evelyn can't help dragging her into an argument about your — what shall I call it? — your confession? What has Hetty to do with it? To do with you?' He thought coolly: I'm making a pretty good beast of myself. And went on, 'Forgive me, but how friendly were you with her?'

Rigden allowed himself the relief of a contemptuous grin.
'If you mean, had Evelyn any reason to be jealous——'

'I'm not a fool,' Gurney said. 'Tell me the facts.'

Rigden's hesitation was very brief. A flame of excitement
had sprung in his eyes, as though he had only just realised
that he could say what he liked, he was free.

'My God, I'd like to tell you,' he said. 'I'd have given
an ear to tell you the other day — when you were telling
me what Hudson had said. I hated to let you go on thinking — whatever you did think about her . . . The truth is,
she was used. They used her to try to discredit Hudson —
it was a put-up job . . .'

Gurney was too taken aback not to show it. 'What the
hell do you mean?'

His violence pulled Rigden up. 'Are you going to keep
this to yourself?' he said.

'I make no promises,' Gurney said. Then, because he
wanted the story, he said, 'You can trust me not to do anything that might make things worse for Hetty.' He almost
added: Or for you. But he held that back.

Almost humbly Rigden said, 'Yes, I know that.'

His excitement had died, but he began talking easily
enough, as though it really was a relief to talk . . . He's
fonder of the girl than he knows, Gurney thought. He
found it difficult to follow the story — since not only was
Rigden being careful (for all his frankness) not to drop the
names of the people involved, but the story itself was so
grotesque, so hard to credit as happening anywhere, at any
time, let alone among people who were not thugs, not the
rough animals you catch a glimpse of when something, a
murder, disturbs the mud hidden under society. It went
back, or Rigden chose to start it then, to a day in June,
immediately after Hudson's book was published. He had
been summoned to London that day by a man he called Green,
after telling Gurney that Green was not his real name. He

described this man with a venom which seemed to give him satisfaction.

'. . . a big slack-bodied man, with a large face and a stomach falling to his knees. Looks older than he is. I should think he's between forty and forty-five. He's high up in his Ministry, and he has a smooth supercilious arrogance he must have practised on his way up; he's like me, a winner of scholarships, except that he started a little better off; his father was a postman. I never saw him without remembering a grocer in Deptford who used to make me cringe every time I had to go an errand for my mother: we were bad customers, and there was always the chance that he would turn me away, but I think he enjoyed my agonies — he only refused me once . . . Green is like him — capable, aggressive, intolerably self-satisfied . . .'

Has he, Gurney wondered, the least idea that he's describing the impression he has made on me ever since I knew him?

'He told me he had a scheme ready for dealing with Hudson, and that it involved making use of Hetty. I asked him what the devil, and he said that with ordinary luck — the actual words he used — it would end in Hudson seducing her. And my share in it was to arrange, after it happened, for all possible publicity.'

He stopped. As drily as he could, Gurney asked, 'What did you say?'

'Everything,' Rigden said violently, 'every damned thing. I said she was eighteen, a young eighteen, I said that her father had been killed in Spain, she was so to speak in trust to the Party, to his friends in the Party — and so on and so on . . . Green was as cool as you like — he might have been a general sending his division into an attack. He said: "I fail to see what her father has to do with it. The girl has to lose her virginity some time, and if what you say about her is true she's probably too naive to be used in any better way. Besides, you couldn't catch Hudson with anything not perfectly fresh." He sniggered a little at himself and said, "And you'll find plenty of people to help you to spread the story. People like Dr. George Craddock, who are *with us in mind*, God bless their holy simplicity, will rush forward to do their bit."'

'He knew his Craddock,' Gurney murmured.

'Yes . . . I put it to him that Hudson had done his worst now, there was little more he could do, he knew nothing that wasn't known to every ordinary member of the Party. Green didn't deny this. He has as much contempt for party members as he has for sympathisers and fellow-travellers. But — you could see it — Hudson had got under his skin, and he kept on saying that the fact that Hudson was an important writer made his defection as serious as his name had been useful in dressing the window: he *must* be discredited . . . What he really wanted was to punish Hudson. At one point he rolled his eyes up so that all you saw was the whites, and said: I should like to flog him . . .'

Am I going to have to tell Vančura that I'm an ass? Gurney thought. 'This man you call Green — what sort of a communist is he? Isn't he a member of the Party?'

Rigden's eyelids flickered, and he said rapidly,

'No. No more than I was. The fact is there's what is called an organising committee, it can overrule the official leaders, and these don't know the men on the committee. No, that's not quite it — one of them would know Green as a telephone number or as a man called Smith or Robert, and would take any instructions from him without arguing. It's quite simple.'

Gurney thought in the same half-derisive half-sceptical instant of Vančura and the White Queen. It should have been the Red Queen, he thought mockingly. 'Almost too simple. Is Green the head of this grotesque committee?'

'Oh, no,' Rigden said.

'Who is?'

Moving his hands in an evasive gesture, Rigden said,

'He was much more friendly than he usually was. Usually he told you what he wanted with the same sort of rudeness as an officer I knew in the war, an ex-sergeant, used when he talked to his batman. But this time he was almost amiable. He explained to me that they were going to put it out that Hudson hadn't resigned from the Party, but had been kicked out because of his sexual immorality: that was why they needed a scandal, of a sort that would make headlines. He said, "Hudson, you know, will make a dangerous enemy. If we can discredit him at once, so much the better." Then he gave me what I can only think of as an ecclesiastical smile and said, "And in this case, my dear Rigden, you need feel no pity. I could give you instances of men who had been devoted self-sacrificing communists for years, and then something happened and they began criticising the Party — and had to be discredited by some — any — means. There was a French writer, I forget his name, who volunteered in 1939, when the Party was against the war; they accused him of every sort of filthy treachery, not a word of it true: he was killed, but they still do it." He sniggered again. "Stinkweed for remembrance . . . That's a mild instance. There are plenty of others, not so mild . . . However superbly a man may have behaved in the past, however convinced one may be of his personal honesty, if he disagrees with the Party on an essential point, at any moment, he becomes a liability and must be got rid of or have his sting drawn. Not that friend Hudson falls into this honourable class. You don't care what happens to this rich aristocrat — who is, after all, really a rat — do you?" I said: No, what I cared about was ourselves, our decency. I said something about dirty weapons, and he laughed, his stomach shaking in the creases of his trousers. "Rot. Boy Scout rot. He that is not with me is against me. You and I, my boy, both learned that in scripture lesson." I think I said then that some things are morally too degrading to be done for any cause. He looked at me with the same smile, almost as though he were sorry for me, and said, "I don't want to pry, but my experience has been that one feels moral distaste as a cover for some shabbier emotion. Perhaps you're personally interested in this girl? Or Hudson has been useful to you, or . . ." I lost my temper and said, "You don't begin to understand what I'm saying."'

He stopped. Gurney noticed the twitching muscle under his left eye. Not so steady as he sounds, he thought coldly. 'Well?'

'Oh, all he said was, "Perhaps I understand you better than you understand yourself", but he said it so mildly that at the time it made no impression on me. And another thing—' Rigden hesitated, frowning, and dropped his voice to a hurried gabble, not easy to catch — 'the real head of the organising committee, a man superior to Green — superior in every way — was abroad. I felt certain — *I knew* — that he would put his foot down on the whole thing as easily as squashing a cockroach. I asked Green to make no plans until this man got back. I even offered——'

Gurney interrupted him. 'Who is this man?'

As he expected, Rigden said, 'I can't tell you either his name or anything about him.' He went on abruptly, 'I was sickened by Green; I told him that if he started any filthy talk about Hudson I would write something denying it, and that I wouldn't have Hetty used in any way, any way at all. He surprised me by taking this well. There was no question, he said, of doing anything without proper authority. That satisfied me — and I came away thanking God I'd been called in.'

Do I believe a word of this? Gurney asked himself

violently. The thought was a sop thrown to his dislike of the grotesquely irrational. With his whole mind he wanted to disbelieve Rigden. And he had not the least doubt that Rigden was telling the truth. He thought swiftly: Telling me part of the truth.

'Why did you believe him?' he asked.

Rigden said savagely, 'Why shouldn't I have believed him? He had to do as he was told like the rest of us — and the other man was as much his boss as mine . . . I supposed . . .'

'Well?'

Rigden sat for a moment with twitching face. He passed his hands down it. 'In about three weeks he sent for me again. I'd written to him, repeating what I felt about the way our chaps were handling Hudson's book by attacking him personally, not his arguments. I expected he was going to tear a strip off me. Not a bit of it. He was polite, and I tried to get across to him that all, absolutely all, I felt was that we should behave openly and decently with an open enemy, meet him on his level — the level of intellectual argument. I told him I disliked the feeling I got from him that he really preferred a dirty weapon. He smiled in a way that could have meant anything and said, "My dear fellow, a good communist has no personal feelings about an opponent. Or if he has — if he finds himself in the awkward position of distrusting his closest friend, or his wife — he isn't facing a problem. The problem has been solved for him; he has only to act in good faith with the Party. You can leave all that conflict-of-loyalties drip to the novelists." He put his fat white grocer's hand on my knee and said, "There are two unmistakable signs of *unconscious bad faith*. One is to hesitate about obeying an instruction. The second is the feeling that to carry out an unpleasant instruction degrades you. You see, I'm using your language. My dear boy, you must be careful, you're on a slope." He might have been warning me that my fly was undone; he was as friendly and casual.'

'Where did you meet?' Gurney asked. 'In his office?' He thought that the answer might give him some idea in which Ministry this sublime grocer worked.

'No. Neither his office nor his home. We met at a little newspaper and tobacco shop in Battersea.' With the eagerness to run off down a side-street he had shown before, he said, 'The chap who runs it has been a commando. Before that he was a barrow-boy, and before that in an institution. He's a brute, but an innocent brute; in the whole of his eighteen odd years before the war no one managed to give him any needs beyond food, drink, a woman; it must have been sheer luck that he wasn't a criminal, or wasn't caught. He enjoyed the war: when that outlet suddenly closed he must have felt as though he'd run head on into a wall: he was in a state of dazed anger when someone got hold of him and made a party member of him; he could as easily have been turned into a fascist, or a commonplace killer . . . If there are many others of his kind in the Party, our honest decent Pollitt is in for some surprises when he calls his troops out — if ever he does . . . But you can't hate the fellow. And he has a young boy he picked up to help in the shop and deliver papers who looks on him as a splendid heroic figure — loves him, in fact. I've seen him watching Bell, that's the chap's name, with the adoring eyes of a dog. A skinny dog, unfriendly with other people——'

That's enough, thought Gurney. He asked drily, 'Was that all Green said to you?'

Brought up with a jerk, Rigden caught his breath. 'No, it wasn't . . . He told me — before I'd asked — that he had given up any idea of using Hotty. He would try, he said, to think of a way of discrediting Hudson, and — this came out with his normal roughness — he would still need my help . . . That didn't worry me, I was absolutely confident

that the other man when he came home would put a stop
to the whole mean business of dropping filth on Hudson.
I felt quite safe.'

A grin of misery and self-contempt touched his mouth.

Gurney waited, and at last said, 'And then?'

'That was the evening she went to his flat,' Rigden said.
His voice rose — and thickened, as though his tongue had
swollen. 'And my God, I still don't know what they did.
I don't know how they got her there, I don't know . . .
All I know is that she came to Green and told him what had
happened. She agreed with him — or so he says — that
she would stand up in court and say that Hudson had raped
her. And then she disappeared.'

Gurney felt no impulse to ask him why he had trusted a
man for whom he felt so little liking. With a flicker of sympathy, he thought: The poor silly devil must have asked
himself that question too many times.

'About as ugly a shock as you'll get,' he said.

Rigden looked at him. 'Yes. No, that wasn't the final
score.' His mouth widened in the same tortured grin.
'D'you want to hear it?'

Gurney's brief sympathy for him became that sort of
pity which is neither kindness nor compassion, but only a
nervous shrinking from the sight of another person's
humiliation. He made an effort to speak kindly. 'If you
like.'

Rigden said,

'You'll think I'm a fool — an obtuse fool . . . My friend
was due at Waterloo the very next night. I went there to
meet him — to tell him before anyone else could . . .' He
was beginning to lose self-control: he had slipped from
'boss' to 'friend' without noticing it . . . 'I'd gone to the
trouble of taking a room in a hotel for the night — not
just to have somewhere to talk to him at once, but to let
him get over the worst of his — his anger, with only me

there to see it.' He stopped, and looked at Gurney with
an expression of hatred. Gurney thought: It isn't me he
hates, nor the other; it's himself . . . Rigden made a brief
rough sound that might have been a laugh, and said, 'I
could have saved my money. He was angry, yes, but not
my God in the way I'd dreaded . . . My anger and wretched-
ness amused him — annoyed him a little, too — the way
you can be annoyed by an hysterical child. He told me to
pull myself together; if he'd been at home he certainly
wouldn't have allowed it, the girl was much too young —
but after all, the incident was of no very profound importance, even to her. The only important thing was to find
her quickly and talk to her . . . "Put her right with herself,"
he said, "praise her a little, make her see that she has
nothing to be ashamed of. On the contrary."' He laughed
again, with the same sound. 'Clever, eh? . . . I made rather
a fool of myself — and he laughed at me, kindly, at my
naïveté and lack of moral backbone. "Don't think I'm not
sorry about it," he said, "I'm extremely sorry, but . . . ask
yourself how one young woman's misadventure measures
up to the issues involved". . . In fact, he took enormous
trouble with me. He was gentle, affectionate, reasonable —
as always. After all, he's an important man, infinitely
more important and intelligent than that bastard Green,
or than I am — and he sat up with me in that dreary bedroom half the night — at the end of a day's travelling —
talking to me, trying, he said, to make me come to my
senses quickly. And I . . .'

He was shaking — his hands. He looked at them for a
moment, frowning. With deliberate surgical brutality,
Gurney said,

'He was putting you right with yourself, eh?'

'My God,' Rigden said. 'Yes — wait a minute.'

Gurney turned his head, to avoid seeing his distorted face.
He felt no impulse to spare the young man any of his

humiliation. If it softened him into giving himself away, so much the better. A very little more, Gurney thought coldly, and he may reach the point of giving away other people. Only may . . . With a cruel pleasure, his mind felt round the silhouette of a 'gentle reasonable affectionate' man. Who was he? What was he? . . . For some reason — to anyone who has had any dealings with them, not in the least far-fetched — he had the strongest possible impression that the fellow was a naturalised Central European, probably a Jew — a professor of economics in London, or employed in a financial house. He knew two of the breed in London and one in Oxford: they are what our shop-keeping instinct calls *intellectual assets*, brilliantly clever, unashamedly vain and self-confident, machines for grinding to a fine arid dust any wheat fed to them. Nothing more likely than that Rigden's friend was one of these valuable *assets*. The astonishing thing, he thought, is that he should have given himself so much trouble for our energetic young thruster. Why? Out of real affection? Out of pity for a bewildered dupe? Out of mere pleasure in exercising a subtle rapacious mind, like a groom showing off a thoroughbred — a very natural vanity?

Rigden had recovered his self-control. He even brought a touch of derision to his account of what his brilliant friend had said during the hours in a hotel bedroom, with heavy curtains drawn, an electric bar glowing in the empty fireplace, the glass doors of the wardrobe giving back his reflection as he walked about in front of it, stopped to put a hand on the young man's shoulder or mark a point by smiling finely . . . He gave Rigden a run round the theme of choice . . . When you have chosen to serve communism — really serve it, in the only way you can be effective, by loyalty to the one existing communist nation, the one single road to an united world and the end of history — your choice cuts out all smaller things, such as worrying about a girl's virginity, or a family, or weakly polite liberal gestures, or purely formal notions of truth or justice, or what have you. As a simple member of the Party or a sympathiser you can, if you want to poultice yourself, believe that purges, deportations, slavery, are straws along the road to an earthly heaven. As a sane man, a cynic or stoic of the cause, you empty innocence and truth of their meaning: the innocents it is necessary to kill are not innocent, they are expendable; lies are not lies, but expressions of will, simple statements of what has been planned and will therefore happen. Machiavellian? Not in the least. Machiavelli would not be tolerated in any communist state. He wrote to please himself; the moment in which it became necessary to stuff his words back down his throat would kill him . . .

'Tell me something,' Gurney said. 'Was there a time — there must have been — when being talked to like that excited you? You felt you were above the mob. Too clever to be fooled by blah-blah.'

Rigden did not smile. 'Yes.'

'All right, I'm not jeering at you. Go on . . . Your man must have enjoyed himself . . .'

'He laughed at me but he was serious enough,' Rigden said. 'He told me, "You've chosen obedience, and the privilege of knowing what's going to happen next. A communist gambles with his own life and other people's, but he's gambling on a certainty. Like any saint . . . It's the road *after* Damascus that is hard, too bloodily hard to leave one any pity to spare for the obscure people it kills off, or for friends who make mistakes. Let alone for the worthless. Hudson, for all his intelligence, has the mind of a tart: he chose — and then hadn't the seriousness or the moral guts to stick it. A pity. Our communist writers in this country are a scruffy lot . . ."'

He yawned, abruptly and uncontrollably. 'I'm sorry,' he muttered.

'When you went to Waterloo station to meet this fellow,' Gurney said — he was careful not to say: your friend — 'had you decided to cut loose?'

'No.'

'When did you make up your mind?'

'I don't know,' Rigden said wearily. 'I don't think there was any one moment . . . unless . . . He had made me feel small and cheap, he knew it, and he let himself go — as he could with me.' He paused, and with an indescribable intonation of grief said again, 'As he could with me . . . Talking to me was like talking to himself: he knew that I — respected him. He said, "You've got this business" — he meant Hetty — "out of all proportion. Think of yourself as belonging to an Order, a great secular Order which sooner or later is going to be running the world, the whole fermenting mass of human beings as little able to run their own lives as children or savages. In the end we shall be doing everything for them, they'll eat what we give them, kill each other only when we let them; they'll have no responsibility, we shan't ask them to do anything except work, breed, play. *We* — a comparatively few men carrying the unspeakable burden of thinking for all the others, acting as their *Lord is my shepherd, I shall not want*, and the rest of it . . ." '

'But he's mad,' Gurney exclaimed, 'mad as your hat.'

'No,' Rigden said, with sudden energy, 'no. Or if he is, it's a catching madness.' He pressed a hand over his eyes, as if he knew that he was twitching. 'I felt — trapped. The thought of any man having all of us completely at his mercy, even——'

He stopped, swallowing the name at the end of his tongue.

Gurney thought: Man at the mercy of man: far more terrifying than being at the mercy of God, as Hiroshima is worse than an earthquake. Or as torture, a death coldly carried out, is worse than the plague.

'Was that the end of it?' he asked.

'No . . . It was getting late. That is, early morning. I pulled the curtains back to let in the daylight. The room looked out over a station platform, a train was just in, and there were people — men, a woman carrying a child, another child running. I thought: Expendable, every living soul of them, and I said, I was shouting, "No one can make such monstrous claims."'

The other man had looked at him with a friendly smile. 'If you knew that by sacrificing Hetty you were ensuring the happiness of a million children not yet born, wouldn't you do it?'

'You can't know any such thing,' Rigden had shouted.

'But if you did know it,' his friend persisted, 'wouldn't you — even against your heart, surely you would hand her over?'

'No!'

His friend laughed. 'I didn't know you were a sentimentalist.'

'I'd sooner be sentimental than turn pimp — which is what Green did,' Rigden said. 'Oh, from the highest motives — but he did it. And you say it's all right. You talk about happiness and the necessities of history, and it comes down to the necessity of arranging for a child to be raped.' He heard himself shouting, and stopped.

His friend said quietly,

'So you're going to rat.'

His quietness brought the young man up with a jerk, and he had made an immense effort to seem calm and rational. He tried to say sensibly that he had always found it a little difficult to swallow that the way to universal happiness lies through the misery and ghastly indignity of purges and death camps and the rest. His friend heard him out to a stuttering end, and said,

'So you might have ratted any time before this?'

Shocked, his self-control gone, he said, '*No!*'

With the same gentleness, the other said, 'What I don't understand is why you waited for such a trivial incident before admitting your treachery — admitting it to yourself and me.'

Stung into anger by the injustice of this, Rigden said, 'What do the weak humble people we are supposed to be saving get out of it if we think of their suffering as trivial? What do we leave them?'

'Their innocence.'

'*Hetty?*'

'Hetty kept hers,' his friend said calmly. 'She was ordered to throw it away, which means that she remains innocent. The guilt, if you want to call it that, is Green's. It might have been mine — and would be yours if you hadn't lost your nerve . . .'

Gurney thought: This may have been the moment when he knew, knew for certain, that he had had enough: the thing he believed in had become, not loathsome — a machine for turning out unhappiness, lies, death, a superb face and behind it an indecent void — but absurd. Absurd *because* of the frightful ludicrous disparity between the great cause, the great secular Order, and poor Hetty . . . Involuntarily, he said,

'Clever. Clever and inhuman.'

Rigden looked at him with a young grief. 'No. No, I can't make you see him. He isn't inhuman. He's very human and charming. More than charming. A charmer . . . Even then he didn't give me up. He reminded me, affectionately, of things we'd done together — and he'd done for me. He implored me to not break on such small personal grounds. My God, you don't know what I felt, hearing him, him of all people in the world, say: I implore you, Nevil . . . I felt sick with shame. I tried to tell him that I hadn't joined to do things like driving a young girl to who knows what. He said gently, "Why did you join? To ask questions? To pick and choose what you'd do? To have an easy mind?" He said, "Go away and think about it before you do anything." . . . You can think what you like of me — but at that moment I wished to God I'd held my tongue. I wished — God knows what I wished.'

He was shaking again, violently. With a slight feeling of shame, because he was using Rigden's grief to trick him into giving himself away, he asked,

'Did you tell Evelyn about it?'

Rigden was silent for a moment. With a touch of irony he said,

'No, how could I? She didn't know I was involved. She knew nothing.'

After all, he may not be lying, Gurney thought. 'You went home. Did you think about it?'

'No.'

'Why not?'

A long silence. Then Rigden said, 'It's no use trying to tell you. You wouldn't understand it.'

There was no insolence in his voice, no decent reason for Gurney's sudden wish to hurt him. It sprang from an obscure jealousy. He'll get over this easily enough, he thought coldly. Why be sorry for the young? They have time . . .

'Were you afraid that if it came out you would lose the Readership?'

'You have the right to say that,' Rigden said steadily.

'No,' Gurney said, 'I haven't . . . When *did* you make up your mind?'

Rigden frowned and twitched. 'I didn't. I kept myself from thinking by trying to find Hetty . . . Any time I forced myself to think what it would be like to break — as he said, to rat — I felt that it would be easier to kill myself.'

Gurney looked at him with a gleam of malice. 'No, that's too much for me,' he said, 'I don't understand you.'

'How could you?' Rigden said with a stupefying bitterness.
'You were never a skinny yellow-faced Nev Rigden, working feverishly for a scholarship, terrified of missing the next
step up; you didn't turn up in Oxford with this — this
servility — in your spine — still afraid, angry with yourself
for being afraid, and as meanly bitter as any other freed
slave when you remembered certain things I shouldn't
dream of talking to you about . . .' He smiled with the
same bitterness and self-contempt. 'Let me tell you —
communism is a great many powerful things, not one.
Among the rest, it's a religion for freed slaves. It stiffens
their spine and draws the poisons of humiliation and
timidity out of them. It offers — it seems to offer — a short
bloody cut to a world where the Nev Rigdens are born free
. . . You think I'm crazy, don't you? Maybe I am — I can
only tell you that to throw it away was more like suicide than
you think. I didn't even face it . . . There was one evening
in London when I thought I'd seen Hetty in the street; I
was in a bus, I jumped out and ran back. It was a girl
very like her, a tart . . . I walked about the whole of that
night, seeing Hetty herself everywhere — her poor young
clear face — seeing nothing else. Talk about a secular
Order, necessity, and the rest of it, shrivelled. What had
been done to her was evil, and done for evil reasons. I
knew it. I was through . . . I didn't make any decisions, I
didn't even decide to tell the Master — or anyone.'

'Why did you tell him?' Gurney asked.

Rigden's face became suddenly and pitiably young. 'Do
you know, I don't know . . . At the moment it was impossible to do anything else. It seemed a way — absolutely the only way — to get free.' He smiled weakly.
'Perhaps Evelyn is right — it was an act of individual folly.
And do you know, in the very moment of telling him I
remembered something my friend said. He said, ''Don't
make the mistake of thinking that the other side will

welcome you — you're not interesting enough; as a repentant sinner you're no catch. You'll be committing suicide — and for what? For what?'"

A sharp feeling of dismay seized Gurney — dismay, ignorance, something like a foreboding. To rid himself of it, he asked,

'Do you regret doing it?'

Rigden's laugh was unforced. 'I'm perfectly happy I did it,' he said.

'And Evelyn?'

After a moment, Rigden said smoothly,

'Well, it was a shock to her, a bad shock. It will take her time to get used to it.'

'Used to——?'

A flash of anger crossed Rigden's face. 'After all, she didn't know what I'd been doing for thirteen years.'

For no reason at all Gurney did not believe now that Evelyn had not known. Or rather there were too many reasons. A quick-witted dominating young woman and a husband passionately in love with her — it was, to say the least of it, unlikely that not once in all this time had she had a suspicion that he was up to something. And with Evelyn, suspicion would have been enough: she would have had the truth out of him if she had had to use a knife . . . His doubts about letting Vančura talk to Rigden vanished abruptly. This settles it, he thought.

He stood up. 'Some day I want to take you to see a man I know very well, a Czech — his name is Vančura. You may know the man I mean. He's a mathematician.'

Rigden said slowly, 'I've heard a little about him — yes.'

Of course, Gurney thought. As an exile, he'd be sure to get into the Red King's dream. 'He would like to talk to you.'

Rigden shivered suddenly.

'Goose walking over my grave,' he said with a young smile. 'All right. Yes, certainly. I'll see anyone you like.'

Chapter 23

WHEN he was alone, Rigden thought uneasily: He
didn't believe me about Evelyn.

To be forced to go on telling lies exasperated him:
he saw no end to it, no end to the insecurity, the sense of
belonging to an inferior class, which lying involves. Yet . . .
The very least I can do, he thought savagely, is to see to it
that neither she nor any other person pays in any way for
my *individual folly*.

In the letters he had written to her in Spain during the
summer, he had said nothing about his search for Hetty.
And nothing about the debate going on, with the dull pain
of an ulcer, behind it. He could see now that this had been
needlessly cruel. I should have given her some sort of
warning, he thought with remorse, not let her come back
utterly and gaily unprepared for what she couldn't help
seeing as treachery. Treachery to her, too . . .

She came home two nights before he expected her. He
had gone to bed: when she rang the bell he was asleep, and
he got up to open the door without giving himself time to
wonder who could want him at this hour. Before falling
asleep he had been tormenting himself with the thought
of telling her, almost wishing she would stay away until
he had done something irrevocable. He dreaded the pain
he was going to give her, and her anger . . . The shock of
surprise and joy swept everything else from his mind.

She pushed her coat out of the way to press her body
against his in its thin covering. She was laughing a little, as
as though her return in this way were a triumph she had
prepared for herself.

Reluctantly he asked, 'Do you want anything to eat?'

She shook her head. 'No, no, not now.' She ran ahead of him into the bedroom, and burst out laughing. 'Oh, Nevil, the window. How can you?'

He never remembered to open it when he slept alone. The window in the bedroom had always been shut when he was a child, and secretly he preferred sleeping with it shut. He opened it, and turned back to her. She threw herself at him like a child, but with a fierce impatience, as if she had been thinking about it as she came. He had the sense that he was plunging into the hot clear Spanish sunlight; the whole of her body was brown, from her wide smooth shoulders to her narrow feet and long narrow legs.

Later he asked her again, 'Aren't you hungry?'

'Ravenous.'

There was very little to eat in the place: he put cheese, part of a loaf, a bottle of wine, on a tray and carried it in to her in bed. She ate with greedy pleasure; he watched her, and drank two glasses of the claret, and suddenly it seemed perfectly easy to tell her.

The change in her as he talked should have silenced him sooner than it did. Her eyes took on the fixed stare he knew well, too well — as though the thought behind them had hardened into a fanatical obstinacy. All at once, pushing the tray aside, she got up and looked round her for something to put over her naked body. There was only his shabby dressing-gown. She pulled it on and said quietly,

'No, I don't believe you.'

'You must believe me,' he said. He added foolhardily, 'It needn't make any difference to us, except that I——'

She did not let him finish. 'Oh, don't be damned silly It makes all the difference in the world, to me as well as you. How d'you think I can bear to live with a dull beast of a Tory?'

In spite of the painful constriction in his chest, this made

166

him laugh. 'I didn't think you were so simple,' he said. 'I haven't gone over to the other side — merely because I don't believe any longer that mercy and kindness are of no importance when they get in the way of tactics. Don't be absurd, my darling.'

He reflected afterwards that if he hadn't laughed she could have gone on a little longer comforting herself with the idea that he could be talked out of it. She was preparing to be contemptuous, to argue: his laughter threw her out, with an almost brutal want of tact. She stared at him for a minute, then said curtly,

'You wouldn't have made this fool of yourself if I'd been here all summer.'

'You think not?'

'I know.'

With something between grief and irony he thought: You know one or two things about me: you know that when I first met you you dominated me by your headstrong will and fearlessness, and your contempt for people who don't think as you do. My self-confidence — the hollow self-confidence of the clever *boursier* — was no match for your innate arrogance — you don't even know you're arrogant. But you don't know, you don't realise — and by God until this summer I didn't realise it myself — that living with you has given me, not just the impulse to grow out of you, but an absolutely irresistible need to do it . . . He felt a sudden rush of pity for her, only because she didn't know about this involuntary — what was it? evasion? disloyalty?

'My love, my only love, don't be so angry with me,' he said gently. 'I can make you see how it happened. And that it doesn't matter to us. Nothing matters.'

She was silent, frowning. At last she asked almost calmly, 'What are you going to do?'

He wasn't certain that he knew what she meant. 'Do? What about?'

With savage contempt, she said, 'Are you going to make a good thing of your change of heart — like Hudson?'

Her bitterness stupefied him. 'I don't propose to write a book about it,' he said. 'Is that what you mean? But——'

She cut him roughly short. 'That's not all I mean. Are you going to slip out of things quietly, without telling anyone that you were once inside — and all that?'

Again he did not see clearly what she was getting at. 'That might not be possible . . .'

'Listen to me, Nevil,' she said. 'If you start telling people about yourself——' she hesitated, and went on with sudden energy. 'Don't tell anyone. So long as you hold your tongue, no one will give you away — it needn't come out at all. It need never come out that you had anything to do with them.'

He thought sharply: And spend the rest of my life covering up, never safe from the threat of being denounced if they wanted to punish me. Or make use of me . . . He felt a flash of anger. Had she seen that danger? She must have; she was not a fool.

He said nothing.

She laid her hand on him for a moment. 'Is it too late? Have you been telling a lot of people already?'

'Too late for what?' he asked drily.

'To come to your senses, and go on as you were — working——'

'Doing what I was told.'

'Why not?' she cried. 'Why the devil not? What's wrong with obeying orders? There must be orders and an organisation and discipline. You never objected to it before.'

Groping in himself, he said slowly, 'They were right about me. Even that bastard Green was right. I took good care never to think about it too clearly —' like avoiding a nail sticking out of the wall — 'I might never have objected — or not yet — but for the use made of Hetty.'

She looked at him with a clear fury. 'Why do you mind so much about this girl?' she asked fiercely. 'Are you in love with her?'

'Don't be foolish.' He hesitated, trying to find words to make her see Hetty's face as he saw it, the face of a child drowning out of reach.

'Why is one not very intelligent girl so important?' she said in a hard voice. 'When did you turn feeble-minded and squeamish, like the silly fellow who said he wouldn't make everyone in the world happy if it meant first killing one child? I would kill a million of them to make the rest safe and happy!'

He laughed shortly. 'Oh, no, you wouldn't. And I don't for a moment believe — if you had been asked about it — that you would have sacrificed Hetty——'

'I would!'

' — or anyone, anyone at all. Think——' He was seized by an impatience and an exasperated pity for her and her disappointment that drove him nearly mad. 'I can't go on arguing now. Tomorrow — I'll talk to you about it to-morrow. But I'm through. Get that into your head. Finished. Through. And now for God's sake let's go to sleep.'

He lay down on the bed. For a moment she stood watching him, with the dressing-gown held round her. Suddenly she threw it off and came to him, slipping her hands inside the jacket of his pyjamas.

'Nevil,' she said very gently, 'Nevil my darling. You do still love me?'

His need of her became unbearable, and drew them both under. Half asleep, she said drowsily, 'Don't tell anyone. Promise.' He promised — and less than a week later, without warning her that he might break his promise, without knowing when he was going to do it, he told the Master, and Gurney . . .

And thank heaven I did, he thought. A few minutes ago, when Gurney had asked him if he regretted it, he had felt, for the first time, an extraordinary exultance and lightness of heart. He thought: I regret nothing. I've escaped. I know the worst that can happen to me: I've lost all chance of the Readership, I may even lose my job — but I'm free. What shall it profit a man . . . ?

In his heart of hearts he did not for a moment believe that he would lose his fellowship, nor that the future did not hold compensations for the Readership he had lost. Some exciting success or other would turn up. Nothing else was thinkable.

Chapter 24

GURNEY watched Vančura's hands as he talked to Rigden — butcher's hands and wrists, covered with long fine black hairs. He had folded them together on his knees. Now they were gripping the edge of the table between him and Rigden, as though he suspected Rigden of trying to cheat him. Yet the young man had let himself be taken between this pair of butcher's hands and questioned, sharply and brutally, without a sign that he resented the inquisition or had anything he meant to hide.

'Why,' Vančura asked him, 'did you leave the Party five minutes after you had joined it? Because you were advised you could do better work outside. Who advised you?'

'Friends,' Rigden said.

'Yes, yes, but who were they? What are their names?'

Rigden smiled very slightly. 'You don't expect me to answer that,' he said.

'They were the men you talked to me about,' Gurney said. 'The fellow you called Green, and the other.'

'I don't call Green a friend,' Rigden said.

Vančura said impatiently, 'I know, I know — they belong, your advisers, friends, call them what the devil you like, to the communist world, but they're not members of the local Party, they work with the Soviet Intelligence or——'

Rigden cut him short. 'I had nothing to do with the Soviet or any Intelligence,' he said calmly.

Vančura relaxed his grip on the table. 'Why lie about it? It's stupid.'

Is he lying? Gurney asked himself coolly . . . If he were,

then he was so monstrously skilful a liar that everything he had so far told them would have to be discounted. And that was surely lunacy? Why should he have ruined himself with the Master, jeopardised his whole career, unless he were driven to it by what he would probably *not* call his conscience? It was the only sane conclusion. But what, in the world Rigden had been living in, was sane, and what was a habit of lying so corrosive, so twisted round the very roots of thought and feeling that it was ineradicable, incurable?

Raising his eyebrows, Vančura said, 'Then what the devil did you do, to justify your existence as a communist?'

'A good deal of writing,' Rigden said. 'Pamphlets — articles about conditions in England — and so forth.'

Vančura stared. 'Wonderful,' he said with bland sarcasm. 'And what became of these exercises?'

Unmoved, Rigden said, 'They were sent to Russia. I suppose they were published there — in Russian or English. I never saw any of them in print.'

'Do you expect us to believe this nonsense?' Vančura smiled.

Rigden did not answer at once. Then he said quietly, 'You don't have to believe me. But if you don't — what is the use of my talking to you? You're wasting your time.' With an involuntary bitterness he added, 'Time? I could have finished a couple of books in the time I spent working on the things.'

Vančura's eyes, hard and fixed as stones, gave nothing away, neither derision nor irony. 'You must be telling the truth,' he said under his breath. 'No one would invent such a stupid bloody lie.'

'Thank you,' Rigden said.

But it would make a cow laugh. They were amusing themselves. Or — what is this man Green? A pederast?'

Rigden did not answer.

'A civil servant,' Gurney said.

Rigden looked at him. 'Did I tell you that?'

'You did.'

'And the other?' Vančura asked. 'What is he? A comedian?'

Rigden said, 'You know perfectly well, unless you're a complete fool, that there were a dozen more intelligent ways I could have got out than the one I chose——' A look, half surprise, half derision, crossed his face — he might for the first time have been wondering why he had chosen it — 'more intelligent and more profitable. If I had wanted to pull other people in with me I should have done it at the start, to cover myself . . . I don't think you're a fool, are you?'

He was speaking in his most irritatingly offensive voice. Yet what, for a moment, Gurney felt was not irritation: it was nearer compunction. He said gently,

'You're asking us to swallow a lot, you know.'

'The fact remains,' Rigden said, 'I was never asked to do anything except write.' He paused and said roughly, 'Never, that is, until Green wanted me to help him to discredit Hudson——'

Vančura interrupted him. 'And you were as offended as a . . .' he swallowed a word and said grimly, 'Oh, never mind — to hell with it, and you.'

'You're probably right,' Rigden said calmly.

'It was a piece of bad timing on their part,' Vančura said. 'You should have been led into committing yourself in some easier way first . . . There are all sorts of forms of treason — to a country, to another person, to oneself. They all taste sour — until you get so used to the taste that you don't notice it any longer. Or you get drunk on the *other* taste — the taste of power, real or spiritual, the pleasure of being in the know. The sort of pleasure a time bomb might feel if it could think.' He was speaking quietly, with half-closed eyes, like a man listening to himself. 'There was a man I knew in Prague, a career diplomat, an upright scrupulous man, who excused himself to me for what he had done to betray our country to Russia by telling me: My real country is the country of the poor, and Russia is its only friend and powerful ally . . . He's dead now — executed. His powerful friend turned against him . . .' He turned the glare of his narrowed eyes on Rigden. 'Tell me, you. What would you have done — suppose that at the end of the war England had swung round, as some of your people and some of mine hoped she would, to fight Russia — would you have said the same thing as he did? Made the same excuse?'

After a minute, Rigden said,

'I might.'

'So — potentially you were a traitor?'

'Perhaps——' he smiled, a stretch of the lips. 'Yes.'

Vančura dropped his broad head for the charge. 'Then what about your two friends, or whatever you choose to call them? Could they — if the next war happens to be a war against the friend and ally of the poor and all that — could they do serious damage?'

It struck Gurney at this moment that the pleasure he was feeling must be very like the pleasure his more distant ancestors got out of a cock-fight. Coldly annoyed with himself, he went on watching Rigden with no slackening of curiosity. The young man's features seemed to have lost some of their fineness under the strain he must be enduring: he looked blunted. He spoke as if he needed time to reflect.

'One of them could, I suppose.'

'Because of his position?' Vančura persisted.

'Yes.'

'Ah — he's in the government or a war industry?'

Rigden spread his hands, as though he were pushing someone aside. Getting him out of our sight, Gurney thought.

'I've no reason to think he would behave as badly as that,' he mumbled. 'He's not that sort.'

Vančura's voice rose and became cruelly jeering. 'He would be too scrupulous, too, as you say, decent . . . You are bloodily a fool. There have been three or four generations of idealists, willing to accept torture and ugly deaths for themselves — and others — to bring alive a society of brothers. These are all dead, all, all, all. The last of them was shot in the neck in a Spanish or Russian prison, or he died in an Arctic camp. Remain men like your friends, remain the self-deceivers, remain the naive. Which are you? Not that I care. The day you told yourself bravely: I accept the need for cruelty and judicial murders, that day you crossed the line separating you from decency. You're damned lucky that what jerked you back was a single act of — of what shall I say? — I mustn't exaggerate — of indifference to suffering. To a child's shame and unhappiness. Luckier than you deserve. For some of the things done there is no atoning. None, none. Never. Never in any future. But you — you want to be praised and forgiven because you were lucky. You've been playing in a farce — God knows what sort of farce — I don't. And now you walk out, smiling. *Me innocent, me good boy now.* A-ah, you sicken me.'

Rigden had lost his calm. 'As you like,' he said in a distorted voice. 'But I'm not turning informer.'

Vančura laughed. 'No, it would be too uncomfortable for you — and you have the right to be comfortable. That's what you think, isn't it?'

The impulse to interfere, to stop Vančura from baiting Rigden any longer, was stronger in Gurney than his curiosity. He leaned forward, smiling. 'Surely you know the English well enough by now to know that we never let ourselves think to the point of discomfort?'

Vančura looked at him from his dulled black eyes with something like longing — very strange.

'This is a fortunate island. You say these things . . . You don't know what you are and have.'

With a sudden noisy movement Rigden pushed his chair back, and stood up. Looking at Gurney without friendliness, he said,

'If you don't mind, I'll go now.'

He walked out without waiting for Gurney to answer, and without glancing at Vančura.

'You weren't gentle with him,' Gurney said.

'Listen to me,' Vančura said, 'he isn't broken yet. You must break him. You must break open his skull and read what is inside.'

His ugly face was alive with an almost affectionate cruelty. He looked imploringly at his friend, as if Gurney had held him back in the act of pouncing. Gurney thought: He's more innocent of cruelty than I am. I swear it. He has a decent political motive for wanting to turn our young gib-cat inside out and read the names he's keeping back . . . He himself had no such rational motive. He had just been watching, with positively indecent interest, an attempt at vivisection, and he was willing to see it go deeper, without caring very much what, when the patient was lying cut open, he might see. He thought: I should like to know whether a man who informs on his friends — oh, from the highest purest motives — does it more easily, with fewer qualms, than a man who is simply betraying his country to one he likes better. Probably not. Loyalty to your friends or your own blood must have older deeper roots, more agonising to tear out, than loyalty to a country . . . Nor could he feel with his heart that to betray your country is the worst of treacheries. It may be. If it lets into the city merciless men, men to whom freedom is a provocation, it may be. But between this vast gesture of betrayal, reasoned and conscious, and the first small act of treachery a child commits without thinking and without remorse, there is an infinity of worse deeds, dark movements of the heart, evasions of the mind, spiritual cruelties . . . No, he thought, I don't know. But one man who has no right to complain of being informed on is the communist, whose first copybook begins: Thou shalt denounce when required thine own father and mother.

How comfortable does Rigden feel at this moment? he wondered. His mind was torn between an impulse to spare the younger man any more anguish and a savage desire to make him come clean. Strangely, he had never been so near liking him.

Vančura was humming under his breath as he did when he was working out a problem. 'Are you,' Gurney asked him, 'one of the people who hope we shall fight Russia?'

'No.'

'Why not?'

'I like the Russians, as you like the French, for the same reason; they're intolerable, but they have so much *nature*. And even if I didn't — I can't hope for the death of the world.' He added in a soft voice, 'Death of my good little Bella.'

'Then what do you hope we shall do?'

'You? This country?' Vančura grinned. 'I take bloody care not to think about it. You are like a nice old lady who doesn't believe her banker when he tells her she has no more money. But why should I care? It's not my country.'

'No,' Gurney said with a fine smile, 'but you make use of it to live in.'

'Damn you and your prying probing tongue,' Vančura said. 'When I bolted here I thought you were a strong people. I only knew you during the war, remember. And I didn't know then how many kinds of courage there are. I thought you would lead Europe. Now I know that you can't even lead yourselves, you let the Americans do it — and Europe doesn't exist . . . Yet this is still the best people

in the world, the kindest, the gentlest, the most decent —
for all that a handful of you have caught the infection I
bolted from . . . All I hope for now is time. Time and a
miracle. I — *I* — Jan Vančura, reduced to hoping for a
miracle.' He looked at Gurney with amusement and rage
exploding behind his eyes. 'That's what I've come to.'

'It comes of living in England,' Gurney said.

'It comes of liking and being sorry for a country where
grown men quote nursery tales, and are mortally shocked
when a young woman gets herself . . .'

Gurney said, 'You're right, of course. It was the mildest
of atrocities. Nothing. But we're not — not yet — blasé
here.'

'No, no, it is you who are right,' Vančura said calmly.
'My mind is a corner of a vast graveyard — friends eaten
by quick-lime, friends forced to perpetual silence and the
self-mutilation of their minds. And the others, who turned
hangmen in fear or self-defence . . . If I talked about it I
should bore people. That's the last word about our age —
that the victims have become bores. Even you, my dear
Henry, would yawn if I insisted on dragging you into the
desert I live in when I am most at home.'

Chapter 25

D URING the rest of the month Gurney had too much
work to get through to bother with Vančura's itch
to get his hands into Nevil Rigden. He went no-
where, saw none but the drier-minded of his colleagues, and
heard nothing about the young man except a little spiteful
or shrewd gossip, echoes from Retta Spencer-Savage's
version of the scene with the Master — not always believed.
Without knowing it, she had suffered the fate of witty liars:
even friends had got into the habit of knocking off a heavy
discount of malice from her stories . . . The Master himself
had done what, in any difficult situation, he always did for as
long as possible: nothing.

Then, late one afternoon, he had a telephone call from
Retta Spencer-Savage herself. Her harsh deep voice,
breathless from the excitement she was enjoying, irritated
him, and he told her he was busy. She didn't let him finish
the sentence.

'No, no, don't try to put me off. I must see you. I'm
only just back from London . . . I've found Hetty Smith.'

'Thank God,' Gurney said. 'Have you told Paget?'

'No. That's why I want to see you at once. I can't tell
you now. Come round as soon as you can — and don't,
this is really necessary, tell anyone I've found her.'

'What——'

'My dear man,' she cut in, 'I'm not making a fuss. I'll
tell you the story when you come.'

She rang off. Puzzled and more than a little angry,
Gurney set off to walk to her house, across the Parks. It
was one of those days our intolerable climate throws off

now and again in early November: warm, gentle, with weak
sunlight striking across long dove-coloured dunes of cloud,
and the earth giving up stored tangy scents. Without
knowing that he was doing it, Gurney walked slowly. On
such a day, the thought of dying and losing the world
saddened him. Though sadness is not the right word for
what, after all, sharpened by regret, is the most acute
happiness.

Athene met him with a triumphant smile, very lightly
subdued by guilt, as though she were not certain of his
approval. She began at once, rolling her lips back from her
teeth.

'It was entirely an accident I found her. I might not
have gone up to London yesterday, and I didn't know when
I went that I should have to go all the way to Holland Park
to see a tiresome woman. I took a short cut through all
those unspeakably dreary streets, slices of stale cheese full
of maggots, off Addison Road, and saw her coming towards
me. I said, "Hetty Smith! It's you!" and gripped her
arm.'

She gripped Gurney's. Her savagely stretched mouth
was too near. He freed himself as amiably as he could.

'Why haven't you told Paget?' he asked her.

'Let me finish telling you,' she said. 'I want your
advice . . .'

For a time the girl refused to tell her anything, where
she was living, what she had been doing since July. At
last, realising that she was defeated by a will more ferocious
than her own, she took her captor into a house as seedy as
the others in the same street, and presented her to its
tenant, a middle-aged German Jewess, with a bold dissant
face, smothered in four or five cardigans and smelling
strongly of cats.

'Not a bad woman. The house is a boarding-house; it
seems she picked Hetty up in the street and brought her

there. I don't know how much she knows about the girl — the fact is, she was thankful to get a servant. The smell of cats in the place was suffocating, but she gave us coffee in her own room, and left us to talk. No, no, not a bad creature.'

'Is she — Hetty — all right?' Gurney asked.

'She seems to be, but . . .'

The moment they were alone in the dingy little room, the girl had dropped to her knees beside Athene's chair and implored her not to tell a soul where she was, or anything about her. She clutched both the older woman's hands. Athene was curiously disturbed by the sight of her stained roughened fingers, 'the fingers of a charwoman, all the nails broken or blunted.' Looking away from them, she said,

'My dear girl, I must tell your guardian I've seen you.'

'If you tell him, or anyone, and they come for me, I'll kill myself,' Hetty said in a quiet steady voice.

She was not hysterical: she listened with a polite face to all Athene had to say, and repeated, 'I shall kill myself if you send anyone here,' with the same quietness and with a touch of cold anger unlike the anger of a girl.

'Did you speak to her about Primrose?' Gurney asked.

'Yes, of course — and all she said, in that calm voice, was, "I don't want to think about her" . . . My dear Gurney, I was defeated, I——' She hesitated: a dark ugly flush spread through her sallow skin. 'The truth is I felt sorry for her. For all her self-possession she looked beaten. And if you had seen her hands . . . She was thin, too . . . Do you know, I felt convinced she would do it — kill herself, I mean. In the end I said, "Very well, I won't give you away to anyone." She said, "Thank you, thank you very much, you're a good woman."' She looked at Gurney with an extraordinary air of shamefaced fury. 'Now, of course, I feel I've made a ridiculous fool of myself,

promising her any such thing. What's more, I've broken
my promise already, by telling you — but I must know
what you think. I must have *some* advice. Surely I ought
to tell Paget? . . . What am I to do?'

Gurney looked at her. We all have our moment of grace,
he thought sharply, and this was yours — the moment
when you forgave Hetty her youth and promise of beauty
because she looked beaten . . . He had always imagined
Athene's heart pumping blood and malice in equal quanti-
ties. Once again, he told himself, you forgot to allow for
the moment of grace.

'Tell me what to do,' she repeated irritably.

He hesitated — and let an irrational impulse decide for
him. 'Keep your promise — at any rate for the present . . .
She won't come to any harm with this German woman?'

'No, no, I'm sure of that,' Athene said.

'If Primrose had been alive . . .'

'Yes, I thought that myself,' Athene murmured. She
looked away. 'That poor woman.'

There was a film of tears in her dark eyes. Gurney
scarcely believed it. Who had ever seen tears, except of self-
pity, in Athene's eyes?

'You took the name of the street and all that?' he said.
Athene nodded. 'Right. Let me have it. I shan't make
use of it unless——' He stopped. He had no coherent
reason to give her. In a confused way he was thinking of
Rigden — less thought than an obscure feeling that at some
time Rigden's peace of mind might depend on knowing
that the girl was alive and safe . . . At this moment he did
not give a curse for the young man's peace of mind. As
Vančura did, he felt that he was getting off very lightly. At
the same time he wanted unhappily to have something in
reserve — for the day when Rigden's luck failed. Though
why I should care what happens to him, God alone knows,
he thought ironically.

A Cup of Tea for Mr. Thorgill

Gilmore came in with the sherry: as he drank, he turned over the pages of a monthly review lying on the table, and came on a long article that Rigden must have written immediately after his interview with the Master. Bravado or conscience? he wondered unkindly. He had heard about it already. Glancing without trying to read it at the opening paragraph, he caught phrases.

'. . . historical necessity — most dangerous and powerful of modern heresies since the Cathars, and infinitely more fatal to happiness . . . our new Manichees believe they have the right to cut the living unanaesthetised flesh of men and women into shapes demanded by what they assume to be the end of history . . . if a single man is worth no more than a stone in the road, then a million stones can be mortared to dust to make the road, the final end of which will need to be magnificent to justify the misery of so many humble men and women now. The road is marked: To a peaceful happy future, and all the way along it you kill and kill and kill. At what point do you reach the last body lying face downwards, and step over it to . . .'

'I have an idea,' he said lightly, 'that the believers in historical necessity have returned to one of the oldest sources of sensual pleasure — the supreme thrill of human sacrifice. Spiritual pleasure, too, perhaps.' He pushed the review across the table. 'This article by Nevil Rigden . . . Have you seen it? Your side, my dear Athene, has a brave new recruit.'

Athene made a sourly contemptuous face. 'Thanks. I don't trust him an inch. And I'm horribly bored by all these ex-communists turning their hair-shirts inside out, lice and all, for our benefit.'

'You haven't forgiven him, have you?' Gurney said with a touch of malice.

'For what?'

'For impudently contradicting one of your stories.'

She gave him a look of morose annoyance, but before she

183

could punish him, the door opened and Gilmore showed in Herbert West.

Athene did not give him time to open his mouth.

'Oh, it's you,' she said. 'You're early . . . What do *you* think of our Saint Nevil?'

West looked at her with his charming timid smile, as if trying to propitiate her by his air of ineptitude. 'Saint Nevil?' His eye caught the review open on the table. 'Oh, I see. Well, I think he's shown great courage.'

She said disagreeably,

'Courage? All these years of dishonesty and lying — is that what you call courage?'

He sent Gurney an imploring glance. 'What do you say, my dear fellow?'

Gurney smiled and did not help him. By this time, he thought mockingly, he's feeling fairly certain that he'll get the Readership, but he won't run too many risks . . . West's face, as guilelessly doting as a sheep's — half sheep, half hang-dog — gave away his struggle to find some way of speaking kindly about Rigden without exasperating Athene's unsleeping vanity. But he's not even faintly embarrassed, Gurney realised suddenly. Certain of the purity of his heart, he can afford to be amiable, since it commits him to nothing, and may pay a dividend.

West's clouded eyes brightened. 'Of course, *you* saw through him, it's no surprise to you that he turns out to have been a communist. But the rest of us were taken in, he needn't have given himself away, and it must have needed a lot of courage to do it. I don't think I should have been so brave.'

'Oh, I saw through him,' Athene said, with a sharp smile. 'It says very little for the rest of you that you didn't. It was written all over him. And I must say I shall be surprised and alarmed if anyone takes him seriously now.' Moistening her lips, she went on, 'He was getting large sums of money for his treachery. Quite extraordinary. Then — I haven't found out why — these stopped, and our shrewd galloper decided to offer himself in another market.'

'Where on earth did you hear this story?' Gurney asked.

'Why, from George Craddock.'

'My dear girl,' he said with contempt, 'why do you believe him? You're not in the habit of swallowing what a fellow-traveller tells you.'

Athene's eyes dilated. In a bleakly innocent voice she said, 'But that's just it. He would know.'

Gurney laughed. 'He may even believe it himself. When they're ordered an unpleasant dose the Craddocks can always tell themselves comfortably that it's doing them good. Or they can admire their Pope for the audacity with which he tells his lies. They can be led by the nose and kicked behind; they can adorn platforms, and burn incense to keep down a bad smell. No end to their uses.'

'One can trust you to take a perverse line on anything,' Athene said. 'I suppose you do it to make sure you're noticed. You always disliked Rigden — until there was good reason for disliking him. Now you defend him. I wouldn't, if I were Rigden, thank you. Being praised by you is the equivalent of being damned by any sensible person.'

Gurney laughed again, a bellow of real amusement. 'I'll leave you and West to admire each other's good sense,' he said, and left.

Outside it was almost dark. As he walked home, a faint, very faint scent of jasmine came from one of the gardens on the edge of the Parks, and before he could do anything to guard himself, he saw Anne holding out to him on her palm a few flowers from the bush of white jasmine on the verandah of a house in Cyprus where they were staying. An extraordinary sense of peace invaded him. A certitude. Ecstasy. 'My love, my love,' he said under his breath.

Oh, fool, fool, fool, he mocked himself.

Chapter 26

RIGDEN had expected the Master's curt summons. None the less it caught him in the pit of his stomach and made him feel physically ill. Towey showed him into the library with a smiling air of indulgence that told him she had heard the gossip and believed none of it. The Master was at the far end of the long room, at his desk: he was writing and did not look up. His body stiffened to hold in its panic, Rigden walked the length of the room, and stood, waiting. To steady his thoughts, he looked along line after line of the books in their recessed shelves, reading the titles, and at the large Courbet over the chimney-piece and the several smaller paintings above the bookcases: directly in front of him on the wide desk were two finely-bound volumes whose titles he could not see, a couple of old silver candlesticks, a small ivory Buddha, and a pair of embossed snuffers. With crude bitterness he thought: What difference is there, what difference of spirit, between my sister's craving for a 'telly' and his collector's passion for these things? He visits Washington and Paris, taking with him in his bags one of his subtly eloquent speeches about the *defence of spiritual values*; they include his right to be invited to stay in the Embassy; they include the past so far as it created the graces he enjoys as he enjoys a good claret, and the future if it can be counted on to preserve them and them only. It's a confidence trick they play on us with their bankrupt *spiritual values*. All lies. A cheque drawn on an empty account. As gross and vulgar a fraud as — as he thinks I am . . . The sickness in the centre of his body was still there. It vanished, or he ceased to notice it, as soon as the Master dropped his pen and began speaking in the brusquely aloof voice he used when he had brought himself to the point of behaving roughly.

'I asked you here to tell you that you're not a candidate for the Readership — as you no doubt knew. I must tell you, too, that you're not likely to get any help in the future in your career.'

This was nothing worse than he had expected, and it was a relief to have it said. Looking at the Master, he said calmly,

'Yes, I understand.'

'Oh, you do, do you?' the Master said. 'Well, I daresay you understand as well that I'm still not able to make up my mind whether you're fit to go on teaching or not.'

His contemptuous voice stung Rigden. 'Why is my tutoring worth less than it was because I no longer believe——'

The Master struck the desk lightly with the side of his hand: he had singularly fine white hands. 'Oh, nonsense. What you happen to believe, as you call it, at the moment, isn't the point. The point is that you've been behaving in a way many people do behave — dishonestly and quite irresponsibly. I made a mistake in supposing that you were less — what shall I say? — less ill-bred.'

Rigden did not speak. Under his raw scalding resentment, he felt humiliated and afraid. It was an old fear — a child's furtive sense of failure. Something in him cringed, in the same moment as he forced himself to go on looking the other man in the face.

'That's all I wanted of you,' the Master said carelessly. 'You can go.' He got up and sauntered towards a window, turning his back on the young man.

Rigden walked out quickly. His face was flushed, but the shock and his self-contempt gave him an extraordinary feeling of lucidity. He thought drily: I've made a fool of myself, thrown away my future, everything I'm trained to do, everything I've managed to get myself by years of hard work — and for what? To live in the same dead corrupt world, on the same side, as Spencer-Savage and his spurious decencies and unforgiveable blind ignorance. I'm a fool, a clumsy fool. I've lost far more than my career — my certainties, my hope, the meaning of my life . . .

He stood still in the crowded street. The hatred he felt for the Master sent a ball of blood through his head behind his eyes. It cleared suddenly, and he thought: You were willing enough to accept kindness and help from him when you were deceiving him. Are you regretting your break? Or are you furious with disappointment because you haven't been met with a fatted calf? . . . Who urged you to break? No one. You did it to satisfy yourself, and if you're not satisfied, whose fault is it? You knew what to expect.

In the same vile-tasting moment, he knew that it had never for one instant entered his head that he would be treated as useless, unfit to teach, a discredited nobody.

The very bleakness and danger of his position drove him out of it. He thought coldly: Surely, if he had any serious intention of getting rid of me he wouldn't tell me in this casual way? If I keep out of his sight and keep quiet — no more scandal — he'll leave me alone. Almost certainly he'll leave me alone . . . Excitement and fear beat in him like a strong pulse. Oh, forget it, forget it, he thought violently.

Forcing himself to move, he walked on. As he passed Blackwell's windows a book lying in the front reminded him of one he needed, and he went in. He was searching the shelves at the back of the shop when he heard George Craddock's unctuous voice, immediately behind him. He turned.

Craddock smiled at him. 'Ah, Rigden. Taking a little time off from your, ah, labour of hate?'

He had three people with him. Rigden knew all of them.
Pebsworth, teacher of some obscure language — Tamil?
Sanskrit? — a charming old fellow in his seventies, a
liberal of the oldest and most uncompromising school, a
sea-green incorruptible with a sensitive horror of anything
he could see as 'a threat to the liberty of the mind', and a
religious belief that men are born good: almost an old
anarchist, but a sweet-natured generous cultivated anarchist
who boiled with rage when he heard of injustice and cruelty
— except in those moments when he contrived to tell
himself that injustice and cruelty are stepping-stones to a
liberty laid up in heaven and revealed to only a new race of
brutal saints. Or saintly brutes. The man smiling beside
him, his tall plump body characteristically half drawn back
behind Pebsworth's, was Bernard Nader — a scientist,
young, a Jew born in England of German parents; an
affably scheming creature with the forehead of a musician
and corrupt brown eyes. He took a frivolous interest in
advanced politics, and was one of Craddock's intimate
disciples, the amiable Judas who would lightheartedly
betray him if he became a liability. In the meantime he
rehearsed for it by making fun of him at other dinner-tables.

The third was an undergraduate — young Howard. He
stood a little away from the others, face half averted. He
had, as Rigden knew already, been taken up this term by
Craddock: he spent most of his spare time in Craddock's
house, eating his admirable food — it must be doing his
under-nourished body good — and playing his magnificent
gramophone. He was working, too, with a voracious energy
that reminded Rigden of his own first year in Oxford.

'Hullo, Craddock,' Rigden said, grinning. 'I hear you
don't approve of me.'

Craddock peered at him with his myopic little eyes
blinking behind colourless lashes. 'Well, my good Rigden,
I'm sure you didn't expect me to enjoy your latest, ah,

exercises — spiritual exercises is no doubt the correct term. It distresses me to notice how your judgment has been weakened — I won't be unkind enough to say anything about your literary style — by your, ah, conversion. You shouldn't, you know, have rushed into print about it. You really should wait until you feel less exalted, less, if I may say so, hysterical.'

'Yes, yes, a pity,' Pebsworth said in his gentle old voice. 'You should hold your tongue, my boy. Much the most decent thing to do.'

Nader smiled maliciously. 'But then he wouldn't be able to show us his pierced hands and sides!'

Ignoring Nader, Rigden said,

'Decent? You're not a communist, are you, Pebsworth?'

'No, no, you know I'm not. But I don't like to see a man making a good thing out of turning his coat. Thirty pieces of silver and the rest of it, you know.'

'I'm sorry you believe that's what I'm doing,' Rigden said quietly.

He meant it. He liked Pebsworth, even though the old fellow belonged, by birth and social habits, to Spencer-Savage's side of the ditch . . . He glanced at Howard. The boy did not open his mouth: he stared directly into Rigden's face, his own shut like a back-door slammed against the outstretched hand of a tramp. Rigden thought: As soon as he's alone, he'll feel sickeningly ashamed of himself . . . He wanted to save the boy — spare him the humiliation of looking at himself and seeing a coward. He smiled and said lightly,

'I have a book of yours, Howard. Come and get it whenever you like. I'm always in at the usual time.'

Howard's lips parted, but he did not answer. Rigden turned away from them, found the book he was looking for, and left the shop.

He went straight from there to keep the appointment he

had put off, dreading it, for two days: the message he got asked him to come at once, but that was more than he could make himself do. He smiled bleakly. I'm as bad as Howard, with less excuse . . . The encounter — you couldn't, he thought drily, call it an argument — with Craddock had helped to steady him, but not enough: when he was nearly at the house, dread, like the dread of being publicly exposed, seized and drove him to walk past it. He had reached the end of the street before he could force himself to turn back to the door, ring, wait there for it to be opened, and speak in an ordinary voice to the servant who must (he thought ridiculously) know that he was here because he had been sent for in disgrace, and be sniggering behind his face. If he were, he hid it very well. He greeted Rigden with all his usual friendliness, as though nothing had changed, as though this were any day months, years, ago.

'Go up to the library, sir, will you?'

He stood for a moment outside the room, his mind jerking spasmodically, like a severed nerve, then pushed open the heavy door.

'Well, Tom, you wanted to see me,' he said jauntily. 'Here I am.'

Paget stood up, smiling his kind smile. 'Come in and sit down. Just let me finish this note. I shan't be a second.'

He turned back to his noisy little typewriter and rattled away. Rigden took the chair he always took in this room, a shabby affair of red leather with one broken spring. It was so familiar, his body knew it so well — it had been in the room where he had first met Thomas Paget, a third-year man of incredible kindness, willing to take a grave interest in the awkward young lout he had picked up — that he felt himself growing less tense. The impatience to get it over that he had felt as he came in vanished, and a familiar warm ease took possession of him. During the whole of his time as an undergraduate, and afterwards, before he married, wherever Paget was living was his home, the kind of home he had never before had, with large solid bookcases, bottles of wine brought out from the lower half of an old cupboard filled above with gramophone records, and endless talk. Talk that was like a delirium; it started in him a fever that ran into and heightened the fevers of success and youth, and let him feel that he had the world between his hands, to do what he liked with, understand, enjoy, change...

Paget had finished his letter, and was looking at him without a trace of hostility. He said gently,

'Well, Nevil, you've done it. Are you as comfortable as you expected to be?'

He was not tempted to lie. 'No.'

'You've committed suicide, haven't you?' said Paget, in the same gentle voice. 'I warned you, you know.'

'I know you did.'

'Well — so what now? All the fun of the fair as an ex-communist? Clean breast and all that — at so much a word? It's a career, of course, though not the one you trained for.'

It was a knife sent into his momentary self-assurance. He said as calmly as he could,

'You know I'm not going to start a career as an ex-communist. I'm not that sort of animal.'

His brother-in-law leaned back, with the look of tolerance he wore easily. As easily, Rigden thought, as though it were part of his nature. And then thought quickly: Now I'm beginning to tell lies about him: he *is* tolerant, just as he is angelically kind, good, rational — up to the moment when goodness, reason, kindness, run head on into his creed.

'In any case, you know,' Paget said, 'England is a thin field for such a career — even if you were a novelist, and you're not, you're a scholar. You can, of course, attack communism on philosophical grounds — on the lines of your latest little essay — but only a few people will bother to read you. We English are immune to philosophical arguments. And we don't seriously believe in the danger communism represents to our rotted liberalism. Rotten in the way a tree can go on standing for years, and suddenly collapse in a high wind, completely gone inside . . . No, no, my dear Nevil, you won't make any mark as a subtle scholarly crusader. You'll be forced to go farther — and betray your friends.' He paused and said delicately, 'Your former friends.'

Rigden felt the inside of his mouth dry and rough. 'So you think I'd turn informer?'

'Why not?'

'You know me better than that.'

'I thought I knew you,' Paget said mildly, 'but I realise now that you were always a traitor — potentially.'

Word for word what the Czech brute said, thought Rigden. He laughed. He saw that his laughter had surprised the other man, and this gave him a childish satisfaction.

'How d'you make that out?' he asked lightly, almost merrily.

'Partly the rabid nonsense you talked about arguing openly — as you would say, decently — with an open enemy. Hudson. And about wanting to save a young woman's happiness. Or was it innocence you said? I forget. I'll give you the benefit of the doubt — perhaps you really believed then that that was all you wanted. But, my dear boy, the mere impulse in you to do these things proves what a long way you had gone towards being utterly untrustworthy. Untrustworthy, unreliable, vain. You to set up your little personal ideas of what is decent against the movement! The movement doesn't make errors. *I* can make an error — I made one in trusting you and taking you inside. *It* doesn't. In any case you're not in a position to decide anything. Nor am I. Who are you, who am I, to

think we know better?' He might, Rigden thought in-
congruously, be a Superior rebuking a lax priest. 'My
dear Nevil, you gave yourself away with both hands the
moment you opened your mouth about Hudson. And you
can be sure — as sure as I am — that an impulse of that sort
isn't any sudden flaw. You'd been sick — a sick mind and
conscience — for a long time.'

A constriction in Rigden's throat made it difficult to
speak. 'You believe that, do you?'

'Certainly,' Paget said. 'It's ABC. Fortunately—' he
narrowed his eyes in a gently ironical smile — 'you were
never trusted far. We could use you because of your influence on young men. Beyond that — no. I never believed
that you had what my ecclesiastical friends would call a
vocation. You have neither the intellect nor the guts for the
hard, essential work. You're too soft.'

For the first time since he came in Rigden felt a prick of
contempt. 'Too soft to make a conspirator, do you mean?'

Paget looked at him with something between distaste and
commiseration. 'If that's what your sick conscience likes to
call it . . . What will you call it when you begin trying to
denounce me?'

Did they, in fact, never trust me? Rigden wondered. Or
were they gentling me into a position I couldn't have
escaped from? Was the whole Hudson business — so
cheap, so puerile in its wickedness, like the cruelties of
schoolboys — meant only to try me out? (Added to the
satisfaction it gave them to punish Hudson for his apostasy
— for the trick he played on them.) Or was it the first jerk
of the bit applied at a moment when Green believed I was
ready for it?

He thought: I shall never know.

The pain he felt surprised him. 'You know I shan't do
anything of the sort,' he muttered.

Paget leaned forward. Like his sister, like Evelyn, he had

a trick of touching his listener with one finger to mark a point: he began to do this now, and drew back as though he preferred not to come too near Rigden. He spoke quite dispassionately.

'Because of your — shall we go on calling it conscience? — you'll be driven farther along the road you've started on. And you're not an ignorant Party member, you've been treated — up to a point — as though you were a useful and intelligent man. I, to my cost, treated you as such——'

Rigden interrupted him eagerly — an eagerness he knew would be cut down. 'You did more for me than anyone in the world.'

Paget glanced at him with what he recognised as hatred, dry cold hate. He felt sick.

Looking away, he thought: He's not an emotional or a passionate man: he really is what most people think he is — immensely reasonable, cultivated, a little austere in his habits, except that he enjoys wine, a little impatient with fools, gay. The single thread in him of vanity is his certainty that he can sum up any situation, and any man, at a glance. And that thread, that nerve, is exactly where I've wounded him. He liked me. Not — not even at first — only because his sister was in love with me. His affection for me was a weakness. And now — now that he's paying for it — naturally he hates me.

At this moment he would have given an ear to convince Paget that he was sorry. He said,

'Can't you believe that my — my affection for you — gratitude — all that — can be trusted?'

Paget smiled. 'Only a fool trusts himself to gratitude. You read about the shepherd and the adder when you were a child. The silly fellow should have drawn its sting.'

Watching him with useless grief, Rigden said, 'What do you mean? That you wouldn't save me from being discredited in some unpleasant way — like Hudson?'

'No, I wouldn't,' Paget said gently.

'What are you afraid of?' He knew.

'My dear Nevil,' Paget said almost lightly, 'I'm not afraid, as you call it, of anything — except that you'll undo all my work of years.'

Extraordinary how many totally blind spots one can go about with, and still appear clearsighted and sane. This was the first moment when Rigden realised clearly that to two men, one of them his dear Tom, he had become nothing but a threat: a very disturbing threat. And that Tom had been savagely cursed for laying himself and Green open to it. When he looks at me, he sees a sordid humiliation, Rigden thought; an error he ought never to have made . . . It needed no effort to imagine Green's brutal comments on it. Or the depth of their fears.

He said slowly, 'I've always known that you are infinitely more intelligent than I am. Why can't you grasp that I loathed the thought of doing for the movement something I could never bring myself to do —' he added swiftly, 'nor could you, either — for myself, my own profit?'

An expression he knew well came over his brother-in-law's face: it was a little like watching, from outside, a lamp brought close to a thin blind: when it reached a certain point of excitement his intellect seemed able to make the fine bones of his face transparent. His eyes gleamed; the delicacy of his features became more noticeable, as did the hollows like a thumb-mark under his cheekbones. As he had done before, Rigden thought of a mediaeval monk, flaying his congregation with his diabolical eloquence.

'You're not pretending, are you, that private virtues are — ever have been, ever will be — used in politics or business? The only — I say: the only — virtues of social life are power, violence, what you would call cruelty. Anything else is sham — a faked culture and hypocrisy. Socially, as privately, you are what you do. If you have power, you use it. You know that — or you did.'

'But you use it, if you are an honest man——' began Rigden.

Paget cut him short with another glance of almost pitying distaste. He's amusing himself, Rigden thought suddenly. In a perverse way it amuses him to expose himself to me nakedly at the moment when he is cutting me off for good . . . An image from the afternoon when he had watched his wife and Tom bathing in the young Thames — it seemed in another lifetime — struck him a glancing blow. He winced.

'Honest? Honesty?' Paget said, smiling. 'Are you honest when you talk about freedom and justice as if they can exist apart from power? You know they can't. The sane man — the man who knows, by the lucid exercise of his reason, what *must* happen — is free to do anything, commit any so-called sin in the book, use any severity, even the most merciless, that may be needed to bring greedy or irresponsible or merely stupid men and women into line with this *what-must-happen*. History has already been written, and the few who can see the road ahead clearly *must* lead. The rest can only trot after them. A leader who was so sorry for his followers' shortness of breath that he let them stray off the road to pick buttercups would be betraying them — just as unforgiveably as if he were a disobedient weakling. And in fact pity would imply that he had a streak of servility — that he couldn't help his nerve breaking when he had to take on an unpleasant responsibility. A supremely good leader gets rid of disobedient, useless, or unwanted men and women as naturally as a gardener thins out his seedlings. What would you think of a gardener too squeamish to do his job? You will soon be maundering in print about slave-camps and famines and shootings and the rest of it, forgetting what you once knew — that they manure the ground for next near——'

'No!' Rigden said. He added weakly, 'That's too horrible.'

'Well, yes, I suppose you feel that,' Paget said in his quiet voice. 'But can you seriously think of a better use for at least half the inhabitants of this or any country—uneducable, dull-witted, grossly or feebly vulgar? Seriously?'

Rigden felt a momentary giddiness, as if his foot had stopped on the crumbling edge of a cliff. He thought: He's not mad, not in the least mad. He's a Pure. Dedicated — to what? To complete sanity — the lucid exercise of his reason, and all that. To taking responsibility for *the others* . . . It was a kind of parody of Christ taking on himself the sins of the world. Paget taking on himself the guilt of all the deaths, the purges, deportations, tortures . . . A refusal of humility so instinctive that it was not cynical — as Green would have been cynical if he had talked as Paget was talking. A pride it would be stupid to call inhuman: proud to be giving up to his faith (it included faith in a few men in Russia) the inmost core of heart, mind, spirit — the ultimate sacrifice. And the last treachery. A sickness of the spirit. The heart can remain sensitive and delicate — he remembered the letter Paget had written to him about his mother — right up to the point where the evil mechanism comes into play. The mind, too, can reason sanely to the same point. Mechanism? No. More an evil dream . . . And it is the exceptionally intelligent and subtle who are wholly ruined by it, he thought: corroded, tainted in their essence. And perhaps the very simple and animal. Between them, given the chance, they crush the blind, halt, maimed, the childlike, the patient submissive nobodies.

His mind took a sudden blind step. He thought: I want nothing: no possessions, no power over anything or anyone.

'I'm not an informer,' he said coolly. 'The only thing I want is to be left in peace — to go my own way.'

In the long look Paget gave him there was neither liking

nor disapproval. It was not a direct look: in an odd way
it by-passed him and rested on some remote object or place.

'And what is your way?' he asked.

'An ordinary life, among ordinary people.'

With a flash of his vivid gaiety, Paget said, 'You haven't,
have you, been made terribly welcome as a traitor?'

'Why do you think I want to be welcomed?' Rigden
muttered.

'Because you are weak. You need to be approved of.
You're always, somewhere, afraid that you'll be a failure.'

Rigden shook his head.

'Shall I give you some advice?' said Paget calmly. 'No
doubt the last I shall be able to give you. The wisest thing
you can do — the only wise thing — is to write nothing, no
more clever noble articles. And hold your tongue. Let
sleeping dogs lie, Nevil.' He laughed and said gently, 'Or
sleeping enemies.'

Chapter 27

Whenever Rigden left the house it was beginning to get dark, the early darkness of a November afternoon, cold, the air still and heavy, with low uniformly grey clouds. He walked home, feeling at each step that he was leaving behind him not only the complexities and the deceit but all the little splendour of his life. Against his reason, against even his instinct, he was ashamed. He had, he felt, cut a poor figure.

Walking up the stairs to his flat, he was conscious of weakness in his knees and wrists, as though the strength had drained out of them. Evelyn was in the kitchen. It was one of the days when their Finn left at twelve o'clock and vanished into whatever likeness of a private life she had contrived for herself in a city where she knew no one and never spoke her own language.

She came out into the hall on her way to the sitting-room, carrying a jug of coffee and two mugs. 'Where have you been all this time?' she demanded.

'I went to see Tom.'

'Oh.' She handed him his coffee. 'Well, you look tired. Let's sit down. Drink this, and then tell me about it.'

She took her own mug to a chair under the lamp, and sat there with her long legs folded under, the light throwing a shadow over her face and throat. Suddenly he saw her for a moment as the very young very frank girl he had fallen in love with in a room crowded with girls and young men after some meeting they had all attended. His heart dropped. In a confused way he realised that he had been resenting her hold on him, half-consciously rebelling against

it, for a long time: and in the same instant he caught
sight of another feeling he hadn't yet touched, but he knew
obscurely that it was waiting on the other side of a darkness
that might reveal anything — as a death suddenly tears off
a mask, and turns a lifetime of resentment into a grief
poisoned by remorse and the terrible dismay of finding
that one is alone in a desert . . . Don't leave me, he thought
dully.

She said nothing until she had drunk her coffee, then
she came over to him and stood looking down at him with
a friendly smile.

'What did Tom say?'

'You don't need to be told,' he answered. 'According to
him I've always been unreliable and untrustworthy. He
can prove it . . . He even took the trouble to explain why
he and a few others have the right to play chess with human
beings who only want to be left alone to plant begonias and
save up for a new wireless.'

'I don't understand you,' Evelyn said lightly.

He put up his hand and touched her. 'Oh, yes, you do
. . . How would you like it if you — and your child if you
had a child — were one of the odd millions used to manure
the ground for next year, as Tom says? Or the next fifty
years . . . No one, not even Tom, has the right to play like
that with people.'

His wife moved away from him. 'I don't see anything
wrong in it. Someone has to know best. And Tom and
the others do know.' She gave him a hard glance. 'You
wouldn't say that people like your sister know better?'

He felt a flash of anger. It was swept aside by a rush of
grief and the need, as sharp as his physical need of her, to
make her believe him. Believe me, he thought, me, not
your brother. He said as calmly as he could,

'You're still that angry little girl who resented being
shut up in a fashionable school and prepared for a good

marriage. You look at poor people, and shudder because you imagine yourself wearing their shoddy half-washed clothes and living in a dingy street — but you can't work yourself into the skin of their poverty, you don't know that they live, yes, live in their shoddy dresses and sordid streets, you don't know that the really galling thing is being looked on by politicians — any sort of politician, even generous-minded young women from the upper classes — as a species — "the poor".'

'You're being horribly unfair,' she said.

'Yes, I am. I am. A boy out of the slums or the mines can scramble to a height where he ceases to *feel* with his own sort and begins to make use of them. If he's only an English labour leader, he hasn't the ruthless efficiency and arrogance of a man like Tom: he does less harm.'

He stopped, feeling the utter uselessness of anything he said to her. She was standing a short distance from him, watching him intently — but it was a look, an intentness, he knew too well to expect that she would understand what he was desperately trying to say. She was refusing to understand. At these moments a sort of exultance took possession of her, the bigotry and simplicity of a true believer: her mind shut like a fist round what she believed, what she felt. He was talking to that closed fist.

'Nothing alters the simple fact that you've changed sides,' she said roughly.

'Yes, that's true,' he said, 'but it's not simple. When I was much younger I thought it was. I thought one had to be on the side of my mother against the people who were quite content to let her *go without*. Now you and Tom insist that the guards with machine-guns in prison-camps are on her side, but their half-dead inmates aren't. It's nonsense — wilful murderous nonsense——'

She interrupted him. 'Whose side are you on?'

'The side of the weak,' he said swiftly. 'Even when I

have to change sides to stay with them.' Suddenly he was sure of himself again, and almost happy. 'Can't you see?'

Still looking at him with her fixed stare of denial — of his meaning, of him — she said,

'I can see that we don't think alike now. You've changed. You're different.'

'The only difference is that you can't make me do what you want,' he said.

'You've turned against everything we believed — and I can't bear it.'

Sometimes in nightmares you are talking, talking, from a dry throat, to an accuser you can't see. He felt this happening to him now.

'That's not true,' he said with despair.

In a lower, savage voice she said,

'Think of the harm you've done Tom. You knew that Green is only waiting for a chance to take his place; he's always resented it that Tom deals with the Embassy and that he gets orders through Tom. You can be sure he's making use of your idiocy to discredit him. And for that I'll never forgive you. Never. It makes me too angry, angrier than I've ever been in my life, with anyone.'

Compared with him, how little I matter, he thought. It was as though she had struck him an actual blow on the chest. He waited for the feeling of constriction to pass, and in the middle of it thought: How do I know whether the whole miserable grotesque scheme to use Hetty started in anything but Green's jealousy? He might have thought of it, Tom being away, as a chance to embarrass him, or hurt him, and then, when he was talking to me, perhaps seeing the chance of another embarrassment for him — if I made a nuisance of myself . . . Far-fetched — but in such a morass who knows? he thought with sudden weariness.

'I know how you feel,' he said.

Her face changed slightly: something, some thought, moved across her eyes, softening their cold brightness. 'You wouldn't have done this if you'd loved me,' she said.

'Do I have to do everything you tell me?'

'Oh, don't talk fudge,' she cried. 'Some things we must agree on. Must. This is one of them.'

'There are very few things in our life that you haven't insisted on my seeing exactly as you see them,' he said bitterly.

'You're talking like an idiot.'

For a moment his fear of losing her drove all other feeling out.

'You . . .' he said. 'My dear Evelyn, I love you more than anything in this world. Don't turn against me because of this. Don't. I haven't harmed you, and I can't believe I've done Tom any real harm. Why should they distrust him only because I've discovered something — about myself — that I oughtn't to have taken so long to discover? Why on earth should they?'

She frowned. 'What do you mean? What have you discovered?'

'That I'm not able to be obedient,' he said. 'Obedience without questions, without shame, without pity — I can't manage it. My mind — what Tom calls my sick conscience — talks back at me . . . But why should they punish him for my defection? I was very little use to them — as he reminded me this afternoon.'

She did not answer for a moment. Then she said,

'You're going to inform against him.'

This was worse than anything else she had said to him. It was the final humiliation. He succeeded in saying,

'You know I'm not.'

'Yes. You will. I'm absolutely sure.'

She was saying in effect: Yes, yes, I know you, I sleep beside you at night, and I know you to be the kind of man

A Cup of Tea for Mr. Thorgill

who denounces his friends. When he tried to move it, his tongue seemed paralysed He thought he had said again: You know I shan't. But he was not sure.

His wife moved, and he supposed she was going away. Instead, she said gently, 'Come here, my darling.'

He stumbled across the room. She put both arms round him and pulled him down with her on the sofa, rocking him against her as though he were a child she was comforting after a beating. He felt an overwhelming relief, the relief of being wanted: the ache of isolation left him, swept away by the warmth and pressure of her body on his. She pushed his hand aside, and took off her jersey. Then, lifting both his hands, she held them over her breasts. 'You see — we can still be happy.'

'Why not?' he said under his breath.

'Promise me something,' she said quietly. 'Promise never to give anyone Tom's name — or tell them anything about him. We can go on being happy. We could have a child.'

His body caught the sense of her words before they reached his far slower mind. He got up, and stood looking at her stretched out half-naked. Quite lucidly he thought: She must be far more anxious about Tom than I knew — to be willing to pay me to hold my tongue.

She was looking up at him through her eyelashes, frowning slightly, her short full upper lip caught by her teeth. He felt a violent anger and contempt — was it for her or himself? — and turned and went out.

o   205

Chapter 28

VANČURA was in bed with a sharp attack of influenza, and Bella had sent Gurney an imploring letter, asking him to come in after dinner when she went to her class: left alone, she said, Jan got up and wandered about the flat, and it was making his fever worse.

When he turned down their street, Gurney saw a man coming towards him; he was walking in the centre of the road and stumbling as though he were drunk. The street was poorly lit, and he had drawn level with the man before he recognised Rigden. The young man must have been walking fast; his mouth was half-open as though he had run out of breath. He stumbled past the Senior Tutor without seeing him. After a second's hesitation Gurney ran after him.

'Where are you going?' he asked. 'What's the matter?'

Rigden looked at him blankly. 'I'm not going anywhere.' Could he tell this man that he had been following — it seemed for hours, but was probably not one hour — an edge between a frightful cold solitude and the fear of sinking back into submission and warmth?

'Then come and help me talk to Vančura,' Gurney said.

Why not? Rigden thought. He turned and walked, saying nothing, to the house. The staircase, unlit beyond the lowest half-flight, pressed against his hand a wall smelling of dust; he had the sensation of pushing with his head against the blackness of a shaft, and his feet caught worn places in the carpet, so that once he almost fell. Like a clumsy dog, he thought.

The bedroom struck him as being colder than the street.

He shivered, and for the first time realised that he had rushed out without his overcoat. There was nothing in the room except the bed, a hanging cupboard formed of a shelf and a scrofulous curtain, and two chairs. Vančura was sitting up in bed: he looked yellow and ill-tempered, his fringe sticking to his forehead, the bones of his wrists more prominent than usual under their covering of black hair. When he saw Rigden coming in behind Gurney, his eyes for a moment lost their leaden dullness, but he did not smile.

Gurney said genially, 'I picked him up in the street and brought him in. Do you mind?'

'Not in the least,' Vančura said. 'I'm even very pleased.'

He believes I've come to give myself up, Rigden thought. He felt a jeering laugh rising in him, and suppressed it.

'I've been expecting you to come,' Vančura said, with the same friendliness. 'I read your article. It was admirable.'

'Kind of you.'

'Not,' Vančura said quietly, 'that it will do a bloody ha'porth of good. Your readers are people who believe what you say and can't help yawning. You might as well save your breath.'

Taken aback, Rigden said, 'I've had exactly the same thing said to me by — by the other side.'

'By the man you call your friend.'

'Yes.'

'Tell me something more about him,' Vančura said. 'I can't place him.'

Rigden looked at him with a curious smile, at once very young and very sorrowfully ironic. 'No, how could you? He's very kind, very lively, gay, very generous. To me, that is. No one did half for me what he did. He behaved like a splendid older brother.'

'You were fond of him,' Vančura said, 'eh? Quarrelling with him gives you a bloody pain.'

A Cup of Tea for Mr. Thorgill

Vexed that he had given away his grief to these blood-shot sardonic eyes, Rigden said drily,

'What do you think?'

Vančura leaned forward. 'I think that you were a kind of house-friend and playmate and pet of this splendid chap, never asked to do anything that might have shocked you, advised against staying in the wretched little local Party, treated as a superior breed of conspirator, one of an inner circle, ordered to say nothing that might lessen your usefulness as a softener-up and indoctrinator of young men — is that a correct picture?'

The suddenness of the attack had brought the blood up in Rigden's face. 'Yes.'

'Don't think I don't understand the enormous satisfaction of living with a certainty,' Vančura said softly. 'You were living with people — you were one of them yourself — who knew what is going to happen: your life had glory and meaning. Now you know nothing more than the rest of us infidels. A frightful let-down.'

'I suppose you mean something,' Gurney said mockingly. 'It strikes me as meaning nothing at all. Sheer nonsense.'

'No, he's right,' Rigden muttered.

It gave him no pleasure to feel that this East European brute could see into him: it was like being invited to stretch himself out to be amputated, without an anaesthetic.

'You left something out of your article,' Vanurča said. 'When you let the wind out of the theory — not by the way new — very old — that mercy, goodness and justice are founded by slitting the throats of every doubter you meet, you forgot one thing. You didn't explain how intelligent people come to fall for it. You — why did you?'

Rigden had a sudden conviction that Vančura was playing with him. It made him angry, and he said,

208

'If you know so much about me, you know that I didn't quarrel with my friends because they're the only people in the world who go in for cruelty and injustice. I haven't joined the—' he hesitated — 'the Spencer-Savages and their corpse candles. I'm still a rebel, I——'

'I know all that,' Vančura interrupted him. He went on with contemptuous sharpness, 'Even now you're prepared to leave your late friends in positions where they can harm this country. Your country, not mine.'

Rigden's anger drained out of him. He could only feel his fatigue. He said, 'I'm not an informer. It's the only certainty I have left. D'you want me to give that up, too?'

Vančura's forehead was wet. A drop ran down his face, followed by another and another. With some anxiety, Gurney reflected that if Bella knew just how he was carrying out her orders to keep him quiet, she would be extremely angry.

'You're tiring yourself,' he said.

'No, I'm not,' Vančura told him irritably. He passed his hand over his forehead. 'Mere human beings can't afford to be fanatical about anything, Mr. Rigden. Not even about justice or loyalty. The fanatic for justice ends by murdering a million helpless people to clear a space for his law-courts. If we are to survive on this planet, there must be compromises. You can't even be fanatical about friendship. You can't trust all men. To save the others you must betray some.'

Rigden's exhaustion had become something far deeper than bodily weariness: he could feel it moving in his veins and behind his eyes, paralysing him. With immense trouble he forced himself to grin sarcastically.

'That's their argument,' he said. 'It was the argument for making use of Hetty.'

'She was harmless,' Vančura said swiftly, 'she shouldn't

have been betrayed. It was an evil act. You don't deny
that, do you?'

'No.'

'Your friends are not harmless. Why do you protect
them?' Vančura asked coldly. 'What are you afraid of?'

Rigden was silent for a moment. 'Why do you imagine
I'm afraid?' he said at last.

Scrutinising him with an off-hand insolence, Vančura
said,

'You're not an ordinary coward, afraid of unpleasantness.
It's something more.' He leaned forward, to say in a cold
gentle voice, 'Are you afraid of being alone?'

Rigden did not answer.

Vančura looked at him with an ironical smile. 'What
is your wife's attitude to all this?'

Rigden remained silent. He was struggling against a
feeling of dizziness which was only partly fatigue. The rest
was a sensation that was becoming familiar to him — an
obscure sense that he was standing on the edge of a cliff
in total darkness: until this moment he had been afraid
of falling; now he was seized by a crazy longing to throw
himself down. He had only to let himself go, and all his
troubles would be at an end. He made an effort to rouse in
himself a conscious feeling of danger. Glancing furtively
at Gurney, he said in a low voice,

'Help me.'

Gurney shrugged his shoulders. 'Of course you want
to keep your mouth shut about your friends,' he said.
'But d'you think you have a right to the feelings of a
decent man?'

He watched Rigden trying to steady himself. After a
minute Rigden said, 'Perhaps not, but I have to live with
myself afterwards . . . a life without meaning, without
hope . . .'

'Oh, if you want hope,' Vančura said contemptuously.

Against his will, Rigden's voice rose. 'I must be able to believe in something!'

'Then believe in Christ and the life everlasting. It's the only hope there is. If you need hope.'

He stared at the young man with a fixed grin, certainly not of amusement. Rigden turned his eyes away from it. He turned them on Gurney. There was nothing in the Senior Tutor's face either, to encourage belief in the prevalence of kindness between human beings, nothing but a scalpel-sharp curiosity.

Rigden's mouth felt dry. 'You think I'm capable of anything, don't you?' he said.

'Anyone is,' Gurney said. 'The woman or man nearest you. Anyone.' He thought: And when they can't think of any other way of betraying you, they die. 'You yourself are capable of leaving loose in the world two men you know to be treacherous. I don't mean treason to the country — that's an old habit of men, good or bad, who happen to have been born without a certain simplicity and humility. I mean the lowest form of treason — betrayal of a weak creature who is in their hands.'

Rigden looked at him. 'Could you turn informer?' he said.

'I could do it if I had to,' Gurney said. Ashamed of this evasion, he said, 'No.'

'You — you egoist,' Vančura said softly and angrily.

Gurney smiled at him. He turned back to Rigden, seeing him for a moment as terribly vulnerable, a small animal caught by a pair of vultures. He drove the image out of his mind.

'Do as you like,' he said roughly. 'You've been lying and cheating for more than ten years. If you think you've done enough to take the taste of it out of your mouth, that's your business. I won't try to persuade you.'

With a strange simplicity, Rigden said,

'What kind of taste do you suppose an informer has in his mouth?'

'Would you be able to tell any difference?' Gurney asked him, smiling.

Rigden closed his eyes. At once he saw in the darkness behind them his mother's face sunk in the pillow. He pushed brutally at her fingers and heard her murmur: Don't go . . . He opened his eyes, and said,

'The man Green — his real name is Toller. Bertram Toller. He's an Under-Secretary in the Ministry of Economic Affairs.'

Gurney said calmly,

'Good. And the other one? Your friend?'

Rigden sighed — a sound between exhaustion and tearless grief.

'Paget,' he said, 'the second man is Paget.'

'I ought to have guessed it . . . No, no, it's ridiculous,' Gurney said. 'Impossible.'

The relief Rigden felt was overwhelming: his body had got rid of a nearly intolerable strain; he felt weak, as after an illness, but light and empty. His own voice surprised him by its lightness. 'Impossible and a fact,' he said.

'But — my God — Hetty was almost his own child.'

'Why does that surprise you?' Vančura said drily. 'Look at it dialectically, in its context.'

'How much did Primrose know?' Gurney asked brusquely.

Rigden's exhaustion clouded his mind, not unpleasantly: he had to force himself to take an interest in the question. 'Nothing. Nothing at first. She didn't, I mean, know that it was anything more than an accident. I don't know why Tom told her the truth. Perhaps she found it out for herself.'

'And then killed herself,' Gurney said.

The murderous rage in his voice pierced the cloud in

Rigden's mind; with something like dread he felt his lucidity coming back: his pleasant feeling of relief lessened. He made an immense effort to explain as much as he could.

'Yes — but not because of Hetty.' He smiled, a curiously absent malicious smile. 'You're all wrong. I saw the letter she wrote — not the one Tom handed to the police — that was a fake. In the real letter she told him that she could have endured anything except his indifference — not simply to Hetty, but to *her* agony when she knew the truth. She said it meant nothing to him, or no more than a child's tears when you tell it something it doesn't like . . . Primrose wasn't a communist, you know; she didn't understand it, and wasn't interested; she accepted it out of love . . . The only part of the letter I remember exactly came at the end — "I didn't know you were like this, I didn't know I was nothing more than a useful thing in your life" . . .'

'Who has that letter?' Vančura asked quickly.

Rigden's head had dropped forward. He answered without lifting it. 'No one. Evelyn had it. She showed it to me, and then burned it.'

Gurney said, 'Then your wife did know you were a communist.'

'No,' Rigden said. He looked up sharply. 'She's out of this. Leave her out of it — I'm responsible for enough damage, without dragging her in . . . She's very emotional about Russia — you've heard her — but it's only sentimentality.' He tried to smile. 'She's a romantic.'

We'll leave him that one of his lies, Gurney thought: it's not of any importance. He said gently,

'Are you prepared to give other people Paget's name — and the other fellow's — what's it? — Toller?'

'What are you going to do?' Rigden asked in a nearly inaudible voice.

Vančura sat up sharply in bed, frowning. 'Wait a minute,' he said. 'Have you any proof of all this?'

Rigden turned his head to look at him. 'Proof?'

'Yes, yes, proof — papers, a letter, anything,' Vančura said impatiently. 'Anything at all to back your word.'

Rigden continued to look at him for a minute with the utmost attentiveness, as though he were not certain what he was being asked. Then he said,

'No.'

'Think carefully,' Vančura said.

'No.'

Vančura leaned back again among his pillows. The sweat was running over his face; he let it run, his hands lying loosely on the sheet as though he had forgotten them.

'That finishes it,' he said briefly, and very drily.

'What d'you mean?' Gurney asked.

Vančura's mouth stretched in a vindictive smile. 'D'you see yourself telling anyone not an imbecile that two respected and apparently sane men are communists of the least pleasant sort, with no evidence except the story told you by a man we all know to be a liar? Who's going to believe it — or him? You might as well save your breath — and your own reputation, such as it is.'

Gurney looked swiftly at Rigden. The young man closed his eyes — not quite in time to hide the flame of relief and hope that sprang in them. He sees himself escaping the worst, Gurney thought. Suddenly he felt that he would rather have Rigden overconfident, aggressive, brash, all the things that used to irritate him in the younger man — and happy. Was this the first and only trace in him of the feeling a father has for his child, the pity he felt for the grey-faced broken young man facing him? . . . He held his tongue.

Rigden got up, slowly. 'May I go now?' he said, moving towards the door.

'Don't tell anybody that you gave us the names,' Vančura said sharply.

Rigden glanced at him without speaking.

'Did you hear me?' Vančura asked.

Rigden said impatiently, 'Yes, yes.' He opened the door and went out without looking at either of them again.

Gurney listened to his footsteps going hesitantly away down the staircase. 'Poor devil.'

'We've ruined him,' Vančura said.

'Or saved his soul,' Gurney said, smiling.

'And when, my friend, were we made dispensers of grace?' Vančura said, with surprising bitterness. 'I may say I got a good deal of pleasure out of needling and tormenting him. So did you.'

Gurney nodded. 'Yes, that's true,' he said calmly.

'And all to no purpose. Inoperable . . . I'm bloodily thirsty. Parched. Get me some water, will you?'

Gurney fetched it from the kitchen, together with a towel he found hanging from a nail behind the door. He dried Vančura's face and the back of his neck with it, and caught the sour smell of fever and sweat from his body. 'Your pyjamas are soaked, aren't they? Let me get you a dry lot.'

'No, no, don't bother,' Vančura said irritably. 'Bella will be home any minute. She'll see to it.' He went on in a malicious voice, 'Sit down. You can't go to the police tonight.' A yawn seized him. 'Or any night.'

Gurney made a bored face. 'I dislike policemen — all of them except the fellows in villages. I'm not sorry for once that the man I must go to is the Master — this concerns the college: it's not anything I can handle alone.'

'I wouldn't talk to him — but do as you like,' Vančura said with indifference.

'Why not?'

'Surely you know your own countrymen?' Vančura said with a spiteful grin. 'They'll listen — since it's you. And you'll convince them of nothing except that it amuses you to tell shockingly improbable stories — which they know

about you already. If you take my advice, my friend, you'll
hold your tongue. Unless you enjoy making a fool of
yourself.'

'I don't,' Gurney said drily, 'but does it matter? You
may be right, but——'

Vančura laughed. 'Oh, I'm right.'

Gurney was reluctant to go on talking to him about it —
not only because he was looking more ill and yellow than
ever: he felt that it was a side of the matter on which
Vančura's opinion was worthless. To hide this feeling, he
said abruptly,

'Why were you so anxious for him to hold his tongue?'

'Why? My dear Henry, do you want him to be accidentally killed — perhaps run over on a country road, as happened to a woman I knew in France, one of our exiles?'

'Oh, nonsense,' Gurney exclaimed.

His friend looked at him with an expression between
mockery and amusement. 'You have so few prejudices —
or they are so well hidden — that there are moments when
I forget you are English. Sooner or later you remind me.
You believe, don't you, that murder is something outside
society, an aberration, the act of a criminal or a man half
out of his mind. But there happens to be a society under
your respectable society, just as highly organised, where
the normal way of getting rid of a nuisance, as normal as
your giving a clerk the sack, is to have him killed.' His
expression became strangely arrogant. 'And another thing
— you think, because you know a little now about the well-
padded dishonesty of a Craddock, or the spiritual corrup-
tion of a Thomas Paget, that you know all about communists. You don't. You don't know anything about the
courage, devotion and, yes, humility poured out in the
name of communism. The farce is that so many of these
devoted modest incredibly heroic men and women ended
in the mass-graves dug on their own side of the line —

Goya's Saturn devouring his child should have been holding a copy of the Communist Manifesto. A heretic — some of them were five per cent heretical — is infinitely more detestable and dangerous than a heathen: any militant Church knows that. The newest Church will become tolerant only when, like the old one, it has lost its teeth. I've heard Lenin spoken of as a saint. It's possible — and an immense yawning mocking irrelevance. The revolutions started by saints fall inevitably at their death into the hands of the *administrators*: then begin the crazy suspicions, the arrests, the purges, the tortures — which go on until even the stones of prisons sicken of blood and refuse more. Then an interval of peace, or apathy, or a Renaissance, before the next . . . saint. Human beings are the most heroic, the most disgusting creatures imaginable——'

'Isn't that Bella coming upstairs?' said Gurney.

Vančura lay back, watching the door of the bedroom. The change in his face when she came into the room would have been laughable if it had not been infinitely moving.

'Ah, there you are,' he said in a voice of trust and relief . . .

Groping his way down the dark staircase, Gurney thought suddenly of Primrose, seeing with terrible distinctness her clown's face and wide equivocal smile. With that smile, he thought, that face neither wholly tragic nor grotesque nor vacant nor sly but all these things at once, she might stand for all the human debris of our century.

He wished he had some reason — or simply the energy — to believe that her life and death meant something.

Chapter 29

WHEN Rigden left Vančura's house he had come to an end of himself: he felt nothing, neither relief nor shame. He turned home only because he was tired. The idea of driving down to the cottage came into his mind like a dog nosing open the door of an empty room.

In a vague way he hoped that Evelyn had gone to see her brother, to complain about him, but she was there, sitting cross-legged in her armchair at the side of the fire, a book open on her knee. She looked at him with a placid face, and asked,

'Do you want anything? Some coffee?'

He shook his head. 'No, thanks.'

'Where have you been, what have you been doing?'

'Walking,' he said. 'Trying to think.'

'What about?' She kept her eyes on his face, with no anger or excitement in them. 'Have you decided to inform?'

He would have told her the truth if he had not known that it meant letting her pick over his brain with a fine knife: he had had enough of that for one evening, and the thought of going through any more of it made him shudder. Yet he wanted to warn her, so that she would have time to make up her mind about him before he came back. He said calmly,

'I may do. I don't know yet. Do you mind if I go down to the cottage for two nights? I'll be back Monday before breakfast. Do you mind? I want to think things out.'

She had listened with her fixed stare. 'I think it would be a good thing,' she said quietly. 'I'll pack your bag for you.'

When he came back from the garage with the car, she had it ready and gave it to him without a word. He made a movement to kiss her, but she drew back, with a calm 'No.' He had reached the foot of the stairs when he heard her running after him. He waited. She put her arms round him and kissed him, unsmiling, and pushed him away. Suddenly he could not go leaving her uncertain, and he said,

'Forgive me.'

She was standing sideways to him. The light coming through a lampshade of torn yellow silk threw across her face a pattern like that of sunlight falling through leaves. She asked, 'Forgive you for what? Nevil — you mean you've made up your mind? You're really going to tell them about Tom?'

His mind had gone dark and blank. He couldn't remember what he had just said to her. The image of a naked woman, one breast silhouetted against a tree, moved across the darkness behind his eyes, dwindling, spinning rapidly away out of sight, thinned to a faint mark, vanished.

'I'll talk to you when I come back,' he said, turning away.

As he got into the car he felt that any incautious movement would start up the pain waiting somewhere in his numbed brain, and he drove slowly, nursing the worn clutch as carefully as though an accident were the only thing he had to worry about. After the last street-lamp the night was completely black, with heavy low-sagging clouds: a thin icy wind moved along the top of the hedges. It was one o'clock when he reached the cottage, and he went to bed at once.

He slept for over eight hours, deep dreamless sleep, and woke feeling happy for a moment, as though he had come home. It was too much trouble to light the fire; he ate, standing up, part of the loaf and cold fried bacon Evelyn

had given him, pumped two buckets of water, and set out
to walk across country. The cart-tracks and narrow roads
he followed were empty, crackling underfoot with new
frost, but not emptier nor colder than the feeling inside
his skull. By mid-afternoon he had gone ten or a dozen
miles. He turned back. His mind abruptly began working
again — not to much purpose — grinding the last few days
to a fine dust, without reaching any conclusion, except that
Tom had been right: all along he had been a traitor. A man
wholly committed might have disliked the use they had
made of Hetty — as Tom himself disliked it — but he
would have swallowed it for the sake of the greater issue.
It was, Tom would tell him, his weakness that he couldn't
believe in the grandeur of an issue that needed so many
human victims. He thought: A less self-centred man, less
proud of his intellect, less twisted than I am — or simply
humbler — would have felt this without needing to have
one victim's pain thrust under his eyes . . . A sharper
thought stabbed him: I'm committed now all right. Committed to living with what I did yesterday . . . All thought,
all feeling stopped, as though he had run his head against
a wall.

It was dark long before he got back to the cottage. He
ate a meal of sorts, and went upstairs. He felt peaceful —
the peace of bodily exhaustion. Without undressing, except
to take off his muddy shoes, he lay down on the bed and
waited for sleep. It was the time of night in this empty
countryside when a light sound is audible for miles. He
heard a motor-cycle on the main road two miles away by
air. Then he fell asleep.

When he woke, a star which had been directly opposite
the window in a square of frosty sky had moved on. He
noticed its absence; then, in the silence, he noticed something else: a sound so nearly no sound at all that it could
not have wakened him. Lying on the bed, he held his

breath to listen. It came again, outside the bedroom — the nearly inaudible creak of old wood. There were no footsteps. But someone had come into the cottage while he slept, and was climbing the stairs with the stealth of an animal. For less than a second he thought that a tramp had got in through the door he had left unbolted. He knew at once that this was nonsense: no tramp, thinking himself in an uninhabited cottage, would be taking such pains to walk noiselessly. Fear broke through his skin. He got up and took two or three cautious steps to the door and pressed himself close to it: his mind, or his fear, told him there was nothing he could do, he had nothing to defend himself with — there was not even a chair in the room. The intruder would have it all his own way.

In the darkness, he was just able to see the door-handle turning, a few inches below his hand. A very faint sound — the man outside pushing the door. It ceased at once, and Rigden felt the man's instantaneous realisation that *this* door opened outwards on to two feet of landing between it and the head of the stairs. He caught his breath as the door began to be pulled, slowly. In the same instant his body acted without waiting to be told. He flung his whole weight against the door, knocking the man on the other side violently backwards. He fell without a sound out of him.

At the bottom of the steep stairs Rigden stumbled over his body. His hands felt a face and a throat. In the revulsion from his fear he began trying to choke the fellow, banging his head against the floor in frenzied rage as if it were the head of a puppet.

He became conscious of a third person, who pulled himself from under them both and struck out with his fists, shouting and sobbing. To deal with him, he let go of the man's neck, and found that he had a thin light body in his hands: it collapsed quickly, but went on sobbing in the darkness . . . Rigden's mind cleared. He got up and went into the room to find and light the single oil lamp they had in the cottage. When he came back with it, he saw that the man huddled on the floor was Bell, the ex-commando from the little Battersea cover-shop. The boy kneeling beside him lifted to the light a face twitching with grief and hatred. 'You've killed him,' he said, 'you——' He laid his white pinched face against Bell's, imploring him. 'You're not dead, are you, Bell?'

Rigden pulled him out of the way, and worked his hand under the man's sweater and inside his shirt. To his relief he found a strong regular heart-beat.

'He's only stunned,' he said, 'perhaps concussed. Anyway, not dead.'

He touched the boy's arm. Still weeping too noisily to hear anything said to him, the boy spat like a wild cat. Angry, and sorry, Rigden slapped his face. 'He isn't dead, I tell you.' Must give him something to do, he thought. 'Here — get away up those stairs and fetch the blankets from the bed. And my shoes. Get on.'

Shocked into obedience, the boy stumbled off up the stairs. Rigden dragged Bell's heavy body into the room, and when the boy came back with the blankets he let him cover Bell with them. He did it gently and clumsily, then squatted close to the body, now and then touching Bell's face or his hand with a light fluttering gesture, like a very young child's.

'Who told you I was here?' Rigden asked him. 'Who sent you?'

The boy did not answer: only looked at him with more hatred than anyone as young as he was ought to have had in him. Rigden noticed after a time that he was shivering violently, his skinny little body shaking inside a jersey so much too large for it and so worn-out that it must have been one of Bell's handed down.

'We'll have a fire,' he said.

He got it going and made tea, but the boy refused to take it from him. Rigden gave up trying to tame him, and they sat in complete silence, waiting. All that Rigden was waiting for was enough daylight, so that he could go: he did not want to leave the boy to spend the rest of the night there alone with the unconscious Bell. He thought coldly: I'm making an ass of myself; he'd be no more afraid of that than he is of me . . . But he stayed.

The light came devilishly slowly, a grey mist discolouring the darkness; then the first solitary bird note, then others, then a distant creaking noise of rooks. Bell was still lying inert, and Rigden began to wonder uneasily whether the fellow were worse injured than he had imagined. I did my best to choke him, he thought . . . In the greyness, his face had the innocence of the brute in its thick pouting lips and wide cheekbones; there was even something of the child in it, more than in the boy's ruined face. There ought to have been some use for him better than the one being made of him, Rigden thought. All he wants, of course, is to be respected, and if he can't make himself valued, can't earn respect and admiration any other way, he'll do it by being as toughly ready to kill in private life — call it that — as he was when he was killing under licence as a commando. I was a murderer myself when I had my hands on him a few hours ago . . . There is a magnificent reservoir of impulses on which the apostles of the police state can draw. Besides which — and besides exacting respect — skill in being cruel can give its possessor acute pleasure.

As for the boy, he thought — so long as he could devote himself, he would be happy. Without benefit of ideological crimes and follies.

He caught the movement of Bell's eyelids. The boy had seen it at the same time, and he began a half-incoherent babble — cut short by something Bell muttered, which Rigden did not catch. He got up and said,

'I'm going.'

The boy looked at him with a trace of fear in his eyes, the first he had shown. 'How am I to get him home?' he asked.

'That's his look-out,' Rigden said.

In the doorway, he turned. His lips trembling a little, the boy was watching Bell, not him. 'If you look in the scullery you'll find water and a tin or two of soup,' Rigden said. 'You could heat that up and give it to him. There's more wood.'

Outside, a cold mist hid everything except a few feet of grass verge and the stone wall. It took him a long time to start the car, and once started it coughed and jerked down the cart-track into the valley so unwillingly that he thought it unlikely they would get up the other side. At the bottom, close to the bridge, he came on the motor-cycle. They slid down, he thought, the engine cut off, and walked up-hill to the cottage on the grass between the track and the wall. It was probably a clumsy step made by the boy that wakened me.

Grinding in bottom gear, the car reached the top of the hill and the main road. He stopped and looked at his watch: it was a quarter to eight. The light was clearer now, with black trees scrawled with Chinese delicacy on the wall of mist. He drove on. A feeling half of derision, half angry excitement, startled a nervous laugh from him. You couldn't have had a simpler murder, he thought; it wouldn't have taken the police five minutes — when they'd discovered it — to reconstruct the whole thing: a tramp sneaking out of the cold into a place that ought to have been empty, and killing accidentally, in a struggle. Clear as daylight . . . He grinned. The grin froze into a grimace. As if the knowledge had been waiting for him up here, he thought: Unless Evelyn told them I was at the cottage they couldn't have known; no one else knew I was going . . .

His mind went out for a moment, pinched out like a wick, then began frenziedly to rearrange things. She would tell her brother — why not? And he — without warning her, of course — had acted, simply and ruthlessly.

That was certainly what had happened. Nothing else was thinkable.

Chapter 30

A s HE went up the stairs he thought foolishly: When she sees me, her face will give her away. He walked in, and her face showed nothing, neither surprise nor relief: no feeling except one that might be sullen resentment. It was to that he had to talk. He told her at once what had happened in the cottage, and asked,

'Did you tell Tom I was going?'

She said drily, 'No.'

'Then how did they know I was there?'

Her face did not change even a little. 'How do I know? Perhaps they were following you. Perhaps Green . . .'

If she had said: Yes, I told Tom, of course I told him, why shouldn't I? — he would have believed her. And believed as well that she had nothing to do with sending Bell and his skinny boy. It would have been perfectly natural for her to tell her brother. Perhaps she's trying to defend him, he thought. A familiar and more atrocious sense of being excluded invaded him. Obeying a violently irrational impulse he said,

'Can't we drop this now? We've had, yes, something all these years — a marriage is something — it was a good marriage. Isn't it worth trying to mend it and start again?'

His wife gave him a clear look. 'I could never feel the same about you.'

'The other night——'

She interrupted him. 'The other night I was ready for us to begin again. You've always pretended you wanted us to have children.' She paused, and said calmly, 'I'd rather have a child with somebody picked out of the street than with you.'

Until this moment he had had no idea how bitterly he had humiliated her by rejecting her. He thought sorrowfully: I ought to have known. Poor girl . . .

'Forgive me,' he said, 'I didn't mean to hurt you.'

He knew as soon as he had said it that he had made another mistake with her. His unhappiness confused him.

'You couldn't hurt me,' she said, smiling. 'It's when I think what you've done to Tom that I want to punish you. If it weren't for that I shouldn't care half so much.'

And that's nearly true, he thought. What you feel for Tom engages more of your heart and mind — or is it, in some way it would only be stupid to call incestuous, your body? — than I ever did — for all the pleasure we took in each other, and for all the warmth and the kindness. You won't forgive me for harming him — just as you won't forgive me for slipping through your fingers . . . With a little pity for her, he thought that the sexual insult was less than half his crime: her anger with him went very deep, starting in her at a profound level where personal bitterness could twist itself round her jealous love for her brother and jealous fanatical belief in his religion . . . It may have hardened her to the point of being willing to get rid of me: she may — at any rate for long enough to get her through the unpleasantness of it — she may have seen herself playing a noble role, a female St. Just. She has that in her . . . He didn't believe any of this.

He thought: Another of the things I shall never know.

'If I'd had the courage I'd have told you, on Saturday evening, that I'd already given Tom away.' He stopped. And looked with a little horror at what he had said. 'I told Gurney about him — Gurney and another man, a friend of his.'

Her face told him that she had almost believed it would never happen, he wouldn't do it. 'You——' she began. 'What did they say?'

My poor girl, he thought again. 'I'm not certain that they believed me,' he said, with an effort. 'They asked for proofs.'

'Well?'

'I told them I had none. One of them, I forget which, said: That settles it.'

She had controlled herself. 'I see. And what are they going to do?'

'I have no idea. I think — probably nothing.' He waited a minute, and said, 'Perhaps — since I've done all the damage I can — I might be left alone now? No more Bell, I mean. What do you think?'

Watching her closely he saw a strange look, half flinching, half — he didn't know what — pitying? regretful? — flicker across her eyes. 'You're talking nonsense,' she said in an even voice. 'Let's drop it. I can't say anything. It's no use.'

'Very well,' he said.

'Have you had anything to eat? Do you want breakfast?'

'No,' he said, 'and I must go, I shall be late.'

'What time shall you be back?'

'Oh, between four and five.'

She nodded, turned, and went into the bedroom, and closed the door. He had an impulse to go after her, and force her to listen to him with something more than her fanaticism and her resentment. But there was no time. And he had no energy.

He came home later than he had intended. As he opened the door, he knew that she was out — the place felt empty and rather cold. He went into the bedroom. The door of the wardrobe was open, and her clothes had gone: so had all the things on the dressing-table belonging to her. He stood for a minute, not thinking. Nothing more could happen. He turned and went back into the other room and saw the letter he had missed, lying on a heap of papers on his desk. It was short.

My dear Nevil,
  You won't be surprised that I've left. As I told you, I don't want to touch or be touched by you again. It would revolt me. Until I've decided what to do with myself, and where to live, I shall stay with Tom — and until I know if he's going to be all right, or if you've ruined him by your lies. If you like you can divorce me for deserting you, but I should like it to happen quicker than that, and I don't see why you can't pick up a girl in the street and let me divorce you — that would be easiest and quickest of all. Goodbye. Don't try to see me. It's over.

Below her name she had written, it seemed hurriedly, 'Don't think I'm happy about this, and don't think I shall change my mind. E.'
He read the letter through twice, the first time without any feeling except an obscure excitement, then with the sense that she was, after all, suffering. . . . Without giving the inferior in his spine time to be afraid, he went out again into the clammy November darkness and walked to his brother-in-law's house, half running. Not until he had rung and was waiting for the door to be opened did he let himself think that it was useless. A moment later he knew from the look on the servant's face just how useless it was. Before he could ask for her the man said,
  'I'm sorry. Mr. Paget's out.'
  'My wife is here,' Rigden said. The man was shutting the door. He pushed against it with a hand and said, 'Don't do that.'

'I'm sorry, sir,' the man said again. He gave the door a sudden jerk, slamming it in Rigden's face, with a sharp click of the Yale lock.

Rigden stepped back. His face burned: he felt all the sensations, the disgrace, the shame and fear, of the moments when he had expected to be turned away from the shop where his mother owed for a month's groceries. Almost in the same instant a cleansing rage filled him. He thought confusedly: That finishes it. I'll never be afraid of anyone again. Never. I'm free.

Rage, and the excitement of complete disaster, gave him a few minutes almost of happiness. Then without warning, as he was climbing the stairs to his flat, he came face to face with himself and his naked hideous failure.

Chapter 31

IT WAS a week before Gurney did anything with his knowledge. There was nothing highminded about his hesitations. They were those any decent man feels about handing others over to the inescapably seedy business of punishment. When he was a child living in the north of England he had helped in more than one rat-hunt in the barns and stables of the house, enjoying himself madly until the moment at the end, which he felt obliged to watch. Since then he had amused himself with the turns and twists made by another beast. *Ondoyant et divers*, yes, but a gulf separated his curiosity about human beings from the gesture of reporting on them to the police. He was violently tempted to wash his hands of the whole thing . . . And leave a singularly odd rat at large? . . . He thought about Paget with a half-sceptical anger. He was nothing so simple as two men in one skin: he was one man capable of the most delicate kindness and brutal indifference, delicacy, cruelty, even tenderness — without a trace of compassion. Yet in no way extraordinary, he thought. If you could empty on to a table the everyday impulses of the most innocent mind, what a tangle of impurities, horrors, treacheries, would tumble out with the rest. What is extraordinary about him is only his intellect. Extraordinary and lethal. Perhaps only a saint — he was thinking of Einstein — can be trusted with his sort of knowledge. So there may be nothing for it but to fetch the police . . . But which is the worst, most unbearable, diseased power in the world today? That of individuals like Thomas Paget or that, growing all the time, of a police which is at the same time bureaucratic and brutal? . . .

Even on the afternoon when he decided to go and see Spencer-Savage he had not made up his mind to tell him. He had other things he could discuss with him.

He had scarcely been in the room two minutes when Towey came in. 'Mrs. Rigden would like a word with the Master, if he can spare the time.'

'Shall I go away?' Gurney said.

'No, no, my dear fellow,' the Master said. He hesitated. 'No, it's just as well you're here. Send her in, Towey.'

Gurney thought he detected a flicker of annoyance in the smile she gave him as she came in. But she was very composed: she pulled off her little fur cap, ran a hand through her dark short hair, and settled herself easily in the armchair the Master drew forward for her.

'I don't want to vex you,' she said calmly, 'and if it will embarrass either of you to talk about Nevil I won't. I'll go away at once.'

'My dear girl, you can't possibly annoy me,' the Master said, 'and as for embarrassing me —' he gave her a sweet smile — 'I shall enjoy it. Shall I send Henry away?'

'No.' Her boyishly candid glance moved from his face to Gurney's. 'I'd like him to hear . . . You know I've left Nevil?'

Gurney did not speak. The Master said brusquely, 'I'm sure you thought it over, and talked to your brother, before taking such a step.'

'Yes.' Her voice was still very calm. 'I've been on the verge of doing it for a long time. Months.'

The glance the Master gave her, and his lazy good-humoured tone, said plainly that he knew she was exaggerating.

'Months?'

'Yes, more than a year.' If she had noticed his scepticism,

she was ignoring it. 'You don't want me to tell you about
his young woman — there has been more than one, of
course — in London. This last summer he wouldn't come
away with me because of some girl he had there. I didn't
mind that sort of thing — well, not very much. You know
I do try to be sensible. I did mind the other thing. Twice
there were boys who — well, you know, Master.' The
sudden dilation of her eyes gave her an air of intense
emotion. 'I didn't believe it at first, but after a time it was
quite obvious what was going on. I was terribly unhappy.
I had to tell him I didn't like it. If it went on after that, he
didn't let me see it.'

The Master had ceased to loll comfortably in his chair.
'My dear, you shock me,' he said quietly.

She moved her hands in a light gesture. 'Oh, but the
intolerable thing isn't any of that. What is quite intolerable,
and I can't bear it, is his perpetual lying. I know he can't
help it, it's an illness, it's really an illness. He romances
about himself and other people, and I know he does it to
make himself important. And I know why. It's because
he was brought up in Deptford and his father was a casual
labourer. He wants to forget that, and he invents wonderful stories about his own exploits — and what I find much
more hateful and unforgivable, about mine — without a
word of truth in them . . . It took me a long time, years, to
find out exactly what was going on all the time. I feel now
— what do I mean? — oh, horribly disgraced by it, as if I
had dirty finger-marks all over me. It's so ill-bred, so——'

For the first time she lost her calm. There were tears in
her eyes; she rubbed them away, and squared her shoulders
against the back of the chair.

Gurney was convinced that the tears were genuine tears;
she was genuinely unhappy. But he did not believe a word
she had said. In spite of her unhappiness he disliked her
at this moment more than he would have believed he could.

233

If she had been lying to protect herself, and even if he had detested her, he would have done anything to help her. Simply out of good manners or kindness, one lies every hour of the day. But lies meant to assassinate — anyone at all — made him very uneasy.

He reassured himself. A pretty woman can get anything out of Spencer-Savage, he thought, except belief in her truthfulness and good sense. He was taken aback to see that the Master was sincerely moved. Getting up, he patted Evelyn's shoulder, and began to walk up and down the room, frowning and pulling at his mouth. What had caught him — Gurney saw it suddenly — was the suggestion, a very clever one, that all Rigden's crimes could be traced back to his start in the gutter. It excuses him, Gurney thought drily, for being taken in by the fellow.

'This explains a great deal . . . My poor Evelyn, I'm far more than shocked . . . I can't imagine anything worse, anything more humiliating, than finding oneself living with a — a diseased creature. No, no, impossible, impossible.'

Evelyn did not look at him. Her gaze fixed and vacant, as though she were trying to control herself — perhaps she was — she waited.

Why, Gurney wondered, is she so anxious to finish her husband off? . . . Some merely sexual motive? Though nothing she had told them about his immorality was likely to be true, he might have hurt her without knowing it, in some unforgivable way — she had a great deal of vanity . . . He remembered Bella, who had none; yet she had wanted to leave Vančura because he distrusted her . . . Perhaps only her vanity, he thought. But he felt certain there was something more. Rigden might — it was just conceivable — have been telling the truth when he insisted that she knew nothing about his politics. And therefore nothing about her brother's. But then why — unless it were to defend Paget — had she come here with this mish-mash of lies?

Or had Paget only now, in the last day or two, told her the truth about himself, and sent her? She would do murder for him, Gurney thought coldly.

Evelyn sat up sharply. 'I forgot one thing. He owes Tom a terrible lot of money. I didn't know this until a few days ago. Tom has been giving it to him because he thought I must need help. But I never saw a penny of it, of course. He was giving it to one of his young women. Or —' she hesitated very briefly — 'the other thing.'

It was at this point that Gurney decided to tell the Master the truth.

'Forgive me,' he said to Evelyn, 'but why are you telling us this?'

She answered placidly. 'I hadn't meant to tell you. It was the Master I wanted to tell. He's been very kind to Nevil, and to me — and after all I don't know at all what Nevil may tell people now. He might say anything. He's very angry with me. He tried to force his way in the other evening — Carr had to throw him out.'

'My dear child, I'm very glad, very touched, that you came here,' the Master said. 'I don't think you need worry about what your husband tells other people. We'll find some discreet way of dealing with him.'

Evelyn stood up. With a charming gaucherie, she made the gesture of a young girl, lifting his hand and laying her cheek against it for a second. 'Thank you, Master,' she said softly. 'But don't punish him. Involuntary lying *is* a disease, you know. It's unpleasant and horrible, but poor Nevil can't help it . . . And now I must go.'

The Master gave her one of his good-natured smiles, the reflection on the surface of his profound indifference and indolence. 'I'll take you to the door.'

If any man had told us these things, Gurney thought, he would dismiss it as improbable (and ill-bred) gossip. I suppose he expects very much less of the women he knows.

When Spencer-Savage came back he said curtly,

'I have a good mind to get rid of Master Rigden altogether — if I can do it without too much trouble. The fellow's intolerable. I haven't paid much attention lately to my sister's stories about him — but I imagine that some of them are true.'

'Are you sure,' Gurney asked, 'that you believe all his wife says?'

'Perhaps not . . . Yes — on the whole I believe her. She may be exaggerating — an unhappy woman does, y'know — but what she says goes a long way to explain his dishonesty and duplicity. Don't you agree?'

'It doesn't explain why he confessed,' Gurney said.

The Master made an abrupt gesture. 'Yes, even that — if we suppose that he wanted to make himself interesting. He may have believed we should be impressed.'

'He was taking a devil of a risk.'

'Well — a fellow with his mental quirks and background . . .'

'You didn't always consider him a lunatic,' Gurney said ironically, 'and only a lunatic would——'

'Oh, I don't profess to understand him,' the Master interrupted in a testy voice, 'and it's a damned unpleasant subject . . . What did you come to see me about?'

For a moment Gurney's doubts returned. He wondered lucidly how far he was moved by a feeling that Paget ought to be taken care of, and how much by curiosity: what would the Master decide to do? Bored by his own indecision, he said,

'In fact, about Rigden.'

The Master yawned widely. 'My dear fellow . . .'

'You'd rather I left it?'

'Is it of the slightest importance?'

'I think so,' Gurney said, 'or I shouldn't be here.'

'Very well,' the Master said impatiently, 'if you must.'

Gurney took no trouble to make the story sound plausible. It always amused him to tell a story, if possible a true one, which shocked the finer feelings and finer prejudices of his listeners. He told it briefly, in few and dry words, careful to appear as unmoved as in fact he was by the Master's obvious distaste. The Master let him finish, and said with another yawn,

'My dear Henry, why are you telling me this cock-and-bull story? Not because you want me to believe it, I'm certain.'

His coolness irritated Gurney all the more because he admired it. Abruptly he realised that it was part of the monument erected by John Spencer-Savage, son of an obscure parson with a great many aristocratic but distant cousins, to John Spencer-Savage, Master of —— College, friend of distinguished statesmen, clever administrator, scholar, impenitent eighteenth-century aristocrat. Like his off-hand kindness and his cultivated, even romantic tastes, his egoism and self-love (both monstrous) had been built securely into the monument; the living man had only to find himself among more than a few intimate friends — if you can call intimacy what in all cases was a useful habit — and at once he withdrew and the monument took his place. A very prudent arrangement, Gurney thought maliciously. A really magnificent piece of humbug and hypocrisy. And only a fool would suppose that it means he has no heart. All it means is that a great many ill-regulated and tiresome emotions are deflected into gratifying his vanity before they can do any serious damage to the fabric.

Rigden's future depended on whether he were seen as a danger, not to the college or any of the young men and women he would be teaching, but to the stability of the monument.

'I should like you to believe that you ought to look into it,' he said coldly. 'Talk to Rigden yourself.'

The Master looked at him with a mild anger. 'No, no, the whole thing is absurd. A young man whose wife tells us he is a pathological liar—and whom we know has been lying to us for years . . . And a highly distinguished scientist, a man of decent family, with his own money. And this other fellow — in a responsible position . . . My dear Gurney, you're asking me to make a complete fool of myself. I won't do it.'

'As you please,' Gurney said.

'It's not only ridiculous, but extremely distasteful. I'm a little shocked that you've had anything to do with it.'

Gurney smiled. 'You're not shocked in the least,' he said, 'except in your public capacity. You're annoyed and bored.'

The Master gave way to one of his sly impulses to laugh at himself — a crack in the monument, making it for an instant likeable. 'You're quite right. I do loathe people who expose themselves. It sets my teeth on edge and quite spoils my appetite . . . I suppose I shall have to talk to the fellow. I'll think it over.'

'He's not in a very happy position,' Gurney said. 'There's a certain amount of spiteful gossip, some of it fairly vicious.'

The Master waved his hands. 'Don't tell me about it,' he said airily.

Chapter 32

It was true that people were talking, almost always the same people — throwing sticks on a fire which, left alone, would probably have gone out fairly quickly: young men at a university have too much to amuse them to talk about the same thing for long, and their elders have their duties and their ruling passions or their pedantic frivolity or their ambitions. But one or two people were taking the trouble to talk day in and day out about Nevil Rigden, and in a way intended to make him at once odious and silly. Gurney had discovered what was going on when he went to see Craddock about one of his young men: he found old Pebsworth there, with Nader — whom he detested — and Herbert West. He congratulated West on his Readership, just announced: West smiled timidly and modestly, and thanked him.

'You have nothing to thank me for,' Gurney said. 'Thank the fact that your most serious rival blotted his copybook at the right moment for you.'

West said simply,

'Yes. But for that, I don't suppose I should have got it. In some ways Rigden is the better man.'

Even in the moment of triumph, thought Gurney, he's able to pull in an extra dividend by being generous and modest . . . He was being thoroughly unjust. He knew it. Both the modesty and the kindness were genuine; West really did admire Rigden, and was sorry for him.

Bernard Nader put on his face of infantile mischief: it sat badly on the predatory one underneath it 'Is he a better *man*?'

'Do you mean——?' Craddock asked, blinking.

'Surely,' Nader drawled, 'everyone here knows that his wife left him because she was tired of living with a queer? After all, it must be, shall we say, a bore.'

'No, I didn't know,' Craddock said avidly. 'But I'm not surprised for a moment.'

Looking at Nader, Gurney asked,

'Did you invent that lie, or are you simply dining out on it?'

Blandly unmoved, Nader laughed at him. 'Does it upset you? I wonder why. I very much wonder why.'

'I can never feel,' Herbert West said in a gentle voice, 'that such people are criminals. You know, there was Leonardo da Vinci. And Gide. The world would be poorer without them.'

Pebsworth's long aquiline face quivered with amused contempt. 'I try to be tolerant, but I don't find it so easy as you do, my dear West. My moral boiling-point must be unfashionably low. I must say I hope Gurney is right, and that it's an unpleasant lie. I find Rigden quite unsavoury enough as a converted sinner, without adding anything more.'

'Do you dislike all converts?' Gurney asked him.

'I don't really know. No, I don't think so. I think I distrust anyone who changes his shirt in public. In the market-place, in fact. I daresay I'd feel the same sort of repugnance for an unfrocked priest, although—' he smiled finely—'I'm a sceptic and I don't like priests. There's something a little ostentatious about it, don't you think? ... I'm a liberal, you know, an almost extinct animal, but I respect your dedicated communist——'

Gurney interrupted, smiling. 'Without giving a damn what he's dedicated himself to?'

Pebsworth ignored him. '—and I can't respect Rigden.'

'If you'll forgive me,' Craddock said, running his

tongue over his upper lip, 'Rigden was *not* a communist. I have that on very good authority. He offered himself to work for them, and wrote some little piece or other — quite imbecile — then, if you please, asked to be paid for it. Naturally they refused — and he decided to, ah, blow them up. Very ingenious.'

'Very,' Gurney said.

He looked round the semi-circle of their faces, from the nearly extinct Pebsworth to Nader's ebullient and pretentiously subtle smile. His mocking amusement became anger. 'I came to talk to you about something,' he said to Craddock. 'I'll call in again. At the moment I can't stand you. I'm as capable as anyone else of committing murder — but only if the victim is able to defend himself a little. You and Nader don't believe what you're saying about Rigden. Or, if you do, you should ask Pebsworth to give you a few lessons in scepticism and sanity. In either case, you're bores.'

Craddock followed him to the door. 'Don't lose your head with your temper, my dear fellow,' he said in a gently protesting voice. 'Rigden's not worth it. I assure you. He's almost certainly done for himself, you know. Not worth your, ah, quixotry.'

'Never waste pity on a failure, eh? Far-seeing little man, aren't you?' Gurney said.

He went off in a savage temper. Between Pebsworth's noble futility and the malice of Nader and George Craddock, it had been a very pretty assassination. Do Herbert West justice, he thought, he didn't take any hand in it. Illogically, he disliked West's shrewd idealism and the mild-eyed integrity of his sheep's head even more than he disliked Craddock. Something about it made his gorge rise.

Sheer prejudice, with a dash of envy, he thought ironically.

Chapter 33

THREE or four weeks of execrable wet cold lasted until the end of term. Gurney was going to spend the vacation in London, in his club. His bedroom would be unwarmed, and the club full of men he was delighted to see once. But he had spent too much money during the summer, and had no foreign currency, licit or illicit, to go abroad.

The Master had done nothing about Rigden. Gurney began to feel certain that thanks to his indolence and aversion from any trouble in which he would be unable to take up a comfortable attitude, let alone an impressive one, he had decided to drop the whole thing, and let the young man live down a not very wide-spread scandal. Paget would be left to his curious amusements but, at any rate for the moment, Gurney felt almost indifferent. One rat more or less, he thought: does it matter?

The day after the end of term, the Master's secretary rang him up and asked him to come round at once. 'D'you know what the Master wants me for?' he asked her.

'I'm afraid I don't. I think he wants to talk to you.'

'I didn't suppose he wanted me to dance for him,' Gurney said amiably.

Nor did he, on the whole, suppose it had anything to do with Rigden. If he had been going to act, he thought, he wouldn't have waited four weeks. When Towey let him in, he asked, 'Anyone else with the Master?'

'Only Mr. Paget,' she said. She looked at him as if she were going to tell him something else, then changed her mind, and said, 'They're in the library. The Master's expecting you.'

Oh, my God, he thought drily: we're off. Rigden, poor devil . . . In the same moment he caught himself thinking: Well, it will be interesting to watch . . . He was slightly, but not very much ashamed of himself.

Thomas Paget was sitting in the corner of a large sofa, his small energetic body pressed into the cushions with an animal neatness. There was a trace of excitement in the smile he gave Gurney, but no anxiety, no concern of any sort that Gurney could detect. His eyes were as friendly and alert as always; he might have been talking across a dinner-table.

The Master spoke in a flippant voice, but he was not, Gurney saw, so much flippant as vexed.

'I wanted you here, Gurney, for the good of your health. I have no doubt you've been having nightmares.' He turned to Paget. 'We're not going to discuss a string of lies. The only point of interest is the one you were raising when Gurney came in — the question of motive or circumstances — extenuating and the rest of it.'

Paget glanced briefly at Gurney, and laughed. 'Thank you, Master.'

'I told Paget a week ago exactly what Rigden said to you, Gurney.' He moved his head impatiently. 'As exactly as possible — I haven't, be damned to it, a very good head for nonsense. He agrees with me that the only sensible thing to do is to confront Rigden with him. Very obliging of him — and frankly I'm obliged . . . I daresay both of you think I've been a little lax, but I have, y'know, other things to do than catch rats. Besides, I dislike rats . . . Paget, I may tell you, will be satisfied if the fellow apologises and says he was drunk or off his head. But we'll see, we'll see . . . D'you mind ringing the bell, my dear boy?'

When Towey came he said, 'Send Mr. Rigden in.'

Gurney had had a good deal of experience of the firmness, almost brutality, lying behind the Master's easy-going manner, but this shocked him. How long, he wondered, has the poor devil been left to stew in his own anxiety in another room?

When Rigden came in, the only person he glanced at in the room was his brother-in-law. Strangely, the look he gave him was one of astonishment: it reminded Gurney sharply of the very young soldier, almost a boy, killed beside him in North Africa; his eyes in the instant he was hit had held the same surprise and doubt.

'Well, are you going to repeat the story you told Gurney a few weeks ago?' the Master said coolly. 'Or d'you want to withdraw it? Do, if you want to.'

With a barely noticeable hesitation, Rigden said,

'I can't withdraw it.'

'Then have the kindness to repeat to us what you said.'

A little to Gurney's surprise, Rigden made his short statement calmly enough. He was haggard and tense, as you expect a criminal in the dock to be, but not aggressive. He's changed, Gurney thought. He could not put his finger on the change, but it was there. He thought that Rigden was a little detached — as though what had been happening to him lately had severed him, not so much from other people as from his anxiety to defend himself or impress them . . . Paget was attending closely, his face grave and very slightly disapproving. Very much, thought Gurney, as though he were being forced to watch a child making a clown of itself. When the young man had finished he asked quietly,

'*Why* have you invented this absurd story?'

Rigden looked at him. 'You know better than anyone that it's not absurd.' In a strangely uncertain voice he added, 'I'm sorry, Tom.'

Paget answered with a touch of contempt. 'You have very good reason to be sorry. What the devil came into you?'

At this moment Rigden smiled, a brief despairing smile that made him younger. 'You said there was nothing else

I could do — that I should be forced to do it. Remember? You were right.'

'If you had, in fact, talked to me about it,' Paget said gently, 'I should probably have asked you whether you had considered the need to provide yourself with some proof . . .'

The Master said abruptly, 'My dear Paget, you're not here to defend yourself. I got you to come partly with the idea that you might discover a reason for the whole of this preposterous business.'

Ignoring him, Rigden said,

'You're quite safe, Tom. I haven't a proof of any sort.'

He said it without a trace of anger or hostility, almost as though he really wanted to reassure the other man, as though it made him happy to do it. Paget's expression did not change. He said quietly,

'Then answer a question or two, will you? Unknown to any of us, you were a communist, weren't you, and——'

'Not unknown to you,' Rigden interrupted.

Paget lifted his hand. 'Just a moment. As a communist — of the peculiar sort you've described — you were willing to work for men you knew were, let's give them their right name, Soviet agents? That's so, isn't it?'

'You know exactly how it was.'

'Yes or no?' Paget said patiently.

'Yes.'

'So that it's only, let's say, an accident that you didn't give them information of military or any other importance? You would have done it if you could, or if you had been asked.'

'I wasn't asked,' Rigden said. 'You know that.'

Paget smiled slightly. 'Couldn't we drop this farce of what I know? I know one thing — we all know it — you were in this potentially treacherous position for a long time, years. During that time you were deceiving everybody, your wife, me, your colleagues and close friends. Ask yourself why we should be surprised that you can't think of any other way out of the trouble you've let yourself in for than by telling more — and more fantastic — lies?'

As a demonstration that a liar is addicted to telling lies it was admirable. Rigden had followed it with an almost expressionless face: unconsciously, his hands closed and unclosed themselves on the arms of his chair. Watching these hands, Gurney felt afraid that he would break down or make a fool of himself in some way. He leaned forward.

'You're forgetting one important point,' he said. 'We only know he is a liar because he told us so himself.'

Rigden did not so much as glance at him. The Master said in an ironical voice,

'I'm by no means certain that he has dropped the habit.'

Paget spoke with the greatest gentleness, as he might have spoken to a man he knew to be dying. 'Nevil, may I ask you one more question? Forgive me — I don't know what kind of sexual trouble you've been having — Evelyn hasn't told me anything. But nothing is more demoralising than a marriage going badly wrong — and if you tell us that you were unhinged . . . a little cracked . . .'

Rigden's sudden loss of self-control looked like a collapse: his hands were trembling convulsively, the knuckles jerking against the rigidity of his hold on the chair.

'Leave Evelyn out of it,' he said. 'I haven't talked to you about Primrose, have I? . . . You killed her.'

That's finished him, Gurney thought. Glancing at Paget, he saw a shutter drop behind his eyes, as though to cut off any image of his wife he kept there. He said nothing.

'Have you completely lost your mind?' the Master said with contempt. He looked away from the young man as instinctively as he would have avoided any offensive sight.

'I'm sorry,' he said to Paget. 'Forgive me for letting you in for it.'

'It's not of the slightest importance,' Paget said.

Then he did a surprising thing. For the first time, he looked at his brother-in-law with what Gurney felt was genuine pity. Or is it, he asked himself, only the cold pity of a priest for a lapsed believer? No, it can't be . . . With a smile of great delicacy and kindness Paget said,

'My poor boy, why, why on earth did you do this? Did you want to commit suicide?'

Before Rigden could answer — if he had been going to answer — Towey opened the door, and said,

'Mr. Bertram Toller.'

Mr. Bertram Toller was astonishingly like the image Gurney had formed of him from Rigden's description — even more unprepossessing, almost repulsively so. A large pale face and sagging belly. An air of supercilious arrogance which seemed less a vice than a natural trick of heavy lightless flesh covering a bad bone structure. Very much at his ease, he nodded with a sour half-smile when the Master stood up to greet him.

'I took the chance,' the Master said airily, 'of Mr. Toller's being in Oxford for the night to talk to him yesterday . . . It's extraordinarily good of you to make time to come here this afternoon,' he said smilingly to Toller. 'You don't know Dr. Paget, do you?'

'I know him by repute, of course,' Toller said. His voice succeeded in being both unctuous and brusque, and he had kept, Gurney noticed, some sort of accent, an unattractive one.

'My Senior Tutor, Mr. Gurney.' Toller nodded. 'And this is Mr. Nevil Rigden.'

Toller moved his head and shoulders clumsily round. 'The fellow you spoke to me about . . .' He stared at Rigden with a kind of official brutality, impersonal and

247

bureaucratic. 'No, I can't recall that I ever met Mr. Rigden. Mind, I don't say it's impossible — I meet hundreds of men every year, but I don't remember them . . . Were you ever a clerk in the Ministry?'

Rigden did not answer.

The Master said urbanely,

'I think I told you that Mr. Rigden is a fellow of the college and teaches history.'

'Yes, yes. You did. Well — I don't know him. Is there anything else you want from me?'

'Nothing,' the Master said, 'except that you should forgive me for wasting your very valuable time.'

Toller's self-taught arrogance was proof against any of the Master's civil graces. He said flatly, 'Right. Then if you'll excuse me I'll go, I have a train to catch.'

Rigden had not opened his mouth. Gurney remembered a phrase he had used about Toller's 'fat white grocer's hands', and with a stab of pity he wondered whether the young man were feeling the impotent despair and anger of the child cringing in a Deptford shop. His face showed no signs of it.

The door had scarcely closed when the Master said,

'You can go, too, Rigden.'

He looked down at his desk, as he might have done after dismissing a servant from the room. For less than a moment Rigden looked round him, with a faint indecipherable smile, not at any person, but at the room itself and its bookcases, tall windows, paintings. Then he walked out.

Gurney was watching Paget. A shadow that might have been sadness crossed his eyes, wide-open and brilliant. He said softly,

'Is there any need, Master, to punish the poor fellow? Punish him any farther, I should have said. Wouldn't the best thing be to let him stay here — rather than turn him loose in his unbalanced state? I'm quite certain you wouldn't hear any more nonsense from him — he'd be only too thankful to be allowed to keep his job and get on with his work. I must say that I hate to think of him being sent adrift.'

'Generous of you,' the Master said warmly. 'We'll see, we'll see.'

'There's something to be said, you know, for keeping a doubtful case under observation,' Paget said, smiling.

'Oh, the fellow's mad,' the Master said carelessly, 'there's no doubt about that. You're being a damned sight too kind to him. I'll think over what you say.'

Paget seemed about to urge him. He smiled instead, and said, 'Well, I'll leave you. You want to talk to Gurney.'

'I'm immensely obliged to you,' the Master said to him. 'I needn't, need I, ask you to keep the whole thing to yourself?'

He saw Paget out. When he came back he said,

'Well, I hope you're satisfied. It was a very unpleasant business for Paget and I'm glad it's over. That young bounder . . .'

Gurney did not answer at once. It would, he thought with cold anger, be worse than useless to say that he believed — even now — that Rigden had told the truth. All the more useless because only one of his reasons was better than instinctive and without any backing in sense or logic. That one was Rigden's entirely unforced confession. He had had no need to confess to the Master. No conceivable reason except one — a desire to cut himself off from his past by an irrevocable stroke. Irrevocable and absolutely gratuitous. It may have been absurdly dramatic, but it was deliberate — and he had known the risk he was running.

'Why did he confess?' he said.

The Master moved his hand irritably. 'How the devil can we know that? He's not sane.'

'He didn't — nor does he,' Gurney said, 'strike me as insane. I find it easier to see him as a young man so anxious to escape from a dishonest situation that he was willing to risk anything — losing his job, anything — to put it out of his power to slip back. Given that desperate anxiety — why should he pile folly on folly by inventing accusations against two men so well able to look after themselves — and ruin him?'

He thought: But they didn't ruin him. We, Vančura and I, did that.

The Master said coldly, 'Have you any reason for believing him that is not — I say: is not — based on the idea that Thomas Paget is an incredible scoundrel and ass?'

Gurney was silent. All his other reasons for believing the young man were wordless and unseizable; they had to do with Rigden's voice when he was talking about his childhood in Deptford.

It was a waste of breath to go on arguing. He said, 'May I ask why you arranged a public execution?'

'My dear fellow,' the Master drawled, 'it arranged itself — after I had seen Paget. He had every right, as an honourable man—' he meant: a man of good family — 'to ask to have Rigden faced with him. I should have done it at once if he hadn't had to go to London for three or four days . . . Yesterday he rang me up to say he was back, and told me he'd heard that the other fellow, Toller, was in Oxford. I got hold of him and talked to him.' With a cool smile, he added, 'What puzzles me is why I was taken in by Rigden. Why, I liked the fellow. I liked him so much that I forgot what kind of stable he comes from. Serves me right.'

'What are you going to do?' Gurney asked.

'Do, my dear fellow, do? Why, get rid of him. What the devil d'you think? My sister has been at me for weeks to throw him out . . . Rids me of her boring persistence, too,' he said gaily.

'Your sister,' Gurney said in his driest voice, 'has never had a better excuse for one of her orgasms of resentment.'

The glance the Master gave him said a great deal about his own resentful liking for a man able to allow himself a liberty of this sort. 'Nonsense. This time she's right. No question. The way the fellow behaved this afternoon nails it.'

With no hope of doing any good, Gurney said, 'Are you sure you're wise?'

'Damned if I understand you,' the Master said abruptly. 'He's utterly unfit to teach.'

Gurney said slowly, 'That's one thing you can't say about him. I'm not talking about his history — an historian can be as painstaking and ignorant as West. What Rigden understands — and an excellent second-rate tradesman like West doesn't — is the enormous intellectual satisfaction and attraction of communism. An idea to end all ideas.'

A mischievous smile altered the Master's face, softening it. 'A damned fine thing if we really could end 'em. Or keep them in their place. Teach the young their manners — and teach a few of them Greek — and leave it at that. Save a devil of a lot of trouble.'

He was speaking flippantly — from one of his most profound convictions. Ideas ought to be a privilege of the well-bred, who can be trusted not to apply them except in extremis.

You have everything, Gurney thought, every talent: urbanity, good manners, intelligence, a scholarly mind, charm, wit — and a vulgar heart.

'I daresay,' he said. 'But I don't agree with you. Anyhow it's too late. An idea has been loosed on us — promising eternal happiness, and in this world, *but not yet*. In the meantime a clever and ambitious young man can have a devil of a run, directing — isn't that the word? — his simpler and less energetic fellows. Not for centuries has there been such a chance to gratify the oldest human lust — for power. It can even serve as a religion, with a sacerdotal grandeur and servitude, if your young man has an itch for devotion as well as vanity. You may not consider it an appetising religion, but neither you nor I are capable of judging. Rigden is — he's been there. Why not make use of him?'

'I wish to God you didn't feel this itch to be clever,' the Master said, exasperated. 'What Rigden knows or doesn't know is completely irrelevant.' He went on in a lighter tone, 'In any case he's a shabby fellow. He couldn't even stick to his own beastly convictions . . . And even apart from his reckless lying, he has behaved abominably. The way he spoke of Primrose Paget was insufferable — even you must admit that. Before this about Paget I hadn't, I may tell you, made up my mind. No question now — I can't be lenient to him. He must resign. I don't want any scandal. I don't want any long-eared cranks getting up on their hind legs to bray at me about academic liberty. No, no, he must resign.' He smiled sharply. 'And you, my dear Henry, must see that he does it — and no nonsense.'

'You realise that it will finish him?' Gurney said.

It struck him suddenly that the Master was speaking with this calm brutality because he refused to let himself think about Rigden's suffering. He hates to be disturbed, Gurney thought: he's thin-skinned, he feels pain acutely, and — practised egoist that he is — he spends a fortune of energy and ingenuity on avoiding the sight of it in other people . . . I should know, he mocked himself. Don't I make every effort to do it? . . . Rigden's case is completely hopeless. If I try to force him to look at what he's doing

252

to the poor young devil — and the harder I try — the
more firmly and coldly he'll shut his eyes. I can do nothing.
Nothing more.

'Very well,' he said.

'Thanks,' the Master said. 'I'm obliged to you.' He
smiled and added with an off-hand contempt, 'A very
unlikeable fellow, that man Toller. Mannerless, self-
satisfied. I couldn't stand him. Smells too much of the
ladder.'

Chapter 34

As he left the house, Gurney reflected that he might as well give his friend the pleasure of knowing that he had been perfectly right. He was prepared to be laughed at. He felt that he deserved worse.

Vančura listened to him as though he had come to make a clinical report on a patient, and said,

'You should have listened to me. You can't teach an old cat anything about the jungle, and I warned you . . . And, God help me, you knew as well as I did how Spencer-Savage would behave. He has principles and some wisdom — but they refer entirely to the past. He hasn't the faintest notion that he's living on the doorstep of hell . . . As for your young man——'

'I've brought off an entirely useless murder,' Gurney said.

His friend nodded. 'Well, don't worry. You're not responsible for his happiness.'

Well-meant, this sharpened Gurney's annoyance with himself. He said bitterly, 'I'm responsible for something. If he hadn't given us the names — if I hadn't given them to the Master — there would have been no worse than a manageable scandal. And — Spencer-Savage being what he is — Rigden would probably have kept his job. Between us, we did in fact ruin him. And I shoved him over the edge.'

Vančura smiled without mockery. 'I knew you would give him away.'

'Oh, did you?'

'What else could you do?' Vančura said calmly. 'You

believe, don't you, that he was telling the truth about Paget and the other chap?'

'Don't you?'

'Yes. But you can't save a country against its will — any more than a man. You can murder it — as my country was murdered — but that's another matter. Easier. Much easier . . . My dear Henry, my very dear Henry, don't burden yourself with a corpse — I mean this young man. He'll find some way to be happy. If he doesn't, if he hasn't the sense to give his mind to it, he'll waste his life — as ninety-nine per cent of human beings do. As I've been doing.'

'D'you feel you've wasted your life?' Gurney asked.

Vančura gave him a strange look, lively, sly, gentle. 'I was coming to see you this evening. I want you to witness a marriage. And later on Bella will want you as godfather for the child who is making the marriage necessary. Do you mind?'

Gurney felt an atrocious spasm of jealousy. It was a physical pain, and it laid him open to himself in a way he could not have endured if it had lasted longer than a moment. His liking for Vančura and Bella — call it, more simply, love, he thought — came to his help.

'It's the best piece of news I've had for years,' he said.

As soon as he had said it, it was true. Perfectly true.

Vančura said, 'Did you when you were a child read the fairy-tale about the princess who became a goose-girl? Her only friend is the horse's head nailed over the gate through which she drives her geese every morning: it talks to her and tells her what to do. One night after Bella told me about the child, I dreamed a variant of the story — it was the goose-girl's head that nodded at me and told me that history has no meaning outside the minds and mortal bodies of individual men and women and babies, and that since men are to be loved I shouldn't hate myself . . . That was the sense of it — I couldn't when I woke up remember the exact words . . . Now laugh at me.'

Gurney shook his head. He had no impulse to laugh. The only people he ever wanted to mock were the pretentious and the cruel — or the cruel who have pretensions to knowing how to save humanity at one bloody stroke. These last were too impatient and murderous for his stomach.

Chapter 35

THE sight of Green bringing his ugly stomach into the Master's library (he was too well-trained to think of him, even now, as Toller) froze Rigden's mind against the anguish started in it by his brother-in-law's question — *My poor boy, did you want to commit suicide?* . . . As soon as he was out of the house the ground gave way under him; he sank to his nostrils in a sour mud, suffocating him with the sense of his useless humiliating failure. What Tom warned me would happen is happening, he thought. I've cut myself off from every chance of a decent life open to me, there's nowhere I can go to do any good, I've thrown myself like a stray dog at people who have no use for me; I'm finished; I'm a ridiculous figure, a clumsy shortsighted blundering fool . . . And if he saw himself as ridiculous, what did the others see? For men as far apart as the Master and Pebsworth he was a shabby character, a self-confessed liar and renegade. For the other side, for Paget — for the man who had picked him up when he was a raw friendless young ignoramus, gaping at Oxford, who had been his brother, benefactor, guide, teacher — he was nothing, a harmless impotent failure he could even let himself pity a little.

My dear Tom, he thought, you were right, I've committed suicide.

A sickening despair seized him. It drove him to walk blindly about the streets, trying to outdistance it, until he was lurching with weariness. At one moment he felt panic. It didn't last. One advantage of being born poor is the dull patience, the hungry endurance of life, born with you. He knew that he would go on living, on some level. He thought almost calmly: I shall never sink any lower than this.

Something, some memory as weak and ineradicable as the image of his young mother living on in a recess of his mind, made him, from the other side of shame and despair, a reassuring gesture.

He was too tired to feel any surprise when he found Gurney leaning against the wall at the top of the stairs, outside the door of the flat. Gurney watched him for a minute while he tried to get the key into the lock, then took it from him and unlocked the door himself.

'Have you anything to drink in the place?' he asked, when they were inside.

'I think there's gin,' Rigden said, 'and there may be a bottle of claret of sorts.'

'Where?'

'I'll get it,' he said, stumbling off.

There were two bottles of red wine. They drank the first while Gurney told him with brutal directness that he must resign.

'Why not sack me?' he asked. 'Why should I resign?'

'Better for us,' Gurney said curtly. 'And better, on the whole, for you.' He let Rigden finish laughing, and went on, 'Why make things worse by getting yourself kicked out?'

'Better to go quietly, like a good little cur,' Rigden said.

Gurney looked at him. 'There wasn't much fight in you just now,' he said.

The scalding anger Rigden felt dropped at once, flattened out by the realisation that Gurney was trying to prick courage into him. He thought wearily: He doesn't know that, for my sort, courage is nothing he means by it, nothing active — nothing but a blind hanging on with both hands . . . With an impulse to show his least presentable side, he said,

'I made a fool of myself, I should have held my tongue.'

'Until I squeezed the names out of you,' Gurney said drily, 'you still had a chance. The chance a man with a black mark against him still has — of being left alone.'

'Yes.'

'That makes me more or less responsible.'

Rigden made an effort to think coherently. 'No. No — you said yourself, from the moment I couldn't stick it any longer I had to get out.' He hesitated. The temptation to go on talking — even though he knew he would say things better left unsaid — was too sharp. 'The only thing I could have done was to slip out quietly, without giving myself away to the Master or anyone else. That was what my wife wanted me to do — and if I'd done it——' He realised that he had given her away, and said bitterly, 'Why am I talking to you? I've done enough harm by it already.'

Gurney gave no sign that he had noticed the admission. Decent of him, Rigden thought heavily; and then thought: But he'd guessed, God damn him.

'You're not talking to an inquisitor now,' Gurney said. 'Say anything you like. You're talking to a friend — if you believe it.'

'I'll believe it,' Rigden said with a faintly mocking smile.

'Tell me. Why didn't you just slip out?'

Rigden said slowly, 'Why? I should have been a prisoner for the rest of my life — always afraid of being given away by one or other of them.' That was not the whole reason, but it would do. A weakness — he was exhausted and the wine had made his head swim — prompted him to blurt, 'If I'd held my tongue — not told you about Tom — we were going to have a child.'

In the instant of making this foolish remark he knew, with a wrenching certainty, that he no longer wanted her . . . His sense of release was almost physical. A nerve, stretched beyond endurance, had torn: the pain and the relief were equal. In the same instant he thought confusedly that it had happened some time since. When — how long since? How do I know? he thought: I know nothing . . . Perhaps it had happened at the moment when — his way and Tom's parting — she had not even hesitated before leaving him to go with her brother. Even, he thought, though she was unhappy . . . There was some vanity in my love for her, he thought pitiably; perhaps a great deal of vanity — or I should have forgiven her for it — surely? Does vanity bleed? Well, why not? . . . He had not come anywhere near the truth, the whole truth. He knew that. But he was too close to it still, the pain was too near the surface, for him to do better than refuse to think about it now.

'She offered you that?' Gurney said.

He looked down, ashamed, 'Yes.'

And you refused, Gurney thought, and expected that you would be forgiven. By some other woman, perhaps: not by Evelyn. And perhaps no woman . . . or only one in whom the instinct to console and encourage is stronger than sexual vanity. He said gently,

'The fact remains — illogical and all that — but I feel responsible for you.'

It struck Rigden as ironical that he should be thinking of Gurney as a good man. He has always disliked me, he thought, and I — I was afraid of him and his caustic mocking tongue . . . Strangely, he felt no grudge against the older man for what he had done: it was all part of something he had started himself, not when he confessed, but before that, when he accepted eagerly the life Paget offered him. And perhaps earlier than that . . . Thinking of Gurney again: I know him very little, the distance between us is too wide; I could never be on friendly terms with him, he belongs to another generation, another class, another world — and one I hate . . . All true. But, for the first time, it struck him that the Senior Tutor's harsh reckless irony overlaid something very much simpler — simple, passionate, modest, almost gentle.

How the brute would roar with laughter if he knew what I was thinking, he warned himself. As drily as he could, he said,

'All right. I agree. I'll write to the Master and resign.'

Gurney looked at him sharply. 'I can get you some sort of job. I'll talk to old Thorgill about you — about giving you W.E.A. work.'

With exasperated loathing Rigden recalled the class in history he had taken for Thorgill in the first year of his fellowship: farm labourers with a sprinkling of comfortable elderly women who knitted relentlessly through the lectures. The memory of it filled him with rage.

'Is that what I've come down to?' he said.

'Have you any ideas of your own?' asked Gurney.

'No.'

'Then let me at least speak to Thorgill. Where will you be?'

'Probably London,' Rigden said. 'I don't know yet. I'll write.'

He saw Gurney look at him, measuring his exhaustion, then get up to go away.

Chapter 36

THORGILL lived out of Oxford, in a village which not a great while since — certainly for years after he settled there with his young wife — had been a few modest streets of cottages and houses, some Georgian, a few older: these were now the tiny oppressed heart of a repulsive body of sordid faceless little houses, with the shops and cinemas appropriate to them. Thorgill's cottage was one of the older ones. The woman who opened the door to Gurney was a district nurse: it was her bicycle leaning against the sill of the low window. Before he could ask for Thorgill she said doubtfully,

'Are you from the insurance?'

'No. My name is Gurney. I came to see Mr. Thorgill from the university.'

'Oh. Well, come in. It isn't any good, I'm afraid. You didn't know he'd been ill? He's had congestion of the lungs, we pulled him through that, but he hasn't caught his strength.' She rolled her sleeves down over an heroic pair of arms. 'He's going, you know.'

Gurney saw that for himself when he came into the bedroom. One of the old man's hands, the same colour, even the same texture as the old timbers of the wall, sloping over his bed, moved, pulling at the blanket: the rest of his lined ugly face and stunted body were lifeless. The district nurse spoke to him in the reassuringly loud voice these lion-hearted women use to keep death in his proper place.

'A friend here to see you, Mr. Thorgill.'

'How are you?' Gurney asked gently.

A pause. 'No, I don't know you,' Thorgill said in a

262

weak dry voice — the sound made by dry leaves blown across a road by the wind. 'What can I do for you?'

'Nothing.' Gurney hesitated. 'I came to see if there is anything you want.'

'I've all I want,' Thorgill said. And after a moment, 'Take the books with you and say I'll be along later.'

'He doesn't know where he is, nor what year he's in,' the nurse said, half laughing. 'He says all sorts, to people I don't know by name, and he talks to his wife. Queer what they see, isn't it? . . . If you're going to stay a few minutes I'll slip off home, then I'll come back and look at him again. If you want anything, there's a girl doing for him in the kitchen — Mary. I shan't be long.'

Gurney seated himself near the bed. Thorgill's eyes were shut, but he was not sleeping. His tightly closed lips gave his face a look of hard indifference, not unlike its expression in a roomful of people he suspected of trying to patronise or get round him. The grief Gurney felt surprised him. He knew very well that Thorgill was not a likeable person: he had a sharp temper, he was narrow-minded, unimaginative, suspicious. And he had given a lifetime of ungrudged faithful energy to what in one of his rarely warm moods he called 'bringing light to them that sit in darkness'. That fewer and fewer people wanted the light he cupped between his misshapen hands had been eating into him these last years like an acid. He had kept his innocence of an old socialist, an old rebel — a socialist of the old innocent simple-hearted sort — his belief that, to be happy, men must be free and wise. But he had no weakness for the idea of people being happy *in a mass*. He wanted each one of them to be able to see to his own happiness, in his own style. Any other way of trying to make people happy was fiddle-faddle and charity. He detested charity. He detested conformity and dependence. He hated them more stubbornly than he hated poverty.

263

Gurney thought: Isn't non-conformity the one thing that is going to save the English? Isn't it the oldest of our habits? . . . He did not feel sure. One of his own habits was to joke scandalously about England and the English. Yet the one thing he felt sure of, the thing of which he was always sure, whatever else he doubted, was that a world in which the English are defeated and voiceless — the defeated are voiceless because no one listens to them — will be a poor world . . .

The door opened: a young girl came in carrying a thick white cup. She stooped over the bed, smiling.

'I've brought you a cup of tea, Mr. Thorgill.'

Thorgill opened his eyes. It was a moment before he answered. Then — where did he think he was? — he said brusquely,

'Thanks, but I'll pay for it m'self.'

His eyes closed. He turned his head away. His face changed so swiftly that the girl Mary was still bringing the cup nearer to it when Gurney pushed her aside. He tried to lift Thorgill's head. It was heavy. The eyelids moved once more.

Later, when he had time to remember it, he thought: His whole life was in that one sentence. Seven words. Seven against a new bloodier Thebes.

For less than a moment, he thought: We're all right still.

Chapter 37

H E STAYED in Oxford three days to see Thorgill moved to his long home in a soil the old fellow had never liked: it had no life in it, he always said — by which he meant that it did not smell, under a smoky sunlight, of peat and soot. A youngish W.E.A. organiser, the old man's nephew, came down from Yorkshire for the funeral, and Gurney told him as much about Rigden as he thought would fetch him — and as much as he could ferret out for himself — and asked him to find the young man a job.

The fellow gave him a prudent derisive northern glance. 'It happens I need a good man. He can apply and take his chance . . . I take it you're willing to speak for him.'

'I'm speaking for him now,' Gurney said.

The other looked all round this for the trap before he said,

'M'uncle thought highly of you. Tell Rigden to apply and we'll see. He stands a fair enough chance . . . But keep that to yourself, Mr. Gurney. Least said, eh . . .?'

In the evening, Gurney called in on the Master to tell him that he would be away from Oxford until after the New Year. Rigden's letter of resignation had just come, sent from an address in south-east London. It was briefly cold and formal: he must, Gurney thought, have taken pains to use the fewest number of words possible. A legitimate vanity.

Now that it was all over — no scandal, no more trouble — the Master had softened towards him a little. Enough to inject a drop of contemptuous pity into his distaste for a clumsy liar.

'Y'know, Gurney, it has struck me that the fellow is

mentally as well as morally diseased. These clever freaks, eh? Freaks in every sense — occurring in a class where one doesn't expect them.'

'A fair number of the world's geniuses have been born to peasants and washerwomen,' Gurney said.

'I daresay. And how many of them grew up sound in mind and body? What proportion have been dissolute or deformed, or lost their wits, eh? . . . This young man may end in an asylum.' He looked down his long shapely nose. 'I hope not. But one can't feel more than moderately concerned for a young lout who fumbles away a decent job and a very charming wife.'

'He won't end in an asylum,' Gurney said. He added with an effect of reluctance, 'I wish I knew where in fact he will end.'

'No concern of ours,' the Master said casually. 'Don't give it a thought, my dear boy. I shan't, I assure you.' . . .

Gurney made a note of Rigden's address, and before he left Oxford wrote to tell him that he was coming to London: he invited the young man to come to see him, at his club. It did not cross his mind that Rigden might not want to come. He suggested a day nearly a week later. Before he talked to Rigden there were two other people he wanted to see. Not that he had any plan, or any very clear idea what he was going to say to him. He was groping.

On his first afternoon in London he went to see Hetty Smith. It was turning dark in those sour streets of decaying houses, with a dirty yellowish light from a few windows, and the weaker light drizzling from street-lamps on to the greasy pavement and the dark clothes of the few men and women, hurrying, heads down, through what is no less a desert for being choked with bricks, paving-stones, sewers, and the persistent dull rumour of traffic. It dejected Gurney to the point of wondering whether the atomic bomb is not man's involuntary response to the vast squalor he has created. A door opened, and two women, two old women, stood for a minute talking, silhouetted in the light from a passage; in the house behind them someone, or the wireless, played a few bars of that easy dragging waltz which might not — though he thought it was — be called *Temptation*: one of the old women turned her head back towards the thin sound, and smiled. He felt suddenly, with pity, almost with love, that these common things living on brokenly in the crevices of our minds and hearts will be the real loss when we disappear, not the great monuments: not our grand gestures but our quite worthless toys: not our achievements but our moments of humility — which have become fewer and fewer . . .

He had not made up his mind what he was going to say to Hetty, nor what, if she refused to talk to him, he had better do. She can't, he thought urgently, stay in these streets.

When he saw her, the first thing he noticed was the mark made on her by living here. Her face had fined down. Its extraordinary beauty — wide forehead and narrow chin, immense grey eyes, fine bones — was no longer a conjecture: it was there, but smudged (no other word for it) by fatigue and the stale sour London air, full of dust, petrol fumes, and the breath of too many people. And, he supposed, by the uncertainty and emptiness of her life, nothing in it of her own.

She looked at him with something like fear. 'Aren't you going to ask me in?' he said, smiling.

'Must I?' she murmured.

'I think so. Why not?'

'Very well.'

She led him along a dark passage like the passage he had just seen into, with varnished yellow walls, stained and finger-marked, full of a vaguely disagreeable smell, and down a short staircase to the basement kitchen, its one

barred window looking onto a stone-flagged yard with
milk bottles and dry brown leaves in a corner — no London
street but has a tree (almost certainly a plane-tree) within
air's reach.

'Is this where you sit?' Gurney asked.

'Yes. What do you want?'

'I'm not going to tell anyone you're here. And I won't
do anything you don't want me to. But you must trust me
— more than you trusted Miss Spencer-Savage.' He
paused, wondering whether to press harder on her secret
— whatever it was. She might burst into tears. He glanced
at her. No, she was not going to do that. 'For one thing,
I know more about you than she does. I know that Miles
Hudson didn't invite you to dinner with him that evening
— you went to his flat on your own. Why?'

Roughness had been what she needed, to startle her from
her defensive apathy. She looked at him steadily, now
without any fear.

'Who told you?'

'He did. But it was Nevil Rigden who told me that a
man called Green — or Toller——'

She interrupted him with a cry. 'Nevil? Nevil talked to
you about me?'

'Hadn't you better tell me the whole story?' Gurney
said.

She was silent for a moment, then asked him in a con-
tained voice, 'Do you know Mr. Toller?'

'I've seen him.' How much did she know? he asked
himself. 'He has another name, hasn't he?' he said.

'Has he? I don't know. I know very little about him —
although I lived with him and his mother for three years
when I was very young. My father—' she smiled briefly
at the shadow moving across her mind — 'my father and
he were great friends. He told me he admired my father.
And my father must have liked him, because — after my

mother died, when he volunteered to fight in Spain — he
left me with the Tollers. I was four.' She paused, and said
in a lower voice, 'During the day I was quite happy, but
as soon as I was put to bed at night I cried for him. I remember it. You see, I felt sure he was dead and I shouldn't
see him again. Only at night. In the daytime I forgot
him. When I had cried for a long time old Mrs. Toller
used to come into my room without saying a word,
dry my face, stroke it, and go away again. After a time I
gave up crying at night — you can't go on forever with
anything, even a fear, even grief.' She smiled with the same
lightness. 'I was living with them when he was killed —
after about a year. No one would believe me if I said that
a young child knows perfectly well what it feels like to be
betrayed — by the one person who ought not to betray you
— the shock, the sense of counting for nothing, of being
laughed at . . . Then one day the Pagets came to the house,
and Primrose wanted to take me away with her . . .'

'You were very fond of her, weren't you?'

'Yes.'

Less for the girl's sake than for Primrose's — poor Primrose — Gurney said,

'You're afraid that she knew what Toller wanted to do
with you. You needn't be. She knew nothing about it.
When she did know — when she found out, or her husband
told her — she killed herself.'

The girl's face lost what little colour it had. She said
under her breath,

'Oh, poor Primrose, poor poor Primrose. I thought . . .
Oh, how hateful I am . . .'

'No, no, don't blame yourself,' Gurney said. 'It doesn't
help anyone. And there's no need — you're lucky, she
never knew what you thought.'

'Is that why you came?' Hetty asked. 'To tell me about
her.'

'No,' he said. 'I wasn't thinking about her.' Nor, before I came, very much about you, he thought uncomfortably. 'I came to ask you . . . You didn't go on your own to see Hudson. You were sent. But why did you agree to go? You're not a communist, are you?'

If she said she was, he wouldn't know what to say to her, except to ask: Well then, why aren't you pleased with yourself? But she said at once,

'Oh, no.' A look of irony crossed her face. 'Only because my father wasn't one. If he had been, you know, I should, too. At least——' she blushed hotly, like a child, and mumbled, 'No, I don't know.'

'And Toller?' asked Gurney. 'Was he one?'

'He never said so. I always supposed he was like my father . . .' She pressed her hands over her cheeks. 'This all goes back to my father — the father I invented. To what I supposed he cared for so — so devotedly that he didn't think twice about leaving me alone. As soon as I was old enough to read about the war in Spain, and ask questions, I believed everything I imagined he had believed. His enemies were my enemies.' She laughed, unkindly. 'What a little fool . . . A child builds up the world from what it finds lying about. What I found was the debris of a world, an unreal one. No one, no sentimental poet, ever told himself so many romantic lies, and believed them himself, as I did . . . You don't want to hear about it — it was something else you asked. You asked why I . . . but, don't you see, if it hadn't been for all that, all those ideas and half-truths and my father a hero and his death, could I have been so . . . such a fool?' She looked at him with an adult coldness and directness. 'Mr. Toller told me to go to Miles Hudson's flat and look in his desk for a notebook — he described it to me carefully. He said that Hudson had become a fascist beast, and the notebook had names and addresses in it that we — that is, people like my father

— must have.' Her composure broke down, and she stammered, 'What an idiot you must think me. I never once thought it queer that any list of names Hudson was keeping could be of such deathly importance . . .'

'No, I don't think you were an idiot,' Gurney said.

He watched — pitying her, but with no impulse to let her off — the effort she was making to speak calmly. Toller had told her that Hudson himself was away, in Paris; he gave her a key to the flat and told her to go that evening, when the flat would be empty — no servant. She was there — searching the drawers of the desk for a non-existent notebook — when Hudson came in.

'He came in whistling something,' she said.

She stopped, and looked down at her small reddened hands. Her knees were shaking, very noticeably, and she pressed her hands over them to keep them still or hide them. She went on in a hard steady voice. At first she had felt only fear, and the sickening disgrace of being caught trying to steal. He laughed at her and made her lie down on the sofa, and began to caress her gently. Then another fear seized her. She was afraid of offending him. Afraid of making a clumsy vulgar scene and being laughed at.

'He behaved abominably,' Gurney said.

She gave him an odd look. 'It was very little his fault,' she said coldly. 'If I'd protested — if I'd made a fuss — he would — he might — have let me go away . . . I didn't, you know . . . I didn't move . . . He left me and went away, he said we must both have something to eat, and I got up and ran out of the room and out of the flat and out . . . I walked all the way to Chelsea — I was staying with the Tollers. I don't know why I walked, but I . . .'

The cold, almost light voice in which she had been speaking disconcerted Gurney. Her refusal of pity was something he understood, but he did not understand where, at her age, she had learned it. He said slowly,

'It was a horrible thing to happen——'

'Oh, no,' she interrupted him. 'Nothing was horrible — really horrible — until I got home.' She made a confused gesture. 'It became horrible then. Far worse than the other — far far worse . . . Mr. Toller was in. I told him. I didn't cry or anything, I told him. He asked one or two questions. I answered them, and then he said, "But it's providential——"'

'Is that the word he used?' Gurney asked.

'Yes. He said it was what he had hoped would happen. I said, "But you told me he was away!" He smiled at me, in the soft condescending way he usually did, and said "Would you have gone there if I hadn't?" And he said, "I'm sure you're all right, but you'd better see a doctor to-morrow. I'll take you to him. You must tell him exactly what happened to you. Then we'll tell the police, and——"'

'My poor child,' Gurney said.

'No, it's all right . . . I didn't know what I was doing then, and I said, "You're not going to tell people!" He said, "Yes, of course. What do you think? I wouldn't give a rotten apple for Master Hudson's reputation in this country when you've told the court and the journalists your story. You needn't be nervous — we'll get a good lawyer, a good thoroughly respectable lawyer, none of your Left-wing donkeys. It's all perfectly easy and straightforward . . ."'

She was shaking uncontrollably now. Gurney said very gently,

'Tell me the rest, Hetty, and then try to forget it. It's finished, done with.'

An almost sarcastic smile came on her lips. 'Do you think so? Then why are you asking me about it?'

'I'm sorry,' he muttered. His discomfort became a feeling of shame. He was making use of her — less brutally but hardly less unscrupulously than Toller himself.

A Cup of Tea for Mr. Thorgill

She shook her head. 'I don't mind. And perhaps it's
better to tell someone . . . I cried. I cried in front of him
for — oh, I don't know how long. I cried wildly, like a
mad woman. When I knew it was no use, he wouldn't
change his mind, I thought I must get away. So I agreed.
I said I was sorry I'd made a fuss, and I would do anything.
I said I was going to bed, and I went into the kitchen and
out through the back door. I walked — I didn't know
where to go or what to do. You see, he'd told me when I
was crying that my guardian — that Mr. Paget had known
all about it, and entirely approved——'

'I'm sure that's not true,' Gurney said. Whether it was
true or not, he did not want her to believe it, for her own
sake.

She looked at him with the same sarcasm. 'How can
you be sure of anything in such a world? I didn't trust
even Primrose.'

'But you wrote to them,' he said.

'Oh, no.'

The only thing she had wanted to do was to hide. To
hide and escape the horror of telling her story in court.

'I didn't want anything. Nothing at all. I was nothing.
I had nothing — not even my father.' She looked at Gurney with a puzzled frown. 'I don't know why, but he had
changed, too — he was someone, a stranger, who had left me.'

'Apart from the police, the person who tried hardest to
find you was Nevil Rigden,' Gurney said. 'He tramped
London looking for you.'

The change in her face — to a young soft gaiety — hurt
him: he did not want her to feel a new confidence — this
time in a young man as selfish and self-centred as any other
young man. As roughly and curtly as possible he told her
what had happened, what Rigden had been, what he had
done, and that he had now no job, no future, and no wife
— she had left him.

The girl listened with the single-minded attention of a child listening to a story. She became calm.

'I'm sorry,' she said softly.

'He feels that he's thrown everything away,' Gurney said, 'not only his career and all that, but the respect of his friends, and his loyalty to the friend who——'

She cut him short. 'There are so many ways of being disloyal. You can make use of anything to betray a friend; you can betray them with another person, or with nothing at all, or with an ideal. My father betrayed me with Spain. Anything. You can betray people with anything.'

Gurney thought: Or by dying. By getting yourself killed.

'I didn't come to see you out of curiosity,' he said. 'Nor — not entirely — to help you.' He smiled. 'Don't frown at me, I'm not going to bully you . . . Would you help Nevil Rigden — if you could?'

She looked at him attentively, but she was not, he thought, seeing him at all. 'What could I do?' she said at last.

'I don't know——' this was strictly true. 'You might — possibly you could convince him that there are other things in the world more important than his success — or his failure.'

She said slowly, 'He won't want to see me.'

It was half a question. 'I don't know,' Gurney said. 'But think about it. He's in London — I'll give you his address.'

He tore a page out of his pocketbook and gave it to her. She took it without a word and folded it into the pocket of her jersey. Gurney got up to leave. He knew that, as soon as he was out of the house, he would torment himself with the thought that he had done nothing for her, and he would see her as she was at this moment, a little tired, lips pressed closely together, immense eyes in which he saw, or imagined he saw, a shade of reproach. It was to avoid these torments that he said,

'I have the greatest respect for your courage, my child — but you can't go on living here. You must let me think of something else for you. You don't want to go back to Oxford, do you?'

'I couldn't,' she said violently.

'I'm not suggesting it. But you can't spend the rest of your life as a servant.'

She looked at him with a trace of anger. 'Why not?'

He grinned at her. 'Because sooner or later you would begin to dislike it, and feel sorry for yourself. Self-pity is demoralising and a bore. I should hate you to become a bore . . . I'll think of a way out — difficult enough not to hurt your pride——'

In a voice he could scarcely hear she said, 'What have I to be proud of?'

'The fact remains that you are proud,' he said gently.

She turned red. 'You're very kind.'

'How little you know me,' he said, smiling. 'I'm thoroughly selfish. It's not for your sake, or Rigden's sake, that I want to help you. I detest the sight of other people's suffering. I'd do anything to avoid that.'

Chapter 38

THE other person he intended to see in London was his cousin. Although it was ten years since he had taken the trouble to go near them, neither Hugh Gurney nor his wife would, he knew, punish him for it.

He had spent the first eight years of his life with this cousin, whose father, when his parents were killed in a car accident, became one of his two guardians. When they were separated, packed off to different schools, both boys wept. Hugh's father had been posted to Spain and Hugh spent his holidays there. Later, they went to different universities. They did not meet again until they were young men and Hugh Gurney was already moving towards his secure importance in the Foreign Office. They attended each other's weddings. And after that they met five — six — times: not more. This was not Hugh's fault: it was all his; it was part of the deep tortuous impulse that, after Anne died, drove him to throw away everything he could lay hands on except his two sharp needs, pleasures, instincts — call them what you like . . . He had a great respect for Hugh, a man of taste and intelligence, hard-working, scrupulous, without the most harmless vanity: and he liked Hugh's wife; she had a kind country face, and her voice was gentle enough to have contented old Thorgill. Hugh had taken her from a family closely allied with the older Royal family, and failed to give her — or she failed to give him — the children both of them wanted. Yet the marriage was a good one, and the disquiet and compassion left on their hands was not wasted: Hugh believed that he had a child — England: his wife had a great many others. Her children, if

276

they could all in their various languages have spoken to her, would still have wanted only one thing — not to die of hunger, wounds, cold; or more simply and knowingly, not to live in fear. Neither she nor Hugh supposed that their efforts demanded more courage or more persistence than it takes to be a good gardener or a good surgeon for fifty years.

Their house in South Audley Street did not smell like a town house; there was a faint smell of beeswax on the stairs and of cloves in Hugh's library. Outside the door, Gurney hesitated. For a moment when he walked in he had to push aside the flying shadow of a short merry child to reach the broad-backed man of fifty holding his hands out.

'My dear Henry — what luck, what fun to see you. You look well.'

'So do you,' Gurney said. 'How is Mary?'

'You'll see for yourself in half an hour. You're staying to dinner, aren't you?' Gurney hesitated, and his cousin said smiling, 'You needn't trouble to invent a bad excuse for not dining here. No one else is coming, you'll be alone with us.'

'Good. I'll stay.'

Hugh looked at him with a familiar gaiety. 'I hope you came to-day because you love us, but I'm afraid you had some other less honest reason.'

'You're quite right,' he said, 'I came to tell you a very queer story. Let me finish it before you tell me you don't believe a word of it.'

As briefly as he could without leaving out anything essential, he told his cousin everything Rigden had told him, without giving him the names. At the end he said, 'The two men are Thomas Paget, the deputy head of our Institute of Theoretical Physics, and a Bertram Toller, an Under-Secretary in the Ministry for Economic Affairs.'

Hugh frowned. 'Paget, Paget? Yes, of course . . . But, my dear Henry, he's a brilliant fellow — most attractive. I've met him.'

277

'There is absolutely no proof that any of it is true.'
Gurney said. 'There's no evidence against either of these
men except Rigden's word.'

'Which you believe,' his cousin said.

'Which I believe entirely.'

There was a short silence. Gurney looked round the
room, at a writing-table and an old chair he knew from
childhood. His cousin sat with hands folded in front of
him on the table.

'That's good enough for me,' he said calmly. 'Does
anyone else know?'

'Spencer-Savage, who doesn't believe a word, and only
wants never to hear about it again. And a Czech friend of
mine, a man called Vančura, who believes it.'

'Tell your friend to hold his tongue. And tell your young
man — what's his name? — Rigden — to hold his. Make
him understand that he must.'

'What are you going to do?' Gurney asked.

'Have them watched, of course. The fellow Toller isn't
important. Paget is. It's reasonably easy to keep him out of
Harwell and such places — and keep a finger on him in other
ways.'

'He'll soon enough realise you're doing it,' Gurney said.

'Then he'll begin to make mistakes.'

'I think you underestimate him.'

Hugh moved his hands as if he were clearing a way for
both of them through a hedge. 'Perhaps. And perhaps at
that point he'll do us the kindness of bolting.'

'You'd let him bolt?' Gurney asked. He was startled.

'Of course,' Hugh said in a dry voice. 'What use is he to
us?'

'And his usefulness to another country?' said Gurney.

His cousin had kept some of the gestures and impulses
of a schoolboy: they irritated Ministers who were not sure of
their own dignity, and reassured others. He laughed.

'They're welcome to him. We're not so short of brains yet that we shall miss him.'

'He baffles me,' Gurney said. 'I don't know what makes him tick. I can see — Rigden has made me see how communism attracts — as a way to power or as a discipline. But I don't know why a man like Paget isn't suffocated by his own smell.'

Hugh waved a hand. 'Oh, *that*,' he said. 'Who is? . . . He could be an active idealist — a creature with so much egoism — so much and so unmanageable — that he has to get rid of it somewhere. Our friend Paget may be venting his in what — no doubt thinking of a graveyard — it's fashionable to call the peace movement.'

'As you get rid of your egoism on Europe,' Gurney said.

His cousin said swiftly, 'Don't kid yourself, because you never wanted to have any power, that you're a noble fellow. You're just damned lazy.'

'You may be right,' Gurney said.

Hugh looked at him with a merry loving smile. 'And I may be wrong as hell.'

'So far as I could without unkindness, I've done what I wanted — which is certainly egoism,' Gurney drawled.

'And a million times my God less noxious than the newest sort — which allows you to inflict atrocious pain on other people for no better reason than that you're willing to endure it yourself for your cause — whatever it is . . . I was wrong to call Paget an idealist. An intellectual lust for power isn't idealism. Unless the devil puts ideals into our heads. And why not? It isn't likely he'd fail to make use of such a superb weapon.'

'In your trade you must do a lot of business with the devil,' Gurney said. 'Tell me what's going to happen to us. What do you people think you're doing?'

With something like grief, a grieving anger, Hugh said, 'Trying to avoid war . . . The fact that we are relatively powerless — a raft manoeuvring between two immense battleships — doesn't let us out. And won't excuse us before God if war comes.' He added meditatively, 'My quarrel with politicians — with all our politicians, of all colours, from right to left — and the cleverer the worse — is that they don't trust either the energy or the imagination of common men. Common Englishmen.'

Gurney thought: He has always seen England as a parish of Christendom — so that, to him, loyalty to England is the same thing as loyalty to God. No merely clever man would understand it, because a clever man wouldn't see England as its ancestral memories and the faith of humble men and women in a meaning outside history; he wouldn't see us as fighting on an invisible frontier.

He had an impulse to pry into Hugh's grief. 'How much do you mind that we're living at the end of European history?'

His cousin said calmly, 'So long as we can pass on all we've inherited, does it matter?'

Gurney had a sudden savage wish to destroy this calm. 'If you're talking about those famous *values of English civilisation*, you might be the curator of a provincial museum, proud of his fossils. Tuppence for the lot, if we haven't kept alive our independence and passion, the ravening curiosity and restlessness we once had, the northern reck-lessness, the breeders of men and ideas that we were . . . If you and your like could do that — instead of administrating, regulating, nursing us to death — death by boredom — we might last through the long night ahead of us. Why the devil should anyone care what happens to an England with only lower-middleclass ideas and wants? Why should anyone care if it sinks under its weight of bricks and television sets and dirty newspapers? Do you care?'

Hugh was smiling in an oddly protective way, as though he were listening to a child. Actually he was thinking: With his narrow coldly blue eyes, long blade of a nose, bony hands, he would have passed unnoticed in any twelfth-century English army.

'Of course I care,' he said gaily. 'What's more, I believe that if God needs any human beings He needs His slow stupid English more than any.'

'So much the worse for Him,' Gurney said.

'You're an astonishing chap, you know,' his cousin smiled. What he meant is that it is unusual for a brilliantly clever young man to give up working for the Foreign Office examination merely because he has been seized by a wish to spend a year in a village in the Dordogne; and unusual — whether from laziness, irresponsibility, hatred of bores, timidity, indifference, or God knows what — to drop completely out of the world he was born into, and be content (if he were content) to stay in Oxford as a Senior Tutor with a reputation for cynicism and a mischievous pleasure in annoying solemn or puritanical people. 'Anyone would think you'd deliberately chosen to make mistakes — and make a failure of your life.'

Gurney laughed. 'No, no, I didn't set out to be a failure, it came about naturally — from my form of egoism. I've always hated having to compete: the only life I like used to be within reach of anyone with the energy to travel simply. I was perfectly happy in it . . . I didn't make any absolutely fatal mistake until I was thirty-five. If I'd stayed in Oxford in 1940, Anne wouldn't have been in London to be killed.'

'Why didn't you?'

'Oh, having missed one war I wanted at all costs to get into the second. It cost me Anne. No doubt I've made mistakes since, but they haven't been important.'

He stretched himself in his chair. He felt like a man coming home from a long hard cold journey to find everything as he left it, nothing changed, nothing moved from its place. To no one else in the world could he say what he had just said about Anne, himself, and his horrible error. He felt the nervous relief of not needing to buffoon: he didn't care whether Hugh saw or failed to see the raw agony and resentment he took pains to hide from other people, even other friends. From Hugh he could take anything — even pity.

All Hugh did was to nod, and say,

'Yes . . . Shall we go down now? Mary will be there.'

She was standing in front of the fire in the drawing-room, and for a moment before she turned round Gurney saw a small tired woman with greying hair and bent shoulders. She turned, and smiled, at once years younger, and gay.

'Why, Henry, how pleased I am. But how strange — this morning I was thinking about you.'

They went into dinner, and she apologised because there was only an omelette, vegetables, cheese. The bread had been made in her kitchen, the vegetables had nothing in common with the insipid rubbish served at most English tables.

'One might be in the country in this house,' Gurney said.

Hugh looked at his wife. 'She does what she can, poor girl, to forgive me for condemning her to London.'

After dinner, Mary Gurney played to them: she was an admirable pianist: if she had been willing to give her marriage second-best she could have been a better one and well-known. Except that it was Bach, Gurney did not know what she was playing. He listened with the liveliest possible happiness. There were moments when he believed that music, and only music, justifies our existence on this earth — and will have justified it at the end, when all is silent for ever . . . At any number of other moments he was prepared to feel the same thing about a good claret or a handsome charming baby.

When he left, Mary held his hand for a moment and said, 'Promise not to neglect us.'

He promised. He knew that he had no intention of coming

to the house again, unless in another emergency. He had no notion why he found it easier to visit Vančura, but he knew sharply the difference between his affection and sympathy for Vančura and his closeness to his cousin. One of the two intimacies he had chosen: the other he had been bred into, it was carried in his blood — like that closeness to the north which underlay all his love for the Mediterranean and the happiness he got from its clear hard skies, its disillusioned cruelty, its warmth, its terraces of vines and olives, its voluptuous light.

Hugh took him to the door. They stood for a moment looking at the street, lent a lost elegance by the semi-darkness. 'Just a moment,' Hugh said, 'I've been thinking about your young man. Rigden. What can we do for him?'

Gurney hesitated. 'Nothing. Or nothing yet.'

'Why not?'

'Oh, let him work out of himself this feeling he has that he's made a fool of himself — committed suicide. As well as his feelings of guilt and disloyalty. It won't do him any harm to have to live with himself for a few years. He's young, he has time.'

There was another reason, one he couldn't give his cousin: it had to do obscurely with an old Yorkshireman trying to pay for his last cup of tea.

'Very well. Let me know if there's anything you want me to do for him later.'

'Thanks,' Gurney said.

He walked back to the club, thinking about them, Hugh and his wife, with love, and of Hugh with something strangely like exasperation. He was so decent, so conscientious, such a good man — without being in the least simple. He had never questioned either his duty or his right to govern: and he could be trusted to do it without the least taint of self-interest. But in whose interest? What justified his belief, almost unconscious, that the England he looked on as his child was the real one? . . . Gurney thought: What, after all, does he know about the thoughtless decent unfired masses he helps to govern? Less even than I do. It's not his fault that we have forgotten the taste of freedom, or that the lot of those few who have minds of their own is appalling — they are at the mercy of *babus*. But he can't, even if he wanted to, put fire in our full dull bellies . . . Who can do it, who will? . . . Before long, certainly before the end of the century, this country, and Europe itself, will have what our pride used to call *colonial status*: we shall have been colonised by one or other of the two great powers. Who, or what, will blow on the spark in us so that it stays alive and warm in a world in which, as a power, we count for nothing?

Something like a torrent of light poured through his mind. Power is not the essential. For the essentials of life, for energy, for happiness, for joy, it is less use than a fire at the end of a cold day or the smell of new bread in a house. Nothing, nothing worth a sigh, will be lost if we have kept the idea of a human being as a creature in whom curiosity and freedom are habits — like our English habit of growing daffodils in pots.

Chapter 39

H E was in his bedroom when Rigden came. He went
down at once. Looking over the banisters into the
hall, he saw him standing there looking round him
with a hard insolence. This place intimidates him, thought
Gurney.

'Well,' he said, 'good of you to come.'

'You sent for me,' said Rigden.

Thinking that he would feel easier there, more able to
say what he liked, Gurney said, 'We'll go up to my room,
shall we? It's cold, but not much colder than anywhere
else.'

Rigden followed him without speaking. Nor had he
anything friendly to say when he was sitting facing Gurney
on one of the room's two uncomfortable chairs. He said
almost nothing. He was controlled — and completely
unapproachable. Talking to him was like trying to stroke a
caged animal: he spat rather than talked. Gurney told him
about Thorgill's death, and the job in Yorkshire under the
old fellow's nephew. 'You'll get it if you ask for it. If I
were you, I'd apply at once.'

Rigden listened with a closed face. 'I see.'

Irritated by his sulkiness, Gurney said,

'Well, what d'you see, what d'you think of it?'

'You know what I think,' Rigden said drily.

Gurney felt a jeering impatience — and in the same
moment a rush of pity and warm affection. The young
man's mulish despair exasperated him. The fool had brought
his troubles on himself. True, he had been caught and
twisted, seduced, by Paget (and a little by Paget's sister),

but the choice had been his; he was responsible for himself, and he could hardly have expected not to have to pay for it. But — when you think how many mean crimes go unpunished, or bring their authors the friendship of other men who are past masters of insinuating their greeds and lusts into the public service — the payment struck Gurney as too high.

He would have given a great deal, a year of his life, to be able, not to protect Rigden — he did not want to protect — but to reach him. He doesn't hear me, he thought: I'm too old to get anywhere near him.

'If you don't take this, what will you do?' he asked.

Rigden's mouth twitched. 'I don't know. I'll think about it.'

'Don't be too long, will you?'

'I must go now,' Rigden said.

Glancing at his watch, Gurney saw that it was nearly eight. 'Will you stay and have dinner with me?'

'No, thanks,' Rigden said. He got up.

Gurney took him downstairs, to the front door. As if he did not know how to leave, the young man stood in the doorway, slowly, very slowly, buttoning his overcoat and turning the collar up.

'Let me know what you're going to do,' Gurney said. He felt the futility of his words.

'Yes, all right,' Rigden muttered. He stood a moment longer, staring absently, his lips pressed into a colourless line. 'Good-bye,' he said curtly, and went.

It had begun to rain, a fine penetrating drizzle; in the overhead blackness a cold breath; turning where it touched the street-lamps to a bright cloud. Gurney watched him walk away out of sight, a thin figure becoming indistinct in the bronzed darkness, soon disappearing in it. As he turned back into his club, his sense of failure was unreasonably bitter.

Rigden walked rapidly, an animal making its way home at night — home being a room in the obscure street he had chosen (the hunted animal going back on its own scent) because it was well off the main streets running south of the river, narrow, shabby, a little furtive. The anger and humiliation he was feeling had the effect on him of too much to drink: he saw and felt with a febrile sharpness; at the same time nothing was wholly real, neither the gleaming black surface of the river on either side of Westminster Bridge, nor the lights strung along the embankment, nor the shadowy arches of a naked wall, nor the cars and buses passing him with their rows of heads like the dummies in a shop-window. He thought of Gurney with something like hatred . . . Did I give myself away to the brute? Did he guess that I went to see him hoping, with half my mind, for a miracle? . . . He tried to recall exactly what he had said to Gurney, but he was too furious with himself, too hideously sick and confused. Pray God he didn't see that I hoped he would offer me something better, he thought. I can bear anything but that.

As late as it was, and still raining, there were people crowding the streets, pressing against the lighted fronts of Christmas shops, their dark clothes and white blurred faces reminding him of nothing so much as the display of limbs, freaks, and anatomical fragments in a surgical museum. He pushed through them, and turned with a feeling of escape into empty side-streets, past gaping stumps of houses destroyed in the bombing, to the blackened sliver of No. 29 Khyber Street. When his head came level with the top of the stairs he saw the thread of light under the door of his room. The pit of his stomach turned over; it could only be Evelyn; she was the only person except the Master and Gurney who knew where he was living. He stood a minute on the landing before he went in.

It was Hetty Smith. She was staring towards the door,

and though her lips opened she did not speak. She must
have seen the anger in his face.

It wasn't anger, it was insanity. He had looked for her,
worried about her, for months, and now that she was here
in front of him in the wretched little room, all he felt was a
sour rage — as though she were responsible for the
humiliation clawing him, and for all the other humiliations,
and the disgrace and loss.

He took a step forward. 'What are you doing here?
Who sent you?'

She must, he knew, be horribly hurt by his manner, but
she said calmly,

'No one sent me. I came.'

'Someone sent you. How did you know where I was?
Who told you?' The suspicion that Green had had him
watched became, before she could speak, a certainty in his
mind. 'I know who sent you,' he said.

There was no colour in her face: it might have been a
silhouette cut in greyish paper. 'I got the address
from—' she stumbled fatally over the words — 'from Mr.
Gurney.'

Rigden said drily,

'Nonsense. How could he have given it to you? I
suppose he found you and forgot to tell me . . . Don't try
any more stupid lies. Tell me the truth. Who sent you?'

She stared at him without answering. He was close
enough to her to see the pulse moving at the base of her
throat, almost to feel her warmth. The anger swelling in
him became something else, a lust to humiliate her as he
had been humiliated, as though he could crush his disgrace
out in her body.

'When you went to Hudson's room that evening he
hadn't invited you to come — it wasn't his trick, it was
your own. You went deliberately. That's true, isn't it?'
He saw rather than heard her say, 'Yes.' With what even

at that moment he knew was an inconceivable cruelty, he said, 'You came here with the same idea . . . All right. I'm quite willing.'

When he was lying over her on the bed, she fought against him, her hands trying to drag his away from her clothes: he had to use all his force against these desperate fingers — which gave way suddenly.

'Don't,' she said, 'please don't, Nevil.'

With his mouth over hers he said, 'Yes.'

Then, for the first time, he saw her: a face of blind fear and grief. His rage drained from him and he stood up and tried to pull her blouse together. She shrank away, turning her back on him, her knees drawn up like a child's when it gets into bed, and cried, a hopeless desolate sound: she tried to stifle it against the bedclothes. He watched her. There was nothing he could do to comfort her. He stood loathing himself.

After a minute she sat up and said with a poor smile, 'I'll go away now. Forgive me for coming.'

'No,' he said. 'Stay here as long as you like. I'll go.'

He went at once, stumbling down the stairs to the malodorous passage which led straight from the front door to the communal closet, and out into the dark little street.

Almost without thinking about it he turned east. It had stopped raining, and an icy wind blew from the river through every gap between houses. As he walked, all feeling left him, even the sense of loss. I'll ask Cat to let me sleep there for the night, he thought . . . Since he came to London he had not been near her, but she wouldn't know that. And she would put off asking him any questions until the morning, when they were alone.

But when he reached her street, he saw that it was too late to disturb her. Downstairs was in darkness: in the bedroom there was a single weak light behind the blind; it went out as he watched it. He decided to wait until to-

morrow to see her. Then he would tell her as much of
what had happened and what he had done as she would
understand, and excuse. He had no wish to shock her uselessly. And no illusion that the change in him would
bring the two of them nearer mentally — any more than
his marriage and what she thought about his climbing way
of life had torn apart the primitive roots fastening them
together: these were laid at too deep a level.

When he left her street and was walking back the way
he had come, he passed a mean little shop, still lit up: it
had been decorated for Christmas with artificial snow and a
grotesquely rigged-up crêche: as he passed it, the image
of a shop as small, mean, and shoddily rigged, rose from the
past; for less than a second he saw the child he was then,
speechless with joy in front of the trumpery scene in the
window, seeing it in a huge clear remote light, his hand
warm in the hand of his young mother. Grief tore him,
becoming an agony of regret and loneliness — and then a
jet of prayer. Let me go back, he begged her; let me find
myself: help me.

There was no answer, and he stumbled on. Afterwards
he never knew where he had been during that night. He
crossed the river again and walked through a jungle of
streets, almost all empty, dark between the lamps, the
houses turning to grey cliffs with one lighted window high
up, a single aching point of life. At one moment — he had
turned back again to the river, somewhere in Chelsea, and
was staring down at the black rippling surface with its
undercurrents of light — the thoughts turning like dark
water in his brain settled into stillness, as if drawn to a still
point. He had an image of the life seeped up in this brick
and concrete jungle, a million tributaries of the stream
coming out of the darkness of the past like the Thames
flowing through the long-living past of this island: he saw
himself as infinitely nothing — and yet it was through him

that the Thames ran, and the streets and roads crossed through him.

He remembered abruptly a few words spoken by Gurney's unlikeable friend, the Czech. He had been talking about England. *You don't know what you are and have.*

If I could make them know, he thought. And knew that he was ridiculous. You, he thought with contempt, you to set yourself up as a teacher. Of what? Of a cold egoism and ambition? . . . The knife turned in his vanity: even his pity for women like his mother had been used to feed his egoism . . . Like Tom, and without Tom's intellect, what I wanted was the pleasure of shoving pawns across a board, without flicking an eyelid towards their happiness, the happiness of a clerk, a carpenter, an airman, with his one life, his one liking for green pickles, his one habit of snoring, his one death. A ludicrous and bitter illusion, dark with blood: you start from the idea of freeing the minds and senses of humble people, and end in a vast graveyard where the same quicklime gets rid of the deported, the disobedient, the helpless . . . It struck him sharply that the one unforgiveable evil of Tom's creed was that there is no place in it for forgiveness. You are forbidden to forgive either the wickedness of an enemy or the weakness of your friend — or husband. Yet — out of a blessed laziness, or knowing that they themselves will need forgiveness tomorrow — men long to forgive. Forgive us as we forgive them . . . Logic and reason may or may not be on the side of the new faith. The heart and its millions of reasons and the intelligence of the heart — *no* . . . He thought: There are also a million ways of living and living happily — if the young were trained to take risks, to vomit the pap fed to them by all the political parties, all without exception, and to avoid being castrated for an idea (or a pension). But Christ save me from ever thinking that I know what's good for them, he thought violently.

He began to walk east again towards Westminster and the bridge. 'Time you went home,' he muttered.

For the first time during these hours of blind drifting about London, he thought of Hetty. Her face, as he had last seen it, with its poor smile — the smile of a child defending itself against the cruelty of an adult — brought him up short . . . Tom — if she had behaved (as he said) sensibly — would have kept her with him; he was fond of her: yet in the sum she counted with him for as little as with an insensitive brute like Green. She was expendable, a pinch of the human debris joylessly sacrificed to history . . . At this moment he remembered the story that — with a stupefying cowardice — he had pushed to the back of his mind the instant he heard it, from a Frenchman who had been a German prisoner and had escaped into Russia, and there, made prisoner again, had found himself one day clearing the dead out of a trainload of Balts being deported across Russia to the east: among them were children piled together in their excrement in a compartment of the icy stinking train: he pulled one of these out and — where all the others had died, it seemed, afraid and uncomforted — it was smiling, a lightly ironical smile frozen on its tiny pointed face. A chin made to fit into your hand, the Frenchman said . . . 'Forgive me,' he said under his breath, 'forgive me: I won't forget you again . . .'

Daylight was on him, a thin yellowish light. There were people passing him going to work. It must have rained heavily again; he realised that he was soaked through. He looked for a bus, found one, and got into it. It did not start at once, and after a minute a fat shapeless old woman came along panting and was dragged on board by the conductor. 'Thank you, ducks,' she gasped.

She sat down opposite Rigden. Under a man's shabby topcoat she was wearing a cotton dress with a bold pattern of roses on what had once been a white ground, a hat covered in soiled roses, a stringy blue sash, and a blue necklace: her big pendulous breasts pushed against the buttons of the dress: she sat with her knees apart, hands folded on her charwoman's large bag, and looked up coquettishly at the conductor when he sold her her ticket.

'One of these mornings you'll miss it,' he said.

She fluttered her old eyelids. 'Go on, you'll always wait for me, won't you?'

'When are you going to give up work and stop home — and save us trouble?'

A shameless old cackle. 'Save you trouble? When they come to lay me out, I will. Not sooner.'

Another one I won't forget, he thought. For no reason he could lay his finger on, she had taken her place with the memories, almost all trivial — like the box of sardines shared at the side of a road in North Africa one evening of sun and weariness — that he knew he would carry with him to the end . . . Old, ignorant, unteachable, probably dirty as well as stupid — and with a fierce will to live, not prepared to trust anyone, any authority or politician's hand, to provide her with what she needed to live her life . . . Oh my God, remind me, he thought, and give me a little humility.

When he got off the bus it was full daylight, a December daylight of heavy clouds dwarfing the city, the wind blowing dust and bits of paper into the faces bent downwards. He had no cause to be happy: happiness fell on him like a friend putting a hand on his shoulder: the inconceivable joy of having no reason to hope except hope itself.

It struck him that in the last few hours he had, consciously or unconsciously, asked various people to forgive him: his sister, Hetty, a dead child (one of the tens of thousands trodden into the earth *by order* — to manure the ground for next year). He had still to forgive himself.

Chapter 40

HE opened the door of his room, and saw Hetty. She had fallen asleep kneeling on the floor, her cheek against the side of the bed. He felt an overwhelming relief, as though he had been let off a punishment he deserved. Moving as quietly as he could on the thin worn-out carpet, he crossed the room to look down at her. He had always known, in a careless way, that she was magnificently beautiful: now, through the marks of exhaustion and tears rubbed away by a not too clean hand, he saw it.

She can't, he thought, have been asleep long, or she would have slipped from such an uncomfortable position. She must have kept herself awake. Doing what? Listening for his return? Crying? Why did she wait?

Her breathing, as nearly imperceptible as a child's, moved a strand of hair lying across her cheek. He stooped and lifted it gently back. He felt responsible for her, heavy with her — very much, he thought, as a woman feels heavy with her child, born or unborn. There was no exultance in the thought, only a sort of contentment: the sense of having at last reached and crossed a frontier between a country where he knew no one, where he was unwanted, and another where, poor and free, he could settle down, and live. Of his new country he had still everything to learn, even its language. Nothing would be easy — one can live without the help of lies, yes: but to do it without resentment (even of oneself), with simplicity, with gaiety, is something else. And not easy. Not even something to pat yourself on the back for doing, since in the end he had no choice.

294

Moving to the window, he drew the blind up. When he turned, the girl was looking at him with fear, a look he could not bear to see on her face. She scrambled up stiffly.

'I'll go at once,' she said. 'I didn't mean to stay here.'

That made him smile. 'Why did you stay?'

'I don't know. I was tired. No, I don't know.'

'Perhaps,' he said, 'you knew that I couldn't face losing you again — and this time it would have been my fault.'

The change in her face — from fear to an uncertain wavering question, like a child not yet quite sure that it is safe — gave him a pleasure so acute that he felt suffocated by it: he could have shouted, knocked his head on the wall.

'You're not angry?' she said in a humble voice.

'With myself,' he said with difficulty.

She frowned, as though she had not heard him, or didn't altogether trust what he said. 'You don't despise me, I don't disgust you?'

He forced himself to speak calmly. 'It's my fault you talk like that. For God's sake don't do it, I can't stand it.' He hesitated, and said, 'I love you, dearly, and if you can forgive me for last night——'

She interrupted him. '*I* forgive you? Oh, what nonsense.'

An instinct — the first tentative word in a new language — warned him not to take her in his arms, not to touch her. For less than a second — the time it took for another image to form in his mind, dwindle and dissolve — he felt an agony of regret. It was gone at once, and the colours, scents, hills, valleys, stones of the country he had chosen took possession of him. He knew, he knew very well, that it was useless to expect the same meanings here — nor did he want that. He knew that love here did not mean ecstasy; it meant a responsibility and a tenderness for which he had no words ready, a (so to speak) working

295

tenderness, in everyday use, one for any use, even disagreeable; he knew that a marriage is a sort of bet in which everything is staked; he knew, or he suspected, that the happiness he could give her would be a simple affair of bread eaten together; he had a sense, terribly precise and piercing, of the weakness of a human life, a flicker between birth and death, knowledge of its weakness and brevity masked from it by the warmth, near it, of another short life. He knew humbly that he would have to learn this tenderness, this love not of himself.

'We won't talk now,' he said. 'You're too sleepy. But if you can trust me after last night I promise to look after you all my life . . . You must go, this is a horrible room. But I'll make some tea for us first — look, we have a gas-ring, and I keep cups here.' He opened the wardrobe.

'I'll make it,' she said eagerly.

'No. Let me.'

He filled the kettle from the tap on the landing, and while it boiled he watched her stealthily making herself tidy with quick light movements of her hands, smoothing her hair and shaking her clothes straight. When he gave her her cup, he noticed that one of her fingers was scarred. He did not dare to touch it. He had never felt so deep a satisfaction.

Someone came up the stairs. Since his was the only room at the top of the house he supposed, vexed, that his landlord knew the girl was with him, and was coming to make trouble. Without waiting for the fellow to knock, he opened the door. It was Gurney.

If he were surprised to see Hetty here, he gave no sign of it. Looking at her with a friendly smile he said,

'Well, I was right, wasn't I? I did the right thing?'

She said, 'Yes,' in a serene young voice.

Rigden was sharply annoyed. 'Why didn't you tell me you knew where she was?' he asked.

'I like to choose my own time to break a promise,' Gurney said coolly. 'But I told her where you were. It comes to the same thing. Do you mind?'

'So long as it amused you,' Rigden said with an uncontrollable bitterness.

Gurney looked at him with a gleam of mockery. 'When you told me you'd been looking for her, I didn't know,' he said. 'And after that — well, you weren't thinking very much about anyone but yourself, were you?'

'No, that's true,' Rigden muttered. Ashamed of his rudeness, he said, 'Did you come to ask me whether I've written to old Thorgill's nephew? I——'

Gurney cut him brusquely short. 'No. I came to stop you writing this morning. I've changed my mind . . . I was doing you good—' his mockery this time was for himself — 'sending you to scratch a hard living in Yorkshire. Never mind why. Yesterday after you'd gone I decided that there was no reason why I should do you good. It's not my business, is it? I'm sorry . . . I can, I think, get you a better job, not so —' he hesitated — 'not quite so inadequate.'

Rigden grinned. For the first time since he had known Gurney, he felt himself on an equal footing. It's because I don't want anything from him, he thought drily. But it went deeper. For the first time he knew exactly what he did want, and it was not anything in Gurney's reach.

'Inadequate to my brains, do you mean?'

'Oh, if you want to put it like that,' Gurney said. 'I could, I think, get you a job abroad, in one of our consulates.'

Rigden did not answer at once. He was not considering the offer. He was not even tempted to consider it. His difficulty was to find a way of refusing which would not show him up as naive or a fool. Suddenly he didn't care what sort of figure he cut.

'You've changed your mind,' he said, laughing. 'I don't know why — except that I showed damned little enthusiasm about going to Yorkshire to teach miners history. The fact is I've changed mine. I'm willing to go there. Perfectly willing.'

Gurney stared at him. 'Why?'

'Oh, I've no illusions. I don't believe in the noble heart of the workers, or the noble anything you like. The noble workers have their newspapers now, their paid officials, their paid leaders, and even their boot-lickers. But —' he gave Gurney an unconsciously forbidding glance — 'I can't go any further without first going back part of the way . . . I may be making a complete fool of myself. And I may resent poverty — comparative poverty — for instance, not being able to order a book I want. I don't know . . . I've lost the chance of doing some things I said I was going to do — I meant to give my mother the sort of life she missed when she was young.' He smiled sharply. 'Don't get it into your head that I'm thinking of anyone but myself. And I'm not trying — what's the word — to absolve myself. I come from a class that doesn't attach any great importance to gestures. Does anyone think about making them unless or until he has every other sort of amusement? It's simply that I shan't be organised — if you know what I mean: you don't, but it doesn't matter — I shan't be satisfied, my egoism, if you like, won't be satisfied, until I've gone back . . .'

Gurney had a feeling of triumph. Irrational and ridiculous: this had nothing to do with him.

'Back where?' he asked coolly.

Rigden looked at him with a familiar aggression. 'I shouldn't dream of trying to answer that one. When we look back, you and I don't see the same things.'

Nor at any time, Gurney thought: I'm too much older. The bitterness he felt would have been unendurable if he

'All right,' he said. Taking hold of the finger, he kissed it, and looked her in the face. 'Now go,' he said.

The blood rushed to her face. She turned, and went out without another word.

Gurney moved to follow her. 'You know where to find me,' he said to Rigden.

The young man looked at him absently. 'Yes.' He made an obvious effort to attend. 'Thanks for all you've done.'

Gurney smiled.

He had to walk cautiously down the narrow uneven stairs. Here and there light of a sort came from a half-open door: various smells, quiescent at night, had stirred, rising from cracked rotten wood impregnated with dust, soot, the river damp in the walls, sweat, ashbins, an acid smell which seemed the breath itself of a house impossible to clean. He thought: What a place to begin thinking that life may possibly have a meaning.

He had a moment of pure unmotived joy, one of those laconic moments when the world seems to exist for no other purpose. While it lasted he was reconciled to his life, to the slow treachery of mind and body, to the derisive shortness of the moments between the misery and ecstasy of youth and the long brutally slow decline . . . For a moment he forgave Anne for dying.

THE END

PRINTED BY PURNELL AND SONS, LTD.
PAULTON (SOMERSET) AND LONDON

had not forced himself to see it for what it was: the involuntary envy of a man of fifty confronted by his loss of energy . . . What did you expect? he asked himself coldly. To be thanked for interfering? To be liked?

He glanced at the girl. She was pale, but a new soft liveliness was at work in her; her eyes had a brilliance that was partly want of sleep and partly a tranquil happiness.

He asked gently, 'Are you going to stay here?'

She looked at him with a little surprise. 'Oh, no. I must go back. Mrs. Lemke will have wondered where I am. She's been very kind, too.'

Gurney let her see that he was relieved. The thought that she might stay here had revolted him. Why? He preferred not to ask himself why.

'I'll take you back,' he said easily. 'We'll pick up a taxi somewhere, it's a long way.'

'Yes, you must go,' Rigden said to her. He added in a rougher voice, 'But you haven't told me anything yet. Who is this Mrs. Lemke? Where is she?'

She told him the name of the street, and whereabouts it was. 'The house is number thirty. It's a boarding-house,' she said calmly. 'I work there.'

'What sort of work?'

'Oh, every sort,' she said, smiling. 'I ought to be making beds now. I was a perfect fool when I started. Now I don't cut or scald myself more than once a week.'

Rigden scowled. 'You can't stay there.'

'Why not?'

'I daresay I can find something else for her,' Gurney said. 'For as long as she needs it.'

The girl looked at him. 'Nothing easy, remember,' she said in a low voice. She turned to Rigden, and touched his shoulder lightly with a finger. 'You're soaking, you ought to change.'